MOTHER OF LIGHT

A NOVEL

Elin de Ruyter

YLFA PRESS

This is a work of fiction. Any references to herbal remedies, medicines and/or midwifery techniques are not meant to be considered as a substitute for professional advice. They are not to be considered as viable treatments.

Cover design by 100covers.com

Interior design by Elin de Ruyter

Map and Illustrations by Chaim Holtjer

First edition: July 2023

ISBN 978-0-6457659-1-5 (paperback)

ISBN 978-0-6457659-0-8 (ebook)

www.elinderuyter.com

YLFA PRESS

To my great-great-grandmother,
Guðrún Þórðardóttir,
and the Icelandic midwives whose
true stories inspired this one

Mother of Light is the literal translation
of the Icelandic word for midwife, *ljósmóðir.*

Glossary
Icelandic Words

Afi—Grandfather

Amma—Grandmother

Andskotinn—Icelandic swear word—'the devil'

Askur—A type of Icelandic wooden bowl, with a lid— used for all meals

Baðstofa—Living room; also functioned as a place to eat and sleep and where people undertook various household activities

Búr—Food cellar, pantry

Góðan daginn—Greeting: good morning/good day

Hreppstjóri—Local district councillor

Húsfreyja—The head mistress of a household—she would manage a household

Já—Yes

Kauptíð—Trading season—held at a merchant town

Blessuð og sæl—Greeting to a woman: may you come blessed and well

Mamma—Mother

Nei—No

Pabbi—Father

Peysuföt—Traditional Icelandic clothes worn by women

Séra—Title for a priest

Sixareen—a six-oared timber rowing boat

Skyr—A type of Icelandic cheese, more the consistency of yogurt—made from milk

Slátur—Slaughter, the term used for blood sausage, liver sausage, scorched sheep's head and sheep's head jam

Sæll/Sæl—Greeting, hello

Torfbær (turf croft)—An abode constructed of stone, timber and earth, typically with a grass roof and stone outer walls; the inside is framed with timber

Pronunciation of some Icelandic Names

Þ—This letter is pronounced as *th* as in **th**orn

ð—This letter is pronounced as *th* as in ba**th**

æ—This letter is pronounced as *I* as in m**y**

Major Characters

with pronunciations

Suðureyri

Household 1

Albert Jónsson, *hreppstjóri*, farmer and fisherman, 31

Kristín (Krissa) Ólafsdóttir, *húsfreyja*, his wife, 41

Valdís (Dísa) [dee-sa] Þorðardóttir, her daughter, 10

Halldóra (Dóra) [doe-ra] Albertsdóttir, their daughter, 6

Þorlaug (Tobba) Þorleifsdóttir, Krissa's mother, 62

Þorleifur (Leifi) [lay-fee] Þorkelsson, Tobba's father, 85

Einar [ay-nar] Sveinsson, farmhand and fisherman, Albert's brother, 26

Árni [our-knee] Valdimarsson, farmhand and fisherman, 45

Guðrún (Rúna) [roo-na] Sigurðardóttir, workmaid, 23

Ingibjörg (Inga) Maríasdóttir, workmaid,19

Sólveig [soul-vay] (Veiga, Solla) Pétursdóttir, midwife from Reykjavik, 24

Household 2

Björn [be-yearn] Jóhannesson, farmer and fisherman, 45

Rannveig [run-vay] Þórarinsdóttir, *húsfreyja*, his wife, 43

Jóhannes (Jói) [yo-air] Björnsson, their son, 18

Sigríður (Sigga) Björnsdóttir, their son, 15

Þórarinn (Tóti) [toe-tear] Björnsson 14

Margrét Björnsdóttir, their daughter, 6

Helgi [hel-gear] Sigurðsson, Rúna's brother, farmhand and fisherman, 26

Hansína [hun-seen-a] Ketilsdóttir, workmaid, 15

Þorsteinn (Steinn) [stain] Bjarnason, fosterchild, 9

Botn

Jakob [ya-cob] Jónsson, farmer and fisherman, brother of Albert, 29

María [mar-ee-a] Gestsdottir, *húsfreyja*, his wife, 28

Fríða [free-the] Jóhannsdottir, her daughter, 8

Ásta [ow-sta] Jakobsdóttir, their daughter, 3

Hans Bjarnason, farmhand, 15

Gestur [guest-her] Jóhannesson, María's father, 65

Hulda [hool-da] Geirsdóttir, workmaid, 17

Keflavík

Elisabét (Elsa) Magnúsdóttir, *húsfreyja*, mother of Helgi and Rúna, 54

Magnús [mag-noose] Sigurðsson, farm manager and fisherman, her son, 30

Elías Sigurðsson, [elle-ee-us] farmhand and fisherman, her son, 16

Águstína (Stína) [stee-na] Örnolfsdóttir, workmaid, 15

Salbjörg [sal-be-yorg] Hallgrímsdóttir, workmaid, sister of Elsa, 48

Steindór [stain-door] Jensson, son of Salbjörg, 10

Tómas [toe-mass] Erlendsson, farmhand and fisherman, 52

Bær

Eiríkur [ay-rick-her] Bjarnason, farmer and fisherman, 58
Jósefína [yosef-eena] Sveinsdóttir, *húsfreyja*, his wife, 56
Hafsteinn [half-stain] Eiríksson, farmhand and fisherman, their son, 29
Gróa [grow-wa] Magnúsdóttir, midwife, mother of Eiríkur, 84
Halldóra [hal-door-ra] Jónsdóttir, workmaid, 23

Vatnadal Upper

Grímur [gree-mur] Halldórsson, former *hreppstjóri*, farmer and fisherman, 65
Katla [cut-la] Hansdóttir, húsfreyja, his wife, 60
Hallveig [hal-vay] Grímsdóttir, work maid, their daughter, widowed, 38
Geir [gayr] Sturlason, farmhand, son of Hallveig, 13

Vatnadal - Hraunakot

Júlíus [yule-ee-us] Halldórsson, farmer and fisherman, 60
Björg [be-yorg] Tómasdóttir, *húsfreyja*, his wife, 31
Herdís [hair-deese] Júlíusdóttir, their daughter, 9
Anna María Júlíusdóttir, their daughter, 7

Tómas Júlíusson, their son, 5

Kalli [cull-air] Júlíusson, their son, 3

Júlíus Júlíusson, their son, 2

Soffía Júlíusdóttir, their daughter, 13 months

Gilsbrekka

Bjarni [be-yarn-air] Hannesson, farmer and fisherman, 32

    Arína [a-ree-na] Jóhannesdóttir, húsfreyja, his wife, 37

    Jóhannes [yo-hun-ness] Pallsson, her son, 14

    Hannes [hun-ness] Bjarnsson, their son, 2

Westfjörds

-ANNo 1881-

Keflavik

Göltur Mountain

Göltur

Suðureyri

Norðureyri

SÚGANDAFJÖRÐUR

Skaður

Spillir Mountain

Bær

Framri

Vatnadalur

Laugan

selárdalur

Gilsen

hvíarnes

Botn

Flateyri

ÍSAFJARÐARDJÚP

N

Bolungarvík

Hnífsdalur

Ísafjörður

Súðavík

Chaim 2023

Prologue

December 1880

Njarðvík, South Iceland

People always leave. That was a truth Sólveig had learned long ago. Birth and death lingered together in the dimly lit croft made from earth and stone. The scent of blood filled her nostrils, astringent and metallic, and with it came an almost paralysing dread. She approached the bed in the corner of the room. The small window above it rattled against the gasping wind, or was it a soul trying to escape? She shuddered at the thought.

The sight before Sólveig tore at her, the unfairness of it all. Her sister's still form lay on the narrow cot before her, her long blonde braids limp and lustreless against the waxy hue of her skin. A newborn baby was nestled in the crook of her arm, its tiny face bruised and blue. She hadn't even known Fía was with child.

"There was nothing we could do for them," the house mistress said behind her. There was no emotion behind the words, as if she were talking about something so mundane as making the evening meal. And Sólveig wanted to scream at her. But she didn't.

"It should never have happened in the first place," she said instead.

No doctor. No midwife. Just a man who thought he knew how to deliver babies. And now her sister was gone.

PART ONE

Better to have little light than much darkness.

Betra er lítið ljós en mikið myrkur.

—Old Icelandic proverb

1

September 1881

Ísafjörður, Northwest Iceland

She arrived with the autumn wind, trailing the postman, his son and his dog.

Two weeks it had taken her to get here. Sólveig had walked, ridden and rowed, traversed mountain heaths and crossed precarious fjords, wearing through three pairs of her sheep skin shoes to take up her new posting in the merchant town of Ísafjörður, but now the doctor was telling her he was posting her elsewhere.

"You want me to go to Suðureyri? I'm sorry, I don't quite understand. Is this not where I'm to practice midwifery?"

Doctor Þorvaldur, a greying man in his mid-forties sighed deeply and rubbed a hand through his short neatly trimmed beard.

"*Já*, it was initially, but we're short of midwives in the Westfjörds and the Suðureyri district don't have a learned midwife of their own. I've decided to post you there. It's in the next fjord—not too far."

"The next fjord?" She sighed, trying to quell the disappointment she felt at the prospect of more walking. Her tattered feet ached at the mere thought of it.

They sat in his office, a small room furnished as a doctor's clinic, a shelf full of leather-bound books against one wall, a cabinet with vials of powders and liquids of varying colours, a cot for patients, an examination table and a timber desk by a large square window, lending the room natural light.

"We're trying to make positive changes here, Sólveig," he continued, his tone taking on an edge of exasperation. "Some of the old midwives just don't uphold to proper hygiene, and there are the new laws. We need trained midwives. You'll stay with Albert and his wife in their household. He is *hreppstjóri* for Suðureyri, the local district councillor. They're a respectable family, and you'll be well cared for in their household."

"I haven't delivered a child, Doctor. I was assured I would have more training before heading out on my own."

"Eh!" He waved his hand in the air as if her concerns were of little matter. "You've completed your three months of training. You passed your exams, so you're more than adequately equipped. You'll charge three *kronur* per delivery and receive escort to and from births, as required by law, and the district shall pay you fifty *kronur* per annum." He stood, reaching for a brown leather bag, then peered into it and closed it once more with apparent satisfaction. "Now, my dear, I've got a broken leg to set in Hnífsdalur, so I must take my leave. You have everything you need for your practise—medicine vials, scissors, bands, enema syringes, tubes and the like?"

"*Já*, I believe so. I was given some vials by Doctor Jónas in Reykjavík." Sólveig stood too, indicating her own case near the door.

"When you need more, come see me again. I have a supply here."

A turmoil of uncertainty ran through her. This was too rushed. "And if complications should arise?"

"I'm the only trained doctor for the whole of the Westfjörds, Sólveig." He swept his hand in dramatic exclamation. "It takes me days just to travel to some of the farms in my district. I need all the help I can get. These women are relying on you. Of course, I'm here if any major difficulties arise, but I find that most labours—well, they progress quite adequately if the woman tends to follow the body's natural cues. You'll find that the ladies of the household will be able to assist you also, but you'll know this already." He winked, giving her no room for rebuttal, and called down the hallway: "Þórunn."

The doctor's wife, a refined middle-aged woman whom Sólveig had met upon her arrival, entered the room. She was short and buxom, clothed in a dark-blue Danish-style dress with a high neckline, flowing skirts and long sleeves.

"Please see to it that Sólveig receives some coffee before she heads out with Albert." The doctor reached out to her again, taking her hand in half a shake. "You must forgive me, duty calls. Good day to you and best of luck." He pushed a stiff black crowned hat onto his head, tipped the brim at her in farewell and fled out the door.

⊹

A man, tall and broad of shoulder paced at the side of the doctor's timber house. He sported a short beard and was dressed smartly in a dark grey suit, his brass-coloured hair mostly hidden beneath the black hat marking his status as *hreppstjóri,* though she thought him more like a sea captain in it.

"Albert?" she ventured, making her way towards him. He turned at the sound of her voice, pulling the hat off his head.

"You'll be the midwife, then?" Sky-blue eyes took stock of her, and she was suddenly all too aware of how tattered, and travel worn she must look before him, a man of status.

"Sólveig Pétursdóttir." She nodded in greeting. "And you're the councillor?"

"Albert Jónsson of Suðureyri." He bowed curtly, in a formal manner, then straightened himself. "I wasn't expecting one so young—I'll say that."

His comment took her by surprise. "I'm twenty-four, not too young, I think." The man was surely not much older himself, she wanted to add, but instead, she pulled her shoulders back, steadying her resolve, ready to face whatever objections he thought he had with her age and inexperience.

"Ah, I can see that I've offended you. Don't take it to heart, girl. Most midwives I know are aged old women with broods of ten to twelve children—not young and so easy on the eyes." His held hers, a glint of humour dancing in them, and she couldn't help but think that he was teasing her.

"Well, I'll have you know, the laws have changed. Women no longer need to be married nor have children of their own to become a midwife."

"Já, and we're happy to have you, Sólveig." He placed his hat back onto his head. "You've come a fair journey, I hear, and if all is well, we'll make haste for home."

Tied to a post at the side of the doctor's house, a blue roan coloured beast stomped its hooves impatiently. The horse was loaded heavily with supplies: a couple of large sacks, and an assortment of ropes and tools.

Albert's gaze followed hers to the horse, and he raised his brows in question.

"To be carried by your horse, my feet would be forever grateful." Sólveig was weary to the bone of travel, but it appeared that she must make this one last leg of the journey to reach her destination.

"These mountains aren't good for riding, I'm afraid. The trail's too steep and narrow, but she can take those." He indicated the sack of clothes she carried over one shoulder and the medical bag in her hand, her life's belongings and she passed them gladly to him, watching as he fastened them to the horse. "It's four hours of hard walking," he stated casually over his shoulder. "You think you'll manage it?"

"Já." Sólveig sighed. After all, what was four more hours of walking? She had little choice in the matter, like many things in life. She drew deep, searching for that bit of extra courage, that mental energy more than anything else, to tackle another mountain. But she knew this would all be worth it in the end. Her destination may have changed, but her role, her duty in society was still the same. Women would give birth and she would go where she was needed.

⚜

They left behind the small town nestled in the fjord between mountains. The tang of salt sat sharp in the air, blown straight from the sea along with the smell of fish, carried over from the drying racks they passed along the coastline. Sólveig's black woollen skirt fluttered about her ankles, and she tugged at the ends of the knitted grey shawl she wore, pulling it tighter around her for warmth. The bumpy dirt track narrowed into a path only wide enough to walk in single file, a path that snaked through a valley and ascended the side of a mountain, the very same mountain she had descended only an hour earlier with the postman. When they reached the top, there was more room to walk by Albert's side, but Sólveig stayed back a bit, unsure and subdued in the presence of this man, this stranger she followed blindly towards what seemed like the edge of the world.

It was well into the evening when they stopped at a place Albert called Hvildarklettur—the Resting Cliffs. He assured her that sunset was still a few hours away and they were making good time, but Sólveig could see, well used to life on the road, that the dark gathering of clouds in the distance meant that heavy rain was approaching, so they couldn't tarry for long.

Sólveig sat opposite Albert on the flattened surface of a large rock, twirling her hair aimlessly. Her coffee-coloured hair was plaited into two long, thick braids wrapped under a cream-coloured headscarf to keep the cold from biting her ears. She sensed the *hreppstjóri* taking stock of her once more as the silence of the mountain floated about them, interrupted by the occasional snort of the horse grazing nearby. The heavy awkwardness of strangers lingered keenly between them, so she distracted herself with a bilberry patch near the base of her seat and reached down to tear off a handful of the plump blue berries. Albert pulled out a small square cloth with a slice of rye bread and dried fish, offering her some of his meagre meal.

"I'm not walking too fast for you?" he asked, finally breaking the silence.

She took a strip of the dried fish and offered him some of her berries, touched that he was kind enough to concern himself with her well-being.

"*Nei*, I'm well used to the fast pace the postmen set, but I'm afraid these shoes haven't much wear left in them." She arched her feet, revealing the thin soles of her sheepskin shoes.

He shook his head, whistling his dismay at the state of her footwear. His own footwear consisted of brown leather boots, not the usual skin shoes that most farmers wore.

"You've come a fair way, a petite little thing such as you. Walking from Reykjavík to Ísafjörður is no easy trek." He regarded her quietly again, then: "Why so far north, may I ask? You got family up this way?"

"*Nei*. Though, I'm told my mother was from Ísafjörður." The mention of her mother made her wistful. "But she's long gone from these parts now."

"And what does she say about you trekking so far north?"

She met his gaze and pulled hers away again, seeking to fill her vision instead with mountain, ocean and the darkening sky stretching before them. "They're all gone now. It's just me," she said firmly, neither wanting nor needing his pity. She had volunteered for this post. She could easily have taken a position near her own district in the south, but what was left for her there now? They were all gone, and she had a new path to walk. She could look after herself, and would.

"I'm sorry," Albert said, his tone soft, and then he stood, brushing the dried crumbs from his suit, packing the leftovers into a pocket of one of the sacks sitting atop his mare. "Well, you'll find a new home awaits you here, Sólveig, and a welcome place in our household." His hands moved deftly over the horse, checking the ties holding his goods in place. "We've thirteen farms around our fjord and the valley over, and there's never a shortage of babies being born."

"Do you have children of your own?"

He turned to her. "I do, two daughters—ten and five winters old, and a new one due to arrive near Christmas, but I'm sure my wife, Krissa, can tell you more about that. What do I know of babies apart from how to make them?" He chuckled loudly, clearly amused with himself. Sólveig's cheeks flushed with heat at his bold words, but Albert cast his glance skywards. "We'd best be on our way. This storm is rolling in fast."

2

The mists swirled around them. Sólveig had trouble keeping Albert and his horse in her line of vision as they trailed down the steep mountain path and into the valley she would call home. Her feet slid on loose gravel and mud and her heart pounded in her chest, the constant thought running through her mind that she was wandering on the precipice of a cliff and could slip off its edge at any moment.

Just before their descent, Albert wrapped an oilskin tarp over the horse, sensing rain was imminent. He needed to prevent his goods from becoming wet and vital food supplies spoiling. He informed her he'd been in town for a meeting with some shop merchants, but he'd used the opportunity to pick up extra supplies for his household and carried with him mostly salt for preserving, oats, rye flour, and some tools to make repairs on the croft and his boats.

"Sólveig!" Albert called through the downpour.

"*Já*, Albert," she returned, but the wind caught most of it and she wondered if he'd even heard her at all.

"I haven't lost you down the side of the mountain, have I?"

Rain rolled in rivulets down her face, her scarf was plastered to her hair, her shawl damp and heavy. "*Nei*, Albert," she called back struggling to keep his outline in front of her, hoping the whiteness wouldn't swallow him and the horse whole.

"You're soaked through, girl," Albert remarked, regarding her sodden state when they finally reached the bottom. The fog about them was thin enough that she could make out a stone and turf croft in the distance at the head of a long, narrow fjord, its water an angry grey rippling in the wind, the rain showering down about them almost sideways.

"I'm quite alright, really," she assured him, hoping that this was his farm they could see before them now.

He raised his brows at her in response, and she heard his snort of amusement. He, too, was soaked through, water dripping from him, his beard showered in clear droplets.

"It's getting heavier. We'll have to take shelter at my brother's farm at Botn." And just as Albert spoke, a gust of wind hit them with such force, it stole Sólveig's words from her. She managed a nod and pushed her head into the onslaught, following him towards the outline of the large croft in the distance.

He led the horse straight through a doorway attached to a row of turf crofts.

Warmth enveloped her as they entered the dark room, but with it came the stench of livestock, and hay mingled with a heady dampness. She was out of the wind nonetheless, and the tip of her nose and cheeks tingled as feeling came back to them.

Albert closed the wooden door behind them, latching it shut against the force of the wind.

"We'll stop here until the rain eases. My brother Jakob runs this farm. Suðureyri is another two hours from here," he said.

Sólveig stood in the darkness of the windowless room, water dripping from her, while Albert called down what appeared to be a long hallway adjoining the livery house.

"Anyone home?" He paused, waiting for a response, then turned back to the horse, pulling some of the heavier sacks off its back to lighten its load.

Adjusting to the darkness around her, Sólveig became aware of other life in the room. A dappled brown dairy cow blew through her nose, her large doe eyes wary of the strangers in her house, but she continued chewing at her meagre supply of hay, her udders heavy and full. It was cramped in the room with Albert's horse and its load taking up a good portion, and they soon heard footsteps coming down the hallway, the orange glow of a lamp accompanying it.

"Albert, is that you? Have you been out in this weather?" A young woman appeared in the narrow doorway, a curly red-haired toddler on her hip. She was comely, with high cheekbones and a sprinkle of freckles on her pale skin. Her long hair plaited into two braids was the same fiery red as her child's. There was a weariness about her, and Sólveig could see why as the woman rubbed her hand along her slightly rounded belly. She glanced over at Sólveig with curiosity, and she smiled back tentatively.

Albert leaned in to kiss the woman in greeting and patted the child on her head affectionately. "I've just come from Ísafjörður with supplies and found us a new midwife to boot." He winked at Sólveig as he introduced her. "María, this is Sólveig Pétursdóttir. She's come a long way to be with us. A city girl, all the way from Reykjavík. Sólveig, this is my brother's wife, María, and their daughter, Ásta."

"You are welcome here, Sólveig, please do come in," said María. "Jakob is just sitting down to his supper with the rest of the household. You'll join us, won't you?"

"We won't stop long. Just until the rain eases." Albert pulled off his hat, shaking the excess water off it, and did the same with his coat.

Sólveig had a feeling this stop was more for her benefit than his, but she was grateful, nonetheless.

"Of course, you'll stop for supper. Look at the girl, Albert, she is shivering. You must be chilled to the bone." María put the child down and took Sólveig's wet shawl and Albert's jacket. "I'll take these and dry them by the kitchen hearth and fetch you both a bowl of meat soup. That should warm you up in no time."

❖

Sólveig carefully spooned the warm liquid from her bowl into her mouth, allowing the heat to seep into her from the inside out. She supposed that meat was aplenty now with the slaughter season upon them, and she was delighted to spoon out a few morsels of lamb with the vegetables—chunks of potato and swede in the watery mixture. She sat next to Albert on a narrow timber bed serving as a seat in the *baðstofa*, a communal living room located up a set of steep, narrow steps under the roof loft. There was a small glass window at one end, letting the only stream of natural light into the room.

The household was scattered about them, with some having already finished their meal, with small items of work at hand, knitting, mending, or reading weathered and well-loved books. But Sólveig's attention was on Jakob, Albert's younger brother, who sat with his wife on the bed opposite them. She thought him much like his brother, with the same blue eyes, straight nose, and short beard, but where Albert was fair-haired, he was dark, with short brown hair that fell across his face as he spoke.

Sólveig finished her meal in silence, listening on as Albert entered a discussion with his brother about the poor summer they'd just suffered.

"We're in for another hard winter Albert." Jakob sighed, reaching for a small square tin on the table next to them where they sat. He took a pinch of the dark tobacco granules between his thumb and index finger and placed them on his hand, palm down, blocking one side of his nose while he inhaled the stuff into his other nostril. "This is the last of it for a while," he said, offering some to Albert.

Albert held up a hand, passing on the offer. "Then you need not be so generous, brother."

Jakob shrugged and put the tin away. "Ah, we need to enjoy these small pleasures while we can, what little there is of them. But in truth, we'll barely survive the winter as we are." He shook his head in dismay, leaning back against the wall, his hands interlocked over his belly. "Another bad season. I've had to slaughter more sheep than I wanted to. There's just not enough hay this summer, and we can't buy it in—not that we could afford it even if it were possible."

Albert nodded in understanding. "It's the same story at Suðureyri. We're all just doing the best we can. We've still got the fishing grounds, which is more than some. We'll get out again before the winter sets in."

"That's all well and good for you, Albert, you've got the best coastline at your feet. We moor our boats farther down and the landing is harder," he said for Sólveig's benefit. "Especially if the weather turns bad of a sudden as it's done these years past."

"Come now, that's enough talk of hard times, Jakob," María clucked with disapproval, standing up to gather their empty bowls. "You'll scare the poor girl back to Reykjavík with all this talk of bad winters and struggles. We'll bear it as we always have."

"It's quite alright, María," Sólveig volunteered. "There's talk of this all over the land. Every farm we stopped at from Reykjavík to your very own in the Westfjörds has struggled with poor yields this summer. We had a few families traveling with us part of the way north, heading for the port at Borðeyri to travel west all the way to America. They'd all given up on Iceland, with nothing to yield from the land but death and disease and the inability to pay their rents."

Jakob and Albert both shook their heads.

"And there's naught but hard life and struggle, even in America," she added.

"You speak as if you know personally of such things," said María.

"My father and his wife live there, on the plains somewhere in the north at a place called Mountain, with their only surviving son. I've only had the one letter from my brother, but the winters there are long and hard. They've had to hack a living out of the wilderness, far from civilisation."

"Já," said Jakob. "But at least over there, there's land for the giving and it's up to a man to make what he wants of it. He's free to be his own person and to earn for himself the life he wants."

"Já, there's that," said Albert, considering them. "People are doing it hard here and all over. I, for one, want to see improvements here before running away to the west. Imagine having a store of our own to stock and keep our fish and goods. We spend so much time going to and from the merchant towns for vital goods when I know we could manage something here."

"Well, you're on the council, Albert, you speak for the district," said María. "You can see it done." She squeezed his shoulder and started to stoop to pick up a spoon that had fallen to the ground.

"I'm working on it." He winked at María taking the spoon off the floor for her. "It was one of the reasons for my trip to Ísafjörður."

"Would you like some help, María?" Sólveig offered as she watched the woman pile up the empty bowls and spoons.

"I'll not say *nei* to offered help," she said, leading Sólveig to the kitchen. María dropped the dirty bowls into a tub of warm water, rinsing each one, and Sólveig took them from her for drying.

"María, how long until the new babe arrives?" she asked, indicating the swell of her rounded belly.

María rubbed a hand over her abdomen. "Ah, this one won't arrive until early next year. I know I look like a right lump." She gave her a sheepish look.

"You look lovely, María." Sólveig loved the vibrancy women carried when they were with child. Yes, she looked weary, but her cheeks were rosy and her eyes bright. "I've just received my midwifery license. I'd be happy to attend you when the time comes."

Silence drew up between them, and María focused all her attention on rinsing the bowls. "*Nei*, that won't be necessary. Old Gróa has always delivered the babies around here." She finally looked up at her. "She delivered my Ásta, you see, and even my eldest, Fríða, who is eight now, and the births have always fared well."

"Well, of course," Sólveig managed evenly. "I'd like to meet this Gróa." She smiled at María, though, in truth, she felt a little disheartened. She was surprised to learn there was already a midwife here, and she couldn't help but wonder why the doctor had sent her to this place when they already had a woman the community trusted.

As quickly as it came, the rain abated, and a glorious sunset brightened the glistening valley. It didn't take long for Albert to reload his supplies onto the horse, and they were off, waving their farewells and thanks to Jakob and María.

They walked a path that traced the banks of the fjord, dipping in and jutting out in places, passing a sea croft and two farms, much smaller than Botn. Albert called out their names to her as they passed them, Kvíanes and Laugar. Farther towards the head of the fjord, she caught glimpses of Suðureyri, her new home, when the path snaked out into the waters of the fjord more. Beyond it lay the open sea, and Sólveig fell behind Albert and the horse with the journey's end in sight, but her nerves were a jumble in her exhausted body. Now that she knew about the midwife Gróa, she felt less sure of her place here. But then, she supposed it wasn't unreasonable to think that the women of the community would simply look after each other here, as women had done since the start of time, when there was no doctor, or he was not within quick reach.

"Not much farther to go, Sólveig," Albert said, interrupting her thoughts. He'd slowed his pace for her, and walked by her side, the horse trailing him.

"Albert," she ventured, needing to voice some of her concerns.

"*Já?*" he regarded at her.

"How often does Doctor Þorvaldur come to this fjord? Will I see much of him?"

"Hmph! It's a long trek for the doctor, as you can see yourself now having just walked it. We need someone like you here, Sólveig. Someone young and learned in the ways of doctoring as well as delivering babies."

"I'm not a doctor, Albert." She needed to make sure he wasn't expecting more than she could deliver.

"*Já*, but you're the closest we have to a doctor. Doctor Þorvaldur doesn't come out this way much, even when matters are urgent enough. There's always something holding him up in town, as if their need is more dire than our own. Nope." He shook his head, regarding her with something akin to pride. "We have you here now, all to ourselves."

"But María told me you already have a midwife."

"You mean *old Gróa*? *Já*, she's been around a long time, Sólveig, and the women here love and trust her, but she isn't as able as she used to be. She lives at the farm Bær in the next valley on the other side of Spillir here." He pointed to the mountain rising stark and steep to their left, a mess of browns and mossy greens blended into dark granite with autumn upon them. "Her legs are tired, and she's losing her sight. She's well into her eighties, you see." He glanced across at her as if he had read her unspoken thoughts or, perhaps, he had heard the self-doubt in her voice, and he said to her gently, "Fear not, Sólveig, you will be needed here."

3

The sun was setting. Albert and Sólveig approached Suðureyri farm, the horizon before them a brilliant display of pink and purple clouds sitting just above the line of the ocean. The air had grown cooler, their exhaled breaths floating in white puffs about them. The horse, their beastly companion, in sight of home, picked up its pace, snorting and neighing in pleasure, knowing its journey's end was near and fresh hay the reward. Sólveig smiled at its sudden enthusiasm, feeling she could well relate.

They passed a small lake which Albert said was void of fish, though the children in the community tried their best to prove him wrong. In winter it froze over and was used to store meat and fish in its shallow, icy depths.

The trail then widened to join the home front, a dirt road that ran along a cluster of large and small stone and turf crofts and outbuildings, blending into the landscape, each playing its own function; some would house sheep, cows or horses, others served as a smithy, a dairy house and storage sheds for food. She heard dogs barking and two thick pelted creatures, a mixture of tan and white, with curly tails, wet noses and lapping tongues, ran to greet them as they approached, trotting happily alongside them the rest of the way to the entrance of the largest of the houses. They stopped before the door of the main house, and Sólveig caught a glimpse of curious faces in the windows above them. Shortly after, two small girls in long-sleeved dresses and stockinged feet opened the front door in a flurry of excitement. They could have been twins with their identical sandy-coloured side plaits, round blue eyes and rosy cheeks, but one was a head taller than the other, her expression more severe.

"Dóra, *Mamma* said it was bedtime," she scolded the younger one, trying to hold her back.

"Pabbi!" Dóra squealed with delight.

"Are you little rascals not in bed yet?" Albert laughed, hoisting the younger child up into his arms.

"*Pabbi*, who is the pretty lady?" She nuzzled into her father and peered shyly over at Sólveig.

"Sólveig, these are my daughters, Halldóra and Valdís, but you may call them Dóra and Dísa, as we do."

"It's a pleasure to meet you both," she replied, smiling at them in turn.

"This lady is our new midwife, girls," said Albert.

"Will she bring the baby out of *Mamma*'s tummy, *Pabbi*?" asked Dísa. She had dropped the older responsible sister facade and looked like a child again.

Albert set Dóra to the ground and glanced over at Sólveig. "I sure hope so, Dísa.

The girls ran ahead, and Sólveig followed Albert into the house. They travelled down a dark corridor; the walls and floor clad with timber. At an intersection of doorways was a single wall lamp, and Albert stopped under the flickering orange glow, shadows playing across his face as he turned to her and pointed to a staircase on their left.

"Björn and his household live here. You'll meet them in the morning." He turned again, making his way up a steep staircase on the right, the light from the room above them creeping onto the steps at the top.

Sólveig took a deep breath, feeling suddenly nervous in the face of meeting a household full of new people and having to talk to them in the custom of common courtesy when all she truly wanted was the oblivion of sleep. Pushing down her apprehension, she trailed him, entering a large room—the family *baðstofa*. A wave of warmth and light enveloped her along with an array of smells created from too many bodies in close confine—sweat mingled with tobacco, deep earthy scents with hints of the sea, their livelihood embedded into their clothes, along with the pungent smell of animal fat burning in glass lamps on shelves above beds and on a table at one end of the room.

The timber floor was clothed with woven mats to hold the warmth, and the walls were boarded, unlike some of crofts she had lived in growing up with dirt floors and unclad walls, and the drafts and damp that came with it. This room was painted with colour, the bottom panelling a dark green and the top a fresh white. Though crowded and busy, it was tidy, and Sólveig concluded with satisfaction that Albert's farm was one of good standing and moderate wealth.

People of all ages sat on the row of beds built along the inner and outer walls, all with various items of work in their hands—working wool, mending socks, plaiting ropes of horsehair, or reading by lamp-light. They stared openly and with curiosity at her.

A woman with delicate features stopped the pedal on her timber spinning wheel and stood awkwardly from a bed next to the table by the window. Her dark-blonde hair was streaked with grey, trailing down her back into two long plaits. Her hand supported a heavily swollen belly, and she waddled towards them, a fine crinkling of lines about her eyes, her expression full of relief and joy at the sight of them.

"Albert, it's good to have you home safe. Did all go as expected?" she asked. "I thought you might have been caught up in the rain earlier."

Sólveig noticed the tender smile Albert flattered the woman with, and she guessed that this was his wife as his arm slid around her swollen waistline, and he leaned in to kiss her on the cheek.

"I was hoping to be back sooner, but when the storm hit, we stopped and supped with Jakob and María at Botn. But Ísafjörður? Well, the matter of opening a store in Suðureryi will be a little more complicated than I anticipated, but I was able to get the supplies we needed, and even better, I found us a learned midwife." He turned to Sólveig, where she stood just behind him. "Kristín, this is Sólveig."

"Well, this is quite the surprise," said his wife. "We certainly feel honoured to have a learned midwife come to us." She took Sólveig's hands in her own, kissing her on the cheek in greeting. "It's a pleasure to meet you, Sólveig, and welcome to our household. Please call me Krissa."

"Thank you," she replied, warmed by the welcome. "I'm pleased to be here, and I hope I can be of some use to you when your own little one arrives. Albert tells me the babe is due soon."

"Krissa—" Albert interrupted, before they could get any further. "Would you mind settling Sólveig in while I attend to the horse and supplies?"

Sólveig smiled to herself. She sensed his impatience, and this talk of babies and birth was as good a reason as any for him to excuse himself.

"Of course," said Krissa, and Albert left them.

Krissa turned her attention back to Sólveig, placing a hand on her arm. "*Já*, this baby is due to arrive in about two months' time, if I've calculated correctly. I truly am happy to have you. I think you've relieved the minds of many with your presence here." And she leaned into her, her voice softer, almost a whisper. "I'm not as young as I used to be, and I know Albert worries for me. I'm nearly ten years older than him, you see, an aged old woman at forty-one—too old to be still having babies," she added wryly. "It's been much harder on my body this time around, and I'm more tired than I was with the others." She glanced down at her belly, rubbing it tenderly with her other hand.

"Well, you must take it easy where you can, Krissa," Sólveig said, knowing that pregnancy and birth were often riskier and harder for women past the age of forty. "But I'll be here to help you, of course, and we'll do our best and pray for the safe delivery of this little one."

"Thank you. You are too kind." Krissa blinked hard, but quickly regained her composure.

As mistress of the house, Krissa took her around the room to introduce her to the household. At the far end near the window sat Þorlaug, Krissa's mother, a woman well into her sixties. She went by the name Tobba. She was an older version of her daughter, but where her daughter's nose was small and neat on her face, her mother's was hooked like the beak of a bird. She simply nodded at Sólveig, making her feel small under her scrutiny as she peered up at her, pausing in her task of working a pair of wool combs between her hands to thin the thick wool tufts into thinner strands for spinning. Then there was Þorleifur, Krissa's grandfather, Tobba's father. Four generations in the one household, Sólveig mused and figured he was well into his eighties. He pulled out the pipe he was smoking and smiled to reveal many missing teeth towards the back of his mouth. The hair on his head had thinned out to almost baldness and his hands, large and bony, were knotted with veins.

"All the way from Reykjavík," he said, drawing the words out, in the croaky tone that came about with old age. "That's a long way to go and just to deliver babies." He shook his head in dismay. "Don't we have enough women around here for that, Krissa?"

"Afi!" Krissa admonished. "Of course, we have plenty of women here, but none that are learned!" She clucked her tongue at her grandfather's impertinence. "Pay no mind to him, Sólveig." And she moved her along, leading her to an empty bed close to the entrance of the *baðstofa*.

"Árni normally sleeps here." Krissa pointed to the neatly made bed. "He's just gone out with Albert to unload the horse, along with Einar."

Spread out along the length of the cot was a thick brown and black woven blanket and a flattened cushion used as a pillow up against the partition wall. A timber plank with the name *Árni* etched into it in cursive writing was tucked between the frame and mattress, telling all who slept in this cot. Above the cot, on the wall, sat a small shelf holding various personal items—an *askur*, bowl and spoon, a small box and some tools.

"Árni is one of our workmen, but I'll move him next to Albert's younger brother Einar," said Krissa.

"Please, I don't want to be a hassle to anyone. I don't need a bed to myself. Is there another woman or a child I can share with?" Sólveig had no intention of being the cause of any angst among the household with these new arrangements.

"Well, you'll need the bed closest to the doorway," Krissa insisted "It only makes sense, seeing as you'll be called out at all hours of the night for deliveries. Besides, our work maids, Rúna and Inga, already share a bed." Krissa pointed to another empty bed next to Sólveig's new spot.

"You'll meet our work maids shortly. They're just in the kitchen finishing up after the meal."

⧓

The evening crept on in a whirl of conversation. The people of the household were curious of their new guest and questioned her thoroughly on her journey north with the postman: where in the south she had lived and why she had sought a position so far north. She answered them as best she could, giving them only the barest of details. She knew, after all, how people could talk, desperate for information to dissect and give their opinion on. Sólveig didn't owe these people anything, and she wasn't going to give too much of herself before she got to know them better. She didn't tell them she'd been raised by her *amma*, her father run off to the west, or the reason she had become a midwife was because of her sister's death in childbirth. No, it was safer to say as little as possible—that she had worked in various households in Reykjavik until she had taken her midwifery studies under the assistant head doctor in Reykjavik. That was the safest thing to do.

When the work maids, Guðrún and Ingibjörg, returned from their kitchen duties, they introduced themselves to Sólveig. The one named Ingibjörg called herself Inga. She was young and lively, perhaps eighteen, a pretty girl, with long golden hair, delicately arched brows and full lips.

The other had a stillness about her. She seemed older than Inga, perhaps around Sólveig's own age. She was short and thin, her hair the colour of night, curling in wisps about her face, her skin pale and her eyes a brilliant green.

"Please call me Rúna," she said when Inga finally let her get a word in. "It'll be nice to have another set of hands around here. It's a large household and there's still much to prepare for winter."

"She's a midwife, Rúna, she's not here to clean and serve like we are." Inga scoffed.

"I don't expect to just sit around and wait for a baby to come along." Sólveig laughed. "Of course, I'll make myself useful. I wouldn't think Albert and Krissa expected any less of me."

"Well, in that case, you can switch with me anytime," piped Inga. "I must serve Árni. He's rather a bore and bad-tempered. I can't seem to do anything right for him. Mending his clothes or bringing him his meal. There's always something I'm lacking. I'd much rather someone younger, like Einar or, better yet, your brother Helgi, in Björn's household. He's more fun and better to look at," she said rather wistfully.

"Inga!" Rúna chastised. "Stop giving Árni a reason to scold you. Your head is always in the clouds, and you could certainly do better at mending holes. I've seen how rushed and untidy your stitches are—and leave my brother out of it, for God's sake, let him be."

"Hmph," Inga snorted, clearly none too pleased with being scolded. She stuck her tongue out at the work maid and stood, taking herself to the end of the room to sit by Tobba on her bed.

Rúna rolled her eyes in response, and Sólveig, feeling awkward at being caught in the middle of this, simply shrugged her shoulders.

The men finally returned as the household was settling to bed, the women last to follow them. Albert delivered Sólveig her sack of possessions when he came inside with Árni and Einar.

Einar was a stark contrast to his older brother Albert, of medium build, his hair a shaggy auburn mop, and his jaw free of facial hair. He had an easy smile, his disposition light like Albert's. Árni was a stern-looking man well into his fifties, short and stocky, with dark bushy brows. He wasn't thrilled upon returning inside to find he had to move his things, but muttering under his breath, he snatched his bedclothes, bed board with his name and his possessions from the shelf above the bed and moved them across the room to the cot where Einar slept. Sólveig stood by in discomfort at being the reason for his disgruntled mutterings. The beds were made wide enough for two adults, sleeping head to toe, but after the luxury of having his own bed, she could understand his frustration at the change. Nevertheless, this was the decision of the mistress of the house, so Sólveig took to unpacking her small supply of possessions.

Inga and Rúna took to their own roles, helping the returned workmen to undress them of their shoes, laying out their socks and gloves to allow the dampness on them to dry overnight and folded their day clothes, placing them in a neat pile on a chest near their bed. Sólveig lay in her own cot, dressed in her night-clothes—a simple grey woollen underdress, with long sleeves, reaching down to her ankles. She lay facing the wall, her eyes heavy, ready for sleep, but thinking she was grateful for not having to play this role for once: the role of the work maid, of not having to be the last one in bed because you were waiting for your assigned workman to retire for the night, making sure he had dry clothes and socks for the following day. She had, like most girls at the age of fourteen, gone to work in another household as a maid to earn herself a living until she could marry, bear children, and run a household of her own. But it wasn't a given that she would step down that path—that marriage, babies and her own household were for her. Her own mother had only always been a house maid, her children brought forth in shame, according to the church and her *amma*, her paternal grandmother. Besides, Sólveig had stepped down a different path. It had been brought about in the face of tragedy, but it had led her to a path of learning. Surely, they would be proud to see her now, her mother and sister, even her *amma*. She was, after all, not employed here as a maid but positioned in the household as her own person, employed by the district to be midwife, her food and board paid for by the district, her independence her own.

Her body was weary after weeks of arduous travel, and Sólveig thought sleep would claim her quickly. It had been beckoning her earlier, but now that the house lay in darkness, she found that it evaded her. She never slept well the first few nights at a new place. She tossed and turned in her bed, too many thoughts to attend to and the sudden need to relieve herself only added to her restlessness. She ran over the conversation she had with Doctor Þorvaldur in Ísafjörður, with Albert, with Krissa, even with old Leifur, who'd told her she had all but wasted her time coming here. She supposed it did seem a little unusual, a girl from Reykjavík choosing the far northwest to practise her midwifery, but why should she have to justify her decisions to anyone? Did they not need learned midwives here? By the doctor's accounts, they certainly did. She admitted that it would have been nicer being posted in the town of Ísafjörður, with its bustling activity and the doctor at close hand. She had a feeling that being positioned in this small district between mountains and fjords would require much more of her than she thought. She would truly have to stand on her own two feet and draw on her learning which had only been three months under the doctor's tuition in Reykjavík. She hoped that it would be enough to help these people when the need arose.

She rolled over again in the bed, this time pressing her legs together. She couldn't ignore it much longer. The need to relieve herself was near to the point of becoming uncomfortable. She didn't relish leaving the warmth of her cot, but she was reluctant to use the pan under her bed in front of these strangers, sleeping or not, especially when it was too cold to go out, but it was only September. Wrapping her shawl around her shoulders, she slipped on the sheepskin shoes she'd tucked in the void under her cot and treaded softly down the stairs and silent hallway. The narrow corridor was cold and dark, eery in the silence of the night, but she trailed her hands along the walls of the tunnel until she reached the kitchen. It had been shown to her earlier that night, and she made her way towards it, the burning peat in the hearth like a beacon in the dark and she stepped through the doorway leading outside.

Sólveig hurried back into the kitchen moments later, her fingers and the tip of her nose stinging with exposure to the cold, but feeling lighter, her bed now calling her to the oblivion of sleep.

Making her way through the kitchen with its glowing embers in the cooking hearth, she paused by its warmth, soaking in some of the heat with outstretched hands, relishing the way it radiated up the front of her body. She closed her eyes, allowing the silence of the night to settle around her, but a rustling in the room off the kitchen made her breath catch and her eyes shot open. She strained to hear the sound again, her heart leaping in painful, startled thumps.

"Is someone there?" she ventured weakly. Sólveig knew better than to be caught wandering around in the dark, especially in a house full of strangers. All too often, she'd heard stories of men forcing themselves upon women unawares in the dark of night, but this was a respectable household. Surely, she was safe here.

Perhaps there were ghosts lurking in the house. She shivered, pushing that thought away too. It was likely mice or perhaps a cat, she finally decided, and shuddered with distaste. Most farms had cats. Surely, this one had them, too, to keep away the rodents, but she found herself tiptoeing quietly through the kitchen towards a storeroom full of barrels and the sacks that Albert had brought with him from town. She would let him know in the morning. The last thing anyone wanted was mice eating into their winter supplies.

She peered into the darkness and was ready to leave when she noticed a shadow of movement at the edge of her vision. Heavy breathing sounded from the far corner, and she realised with a sense of dread that the dark shapes in that part of the room were clearly not barrels, nor mice or ghosts of her imagination, but two grown people. From the deep, muffled tone and then the lighter one that caught her ear, Sólveig knew it was a man and a woman. He had her up against a wall, his body melting into hers. She took an abrupt step backwards, shocked to find herself spying on such a thing, though she had not known it for what it was. In her fluster, she turned, and thinking to flee in the same silence she had arrived in, instead walked into a wooden crate, kicking her small toe on its edge, sending a dizzying pain up her leg.

"*Anskotinn,*" she swore under her breath, struggling to rein in more curses, breathing deep and heavy in the effort to not draw attention to herself, but, in truth, wanting to scream out her frustration and jump up and down to cradle her toe. When she looked up again, two startled faces assessed her through the darkness. She could just make out a man with short, dark unruly hair. His brows were raised as if waiting for Sólveig's next move. Was she a threat? Would she scold them or tell the master of the house, or would she leave them be? He must have thought her harmless, because the woman stifled a giggle and pulled at the man's shirt, trying to draw him back to her. He held her gaze for a moment longer, then shrugged his shoulders, turning his attention back to the business of kissing the woman.

Sólveig's face flushed hot with shame, and she made her way back to her bed, her bladder empty, but her toe throbbing and sleep a distant memory.

She lay in bed wondering about the man and woman sneaking to be together in the night. He was clearly not forcing himself upon her. The woman had been an eager participant. They were most likely workers, unmarried, at that, to have to resort to sneaking their kisses in the night while the rest of the household slept, and it made Sólveig reflective and somewhat wistful.

Whenever she closed her eyes, she kept seeing the way the man's body was entwined with the woman's, making their bodies seem one in the darkness. She had never had a man interested in her that way. Never had stolen kisses in the night. Always so focused on doing the right thing, on keeping her head down, and working hard and then later on becoming a midwife, she'd never taken much notice of the men around her. Of course, being a midwife, she knew how babies were made and she'd heard the rustle of bed sheets and soft moans often enough coming from the marriage bed in the *baðstofa*, first growing up in her grandmother's household and then in other households she worked at when she turned fourteen. The thought of a man showing her some interest made her stomach go into knots, and besides, it had been a death sentence for her sister, she reminded herself—as if the memory of what happened to her could be so easily erased. The mere thought of it sent a wave of gooseflesh through her every time. It was simply safer to stay away from the attentions of men.

Quiet footsteps sounded, and through the veil of darkness, she watched a young woman enter the *baðstofa*. The bed creaked and she heard the stirring of the other woman in the bed partitioned next to hers. Back in the storeroom, she hadn't seen the woman's face in clear detail, but she knew it had been one of the work maids from Albert's household, either Rúna or Inga. Whoever it had been was returning from the arms of their secret lover. She had come alone, so Sólveig assumed the man belonged to the other household in the *baðstofa* across the hallway.

4

The work maids left early the next morning before the sun rose, out to the livery to milk the cows. By the time the rest of the household was awake, the men, too, were long gone to see to the task of sorting sheep for the slaughter, old Þorleifur trailing them. Dísa fussed about with Dóra, telling her little sister to sit still while she plaited her hair for her. The younger child kept moving, throwing a toy bone in the air, her hands outstretched to catch it, making the job of plaiting all the harder.

Sólveig sat on her bed, examining her bruised and battered toe, her morning meal done with. Krissa was just entering the room, returning from the kitchen with two bowls of skyr with bilberries for her children, but had halted on her path and now stood over her.

"My word! Sólveig, that looks terrible."

Sólveig tried wriggling her little toe and winced. It was swollen, a black-and-blue bruise colouring her skin.

"Ouch," exclaimed Dóra. She had pulled away from her sister at her mother's remark and made her way over to inspect Sólveig's toe, a hand covering her mouth at the sight of it. Dísa followed suit, and then Tobba came over so that a circle of concerned faces peered down at her.

"And how did you manage that?" asked Tobba, clucking her tongue with distaste.

"Just me being clumsy, is all. I hit it on the end of a wooden crate yesterday in the storeroom." She wasn't going to mention the why of it—that it had been the late of night and the shameful act she had witnessed in the dark corner of that storeroom off the kitchen.

"Best keep it clean so it doesn't go putrid," said Tobba sharply.

"*Nei*, it's under the skin," said Sólveig. "I didn't tear it. I'll make a salve of butterwort to put on it. It may help lessen the swelling. Now, tell me" —she glanced up at Krissa and Tobba— "do you grow or collect any herbs here yourself? If you do, I'd love to have a look at your supply." She had with her some vials of medicine that had been allocated to her for use with her midwifery—cinnamon drops for disinfection and masking smells, Hoffman's drops and *salmiak spiritus* to relieve pain and induce sleep—but she found she relied more on her herbs, as she had grown up doing, under her *amma*'s tutelage. She only had a very meagre supply herself that she'd managed to dry and collect over the summer, but it was useful to have a variety of herbs at hand, helpful with coughs and sore throats as well as inflammation of the skin.

"So, you're an herbalist too, are you?" asked Tobba, regarding her with interest.

"I wouldn't call myself that, but I do find it very interesting the way we can use plants to heal." She smiled at Tobba and continued, "Mostly, it's just knowledge my *amma* passed to me as a child. She delivered babies too, though she was not formally educated."

"We grow vegetables in the garden behind the croft near the kitchen—the usual root vegetables—mostly potatoes and swedes," said Krissa. "The rest we gather off the mountain slopes as the season sees fit to provide—angelica, moss, thyme and sorrel, scurvy grass. Berries come early autumn, and you'll find butterwort near the lake growing on the lower slopes, in the damper patches between crevices in the rocks, and then there's dulse, the red seaweed down by the sea. I try to keep a supply of thyme and angelica for when colds come about, which seems to be all year round." She frowned. "We do have a room off the kitchen set aside for dry goods and herbs, with a spare cot, if we run out of room in here with extra guests. There's a bench there for grinding and you can hang a line for drying. You're more than welcome to create a space for yourself there, Sólveig, to store your herbs and medicines."

It was probably the one and the same room she had stumbled into the night before, Sólveig thought to herself wryly, but she nodded her thanks to Krissa, who took her attention back to her daughters and proceeded to usher them to their places to eat their morning meal.

⊹

Later that day, Krissa introduced Sólveig to some of the household across the hallway. There were so many new names to remember, Sólveig knew she would have to ask a few times before the names stuck. The house mistress was Rannveig, a plump, cheerful woman, close in age to Krissa, with light-brown hair and a mole dominating her cheek. With her were two young women and a child—her timid work maid, Hansína, and Rannveig's two daughters, Sigga and little Margrét, who was the same age as Dóra. They were in the kitchen, a shared space, making *slátur*—blood and liver sausages, trying their best to use every part of the sheep. There were hands everywhere—some were covered in bloody gruel, and Sólveig watched deft fingers fill the thick cream-coloured pouches of stomach lining from the sheep with the meat and blood mixture while other hands were busy sewing the fist-sized pouches shut. The bags of meat would be stored along with sheep's-head jam in barrels of whey liquid left over from making skyr—food that would see them through the long winter when the land was frozen and barren. They all depended on the sheep. They took its meat, head and tongue included, its blood, its woollen coat, and even its bones were utilised as spoons and knife handles and children's playthings. Rannveig's husband, Björn, and his menfolk had slaughtered only the day before. Krissa told Sólveig her girls would be in the kitchen too over the next few days preparing their own *slátur*, and they left Rannveig and her girls to their work, making their way into the storeroom and Krissa's supply of herbs.

That evening, Sólveig was in the room off the kitchen shifting items around to make herself some space for her herbs and medicines and preparing a salve for her bruised toe. The light in the room was dim, there being just one small glass window positioned over a timber bench. Otherwise, the space was filled with barrels of food stores and salt, some stacked on top of the others. A room was attached again to this one, steps going down into a cool dark cellar where they stored more food. It was locked and required the mistress's keys to open.

Peering through the window, she could see a distorted image of the ocean and a small croft on the beach somewhat up from the shoreline, lined with boats.

"I was hoping to find you alone" came a young woman's voice tentatively from the doorway.

"My goodness! You scared me, Inga." Sólveig laughed lightly, clutching the base of her throat.

Inga stepped into the room, glancing over her shoulder a couple of times before approaching her. She peered into the bowl Sólveig held, her nose pinched with distaste. "What's this you're making?"

"A salve for my bruised toe."

"Oh." Silence ensued, and Inga swallowed hard a few times, ceaselessly twirling the long ends of her honey-coloured braids.

Sólveig continued mixing the salve, sensing that the girl wanted to say something but was having a hard time starting. "Is there something I can help you with, Inga?"

"Well, it's just—" She dropped her hands, clasping them together behind her back to still them. "You haven't mentioned to anyone about last night, have you?" she blurted in a hushed tone.

Sólveig stopped the motion of stirring. "Last night?" she asked, slightly baffled, and then it dawned on her. "Ah, so it was *you* in here with that man?"

"Já," Inga replied quickly, "but you mustn't tell anyone about it. If Albert knew we were sneaking about to be together, that would be my job, and I do so like it here. Albert doesn't tolerate that sort of behaviour from his household."

"Well, perhaps you should stop, then."

"I know I should, but I like being with him. I like it when he kisses me." Inga hesitated. "Just please tell me you won't say anything, Sólveig."

"Breathe easy, Inga, I'm not one to tell, but are you being careful? He wasn't forcing himself upon you, was he?"

The young woman shook her head vigorously. "Oh no, not Helgi. He would never."

But Sólveig wasn't convinced. "It's just that you shouldn't let it go too far. Once a man starts, it's sometimes hard to make him stop. You know you could end up with child, Inga, and what then?" She went back to stirring the mixture but kept her attention on the maid, wanting to drive the importance of this into the young woman. "Have you ever seen a child being born? Babies are easy to make, but birthing them and caring for them takes much more of a woman."

Inga shook her head, her face going pale, like the thought of babies had never crossed her mind in all the 'kissing' she was doing with this Helgi. Sólveig wasn't surprised. Many young girls and unmarried women were naive in those aspects of life through no fault of their own, letting a man do with them as they pleased and not understanding the consequences. These matters were of a delicate nature and weren't spoken of aloud, even between mother and daughter. Maybe if they were, Sólveig reckoned there would be a lot less illegitimate children running around. It was assumed that coupling was something a woman just eventually learned about when she married and her husband would teach her what to do, but what about before she married? She had more than once been warned by her *amma* to stay away from men and to never share a blanket with a man other than her husband. When she had tried to question her on why these things were not allowed, her *amma* had scolded her and told her that shame would befall her, like it had her mother, a woman she'd met for the first and only time at the age of fourteen, when she received her confirmation. But it had not been hard to figure out the rest. That what a man did with a woman under the blankets of the marriage bed resulted in a child. If only her own sister had known the truth of it, she thought, a stab of regret filling her.

Sólveig knew she would have to be blunt with the girl.

"So, you haven't shared a bed with him or let him inside you?" she asked.

The girl blushed a darker shade of red. *"Nei*, of course not! We haven't done anything like that." Inga shrugged, her eyes turning soft, and her tone light. "It's just some harmless fun, a bit of kissing, that's all."

Sólveig found that hard to believe after what she had witnessed the night before. It had certainly looked like much more.

"If you say so, Inga," she said, almost dismissively, taking her attention back to the salve. She really didn't want to be drawn into this tangle. "Though, I think a respectable young woman like you knows the smartest decision would be to stop this affair before it goes too far."

The girl blinked hard a few times, as if stunned by the suggestion, but then drew herself up, pulling her shoulders back and lifting her chin high. "He will marry me one day, you know."

Sólveig sighed. She pitied the girl. What man could hold a woman so captivated that she would risk her job for his affections? "I am happy for you, Inga, really, I am, and I hope he does marry you, but in the meantime, please just be careful, and if your menses stop, then you'll have cause to be concerned."

5

Her first few days at Suðureryi passed in a blur of activity as Sólveig settled in with her new family. During those days she was able to let her body rest and recover from her arduous journey, taking on light tasks until she was finally able to walk without too much of a limp.

There was always plenty of work in the running of two large households, and while the women of Albert's household worked in the kitchen, smoking and salting the meat from the sheep for storage and preparing the *slátur*, their hands covered in blood and sheep-innards stuffing and sewing pouches, Sólveig questioned Krissa about the people of the community. She wanted to get an idea of who was currently with child and who may need her assistance in the months to come.

Krissa told her what she knew—that there were thirteen farms in the district, including those over the mountain, Spillir, in a valley called Vatnadalur. Most households had women of childbearing ages, but Krissa said it wasn't something they really spoke about. Sure, you would see an expanding waistline and then news would reach them that a baby had been born, but it wasn't something women would go around announcing to everyone. She mentioned María at Botn, of course, who she had already met, and then there was Björg at the farm Hraunakot in the Vatnadalur valley. Krissa knew her to be with child—there was rarely a time when she wasn't during the past eight years, with six little ones already born, she'd informed her.

Sólveig was eager to meet the other women of her community, to introduce herself and make it known that she was an educated midwife and could help them when their time came, but she also wanted to meet the old midwife Gróa who resided in the valley over at the farm Bær.

Sólveig knew the people of the household were busy with their own tasks, and she didn't feel quite confident enough to just walk about the district on her own, not knowing who lived where, so when she overheard Albert mention to Einar on her fifth day at Suðureyri that one of Björn's workmen was heading over to Vatnadalur that day, she knew her chance had come.

"Could Rúna or Inga not take you?" Albert asked in gruff reply to her request to go to Vatnadalur.

"I'm afraid they're tied up with finishing off the last of the *slátur*. I'm only asking because I overheard you saying someone was heading out that way today."

"Ah *já*, Helgi is out to see Grímur with the matter of writing a letter."

"Surely, he wouldn't mind if I accompanied him?"

"I'm sure he wouldn't, Sólveig, but I think it best I take you or one of the work maids another day." And with that, he considered the matter settled, tipping his head in farewell before she could get another word in.

Sólveig wondered why Helgi couldn't simply take her. She knew Albert was out on the boat with Einar and Árni to bring in a catch, and she figured he would be tied up every day after that too. It was rare that anyone sat idle for long, so she wasn't sure when she would get the chance next. She hated to make trouble where there needn't be any and decided that she would save Albert and the busy housemaids the hassle and ask Helgi herself, if he hadn't already left.

Sólveig stepped outside into the fresh morning air, hoping to seek out the workman. The mistress for the other household, Rannveig, had mentioned they were down by the sea croft doing repairs on one of the boats. The sky was cloudless but the wind was up, blowing salty notes from the sea at her as she strolled towards a group of men gathered around an upended boat near the sea croft and a fish-drying hut.

Four heads were bent down together, inspecting a sixareen—their six-oared ocean vessel. An array of tools lay scattered on the ground around them, with the long poles of the boat's sails. They didn't look up as she approached, too absorbed in their task, but she had met Björn and his sons already, the wiry older man with a brown hat and dark-grey beard. Next to him were his two sons. Jói, who was about eighteen, a young man with ears that stuck out from under his hat, and Tóti, only fourteen, gangly and freckle faced. They were both younger versions of their father, with deep-set eyes and tawny-coloured hair. The fourth man she hadn't met before. He was crouched down on his haunches, his shirtsleeves rolled up, revealing muscled forearms, a couple of iron nails between his lips as he hammered another into the timber at his feet. Most of his face was hidden under a grey cap, and he sported a black moustache, shadowed by a few days' growth across his jawline.

"Góðan daginn," she greeted them, clasping her hands together before her.

The men finally looked up at her and tipped their heads in greeting, accompanied by *"Góðan dag,* Sólveig."

The fourth man pulled the nails from between his lips and stood from his crouch. He was not a tall man, but solid, broad at the shoulders and slim waisted. He smiled at her, and she returned it, sensing amusement in his green gaze. He had the look of the *selkie* about him—those mythical creatures from the old stories she'd heard as a child, of seals that shed their skin for human form when they touched land, with their black hair and green eyes. His were thickly lashed, that same deep green, like moss-covered rocks, and she had a feeling this was the notorious Helgi. He had been elusive thus far, but she was certain that this man was Rúna's brother. They were so alike with their startling eye colour.

"So, this must be the new midwife everyone is talking about." Helgi pulled his cap off, revealing a flattened mess of short curls, black like the darkest of nights.

He had a pleasing face, and she could she see why Inga had made the remarks she had about swapping her workman, the cantankerous Árni, with this light-hearted man, but she was also reminded that this was Helgi, the one and the same man who she had spied with Inga just a few nights ago in the storeroom, breaking all the house rules. Here was a man with no boundaries.

"You must be Helgi. Rannveig said I would find you here." She held her hand out in greeting. "We haven't been properly introduced. I'm Sólveig."

He took her outstretched hand and pulled her towards him, a hand at her waist, and greeted her in the proper custom, a kiss on the cheek. The bristle of his moustache scraped lightly across her skin. She pulled away quickly, catching the gleam in his eyes at her apparent discomfort, his expression betraying the fact that, of course, they had already met before, though under shadier circumstances.

"Albert tells me you're heading into Vatnadalur today? You wouldn't mind me accompanying you, would you?"

He seemed surprised by her request. "By all means, Sólveig, you're more than welcome to join me." He grinned at her, his eyes bright as he added, "The walk over there suddenly seems less of a chore."

She let his remark slide. "When are you planning on leaving? I'd appreciate it if you could direct me to Björg and Gróa's farms while we're there."

"Certainly." He nodded and pushed his hat back onto his head, crouching down again. "We'll make tracks when I've finished up here. I'll come find you when I'm ready to go."

⁂

Sólveig spent the rest of the morning helping Rúna and Inga in the kitchen with the last of the *slátur* preparation. When midmorning came around, Helgi loped into the kitchen, making his sister squeal when he pinched her sides in greeting and almost received a smear of the bloody mixture across his face from her hands.

"*Uff*, Helgi, away with you now. Don't you have better things to do than torment me?" asked Rúna crossly.

"As a matter of fact, I do. I'm here to collect your midwife. She's asked for my escort services over to Vatnadalur," he mocked, bowing formally in front of Sólveig. They all giggled at his playfulness, but at this mention of escort, Sólveig caught the way Inga's lips pressed together in displeasure.

Sólveig wasn't blind to the way the young woman made eyes at Helgi as he entered the room, but he didn't approach her, and she could see that this hurt the girl. Underneath all the jesting, she sensed tension there between the lovers, and Helgi's over-the-top playfulness was a distraction from this.

"I'll just be a moment," Sólveig chimed in, cleaning her hands and disappearing upstairs to the *baðstofa*. She returned quickly, tucking her woollen shawl around the jacket of her bodice to keep her chest warm and finished tying off the cream-coloured kerchief to cover her head. She wore her green chequered apron, with her long black skirt, the only good one she had, and her new sheep-skin shoes. "I'm ready," she declared, clutching her midwifery bag in her hands, with the tools of her calling.

"Stay out of trouble, sister," Helgi teased in departure, tugging at Rúna's plait lightly.

"It's more the other way around, brother. Now take care of our new midwife. Be nice to her." She winked at Sólveig and added, "If he annoys you too much, I give you permission to slap him about the ears."

The clear skies of the morning had turned overcast with thick clouds, and a light drizzle rained down over them as Sólveig and Helgi set off for Vatnadalur. Suðureyri farm sat at the head of the fjord, and they had to take the path around the mountain Spillir to reach the next valley. The wind bit at her ears, and Sólveig shifted her head scarf to cover them better. Helgi wore his cap, the tips of his ears tinged red with the cold, but he had rolled down his sleeves, covering his arms and chest with a brown vest and a black jacket. They passed the seaman's croft where the men were working earlier that day, Björn and Jói still there.

"Were you able to fix it?" she asked Helgi as they passed them. He was just ahead of her, and slowed his pace to walk beside her, making conversation easier against the onslaught of the wind.

"Sure, we'll get her out tomorrow, if the weather holds up." He went quiet again, nothing but the wind and lapping ocean beside them to break the silence.

"Is it far to Vatnadalur?"

"Not so far." He glanced over at her with a smirk, and then: "Not for one such as you, a seasoned traveller of mountains and moors—and a daughter of the French to boot."

She could tell by his tone that he was teasing her, but his remark was befuddling. "Daughter of the French? And what do you mean by that?"

"The brown-eyed beauty." His green ones flashed as they met hers. "It's said they come from the French and Spanish sailors who fish off our coastline."

Did he mock her? She stopped in her tracks. His compliment had turned so suddenly to insult. "Well, I know my father," she said indignantly. "He was neither Frenchman nor Spaniard, thank you, nor my mother."

"You know, it could be there, and you wouldn't even know it, tracing back to your grandparents or theirs—" His tone was teasing, his familiarity with her startling and undignified. "A stranded sailor, an innocent maid," he continued, to her shocked dismay. "Alright, alright, I'll stop. I can tell by that scowl that I've taken it too far. I do apologise." He tipped his head at her, in what she felt was mock sincerity. "It wasn't meant as an insult to your breeding."

"Shall we be on our way, then?" she asked curtly, indicating for him to walk on, so she could follow.

"It's only just over an hour—to Vatnadalur that is," started Helgi, after a few moments of strained silence. He slowed his pace and walked beside her once more, his hands in his pockets, his tone still light, but the teasing edge was gone. "And you're from Reykjavík I hear?"

"*Já*, I guess you could say that," she replied warily. Her earlier indignation had drifted away with the wind, but she felt uncomfortable revealing anything about herself to this man. "I was born at Vogar, the coastal south of Reykjavík, but lived with my *amma* in Hafnarfjörður growing up, and when she died, I was at various households around Reykjavík. I did my midwifery training there."

"How long have you been at Suðureyri?" she asked in return.

He blew out his breath and counted to himself. "It's been about twelve years. Came here when I was just a lad of fourteen." He looked past her, indicating the mountain across the sea on their left. "My people are just over the fjord at Keflavík, high up on the headland, where the ocean stretches beyond the horizon," he said almost wistfully, "but the winters can be hard. My two brothers are helping my mother manage the farm." He glanced over at her, as if considering her. "You've come to a good place, Sólveig. The people here are like my second family. Of course, Rúna is here too. You won't find fairer men than Björn and Albert."

They fell silent again, but she ran over his words, letting them linger, and she found that they brought her comfort.

They reached the headland, the very edge of the mountain Spillir where it stretched its earthly body out into the sea, and they traversed a narrow path that ran along the base of a cliff, the sea a moving torrent below them.

"Be careful here, the waves have a way of sneaking up on the path at times," Helgi cautioned her, steering her by the elbow so that she was closer to the cliff face and he nearer the ocean.

The wind carried flecks of ocean spray onto her face, delicate drops that cooled her cheeks and sat on her eyelashes. The sea was angry below them, throwing itself violently against the coastline, and her thoughts went to Albert and the men out on the water, hoping it was calmer wherever it carried them.

They managed to make safe passage, and Helgi veered left into the head of a valley, stretching long and narrow before them, a vision of reds, yellows, and browns before her, the colours of the season. The mountains crowded in around them, rising stark, their tops laced with white—patches of snow that hadn't managed to melt over the summer. There were crofts scattered along the valley, the largest of them nestled next to a church and graveyard Helgi called by the name Staður.

"This is where we attend church." He pointed to the small timber building surrounded by a stone wall, a cross sitting neatly above the gated entrance and another larger one on the peaked arch of the grass roof.

"Do you attend every Sunday?" she asked, unsure what the custom was here. Back home, they walked to church every Sunday morning.

"*Nei*, we don't have our own priest, but we take Sunday as a day of rest and read the psalms and sing hymns within our own households. Séra Stefán, the priest for Holt in Önundarfjörður walks over to deliver the service, and he does so the second Sunday of the month if weather permits."

It was a good thing that the rules dictating christenings had changed, Sólveig mused as they walked. Old law demanded a child's baptism within three days of being born, but now the law had relaxed, and babies didn't have to be rushed out for this holy blessing, the parents at risk of being fined if it wasn't heeded. When a baby was weak and not long for the world, a baptism was performed at home, and now the rules had extended to three months. What a journey it must have been for any newborn child to travel that distance within three days of birth! This had been the case when she was a child. Her *amma* had told her stories of babies perishing on the journey to church in midwinter, traveling many hours in the bitter cold, just to receive God's blessing.

"There'll be a wedding next month," Helgi interrupted her musings.

She held back a knowing smirk. "You're own?"

His eyes met hers. "Mine?" He scoffed, sounding surprised.

"Why, you and Ingibjörg, of course." She knew full well she was provoking him. In truth, she hadn't planned to bring it up. Perhaps it was in some way a small rebuke to his earlier comment about her brown eyes and breeding. "She's a beautiful young woman."

He narrowed his eyes at her in what she suspected was annoyance. "That she is, though, I'm in no mind to marry Ingibjörg."

"But the other night?" she ventured, a little befuddled by his reaction.

"So, it was *you* the other night." He snorted with amusement at this revelation and then: "How's the toe?"

"It's fine, thank you, and don't you go smirking about it." It suddenly dawned on her that this man was just toying with the work maid. "You know, Helgi, you need to be careful with a young woman like Inga. It may be just harmless fun for you, but it's much more than that to her."

He stopped in his tracks and turned to her, meeting her glare with his own look of disdain. She squirmed under the stern gaze he gave her. It had lost its light playfulness, and she realised that this time it was she who had gone too far with her opinion.

"I'll thank you to mind your own business, Midwife," he said curtly, and continued walking, leaving her to trail him.

She had offended him. Well, good! Perhaps he would think twice before things went further with Inga and she ended up carrying his child. *Amma* was right to warn her away from men, she thought. Men only ever had one thought on their mind, with little consideration of the consequences, and it made her blood boil.

Silence ensued and Sólveig followed behind Helgi as they travelled a well-worn path that snaked into the valley passing a second larger farm called Bær. The path trailed high on the slopes, but the farm was positioned farther down and across a small fast-flowing stream. Helgi informed her this was where the midwife Gróa lived, but they would stop

to see her on their way back. He was in a hurry to get his letter written.
Björg lived on the farm next to Grímur's deep in the valley near the lake.
The valley was rock-strewn, as if a giant had played catch along the slopes
of the mountain, boulders large and small scattered everywhere.

It wasn't long before she caught a glimpse of a body of water, its
surface rippled and grey under the overcast sky, two people in the
distance standing by its edge. She was about to ask Helgi if people fished
the lake, but they came upon a small turf croft, and he stopped at the
entrance.

"Björg and Júlíus live here. I'll find you when I'm done." He nodded
to her in curt farewell, leaving her standing alone by the door.

Sólveig pulled herself upright, straightening her skirts and tugged the
kerchief off her head, patting her plaited hair down neatly and finally
tapped on the front door, calling out *"Halló!"* as she did so.

A young girl with a round face and dimpled cheeks opened the door.
Her light-brown hair was split in the middle with a plait sitting over each
shoulder. Her dress was a little worn for wear, and Sólveig could see it had
been patched in many places, a tattered, thin woollen shawl crisscrossed
over her chest.

"Is Björg home?" Sólveig ventured.

"*Mamma* is in the kitchen. My brother Kalli is sick," the child replied,
unable to meet Sólveig's eyes.

"I'm Sólveig, the new midwife. Perhaps I can have a look at your
brother and talk with your mother."

The girl turned back into the narrow hallway, and Sólveig stood,
waiting in the doorway, her hands clasped around her medical bag. The
girl came running back to the door, tailed by a younger sister, no doubt,
no older than Albert and Krissa's daughter Dóra, her thumb in her

mouth, peering up at her with curiosity, twisting her side plaits nervously with her other hand.

"*Mamma* says you may come in."

Sólveig followed the girls down a short corridor and up a narrow staircase, into the home's *baðstofa*. It was a small room. The walls were unlined, the stone and turf exposed. There wasn't even a proper glass window, just dried sheep bladder spread across the timber panes at the end of the room. Not since she was a child had she seen this. Most of the households that she had managed to find a position in were wealthy enough to have their own glass windows. Two more young children were in bed, sniffling and whining.

A fair-haired woman came bustling towards them from the other end of the room, a crying baby on her hip. She was small of stature with fine features and thin lips, her cheekbones set high and prominent in her long, freckled face. She couldn't be more than thirty years old, but she looked ragged, almost bone weary, and Sólveig felt for the woman.

"You must be Björg."

"What can I do for you?" The woman shushed her irritable baby, patting her bottom and swaying her hips in a rocking motion to calm her.

"Are your children sick?" Sólveig indicated the two little ones lying in the bed together.

"Nothing more than the usual cold. It's too cold for them to be wandering about, so they're kept abed, but this one here, she's been in a right mood all day with the teething." Björg was abrupt and snappy, irritation radiating off her in waves. "So, you're the midwife?" She raised her eyebrows in question. "There's been talk of a fancy learned midwife come all the way from down south."

"I don't know about fancy. I'm Sólveig. Krissa told me that you're expecting." Sólveig glanced at her protruding waistline. She was thin and her belly swelled around her low and neatly to the front, and Sólveig thought she looked more than halfway through her pregnancy. "I just wanted to introduce myself and let you know that I've completed my studies and—"

"Look, Sólveig, I'm sure you mean well and all," she interrupted, shifting the distraught baby to her other hip, "but I don't have no way to pay you, and old Gróa delivers all the babes around these parts. She'll deliver this one, when the time comes, like she always has. Now, if you don't mind, I've got a screaming baby and two sick ones and a whole lot more to do before the day is out, and Júlíus comes in expecting to be fed."

"Oh, I don't need you to pay me, Björg, but, of course, I understand." Sólveig tried not to let her disappointment show at another refusal of her services. "I just want you to know that I'm here and will be staying at Suðureyri farm if ever there is anything you need. Please don't hesitate to make it known to me." It was clear the woman was struggling with all these children on her own. "Is there no one to help you with some of your tasks, Björg?"

"*Nei.*" She scoffed. "Apart from Herdís here, these children, this house, all falls to me." Björg sniffed, her lips pressing into a firm line, and she pulled her gaze away, shifting the baby to the other hip once more, tapping her bottom faster.

"Björg, let me take the child. Just for a couple of hours, and Herdís can show me to the kitchen. You need rest. Helgi won't be back for a while yet." The baby squirmed and screamed louder, reaching desperately for her mother as Björg allowed Sólveig to take her.

Sólveig passed the baby to Herdís, who stood by her mother, and the baby calmed down some, being in the arms of the someone she knew.

"It would be nice to just put my feet up for a little," she admitted to Sólveig, and she allowed herself to be led to a cot by the window. Björg sat on the bed, sighing with relief, but stood up again, shaking her head. "Oh, I don't know about this. Júlíus wouldn't be pleased—"

"Everything will be fine," Sólveig reassured her. "Just rest, even if you can't sleep, just rest your feet for a spell."

"Don't let me stay abed too long," Björg murmured, a soft smile touching her lips. "I may not wish to rise again."

Sólveig checked on the two little boys in the cot next to Björg's. They were no more than toddlers, about two and three winters old. From their noses ran a trail of pale-yellow slime. One had fallen asleep and the other one was sucking his thumb. She brushed her fingers over his soft golden curls and down along a chubby cheek. He smiled at her sleepily behind his thumb, unafraid of this stranger in his house. She had some of her herbs in her bag. She could brew a cold tea for the boys, but whether they would take it was another matter. An older child sat on a bed built into the opposite wall, playing with some sheep bones.

She smiled at him and asked his name.

"Tómas," he replied shyly.

"Well, Tómas, do you think you can watch over *Mamma* and your brothers while they have a little sleep?"

He nodded his small round head. "My tummy hurts."

"Are you hungry?" she asked, wondering if the children had had much of a morning meal or if this one, like many children, was always wanting to snack on a morsel of food. He nodded his head, and she pulled out some rye bread she had wrapped in the satchel in the pocket of her dress and gave it to him. He gobbled it up, smiling his pleasure at her, and she left him, making her way downstairs to the kitchen, where Herdís had taken the crying baby.

Sólveig thought to help with some of the cleaning and wanted to get the evening meal prepared while Björg rested. When she entered the small kitchen, she found a stack of pots and bowls to scrub before the evening meal could get under way.

Herdís held baby Soffía, who was just over twelve months old. She bounced her on her hip as her mother had done with the child. She was still whining, her cheeks flushed red, the front of her long-sleeved dress wet from drool.

"*Mamma* sometimes gives her some dried fish to chew on for her teething, but *Pabbi* says we need to be careful with the food stocks for winter."

Sólveig pulled her little satchel out of her dress pocket and gave the baby some dried fish for her aching gums. She'd packed it along with the rye bread, her own meal for the day. She could go without and wait until suppertime back at Suðureyri. Soffía held the pale, fleshy strip in her little fingers, grabbing at it eagerly, bringing it straight to her mouth. Chewing the tough flesh would relieve some of the child's frustration.

Herdís was a willing helper, and they were able to sit little Soffía in a large empty half barrel on the floor of the kitchen while they boiled water to scrub the pots and bowls clean and made a broth for dinner of haddock from a barrel accompanied with potatoes.

Sólveig was just stirring the warming contents of the soup when she heard shouting coming from the *baðstofa*. Herdís's eyes grew wide.

"It's *Pabbi*! He'll be home from Flateyri."

"Herdís, watch your sister please," Sólveig called to the girl as she rushed down the hallway and upstairs into the *baðstofa*.

"What is the meaning of this? You just sleep the day away, you lazy woman. Get up, get out of bed, and see to your husband and children."

Sólveig entered the *baðstofa* to find a burly man with stringy grey hair and a bushy beard leaning over Björg, but Sólveig couldn't just stand by and watch as he grabbed his wife by the arm, wrenching her up and out of bed. The woman yelped, her eyes large and blinking hard as if in shock.

Sólveig marched up to him. "*Nei*, stop. She needs rest. You let her sleep."

"And who the hell are you?" he demanded, releasing his wife to stand at his full height. Sólveig looked up into the weathered and wrinkled face of a man well into his sixties, his thick, wiry brows knotted together in vexation.

"I'm Sólveig, the new midwife for the community," she managed evenly. "It was I who told Björg to rest. She's on her feet too much. There's some swelling around her ankles and she needs to rest more."

"Gróa's the only midwife around here. We don't need you here with your city learning charging a small fortune for something women have always done for free. People round here have always got by without that, and we'll be fine too."

"I don't expect any sort of payment. That's not why I'm here."

"We don't need your charity, lady, and I'll sure as hell not have a stranger come into my home, let alone a woman, and tell me how I should run it. Now get before I throw you out," he demanded, taking a step towards her.

Sólveig stood her ground, her heart beating hard, unsure whether he would drag her out if she refused, but she held his angry gaze, and stood a little straighter, unwilling to back down to this man who thought he could have his way through intimidation.

"Is everything okay here, Sólveig?" It was Helgi. He stood at the entrance to the *baðstofa,* and she breathed a sigh of relief at the sight of him. He came to stand beside her, his hand resting lightly at her elbow. "Júlíus, is there a problem?"

"It's okay, Júlíus," Björg stated flatly before any more words could be spoken. "Sólveig was just leaving."

Sólveig and Helgi made their way back towards the head of the valley, towards the farm Bær, where she could call in to see Gróa, the old midwife. Though Sólveig wasn't so sure now. Perhaps she should just call it a day. She was unsettled and somewhat deflated after her altercation with Júlíus.

They had left in a hurry, Björg giving Sólveig an apologetic look, over Júlíus's triumphant one of reasserting his authority in his household. She hadn't had time to finish the cold remedy for the boys, and she had wanted to do more for Björg, to help alleviate some of her many tasks. The woman needed a work maid with her full time. Herdís was a great help, but it wasn't enough. The whole thing just made her mad. She sighed through her frustration as she walked beside Helgi, and he glanced in her direction.

"That's about the third time you've sighed like that. You sure know how to stir up trouble. I'll give you that." He gave her a friendly nudge with his elbow.

She didn't respond. She simply kept marching on towards the head of the valley, towards the glistening expanse of the ocean ahead, but Helgi's hand was suddenly at her elbow, pulling her to a stop, forcing her to face him.

"Sólveig, are you okay? Did Júlíus lay a hand on you?" His eyes searched hers, his tone low and oddly dark.

"*Nei*, he didn't hurt me." She shook her head, but, in truth, she was hurt. Her anger hurt, her frustration with herself and what had happened at Björg's hurt. She was shocked that a man could behave so towards his wife and to a stranger who had only offered kindness.

"I'm just so mad," she finally managed. "I'm mad at that brute of a man, but I'm also mad at myself. This wasn't how it was supposed to have gone."

"I should have warned you about Júlíus. He's known about these parts for his temper." The look he gave her was one of pity. "But you've got guts, woman. It's not many would stand up to him the way I saw you do just now."

"Oh, Helgi, but I think I just made things worse, instead of better." Her bottom lip trembled, and she turned from him, ashamed that he should see how upset she was. She took a deep breath. *I am stronger than this.* But he was right, she'd only been here a matter of days and already she was in a state.

"Are you set to give up?" came Helgi's voice from behind. "Don't let the people here scare you off. They need you and they'll call upon you soon enough. Change is hard for many."

"I didn't say I was giving up." Frustrated, she walked on ahead, leaving him to trail her, and he followed her closely.

"Just give people a bit of time to get used to you. Things may seem a bit backwards compared to where you come from but—"

She stopped, turning so suddenly that he almost ran into her. "This has nothing to do with people getting used to me, Helgi. You think I haven't seen other men treat their women this way? You think that men down south don't do the same thing? Your community is not unique to that." She pointed back towards the croft. "That woman is about to give birth to *that* man's child. He gave her that child whether she wanted it or not, and he works her like a slave to an early grave. And then what happens to those children when there is no mother to care for them? She needed rest and I just sought to provide a little reprieve for her—because I could." Sólveig kicked at the ground in frustration, a dizzying pain riding up her leg. She whimpered and turned from him again, her eyes watering, biting back a curse.

"Ah, Sólveig," Helgi sighed. But he'd misunderstood, and before she could stop him he turned her to face him and drew her into his embrace. She couldn't remember the last time anyone had held her so, and that simple act left her sense of propriety and self-pity suddenly battling with each other. He rubbed his hand along her back, with tender strokes. "Don't cry. It was a kind thing you did, and I know Björg was thankful for it."

"I'm not crying, Helgi! *Já*, it upsets me, but—"

He pulled back, his eyes catching hers, holding them as if searching the depths of her. "What, then?"

Sólveig shook her head, not wanting to say it. She noticed a small scar above his right eyebrow and was distracted enough to wonder what he had done to get such a mark, but then, his thumb swam into her vision, and it caught the stray tear rolling shamelessly down her cheek. Her breath hitched.

"Go on," he urged. His hand lingered there, and his lips parted ever so slightly.

Sólveig swallowed hard, Helgi's eyes not releasing their hold on her, and for a moment she forgot all about Júlíus and Björg. For a moment all that was between them was their mingled breaths, and the silence of the valley, and all Sólveig could think was that this felt good, that his touch was comforting and—

She pulled abruptly away, shocked with herself. "It was nothing. I just kicked my sore toe again, and it *really* hurt," she blurted pathetically, glancing down at her clothing, out to the ocean ahead, anywhere, so as not to meet his eyes again. What had she been thinking, letting him hold her that way? She hardly knew the man.

When Sólveig finally did look at him, his eyes were bright. He was trying not to smile, and his shoulders shook with restrained mirth. She pushed at him. "It's not funny, Helgi, it really hurt. I blame *you*, you know."

"Well, maybe nosy midwives should stay out of business that doesn't concern them," he offered with irritating smugness.

She scoffed and started walking again. "So you say, Helgi. My lips are sealed."

He caught up with her and they were able to stroll side by side for a while on the path winding back towards the farms Bær and Staður.

"You know, Sólveig, there's a saying here in fjords— that 'it's not always best to go down the mountain the same way you went up.'" He winked at her and took her hand. "Now come, we must make haste to Bær if you're to see Gróa before dark. There'll be no moon tonight."

While they walked, Sólveig pondered Helgi's words—what he had said about walking down a mountain—and perhaps he was right. She needed to take a different approach with the people here. Perhaps she needed to stop pushing so hard, and let the women seek her out. She needed to be patient, and there was time.

6

Gróa wasn't home.

Helgi walked with Sólveig to the door, taking liberty to knock for her and called out to announce their arrival. It was early afternoon. Voices sounded from indoors, evidence of the household going about their day, but it was an older man who answered their beckoning.

"*Sæll*, Eiríkur." Helgi took the man's outstretched hand in greeting. He was a stocky man with large protruding ears and a short beard more grey than the golden hue Sólveig could see it had once been.

"Helgi! What brings you to Bær, my friend?" he asked jovially, his smile broad and welcoming, revealing some missing teeth.

"Just been to Grímur to see to a letter, but we're seeking Gróa, if she's home."

"Afraid not." He squinted one eyed at them in consideration. "Left late last night to see to a birth over at Staður." He nodded his head in the direction of the farm farther down the valley, sitting on the hill next to the church. "Ástríður had her fourth this morning. A boy, it was. Jósefína went with her to assist."

Sólveig couldn't help the disappointment that rose to the surface at this news of a delivery she hadn't been considered for.

Helgi glanced over at her, his brows raised in question, silently asking her what she wanted to do now. She shrugged in response and he turned back to Eiríkur. "Sólveig is our new midwife. She was hoping to meet the old woman, since she's delivered half the babies in the district. Eiríkur is Gróa's son," he supplied for Sólveig's benefit.

"Well, now, that's to be expected." Eiríkur surveyed her with more interest, nodding his head in apparent approval.

"*Mamma*'s getting too old to be traipsing around the fjord for much longer. 'Tis good to see someone young and lithe." He winked at her. "Travel between the farms is light work in spring through autumn, but once the snow comes, it can be a trial for sure." He leaned in to kiss her in greeting. "It's good to meet you, Sólveig."

"It's a pleasure to meet you too, Eiríkur." Stale tobacco filled her senses as his bristled face brushed against her cheek, stringy and surprisingly soft, and she took his hand, squeezing it. "Please do tell Gróa we stopped by. It's always a blessing to hear the news of the safe arrival of a child."

Helgi and Sólveig took their leave from Eiríkur, declining his offer of hospitality, and decided instead to carry on to Suðureyri. They walked in silence for a while, Sólveig feeling downcast and disheartened, but she knew that there was no use in wallowing. It wouldn't change anything.

"I can hear you from here, Sólveig," called Helgi, walking just behind her.

She peered back at him. "I didn't say anything."

He caught up to her and they walked side by side. "You don't need to." His tone was smug. "I can hear those little thoughts trickling around in your head. Ástríður is Gróa's granddaughter," he explained. "You were never going to be called out for that birth."

"Well, thank you for your honesty, Helgi," she said with sarcasm and nudged him with her elbow.

"*What?*" he asked innocently, losing his balance momentarily.

"Did you get your letter written?" She was eager to change the subject.

"I did," he answered.

"Is Grímur the only one that has the skill with writing?"

"*Nei*, Albert can write some, but Grímur is the best with putting together a letter. He's well read. Used to be *hreppstjóri* before Albert. Had a private tutor as a boy, is what I heard."

"I'm not sure how personal the matter was, Helgi, but you can ask me too. I know how to write."

"Well, what are we doing here, then?" He stopped in his tracks.

"I just don't have the tools to do it." She halted too, explaining. "Paper is hard to come by, and besides, I needed an escort into the valley." She flashed him a doe-eyed smile.

He narrowed his eyes as if considering her and the truth to these supposed 'writing skills' she claimed she had. He shrugged, a smirk etched into the corner of his mouth as he said, "I'm not sure I'd want a nosy midwife writing my letter for me anyway."

"Suit yourself," she rebuked and followed him as they made their way back towards Suðureyri, past the farm Staður, where Gróa watched over Ástríður and her newborn son. She sighed, wishing she could have been there too, even if just to watch, to see what the old woman was like, and how they delivered babies in the Westfjörds.

"And where did you learn to write?" Helgi asked.

"It wasn't easy to come by, trust me," she told him. "The last household I worked in, down south, the mistress had a tutor for her three children, and I was able to sit in with them on some of their lessons, but it wasn't enough. I had to supply my own tools and paper, and I spent many a night after the household had gone to bed, practicing my letters by the lamp light."

"You're lucky," he said, subdued. "It's more than some."

She nodded in response, considering him for a moment, wanting to know more about his education, but holding back in the asking of it.

Had he done his basic church teachings? Most people were educated at least to that extent. Had he been taught to read and recite the psalms and passages from the Bible that were drilled into them from childhood up until confirmation at the age of fourteen?

"I can read, if that's what you're thinking." It was more of a statement than a question, and she wondered if she bore her thoughts so clearly on her face all the time. She needed to learn to school herself better. "Though, I don't need books to tell a good tale. Those are in here." He tapped his head.

"Well, tell me a story, then."

"Stories have to be earned," he replied casually.

"Oh, do they? Please," she begged. "Did I not provide you company on your walk? Go on, tell me a story."

The expanse of the ocean grew large before them, a heavy rippling torrent of grey, and Helgi veered right, trailing back along the narrow path where waves crashed onto the rocks below them, with Sólveig on his right protected from its snatching wet grasp.

The ghost of a smile touched his lips, and she followed his gaze to the cliffs rising stark and abruptly beside them. "You know, walking along this path, by these cliffs, always reminds me of the story of the girl in the mountain dairy and her Hidden man in the cliffs."

"Go on," she said, intrigued. She loved a good story, and there were many twisted tales of the beautiful and wily *Huldufólk*, the hidden people said to live alongside humans, in nature, living inside rocks, canyons and cliffs, only revealing themselves to humans as they pleased.

"There was once a beautiful young maiden named Ólafía," he began, as all good stories did, and she settled in to listen to his tale.

"She lived in the north with her father, a minister who owned a vicarage and a dairy. Over the summer, the sheep were herded into the mountains.

Ólafía was appointed keeper of the mountain dairy and spent her summers there with the shepherd, who was but a boy, and many days she passed there alone in the small hut, turning milk into butter and skyr.

"During the day, after her chores, she would walk along the cliffs near the sea, and one day she happened upon a man who lived there. Hair the colour of fire, eyes the green of emerald, clothes spun fine, embroidered with gold, and on his feet were polished leather boots. He was the most handsome man Ólafía had ever laid eyes upon. He was kind to her and good company on the lonely days, and she went to see him almost every day that summer."

Helgi was a storyteller indeed, his tone low and smooth as he wove his tale of forbidden love. He told of the young woman returning home from her time in the mountains with a child growing in her belly and later when she went into a long and difficult labour. It was during this time that her Hidden man returned to her under the guise of fog and missing sheep, to deliver her of the child and save her life with a magic potion, only to disappear once more, taking the babe with him.

"Some time later, Ólafía's father married her off to a young farmer and they were happy for a time. But then one night, two strangers arrived at their door," Helgi retold dramatically, his own green eyes flashing to hers. Suðureyri farmhouse had just come into view, and they veered right, heading into the fjord.

"It was him, wasn't it? The man from the cliff, the father of her child?"

"Let me finish, woman." He chuckled.

"They sought refuge at the farm, and though his wife had warned her husband before they were married to never to let strangers stay, he did. Ólafía was displeased when she saw the two strangers come into the house. They took a seat on one of the beds and the older-looking one stared at her, taken so by her that he could not look away. Ólafía sensed him watching her all evening, but she kept her eyes downcast, daring not to meet his eyes.

The following morning the farmer and his wife made ready for church to take their communion, and as they were riding away, the farmer asked his wife if she'd had the decency to bid their travellers farewell before they left. She told him she hadn't. He scolded her for this rudeness and insisted that if she was to receive proper communion, she needed to ask their forgiveness."

"What did she do?" asked Sólveig, thinking Ólafía would tell her husband that it was *he* who had broken his promise to her by letting the strangers in, so it was *her* forgiveness he needed.

"Well," said Helgi, *"Ólafía returned to the house and found the strangers in the baðstofa, and when she approached the older of them, her eyes finally locked with his, and she said to him, 'Forgive me, my love. I had hoped to never see you again, for the pain of our separation the first time was almost my undoing, but, here you are, and I'm afraid to ever look away.' With these words they embraced, and there came an anguish so deep that neither could utter a word, and they clung to each other as if their very lives depended upon it.*

Ólafía's husband had been waiting and waiting for her to return, but he finally made his way back to the farm to see what was taking so long. When he entered the croft, he found them both—the stranger with the green eyes and hair as red as fire, and his beautiful wife—lying on the floor. Their faces were solemn, the colour of death marked them, entwined as they were in a lovers embrace, and he remembered her warning and the promise he had made her—the promise he had broken.

The farmer looked up to see the second stranger standing in the corner of the room, his hair, too, the colour of fire, but he saw now that his eyes were that of his wife's. The farmer was saddened and confused, but the young stranger told the man that this Hidden man had been his father and this woman lying before them, she was his mother. Upon reuniting with his father, their hearts had burst with grief and they died in each other's arms."

"Oh, Helgi, how terribly tragic, both beautiful and tragic. But whatever happened to the boy, her son?" she ventured.

"Well, he would live on for his parents. It was said that he ran away to dwell in the cliffs where he had been raised, belonging neither to the Hidden world or to this one and at the same time both."

"That was a good story. Thank you."

They continued side by side in silence, and Sólveig pondered the story he told her and the forbidden love and wondered if this was how Helgi felt about Inga. Was theirs a forbidden love? She supposed it was.

Well, he would just have to marry the girl, she mused. But she knew it wasn't as easy as that, and besides, he had told her that he had no intention of marrying her. Helgi was a puzzle to her, that was for sure, and Sólveig just hoped he didn't break Inga's heart with his indifference.

It was sunset by the time they walked up the road to Suðureyri farm. Sólveig thanked Helgi, and he tipped the brim of his cap in her direction.

"Midwife," he said in parting, making his way towards the back of the house while she made hers towards the front.

She met Albert at the entrance as she undressed of her shoes and head scarf.

"Albert, are you just returning now?"

He closed the door behind him, pulling his hat off his head. "Sólveig," he said in greeting. "*Já*, we've been back at shore for most of the afternoon. Made a good catch today, but we're just home for a spot of supper. We'll be out again afterwards to finish the salting. Are you just returning yourself?"

"*Já*, we've just come in from Vatnadalur," she said.

"Good." He nodded. "So, one of the work maids was able to take you, then?"

"*Nei, nei*, I didn't want to interrupt their day. They've plenty to do without traipsing around the hills and valleys with me," she said lightly. "Helgi took me with him. It was no trouble to him."

"I see," he said, pulling off his shoes and turning to face her, but the smile was gone, and his tone had changed. "So, when I asked you today to wait, you decided to go ahead and ask him anyway?"

"*Já,*" she answered, taken aback. She was greeted with silence and stood for a moment, but before heading into the hallway, she asked him. "What difference did it make whether the work maids or Helgi took me?"

He sighed deeply, rubbing a hand over his eyes. "Look, I'm too tired to argue this with you, Sólveig. You're new to this household, and it's my duty to ensure you're looked after. When I ask you not to do something, I expect my caution to be regarded, is all."

"Well." It was all she could say in response to him at first, but as she stood before him, her arms folded across her chest, she felt a compulsion to say what was bubbling up inside her. She needed to make something clear to him, and she drew in a deep breath and said it before she could think too hard about it.

"I'm not here to make trouble, Albert, but you need to understand that I'm not here as one of your work maids, to do as you bid. I will respect your house rules, but I'm here to do my duty as a midwife. I am my own person, and I'll come and go as the need arises, with or without your permission."

He took a step towards her. "You've got a tongue on you, woman, I'll say that," he said, clearly taken aback. "But you need to understand that you're not in Reykjavík anymore and there's a certain way to going about things up here that I think you may not be accustomed to." He held her eyes and she didn't dare look away. "I'll respect your decisions as a midwife, but you'll also pay heed to my caution in future. Is that understood?"

Her heart was racing, her palms suddenly sweaty. She wasn't used to standing up for herself, not only to a man but to a man of position. This was the second such incident of the day, so she bit her tongue and gave him a curt nod in acknowledgment. After all, it hadn't been like it was with Júlíus. Albert hadn't raised his voice at her, like she expected he might, and she appreciated that he spoke to her like he listened to what she'd had to say whether he had agreed with her or not.

"Come now, supper will be ready, and I'm famished." He held his arm out towards the door, and she moved past him, making her way down the hallway and up the stairs into the *baðstofa*, feeling his presence in the darkness behind her, trailing her towards the light of the room.

⸙

That night, Sólveig lay in her cot mulling over the events of the day. What was it that had irked Albert so about Helgi taking her to Vatnadalur? Was it that he'd taken her? Did he not trust Helgi? Or was it that she had disobeyed him? Albert had tried to assert his authority over her that evening, but she hadn't become a midwife to just deliver babies. Midwifery afforded her independence as a woman. It had gifted her a chance at a higher education, when there was none for women other than the usual church readings. It had opened the doors for her to earn a wage for her skills and the ability to provide for herself. It was her chance to be her own person, to answer only to the likes of herself.

As these thoughts flew through her mind, her irritation with Albert rose. She was a grown woman for Christ's sake, not some silly, giggly maid like Inga, blushing at the slightest smile from a handsome man. She could be trusted—in fact, she prided herself on her chastity and prudence around men.

"Hmph," she grumbled irritably, turning in her bed, unsettled, her mind once again too busy for sleep. But then, she was reminded of that moment in the valley when Helgi had pulled her into his arms, how he had looked into her eyes, how his touch had felt on her face—both tender and warm, and she finally realised why Albert had been reluctant for her to go with Helgi. She remembered how Inga had told her of Albert not tolerating loose behaviour. Helgi was a bachelor, and she, too, was unwed. Albert was a moral man, and he had been concerned with her propriety. It hadn't been seemly for her and Helgi to travel together, two unmarried people, without a third person at least for company. Why couldn't he have just said so to her when she had asked him that morning?

Sólveig turned in the bed again, sighing deeply. She knew that she couldn't say anything to Albert about what she had seen between Helgi and Inga. They would both be sent away if he found out, and for all his sneaking about with Inga, Helgi was a likeable man, light of spirit and a good storyteller. She had found him rather refreshing and easy to talk to when he hadn't been irritating her with his smug comments about her being nosy and untrustworthy.

7

Late September 1881

Sólveig spent the following days after her visit to Vatnadalur helping the women of the house gather and prepare wool for spinning.

It was heavy, backbreaking work, pulling the sodden fibres through the water without losing them to the flow. The stench of urine from which the wool had been soaked in to cleanse it made them all gag at first, but the smell settled, and they grew accustomed to it.

It was a fair day for September, and Sólveig was with Rúna at the stream behind the house, the two of them ankle deep in the cool, shallow water, the hems of their skirts tucked into their waistlines, revealing milky-white legs. Sólveig's feet had gone numb with the cold, and she bent with her load over the flowing water, pounding and twisting the wool so the water and urine was free of it. The work wasn't so bad with good company, and Rúna was light of heart and easy to talk to like her older brother.

It was just past midday when one of the workmen, Einar, walked past them for the third time, his brows raised at the sight of them, the corner of his mouth turned up in a sly smile.

"Off with you now, Einar, and you can stop your gawking," called Rúna to him as he passed them.

"You'd think I have nothing better to do than walk past you women all day and gawk at you, as appealing as that may be," he shouted back.

"Ha! So you say. You'd be far more useful helping with this washing." Rúna stood with her hands on her hips in challenge, but Einar simply kept on walking, his broad shoulders shaking lightly with humour as he made his way towards the sea in the direction of the small croft and line-up of boats.

Sólveig glanced over at her friend, her dark plaits tied together and tucked neatly under her head scarf. Rúna appeared flustered, and she washed more vigorously than before, her arm sleeves rolled up to her elbows as Sólveig's were.

"That man," she fumed and kept dunking and squeezing. "I'll give him a piece of my mind if he dares come back, just you watch me, Sólveig."

"I thought you already did." Sólveig laughed, ducking her hand into the stream again. When she straightened up, wringing the water out of the wool, she noticed Inga heading towards them. The work maid was tasked with spreading the wool they had rinsed, to dry over the stone wall at the back of the house, near the vegetable gardens off the kitchen. Inga had already been twice to collect, but she'd taken her time coming back, and this time, as she approached them, Sólveig noticed how puffy her face was and the tip of her nose red. It looked like she'd been crying. Wading out of the water with her bundle of wool, she dropped it into a tub and stood beside it, waiting to question the girl.

"What is it, Inga? Has something happened?"

"What did you say to him?" Inga snapped, rounding on her, a mixture of anger and hurt in her glistening eyes.

"What did I say to whom?" she asked, confused by this sudden outburst.

"You know exactly who I'm talking about. Helgi told me he didn't think we should be together anymore!"

"Oh, I'm so sorry, Inga—" was all she could say, and she stepped towards the young woman to comfort her, but Inga brushed her off.

"You had to involve yourself, *didn't you?* You were the only one that knew, and you couldn't be trusted to keep your mouth shut."

"Inga, please," she tried. "All I said was that he needed to be more careful, that's all, the same thing I said to you. It was never my intention to see you hurt, you must believe me."

"Well, if you hadn't thought to interfere, then he would still be with me now."

"Oh, Inga, calm yourself, girl. He was never going to marry you," piped in Rúna, approaching them from the bank, dropping her pile of wool in the tub as she reached them. "He was playing with you, that's all, and shame on him for doing so and shame on you for letting him. Sólveig was just looking out for you, you know. You should be thanking her. You know how Albert feels about secret affairs in his household."

"We wouldn't have been caught. We were being careful," said Inga, crossing her arms over her chest.

"Not careful enough, by the sounds of it, if Sólveig knows about you. And you're lucky it *was* Sólveig and not Albert or Krissa that know. If Helgi wanted to marry you, Inga, he would have approached Albert a long time ago."

Inga burst into a sob, picked up the tub of rinsed wool, and marched towards the rock wall over the rise at the back of the farmhouse.

"You knew about them?" Sólveig asked Rúna.

"*Já*, and I wasn't happy to know about it. The way the girl kept asking me about Helgi, it wasn't hard to guess. It was just a matter of time, and

I said as much to Helgi just the other day. I asked him straight up if he'd done anything with her."

"And what did he say?" Sólveig was curious to hear what his response had been. He had been quite clear with her when she had broached the subject with him that it was none of her business.

"He told me to mind my own business." She scoffed. "And that, Sólveig, told me enough. You see, he would have been happy to deny it, if it were otherwise."

"Well, I do feel bad for the girl." She hadn't meant for Inga to be hurt by her nosing about, whether it had been on purpose or not. "She's clearly in love with him."

"Sólveig, if it's not my brother, it will be someone else. That girl will be a mother before the year is out. She throws herself on any man that shows her attention, and trust me, many do turn their heads to her looks. I'd just rather it wasn't my brother."

8

November 1881

The days drifted into weeks and Sólveig marvelled at the ever-changing landscape around her, as winter slowly crept in. The mountains were covered in layers of snow. It trailed down the rocky slopes in tendrils, stretching down into the sea, like veins down the inside of a forearm. The fjord was silent after the departure of the birds. The arctic tern, the golden plover and her favourite little brown bird, the meadow pipit, had flown south for the winter, their singsong replaced by the howl of the wind and violent lapping of the sea.

The household rose in darkness, the work maids emptying bedpans and making their way out early into the gloomy morning to milk the cows by lamplight. Sólveig often joined them later in the dairy, helping to turn the milk they collected into butter and skyr and it was in the dairy house that Albert sought her one evening.

"Well, Sólveig, it's time to put all your learning to use. Krissa says our child is making his way into the world."

"His, huh? You're so sure it's a boy?" she teased.

"This one is surely a boy." He grinned.

She'd had a feeling Krissa would go into labour soon. The swell of Krissa's belly had dropped lower and her face had the puffy look of late pregnancy, her feet and ankles swelled if she was on them for too long. Krissa never wandered far, staying clear of the icy paths around the farm. She spent most of her time upstairs in the *baðstofa*, on her bed, knitting or weaving until she complained of her back aching. Sólveig kept an eye on her, would rub her back for her on occasion and scolded her if she didn't rest enough. The babe was running out of room, Krissa would tell her, her frequent trips to empty her bladder proof of that. She needed help squatting over the bedpan and complained that she couldn't see for the bulge of her belly. Once she was down, she couldn't get back up without assistance.

"Did she tell you she's been having pains for the past few days?" asked Albert.

Sólveig shook her head, concerned that Krissa hadn't thought to mention it to her, though pains were not unusual days, even weeks, before birth, as long as they were mild and infrequent, with no bleeding attached to them.

"You'll have to watch her, she's a quiet one when it comes to birthing and she'll be in a great deal more pain than she'll let on," he said dryly, "but her pains are more intense now, so she's sent for you."

"I thought you said you knew nothing of birthing babies?" Sólveig raised a brow at him in question.

"I still claim I don't," he said. "Not like you do anyhow. I've seen her at it, through the night, two times now, though I try my best to stay out of the way."

"I'll clean up and be out shortly, Albert."

He nodded his head, but she sensed his hesitation as he lingered in the doorway.

"All will be well, Albert." She squeezed his arm in gentle reassurance, sensing his worry.

"Krissa. She's lost three little ones; did she tell you that?" he asked.

"She did mention that this was her sixth baby, but I've only met your two girls."

"*Já*, Krissa was married before," Albert replied, a faraway look in his eyes. "She lost her first husband Þórður, and her father to the sea in '73."

"I'm sorry, Albert. I didn't know. So, Dísa and Dóra—?" she started somewhat awkwardly, unsure if he considered it impolite to ask whether he was the biological father of the girls or not.

"Valdís, our eldest, is his girl," he said, casually. "But Dóra, she's mine. I came to Suðureyri shortly after the accident, as a workman, and took over the management of the farm for Krissa and her mother. Dísa was only three and she's been mine ever since."

"Of course," said Sólveig.

"Krissa gave birth to two other babies before I came here," he continued, "but they didn't survive past a few days old. Born too soon, they were." He sighed deeply. "And then we lost a boy between Dóra and this one. The little fellow was born without breath."

"Stillborn. Oh, Albert, I am sorry for your loss. Krissa has been through much."

He nodded and she sensed again the worry within him for his wife. She took his hand in hers.

"You must hold on to your faith, Albert. We must pray that you will be given a healthy child, but please know that this one is not too early and Krissa says she's been feeling regular movement of the child. All will be well. We *must* believe it to be so."

His mouth turned up in a half smile, his large hand covering hers. It was warm and reassuring.

"I know she's in good hands, Sólveig. I'll be in the smithy if you need me."

Birth took time, Sólveig mused as he left her to clean up and prepare herself. It was better that he stayed out of the way, better that he kept himself busy. Birthing was women's business after all. She appreciated Albert's faith in her. He could just as easily call Gróa over from Bær to assist, like many in the community would do. The old woman certainly had more experience than Sólveig, but Albert seemed to trust her with his wife, regardless of the fact that she was untried and new to the community. She wouldn't let him down. She wouldn't let Krissa down, and though her nerves were all on edge now with this news, excitement ran through her. Finally, her chance had come to put her knowledge and skills to use. This would be her first delivery in her new district, her first outside the few deliveries she had by chance witnessed as a child in her grandmother's household. All her training had been done out of books—theory taught by the head doctor in Reykjavík. Three months of theory. Was it enough? She hoped it would be. She would have loved longer training, would have loved more hands-on experience, but the only way to gain more experience was to attend births. This was her chance to prove herself, and she said a silent prayer to the Almighty to bless the impending birth, and to help guide her hands in the safe delivery of this child into the world.

Sólveig found Rúna in the kitchen preparing the evening meal with Inga.

"Well, your moment of truth is here, Sólveig. Call out if you need an extra hand, though I'm sure Tobba will want to assist. She normally does."

She thanked her friend, changing her apron and cleaning her hands with warm, soapy water, and requested of her some unsalted butter or melted tallow for the examination along with plenty of hot water for the delivery and a tub for bathing the child afterwards.

It was taking too long. Tobba kept muttering this to herself, but it was loud enough that everyone could hear the old woman's grumblings, and it wasn't doing anyone any good. Sólveig wished Krissa's mother would just leave the room and stop interfering, and when she repeated it for what Sólveig had counted as the fifth time, she decided to pull her aside and asked her to keep quiet. It was making Krissa tense, which again was slowing things down. She wondered how Gróa had gotten along with the woman, or was it just that Tobba didn't trust her skills so she felt the need to undermine her and question her ability?

"Her body has done this many times," Sólveig reminded Tobba. "She will find her rhythm." She gave Krissa a reassuring smile. The woman was sweaty, her face flushed, and tendrils of blonde hair had escaped its plait and stuck to her face and neck. She lay on an oilskin cloth propped up against the wall at the head of her bed, her legs bent and knees pulled apart. Krissa smiled wanly in reply, and then her mouth contorted with pain and Sólveig noticed the flicker of fear flash in her eyes. The woman moaned, albeit quietly, closing her eyes, clutching her stomach in effort as another birthing pain passed through her, and this time fluid came with it, trickling out of her and onto the bed. The woman drew the pain into herself, trying to breathe through it. Yes, Krissa had done this many times, alright. The contractions were getting much closer between, but the progress was slow. It was now well into the night; the children and workmen lay asleep in their cots around them. Going by Tobba's and Krissa's own accounts, her births were usually very quick, but this one seemed to be taking his time.

Albert still hadn't come to bed, and Tobba said they weren't likely to see him rest his head until the baby was born and he knew for certain that Krissa was well.

"Good, the waters have come loose now, so if it's okay with you, Krissa, I'd like to have another look to see how the babe is positioned?"

Krissa nodded her head and gasped as Sólveig rubbed some butter on her index and middle fingers, trying to warm them some, and slipped them inside her to check the baby's progress. She had performed an inspection initially but hadn't felt the baby's head, and the waters were still intact then, making it more difficult to determine the baby's position. This time she could feel the child with more clarity—little fingers—no, they were too short to be fingers. She moved her fingers farther along. Was that a heel? With her other hand, she felt along the swollen belly, pressing against the hard flesh to feel the position of the baby.

Something wasn't right, and dread flushed through her as she discovered the hard bulge just near Krissa's rib cage. Krissa waited expectantly for the midwife's assessment of her progress, and Sólveig schooled her face into neutrality.

"Krissa, when you feel the baby move, where is it the strongest?" Sólveig was surprised at how she sounded much more confident than she felt.

Krissa looked slightly baffled and stopped to breathe through another contraction, her hands clutched at the kerchief tied to the timber pole at the head of her bed. Sólveig waited for to her catch her breath and for the pain to pass.

"It's been different with this one. His movements are always very low. Is—is something wrong, Sólveig?" Her voice sounded small and tight.

"All will be well, Krissa," she reassured her. "We'll get this baby born. He just wants to do things a little differently, is all. He's decided to come feetfirst."

Krissa's shoulders slumped, and the woman closed her eyes, her head falling back onto the pillow. Her lips wobbled, a nostril flared, and a stray tear rolled down the side of her face. Sólveig felt for the woman. She could see how this news deflated her, how tired she was. Her strength was waning along with her morale.

"Krissa, your other babies weren't born feetfirst, were they?" she asked. Krissa shook her head. They had already discussed her previous deliveries at the start of her labour, but she just needed to make sure.

Sólveig swallowed hard. She had never delivered a child, let alone a breech one, but she took comfort in the knowledge that they had covered this in her training, even if it was something she had simply read about in a book. She ran over the possible complications they could face with this type of delivery. It was a risky process if the head didn't tilt at precisely the right angle coming through the pelvis. The baby had a higher chance of getting stuck in the birth canal, and the supply of oxygen could get cut off through the umbilical cord. She took a deep breath, pushing away everything that could go wrong, and focused instead on how she could make sure that it went as she wanted it to.

"Krissa, this baby is ready to be born and it's much too late to try and turn the child."

"Does Albert need to fetch the doctor?" asked Krissa, her tone laced heavily with worry.

"Perhaps it's for the best, just as a precaution, but I'm doubtful this baby will wait. He seems in a hurry now. I know what to do." Yes, she knew what to do, but what she didn't say was that she'd only ever done it in theory.

Tobba called down the hall to Rúna, asking Albert to go for the doctor.

Sólveig, meanwhile, watched a ripple of pain pass through Krissa. Though the woman made not a sound, she saw how her body tightened and the way she clenched the cloth tied to the bed post in her fists, the muscles in her arms straining, but with this contraction came the urge to push.

One little foot popped out, and then the other, and a tiny pink body slid down towards the bed, stopping just under the child's arms, which were still inside Krissa.

"You have another girl, Kristin," exclaimed Tobba from where she stood beside Sólveig.

"Keep going. You're doing wonderfully." Sólveig maneuvered her fingers at the folds of stretched vaginal flesh, checking the pressure on the umbilical cord. Then grabbing a linen cloth, she wrapped it around the small torso. There was a slight chill to the air, and she used the cloth to grip the babe's slippery body as she rotated the baby carefully to release each little arm.

"That's it, Krissa. You just have the head left to birth. We must go very carefully now. When you feel the need to push on the next contraction, I want you to do small breaths," she explained and slid two fingers inside the woman, resting them across the child's face to flex the head. It had to be positioned correctly in the birth canal so it didn't get stuck. With the other hand, she hooked two fingers around the neck, grasping the shoulders, applying gentle pressure downwards.

The babe's head was released on a guttural moan from Krissa along with more pink fluid from the sack that had carried the child, and the woman gushed with relief. Sólveig pulled the cord away from her neck, clearing her mouth of mucous, and rubbed the baby on the back to propel her breathing. The baby pulled in a deep breath and let out an angry, startled wail. Sólveig hadn't realised she held her own breath until she let it out at this glorious sound of new life.

She said a silent prayer of thanks over the child as she inspected her quickly. The baby was a good size, with a small tuft of fair hair over her head, full fingered and toed.

"Has Albert left for the doctor?" asked Krissa weakly, closing her eyes briefly.

"We won't need him now," said Sólveig.

"I'll take the horse and catch up to him in no time," came Einar's voice from his cot. He came over to inspect the baby as Sólveig handed the babe to her mother and cut the cord.

"Well done, Krissa," he said, his features soft at the sight of the child, and he left them.

"Oh, my sweet baby." Krissa smiled down at her new daughter and then looked up at Sólveig, her eyes glistening with unshed tears. "When you told me she would come feetfirst, I honestly thought I would die trying. It's happened that way for many."

"I wasn't going to let that happen," said Sólveig, her heart bursting with joy and elation. "I promised Albert."

It was early morning by the time Krissa delivered the placenta.

The afterbirth pains came strong and hard, and Krissa winced and moaned in the bed with each contraction, though they came at longer intervals now.

"They seem to get worse with each child I deliver," said Krissa.

"*Já*, the womb is drawing itself back together," she consoled her. "With every birth, it has to work harder to return it to its original size. We'll make you a tea of chamomile and a hot compress for the cramps." The child squalled when she took her from her mother, unwrapping her from her swaddle. Sólveig lowered her gently into the warm tub of water Rúna had prepared and she cradled the child, its head in her hands and the body submerged in the watery cradle, and the cries died down instantly. She cleaned the birth from her with a wet rag and soap, inspecting the child as she did. When the bathing was done, the baby was dried, and with careful fingers Sólveig massaged oil around the newly cut and tied umbilical cord and covered it with a strip of clean linen to protect it. It would be changed every day until the cord stump fell off in four or five days, and the sore healed completely. Dísa, who'd woken with the squalling, helped dress her new sister, making her a nappy of cloth and swaddling her so she could hold her.

Sólveig helped Krissa strap her breasts to stop the milk coming through, and a bottle was prepared for the babe, a blend of warmed cow's milk diluted with water and a pinch of sugar. Sólveig thought it strange that women didn't want to suckle their babies. Could it really be right that the child sucked all the nutrients from her mother and would make her sickly? It seemed like the most natural thing to do, a woman's body providing milk for her own child like most other creatures—ewes with their lambs and horses with their foals, cows with their calves, but they, too, weren't suckled for long. Doctors only discouraged it if the mother was sickly or incapable, but many house mistresses didn't want to be tied to the demands of breastfeeding when so much other responsibility fell to them.

Other members of the household were rising, the work maids were already up and Rúna and Inga came in with bowls of broth each for Sólveig, Krissa and Tobba, heading back into the kitchen to get more for the girls, the workmen and old Leifur. Albert held his new daughter while his wife ate.

Einar had managed to catch up to his brother just before reaching Botn and all trace of his earlier worry and tension over the birth of his child was gone. He stood and brought the child over to Sólveig, where she sat on her cot, eating her morning meal.

"Congratulations, you have a beautiful new daughter, Albert." She admired the sleeping bundle in his arms and added cheekily, "You'll have to go again for that ever-elusive son."

"Hmph." Krissa scoffed from her cot. "Let's just enjoy this little one for now. I don't want to do that again anytime soon."

"Thank you, Sólveig." Albert dragged his eyes away from his new daughter to meet hers. "I heard she had a hard time of it, but you never faltered," he said with approval. His voice betrayed his emotion, and she could almost feel the utter elation in it.

"Your wife was the courageous one, Albert. She did the hardest work," she reminded him. She appreciated the praise, but what a fine line it was that a child teetered on, between life and death. Birth was the place of in-between. So much could have gone wrong, but today they had been blessed with new life, and she was nothing but grateful for it. Albert stood again, taking the child back to his wife, and Sólveig watched on as the little family enveloped their love around its newest member.

This first delivery of hers for her new district had been more difficult than she anticipated, and she said another silent prayer of thanks to the forces above for guiding her hands, for instilling in her the courage to follow her instincts, but she knew that danger still lingered. She pushed back at the memory of her sister, reminding her that she would need to monitor Krissa closely over the next few days to make sure no childbed fever developed. There was likely nothing to worry about. The placenta had come away cleanly. She had just been able to inspect it before Tobba snatched it from her to burn it in the kitchen fire. It was old superstition that dictated if the placenta was burnt, a beautiful star would follow the child for all its life—the people here were just as superstitious as the ones down south, she thought wryly. It was an age-old custom, and if somewhat strange, Sólveig thought the meaning behind it beautiful.

A short while later, Sólveig left the *baðstofa*, heading for the kitchen with her empty bowl and the hope that coffee was brewing, even if it was slightly watered down. She'd needed it to get through the day, but as she passed through the doorway leading to the corridor, she almost bumped into Helgi entering the room.

"Well done, Midwife." He nodded at her appraisingly. "I told you you'd get your chance." And he stepped back, gesturing for her to go first. She nodded her thanks and moved past him, catching that scent of sea and wind that seemed to be so much a part of him.

9

December 1881

Sólveig stomped her feet, rubbing her gloved hands together to spread some warmth into them. It was cold out. Snow fluttered around her at a slanted angle, blown sideways by the wind. She'd be warmer again once they started walking.

"Krissa's almost ready, Albert. Rúna is just helping her with her *peysuföt* and getting the child wrapped in under her shawl," she informed him. The wind whistled about her ears, even with the shawl covering them, and she noticed Albert push his hat down on his head a little tighter.

"Always waiting on the women." Albert shook his head in dismay.

"Hah! *The women?*" She smirked.

"*Já*, it's always like this when we attend church," he continued. "It's the social event of the month, and everyone wants to look their finest, of course."

"I suppose you're right," she said, making her own assessment of him, seeing how finely dressed he was, out of his usual worn-out farming clothes. His hair was neatly combed beneath his *hreppstjóri* hat, his beard trimmed, and he wore his dark-grey coat and matching pants, with his leather boots. The other workmen were dressed in similar clothes, their faces scrubbed cleaner than she had seen them in a while, their beards and hair combed neatly under hats. Of course, Sunday was not only a day of rest but going to church was a chance for the community to come together, share gossip, talk sheep and farming, boast of new babies and upcoming weddings. This time there would also be a christening, and Krissa would be churched for the first time since the birth of her baby.

"How are you settling into our little corner of the fjords, Sólveig?" Albert asked her, using conversation to while away the time, stamping his own feet to encourage warmth.

"I like it just fine." She smiled. "Though, people here have proved quite reluctant to use my skills as yet, apart from Krissa, of course."

"Ah, you'll be so busy soon enough that you'll wish they called on old Gróa again. You really made an impression on Krissa, you know."

"I did?"

"*Já*, she can't praise you highly enough. She had a tough time of it, and you saw her through it, new as you are to midwifery. You've got the patience and a good sensible head on your shoulders. It looks like you might be stuck with us." He chuckled. "I know Krissa won't let you leave us anytime soon."

"Well, I am pleased to hear that, Albert."

His words warmed her immensely, and she had been truthful when she told him she was content with her new life at Suðureyri. The birth had gone exceptionally well, considering the complication that had arisen, and Krissa was recovering as she should after the birth. She'd risen from her confinement a week after the birth. The child was thriving and only waking a few times at night to be fed. Sólveig was as attentive as she could be, caring for Krissa's every need, helping to feed and settle the child and making sure the mother was easing her way back into the routine of household tasks. Yes, she was content. She felt needed. She felt she had a purpose here.

Sólveig was pulled out of her reverie with the sound of children laughing. Albert's older girls, Dísa and Dóra, played not far from where she stood with Albert, bored with the waiting around, their hair newly braided, and they, too, were clothed in their best dresses with thick woollen stockings and sheepskin shoes.

She watched in amusement now as the girls scooped up soft layers of snow into small mittened hands, shaping them into balls in their palms, aiming them at their uncle Einar, who poked his tongue at them, daring them to hit him. He swerved and swayed, little giggles echoing around them.

This fun, however, was short-lived as Tobba appeared suddenly in the doorway scolding them—Einar included—ordering them to leave the snow be, reminding them that their gloves would be soaked through with melted snow and their fingers would burn with the cold, and Einar should know better besides. Sólveig couldn't help but smirk to herself as the old woman slapped Albert's younger brother about the ears.

"Cranky old woman," she heard Einar mutter as Tobba retreated into the house. The girls kicked their feet sulkily in the snow, but Rannveig's daughter little Magga appeared in the doorway, and they ran to her, disappearing inside. Björn's youngest would be staying behind with her mother, Rannveig and old Leifur. It was too far for the old man's legs, and he was half blind besides, and Rannveig complained that her cough had been aggravating her, so she thought it best to stay out of the cold.

Sólveig sighed, thinking she should have just stayed inside a while longer too. Krissa had told her she was nearly ready.

"A boat's comin' in," Einar called over to his brother. Albert strolled over to him, and she followed, coming to stand where he did at the end of the row of farmhouses closest to the sea. A small boat was approaching the landing on the beach near the sea croft. They watched it pull into shore with the heave of oars. It wasn't one of the fishing sixareens but a smaller wooden vessel, and squinting into the distance, she saw two figures jumping out of the boat.

"Who do you think is coming?" she asked.

"Looks like Helgi," said Albert, narrowing his eyes.

"What's *he* doing back so soon? Not supposed to be back for another week yet. Come on, Alb, something's up," said Einar, rushing past the outer crofts and down the bank towards the visitors.

Sólveig stood back, watching Albert and Einar, make their way to the snow-littered beach, wondering if it was Helgi, and what had kept him away from Suðureyri these past few weeks?

10

Sólveig was needed at Keflavík. Helgi had come for her, and she was surprised to learn that her skills were required again so soon.

"Me?" she responded dumbly when Helgi approached her with Albert, Einar and another younger man in tow.

"*Já*, you! You're the midwife, are you not?" Helgi asked, with more sarcasm than she thought was necessary.

She nodded, feeling that same mixture of anticipation and fear bubbling up inside her at the prospect of delivering another baby, but with it came a stab of disappointment, too, knowing that she would miss the christening of Albert and Krissa's daughter—the first baby she had delivered.

"She's a house maid at Keflavík. The girl is young and it's her first baby," said Helgi, his striking green eyes full of concern.

"The wind's up, but the weather looks fair, so it should be smooth sailing to Keflavík," Albert contributed from where they all stood in front of the farmhouse.

"I'll need to pack a bag. Are we taking the boat or walking?" she asked Helgi, trepidation filling her.

"We'll be taking you across on the boat," he replied. "It's quicker. The mountain passes are too heavy with snow to cross on foot."

"How was the landing when you left Keflavík?" asked Albert. "That coastline can be dangerous, and you'll need a safe place to land the boat, especially with the frost we've been having of late. Some of the lower fjords have iced over fully. We're lucky the open sea is so close and the fjord not so narrow and shallow here, though it's been known to freeze over near Botn on occasion."

"I'm well used to the landings at Keflavík, Albert. Have no fear. I'll bring her home safe."

Sólveig caught the look Helgi gave Albert and could tell by his tone that he was irritated by Albert's second-guessing him.

"I won't be long," she told Helgi, retreating into the *baðstofa* to change and pack extra clothes for herself, along with a clean apron, her *askur*, spoon, and hairbrush. Her medical bag was all ready to go. She'd been told by the doctor in Reykjavík to always carry her medical bag with her, wherever she went. *You never know when a birth will occur or when you'll be called out to assist. You must always be prepared.*

Sólveig could expect to be away for up to a week. It wasn't a requirement for her to stay for more than two days, but she didn't know what the conditions would be like at this household in Keflavík. She recalled that this was where Helgi and Rúna's mother and brothers lived, and she was intrigued to meet the rest of their family.

She bid her farewells to Krissa and Albert and apologised to them for missing their daughter's christening. Krissa told her not to be silly. She was needed, so she must go, and Sólveig turned her attention to the men in front of her. She followed them down to the beach, where their small boat awaited them. With Helgi was another person he introduced as his younger brother, Elías. He was but a boy, gangly in the way of youth, not quite a man, but no longer a child. When Sólveig smiled at him in greeting, she noticed how his neck flushed red with embarrassment, the colour travelling up into his face, and he stumbled over his greeting to her. Helgi ducked him on the head, telling him that she wouldn't bite, but the young man was more comfortable looking at the snow-speckled sand by his feet than at her, it would seem.

"Are we to go in this *little* thing?" she asked with incredulity, indicating the small timber boat before her, a knot of fear growing inside her. They would surely be swallowed by the sea in this.

"*Shh!*" Helgi motioned, bringing a finger to his lips to signal for her to hush, his eyes narrowing. "You just be careful how you talk about *her*, Sólveig. You'll insult the girl. She doesn't like being called *little*." He petted the sides of the boat delicately, smoothing his hands along the curved timber panels.

Sólveig responded with a blank stare.

"*What?*" he asked.

"Well, for starters, you're talking about a boat as if it has feelings!" She wasn't sure whether to laugh or call Albert back to take her instead. Perhaps Helgi was crazy and untrustworthy after all.

"She'll get us there safe, Sólveig. Just you wait and see, and then you'll be eating your words. *She'll* expect an apology from you then."

"Can you please stop talking about the boat as if *she*, I mean *it*, is a person."

Elías was laughing quietly as he dragged the boat with Helgi across the frosty sand to the lapping waters of the shoreline. Helgi, too, was smirking to himself, his moustache twitching at the corners.

"Uff, why do you tease me so?" she said to him sternly, but, in truth, trying her best not to yield a smile to his jesting.

Helgi winked at her. "Because I love seeing the fire in your eyes and the way your mouth sets in that firm line. I think I've missed your scolding." He came up to her, standing all too close, his gloved hand reaching out to take her bags from her.

"How long have you been gone, Helgi? I hadn't even realised you'd left," she lied, letting him take the bags. He placed them inside the boat, where Elías took them, tucking them under the seat.

"Well, that's just hurtful," Helgi said, feigning offense as he turned back to face her. "Alright, in you get," he added, and before she could take another step, he bent down suddenly, wrapping his arms around her legs, and in a most ungracious manner, proceeded to sling her body over his shoulder. She squealed, unable to help the sound that escaped her as he hoisted her into the boat, placing her gently onto her feet. She should have guessed he was up to something. She had seen the gleam in his mossy eyes, the light creases of pleasure at their corners, just before he decided to carry her like a sack of flour onto his shoulders.

She was puffing and ready to scold him again when she remembered his earlier statement about enjoying the fire in her eyes when she was mad at him, so she simply sat down, her back to him, refusing to give him that satisfaction. She heard his hearty chuckle as he pushed the boat that last leg off the beach and into the water, jumping in to take his place at a set of oars, facing her. The boat rocked precariously for a spell, and she clutched the edge of her seat, her heart sitting in her throat. She hated boats, remembering the fjords she'd crossed time and again on her journey north with the postman, and she didn't relish those memories.

"Are you worried, Midwife?" Helgi asked, taking up the oars. "You're looking a little pale."

"I'd prefer to walk there, but I'm fine," she said firmly, still not meeting his eyes. She focused instead on the rhythm Helgi and Elías created with their bodies, moving in sync with the motion of the oars. Their large gloved hands were wrapped tightly around the wood, heaving the long paddles back and forth through the thick water, pulling the boat smoothly across the sea. The power of their strokes reverberated through the motion of the boat, and she reassured herself with the knowledge that they had rowed to get to Suðureyri and had arrived in one piece—had they not? She wished her busy mind would quieten.

She sensed again the heaviness of Helgi's gaze on her, and when she finally looked up at his face, her eyes locked with his. What she saw there made her flush with heat, and she fervently wished she could unsee it. She drew her eyes from his, thinking now that she preferred the usual playful glint she often saw in their depths. This look was serious and calm, desire and angst all at once, and she didn't know what to do with that—what it could possibly mean?

She focused on the horizon ahead. The sky was a hazy blur, tinged with the palest of pink where the sun sat behind thick clouds. The wind was with them, pushing their boat along the smooth surface of the water, but as they reached the end of the fjord and crossed into open ocean, the waters grew choppy—not so much that the men couldn't control the boat, but it rocked harshly. Her morning's meal of porridge sat like a rock in her stomach. She wouldn't have eaten the whole bowl had she known she would be sitting in a boat only a short while later. Making herself a little taller, trying to breathe through the nausea, she closed her eyes briefly, taking a deep breath of cool, salty air through her nose and then releasing it slowly through her mouth, but the rocking grew worse again, and her stomach heaved. She rushed to the side of the boat, where she had no say in the contents coming out of her mouth.

"You've certainly no sea legs, my girl," Helgi observed, his features a mixture of amusement and concern.

Sólveig was mortified that they'd witnessed her weakness.

"You don't need to be embarrassed on our account. Here." Helgi passed her his kerchief, and she took it, wiping her mouth. "Keep it," he said.

"How long until we reach Keflavík?" she asked meekly. The boat rose and lurched again, and she turned quickly, unable to stop herself from heaving out the side of the boat once more.

✦

"Surely, there's nothing left to come up now." Helgi was beside Sólveig, gently rubbing her back. "We're here. We've made land," he reiterated.

She groaned, opening her eyes, and lifted her head from where it lay on the ledge of the boat. "I don't think I can move." Her fingers and toes were numb, and her cheeks burned from the cold.

"Come on, it's over now."

She stood slowly from her crouched position on the floor of the boat, but she was light-headed from the effort of heaving, and the world spun. "Are you sure we're not still in the water?" she asked, throwing her arm out to grab hold of him.

Helgi gripped her upper arm, steadying her. "Nope. I told you she'd get you here. She may look little, but she's a tough old thing, like someone else I know." And he winked at her.

"Pfft," she scoffed weakly. "I'm not old!"

The corner of his lips went up in amusement. "*Nei*, but you're little and tough. The croft is only a short trek up this bank," he said, changing the subject, his hands now rubbing the side of her arms. He peered into her face as if assessing her, his brow furrowed in concern. "And then we can get some coffee into you to warm you up so you can deliver this baby—you look almost frozen."

And then it registered with her. Yes, she was here for a purpose. She needed to get a move on.

"Here, get some of this into you," he said, his hand disappearing quickly into the pocket of his pants. He pulled out a chunk of dried fish.

"Oh, Helgi." She shook her head. "It's too soon. I don't think I can stomach it just yet."

"Come on, Midwife, just a little." He took a bite, tearing at the dried flesh, eyeing her as he did so as if she were a child needing convincing to eat their meal. "Besides, you'll need the strength to walk up that bank." He indicated behind them, where she saw Elías making his way already, adding, "It's narrow and steep."

"Oh, alright." She finally gave in, snatching the leftover strip awkwardly with her thick gloved hands and put it into her mouth.

"Satisfied?" she asked, chewing the tough flesh.

"Good girl," he said with a wink and jumped from the boat. Turning to her, he helped her down and then dragged the boat up the beach towards the base of the small cliff rising before them.

Sólveig followed him, stretching her frozen limbs as she walked, still chewing the fish but admittedly feeling somewhat better to have a small morsel of food in her belly. She peered over at the narrow track up to the headland, where Elías had nearly reached the top. He must have gone ahead to notify the household of their arrival.

The turf croft at Keflavík was only a small one. Helgi informed her it was the northernmost farm in their district, the most isolated and difficult to get to, especially in winter. The croft stood on a flat headland towards the front of the bank, the sea stretched out before it, the land sloping back into a valley blanketed in snow with the mountain Göltur rising tall and stark behind it.

They approached the dwelling, Sólveig puffing hard behind Helgi after their climb up the steep bank, but she stopped short, her ears straining to catch the high-pitched wail on the wind. She couldn't help but shudder at the sound, pondering what sort of eery spirits inhabited this place. She shook her head at her foolish thoughts, thinking the cold had perhaps addled her more than she cared to admit. Surely, it was nothing, but she had almost caught up with Helgi when he, too, stopped. He turned to her, his hand up, halting her. The sound of snow crunching underfoot no longer dominated the silence around them.

Sólveig watched him. His expression was one of intent, his dark brows drawn together in concentration, listening and waiting for something. The wind whistled about them, and then it came again, this time clearer. It was a woman's wail. Her screams were desperate. They told a story of agony and fear.

The rise and fall of Sólveig's breath came faster and her mouth went dry. "What or who was that, Helgi?" she asked. And she saw how his face blanched.

"It's Águstína!" he remarked. "Sólveig, we must hurry." And he ran towards the farmhouse, throwing open the front door, ducking as he rushed through the low frame of the entrance, Sólveig trailing him.

She chased him down a dark hallway and up the staircase, straight into the *baðstofa*. "What's happened?" called Helgi as they burst into the room.

It was a large, dimly lit space, with an oil lamp on a flat-topped trunk by the glass window at the end closest to the entrance. An older woman with silver-streaked black hair sat at the edge of a bed at the opposite end of the room. She turned to them as they entered, and relief flooded the woman's weathered features. She could see her friend Rúna in that face, though her eyes were a deep blue instead of green. The woman tried standing to greet them, but the young woman beside her wailed, clutching desperately to the long sleeve of her shirt to stay her.

"*Nei*, don't leave me," cried the girl. She was indeed young, no more than fifteen, her face still rounded with youth, her breasts small but full, sitting over a bulging belly. She was mostly tucked into herself, her legs brought up awkwardly, her knees clamped together tightly, trying to hide from the pain, though Sólveig knew this was no pain the girl could hide from.

The older woman turned to the girl. "*Shh*, Stína. I'm not going anywhere. I'm right here." She stroked the side of the girl's face tenderly.

"Is there trouble with the baby, *Mamma*?" Helgi lingered in the doorway. "I've brought the midwife. This is Sólveig," he said, and Sólveig stepped forward, tipping her head in greeting.

The older woman smiled at her, beckoning her into the room. "You are a most welcome sight, Sólveig." And then she turned her attention back to Helgi, sighing deeply. "Nothing's the matter, Helgi, other than a woman birthing a child. Thank you for bringing the midwife, son. She can take it from here. Now off you go to the kitchen and bring in the boiled water. I prepared some not long ago."

With that, Helgi left the room and she turned her attention to Sólveig.

"I am Elisabét, but you can call me Elsa. This is Águstína or Stína as we call her," she said, indicating the girl beside her. "She's not being much help to herself, though." Elsa shook her head, a deep line appearing between her greying brows. "It's really not as bad as it seems. It's Stína's first child and she's but a girl and afeared of the pain, is all." Elsa turned back to the girl in question, squeezing her hand. "Look, Stína, she's finally come—the midwife. She'll take the pain away."

Sólveig pitied the girl. She was clearly scared beyond reason. Stína whimpered and thrashed her head about. Like a skittish horse, the fear was stark in her blue eyes, her breath came fast, her chest rose and fell quickly. One hand still clutched Elsa's sleeve. The other was wound tightly in the bedsheets.

"How long has she been like this?" Sólveig asked, dropping her bag and sitting by them on the end of the cot.

"She's been at it since the early hours of the morning, but her waters only just came loose before you and Helgi arrived. That's why she was howlin'—that and the pains are coming quicker and harder now." Just as Elsa spoke the words, the girl tensed, and the wailing increased in volume once more.

"I'm going to die! I'm going to die!" Stína sobbed. Her dark rye-coloured hair sat in two thick plaits, dishevelled and falling loose about her neck and shoulders. She closed her eyes as if by shutting them, she could will it all away, as if by keeping her body tight and closed up, she could stop this child from being born.

The girl was dressed in a long-sleeved underdress. It was soaked through, but it seemed Elsa had managed to get an oilskin over the bed to catch the fluids. Sólveig pulled off her mittens and placed her hands gently on the girl's bare feet. They lay flat on the bed, her knees drawn up and clamped shut.

"Listen to me, Águstína," she said sternly, but not unkindly. Águstína opened her tear-filled eyes, and Sólveig continued, "You are not going to die, do you understand? I won't let that happen. The pain you're feeling right now will go away once the baby is born. But we have to get him out first. Your body is helping you do that. It is helping you to push your baby out. But *you* need to help it too."

The girl looked all misery, her lips wobbling as she said meekly, "I just want my *mamma*—I just want it out. It hurts. It really hurts."

Elsa squeezed her hand. "Listen to the midwife, Stína. All will be well, child."

"We need you to help us, Stína," Sólveig added. "Can you spread your knees apart for me so I can see where the baby's head is positioned. He may be ready to meet you now."

Stína shook her head vigorously. By the frequency of her pains, Sólveig guessed she was close to pushing, but she wanted to check. She just needed the girl to uncurl herself, to stop fighting it so much and allow her body to do the work.

Sólveig said a silent prayer to the Almighty, asking him to guide her hands in the safe delivery of Stína's child, but most of all for the girl to simply cooperate with her.

Helgi came in then with a tub of water, leaving it on the trunk at the window near the entrance to the *baðstofa*. It was farther from the bed where Stína lay, but the room was not long, and the light was slightly better there by the window. Sólveig thanked him and sent him for some more. Everything had to be cleaned well—her hands, the scissors for cutting the cord, a needle for stitching any tears. In the meantime, she stood from the bed, picked up her bag and left Elsa to talk the girl through another contraction as the room filled again with Stína's wailing. Sólveig hurried, heading to the table by the window. She scrubbed her hands clean using the hot water and a bar of soap from her bag, tied a clean apron over her skirt and lay out her tools on the table on a cloth, ready in case she needed them. She also pulled out a small leather pouch from the bag and slipped it into her apron pocket.

Returning to Elsa on the bed again, she explained to Stína what she needed to do, asking for her permission to check inside her, but the young woman was stiff and determined, keeping her knees clamped tightly together, telling Sólveig not to touch her. When another strong pain passed through her, the girl screamed again, begging them to take the baby out, that she just wanted the pain to stop.

"Stína!" Sólveig snapped at the girl. Startled by her tone, Stína's wails quieted down to a whimper. "I know it hurts, but you have to be brave now, you have to be brave like—" Sólveig wracked her brain for a good story, for something inspiring. "Like Gunnhild, the mother of kings."

The girl stopped her sobbing, slightly baffled at this mention of Gunnhild and stories at a time like this, but Sólveig carried on regardless. The girl needed some sort of distraction from the pain.

"Do you know this story, Stína?"

Stína shook her head, her face contorted in misery.

"*Nei*? Well, *Gunnhild was a beautiful young woman, much like you, but she was held captive by two sorcerers who both wanted to marry her, and much like you—she fought her fate. That didn't do her any good, you see, because her captors were the wisest sorcerers of the land, and no matter how she tried to fight them or escape them, she was bested by their magic.* Stína, can you stop trying to escape your pain, stop fighting it so hard?"

"I can't—I can't stop. It just hurts so much," the girl wailed pitifully.

"Oh, but you must! You must endure it, and you can, like Gunnhild did her captivity, and I know you can do it because you will have a happy end to your story, just as she did. The sooner you stop fighting it, the sooner your babe will be born, but, Stína, I have something here that will give you the courage you need to face it."

Helgi appeared again, bringing more water and rags, taking the old water out again. She could see that being in the room was the last place he wanted to be. She thanked him and took the small leather pouch out of her dress pocket. Opening it, she pulled out the birthing stones.

They weren't actually stones but two brown beans, round and flat, that fit neatly into the palm of a hand. They were light and rattled when shaken.

"See these? They are birthing stones. They've been passed down to me from my own *amma* and have provided countless women the courage they need to face childbirth. They hold much power, Stína. The stones will help you expel the baby. Hold them in your hands, and when the pain comes, squeeze them and they'll gift you strength."

The girl unclenched her fist from the bedsheets and looked at Elsa, who nodded her encouragement, and Sólveig placed the stones into her open palm.

The girl relaxed just a little, and when another pain pushed through her, she wailed again, but this time she clenched the stones in her hands. Sólveig spoke to her gently, instructing her to breathe through the pain, and the girl's body began to relax, her wail transmuting into a guttural moan, some of the fear drawing out of her along with the tension in her body. When the pain eased, Stína finally spread her knees apart, allowing Sólveig to examine her progress.

The head was there at the entrance, and when the next contraction pulsed through Stína's body and the pushing began, Sólveig kept her voice calm, her tone soft, as she completed her story of Gunnhild. She told of how her endurance, courage and wit had led to her freedom, and all the while, Águstína, the woman-child, drew on her own courage and birthed her baby.

It was a boy. He was a healthy size, and Stína's opening tore slightly as his head came through, but his cry was strong and echoed throughout the small room which had darkened as daylight slowly left them.

Sólveig checked the babe over, cutting the cord and tying it with string close to the navel to stem the bleeding, then wrapped him in a blanket and held the wailing baby up to the girl, showing her what her courage had produced. The young mother's eyes widened with surprise, and she started crying, this time with joy, holding her arms out to embrace her new son.

"Oh, look at him, he's so small," she said softly, in awe of him. His tiny features were creased in disgruntled anguish, but she hushed him against her chest, popping a finger into his mouth, and he suckled it, the effort tiring him quickly.

Sólveig and Elsa gushed over Stína's bravery and how beautiful her little boy was, but she noticed the girl tense, another pain coursing through her, and Sólveig explained to her about the placenta, the special sack that had carried her baby and the cord attached between them to feed him and help him grow inside her. She told Stína she would have to push one more time to release it from her body.

But it took a while for the placenta to come, and Sólveig resorted to the use of a tincture she carried with her of angelica—angel's root as it was fondly named for its success and versatility with healing. She placed a dropperful under the woman's tongue followed with a mouthful of water, and the placenta finally made an appearance.

Elsa left Stína's side, lighting some oil lamps for Sólveig to brighten up the room so she could inspect the placenta, making sure there were no big sections missing that could cause puerperal fever later. It was a terrible infection that killed many women after childbirth. She also inspected the tear at Stína's opening and was relieved to see that it was only minor and wouldn't need sewing. She would encourage the girl to clean the area daily, however.

"You were right," said Stína, an exhausted smile touching her lips. "The pain is not so bad now."

Sólveig cleaned up after the birth, removing the oilskin cover over the bed, and settled the new mother while Elsa washed the baby, cleaning the birth off him. They wrapped a cloth about his bottom, and he was swaddled in a blanket to keep him warm. She watched the young mother as the baby suckled at her breast. Elsa had informed Sólveig that they had so little milk to spare with the sheep herds being culled so drastically in autumn and they didn't have a dairy cow to provide milk, so Stína would simply have to try and feed her baby by breast.

"That's it, see he's taking the milk, you're doing wonderfully." Sólveig praised the new mother, and she thought to herself, yes, she was young, but she could see the love Stina already had for her new baby.

"I'm not even sure how he got in there," the girl said softly. She dragged her gaze momentarily away from her son to Sólveig, her eyes questioning.

Sólveig was taken aback by this revelation. Of course, she had wondered who the child's father was. But Elsa hadn't mentioned it. Did the girl not know who the child's father was? Was she that naive? To be unaware of how a baby was made.

"Stína, a man helps a woman make a child. Did you not know that?"

She saw how the young woman's cheeks flushed red with embarrassment. "Of course, I know that a child made belongs to a woman and a man. I just wasn't sure of the way of it. I thought perhaps when they married, a baby could be made. But, Sólveig, I am not married." She looked down at her child, unable to meet Sólveig's gaze.

"A marriage is simply a written contract between a man and a woman, but a child can be made when a man gives his body to a woman and she to him, whether she is married or no."

The girl blushed an even deeper shade of red, drawing her breath in quickly as if something had just occurred to her.

"Stína, do you know who the father of this child may be?" She sensed the girl had figured it out.

She nodded her head and whispered the name, her eyes wide with realisation.

Sólveig only just caught it, but the answer took her by complete surprise. She had perhaps expected either of the brothers Magnús, or Elías, but she had not expected her to say Helgi.

"Helgi?" Sólveig repeated dumbly. "Helgi is the father of your boy?" She looked down at the child cradled in Stína's arms, at his dark head of hair and tiny, perfect features.

"*Já*, he only did it the once, and it hurt so I told him I wouldn't do that again with him."

Sólveig struggled with her thoughts and the tangle of emotions that rose within. There was certainly shock at this revelation, but what came the strongest was a deep sense of disappointment in Helgi. It twisted in her gut and left a hard knot there, and then there was a rising, burning anger. How could he do this to the girl? She was barely a woman! Why had he not told her he was to be a father? Did Elsa know about this? Did the other members of the household know? Was this all one big secret they kept to themselves? Keeping Stína even in the dark? Oh, the humiliation! How foolish she'd been for letting her own feelings soften towards Helgi, and she realised that her initial assumptions of him had been correct. He was the worst sort of man! Exactly the sort of man her *amma* had warned her to stay away from.

"Is everything okay, Sólveig?" Stína's eyes were large, full of concern for her.

She petted the girl's hand and stood from the bed.

"It's just been a long day, is all." She smiled at her with reassurance, but, in truth, Sólveig was sick with fury. "I'm just stepping out for some fresh air." Grabbing her shawl off the chair she had draped it over earlier, she rushed down the hallway and out into the darkness, hoping the icy air would dampen the heat of her anger.

She scoffed bitterly into the silence before her, realisation enlightening her. She understood now why it had been Helgi who had to come collect her to Keflavík, why he'd been hidden away up here for the past week—with his child's birth imminent. She recalled the way he had blanched when they heard the girl screaming and knew that the worry she'd seen etched into his features had been for Stína, the mother of *his* child.

Sólveig stood in darkness. Winter days were short, and though it was only early evening, night was upon them, but the sky was clear, the stars bright, the moon reflecting on the snowy landscape around her. She stood with her face to the wind, towards the ocean, where she could hear it breaking onto the shore below them. She embraced the wind, let it surround her, blow over her, push against her, taking small comfort in the way its icy breath numbed her cheeks, the tip of her nose and bare fingers, all the while wondering why she felt so hurt by this? So betrayed by him?

She should be basking in the joy of a successful birth. New life had just entered the world, but it was all tainted now by this revelation that Helgi was the child's father. The girl was barely fifteen, for Christ's sake! He had taken advantage of an innocent young woman, but she knew it was more than that.

She was angry at herself for softening towards him, for having allowed herself to secretly enjoy the mischief in his eyes when he teased her, or the way his hands on her made her catch her breath, whether simply lifting her in and out of a boat or cradling her face tenderly as he had done back in September. But this! Helgi was the child's father! How could she respect a man who was floundering about with other women while he had one at home pregnant—let alone allow herself to fall in love with one?

11

Sólveig was introduced to the rest of Keflavík's inhabitants at suppertime. Elsa's eldest son, Magnús, entered the *baðstofa* first, followed by a much older grey-haired man named Tómas, their workman. Magnús had the same dark curls as his siblings, but he was the tallest of the brothers and he wore a patch over one eye, the result of an accident in childhood, the other eye the blue of his mother's. He was a quiet sort of man, but he welcomed Sólveig to their household and thanked her for delivering the child safely, then headed over to see Stína and her new baby.

Only a moment later, deep voices and cajoling sounded in the hallway as Elías and Helgi came up the stairs and entered the room together, ducking their heads in the low doorway. Helgi had his younger brother in a headlock, Elías squirming and punching at his older brother's arm in a bid to release him. Elsa entered just after them and slapped Helgi about the ears, though he sat a head taller than her.

"I'll have none of that in here now," she reprimanded. "You'll be respectful, boys. Not only is there a new baby and a tired mother in here, but we have a guest with us."

Helgi let go of his brother, glancing over at Sólveig with a devilish grin, and was rewarded with another slap across the ear.

"Já, Mamma," he said quickly, and Sólveig couldn't help but smirk at these grown men still having to be kept in line by their mother.

"Go on, then, go and let Stína show you her new boy," she urged them, bringing the bowl she carried into the room. Magnús took the *askur* from his mother, seating himself on the cot opposite the young woman holding her baby. Stína and Sólveig had already eaten their meal of boiled fish and potatoes, and she took the empty bowls with her, back to the kitchen where Salbjörg and Steindór were cleaning up. Sólveig had met Elsa's recently widowed younger sister and her son in the kitchen earlier after coming in from being outside.

Elías congratulated Stína, and he stroked the child on the head as Magnús had done, taking a seat by his brother as Elsa arrived with two more bowls of food, and finally Helgi was there by Stína's side. The young woman looked up at him, her eyes shining with pride.

Sólveig tried not to be too obvious in her observation of them, wanting to give them some privacy, though to have privacy was, in truth, a foreign notion in a place such as this.

Helgi's expression was tender. "He's a fine boy, Stína."

"Would you like to hold him?" she asked.

Helgi peered at the small bundle in her arms, suddenly unsure. "I'm afraid I might drop him, he's so small."

"Go on," Stína encouraged, lifting the child towards him.

He took the child awkwardly, his hands swimming around the small bundle, and he cradled his son.

The knot inside Sólveig twisted at the sight of him holding the babe. She was still angry with him and hurt by the revelation that he was the child's father, but she was hard-pressed not to admit that she sure enjoyed the sight of a man holding a baby.

The child stirred, mewling and stretching his sleeping limbs, so that his swaddle came loose about his arms, and Helgi suddenly looked panicked.

"Here, he's come loose, you better take him back." He handed the child to his mother, lowering him gently into her arms, and then took his bowl of fish from the table.

Sólveig couldn't help but stiffen when Helgi decided to take a seat next to her on her cot, her knitting needles halting momentarily as his knee brushed hers. He winked at her and sat, then bent over his bowl, scooping the contents into his mouth as if it had been days since he had eaten, rather than hours. Apart from holding the baby just now, he didn't seem at all affected by the momentous event of becoming a father. In fact, it was as if everyone in the room just ignored that important detail. Why was she the only one who was bothered by this lack of acknowledgment?

Sólveig desperately wanted to say something, but she'd been told to mind her own business by him before, so she wasn't as inclined to be the one to point this out.

"Go sit with Stína," she muttered instead, pulling her knee away from his so they no longer touched. Why did he sit with her? He should be over there next to his woman and child.

"Here's just fine. Stína's resting and there's no other space besides. Why? Do I smell or something?" His brows were raised in humour, his mouth full of food.

What is wrong with this man? She shook her head with distaste, her anger still simmering just below the surface.

"Fine, *I'll* leave, then." She threw her knitting needles down and stormed out of the room, but as she rushed down the hallway, Helgi was right there behind her, and he grabbed her by the crook of her elbow, pulling her to a halt.

"Woah, hold on there now, you don't get to flee that easily."

It was dim in the hallway, the light from the room lending them visibility where they stood. Helgi turned her so she was forced to face him, his earlier humour all but vanished from his features. "What's this about, Sólveig?"

"Let go of me." He released her, and she took a step back only to find the cool stone and earth wall hard up against her back. He had her cornered regardless.

"Is there something you want to say to me? All evening you've been looking at me like you want to strangle me. What is it that I've done to offend your senses?" His brows were furrowed into a line, and she caught the flash of muscle in his jaw.

The anger and disappointment she had quashed earlier rose to the forefront. "*Já*, I have something to say to you," she gushed, breathing hard.

"Well, say it, then?" he prodded impatiently.

"How can you just pretend like it's nothing? That's it's no big matter that you've just become a *father*—?"

A look of incredulity crossed his features. "A father?"

"And all this time, you and Inga, and then you had Stína back here—" she sneered, feeling disgusted by it all, her heart thumping so hard it left her almost breathless. She was so exasperated by him, by his indifference and callousness. "How can you be so careless with people?"

It took Helgi a few moments to make sense of her, and then he stepped away from her as if he'd been scalded. "You think I would?"

She pulled her shoulders back, tilting her chin up with defiance as if daring him to contradict her. Her silence was answer enough.

"I see. Well, that explains your frostiness with me." He scoffed, a bitter and twisted sound. Dark amusement and irritation flashed in his eyes, and he tapped his finger lightly on her head. "So, you think in that righteous little head of yours that I'm his *pabbi*?"

"Do you deny it?" she demanded.

Helgi grabbed her by the upper arm, and she stifled a squeal as
he pulled her down the hallway and into the kitchen, away from the
baðstofa so the whole household wouldn't hear them argue.

"Of course, I deny it," he growled, letting her go. "I'm not the child's
father."

"*You* would deny it. You think I haven't seen the way you are with
women, the way it was with Inga. I'm so tired of it, Helgi—" She jabbed
at his chest with her index finger, and he flinched, his jaw clenching
harder. "Of men like you thinking they can just make babies with women
for the fun of it and then leave them to deal with the burden—while they
move on to the next woman no less!"

"Is that what you really think of me?" Helgi looked as he if she
had winded him, but he schooled his features quickly. His unrelenting
gaze burned into her, his eyes betraying his anger, and there it was,
disappointment and hurt—but why did he look at her like that? Why
did he deny the truth? Stína told her he was the child's father. She
steeled herself, holding her ground with him, but he leaned towards her,
standing only a hand's breadth from her face, his breath warm and harsh
against her ear.

"You have it all wrong, Midwife."

Sólveig stood alone in the kitchen, her heart still beating fast and hard,
feeling flustered and irritated and confused—irreparably confused.

When she turned to leave the kitchen, she found Elsa hovering in the
doorway. The woman had surely heard everything.

"Why does he deny it? Stína told me the child's father is Helgi."

Elsa sighed, kindness and understanding mingled in her weathered
features. "I see, except it wasn't *my* son that she was referring to."

"What do you mean?" A sense of dread came over her at those words.

Elsa continued, "The child's father *is* a man named Helgi. Helgi Jónsson is his name. He was with our household as a workman, a drifter come work for us the May before last. He was a likable man, a lot of charm about him. Stína took to him, and I tried my best to never let her be alone with him, but, of course, I simply couldn't be there all the time, minding her like a child when she was a half-grown woman. He was gone by March, went down south, we heard, and by the time summer came, her belly was growing, and we knew he had left her with his child."

"Oh, Elsa, what have I done?" Sólveig despaired, closing her eyes, her fingers rubbing at her temple. It all made sense now, why the family didn't speak it out loud. What use was it when the man was long gone? She sighed, thinking that she should have simply asked Elsa about it earlier, rather than stewing on it as she had, and Helgi—*Andskotinn*, she swore inwardly. She would have to apologise to him. She sighed heavily, recalling how she had just accused him.

Elsa patted her arm. "You weren't to know. It was a simple misunderstanding, is all. Helgi will come around."

Of course, there had to have been another Helgi! She groaned. Just her luck. Well, she conceded that at least he wasn't the lowly scoundrel she had spent the last few hours or so painting him in her mind to be.

Elsa followed her back to the *badstofa* and Sólveig ducked her head through the doorway, but Helgi wasn't there. Magnús told her he'd seen him head out to the sheep house.

Sólveig grabbed her shawl and left through the back door from the kitchen, trudging through the thick snow to the small stone croft on the hill behind the main farmhouse. It was the dark of night, but as it had been earlier, the sky was clear, the stars a twinkling blanket above her, a half-moon lighting her path. The wind blew at her, and she held her face towards it, closing her eyes, the cold sting upon her cheek enlivening.

She went over in her mind how quickly the situation had changed. She had expected Helgi's excuses and indifference, him telling her to mind her own business once again, but she never thought that she would be the one apologizing now. Rushing out, she had left her gloves and head scarf inside, and she could feel the bone-numbing cold crawl up into her fingers as she turned the handle to the door of the sheep croft. Just that short distance walking through the thick snow had left her breathless and her toes numb, and she must have appeared a flushed mess when she entered the warmth of the sheep house.

The smell of fresh hay was comforting, the odour of sheep overwhelming. The light was dim in the croft, a single oil lamp hanging on a hook by the door, casting only a small orange glow around her. The rest of the croft sat mostly in darkness. She stood still, allowing her eyes to adjust to the dimness. Helgi was at the back of the croft, his figure stooped as he spread hay along the feed troughs in the stalls. The ewes swarmed him, reaching for their supper, their little mouths chewing fast, the occasional bleat stirring amongst them.

Surely, he heard her enter the croft, if not seen her. Sólveig waited for him to acknowledge her, but he didn't turn. She sighed in frustration, realising that he was purposely making this hard for her.

"Helgi?" But he kept on with his task. "Stína told me that her baby's father was Helgi. I didn't know there had been another named Helgi staying here. Helgi, please, what I said about you and Inga—"

He stopped.

She finally had his attention. "I shouldn't have said that, and I *am* sorry for it."

He turned to her then. His brows were knotted, the muscle in his jaw twitching as he mulled over what he would say to her.

"You know you may have simply asked me if I was the child's father, but you seem to have this idea about me that I'm some sort of scoundrel."

"And would you have been any less offended if I had simply asked you?" She glanced down at her hands, feeling somewhat embarrassed, hoping the dimness of the room hid the heat flushing her face. "You would have likely told me to mind my own business, would you not?"

He took a moment before speaking again, weighing up her question.

"You know, Magnús and I wanted to find him, but *Mamma* wouldn't have it. I wanted to find the bastard and beat some sense into him for taking advantage of her the way he did. I would have dragged him all the way back here to marry the girl. Made him accountable for her. The best I could do was a letter down to the authorities in Reykjavík, where he's gone. It took a while to track him down, but we got wind of where he was. He'll get a fine at least, and notification that he's obligated to the child if anything should happen to Stína." He shook his head. "She deserved better than him."

"Oh, Helgi." She sighed. It all made sense to her now, the letter he had Grímur write for him back in September, the reason he had left a week ago for Ísafjörður and then back to Keflavík. He'd just been looking out for the girl. She could finally breathe again, but with the air cleared came a sense of her own foolishness. How she had let herself get so worked up about him. How the disappointment of thinking he'd done this had, in truth, just cemented the feelings she had about him.

"Sólveig?" His voice was soft, his eyes both tender and pleading. "I would never do that to a woman. I hope you know that. I would never give her my child and just walk away. That's not the man I am, nor the man my mother raised me to be."

"I know that now, Helgi," she said carefully and let the words sit there between them. She took a few steps towards him, so that they were only arm's length apart, and looked hard into his eyes. A pang of guilt ran through her at the hurt they radiated.

"I truly am sorry for what I said." She slid her hand delicately into his, squeezing it. His long fingers wrapped around her hand in response. His thumb caressed her skin, and she broke his gaze, pulling her hand away, but a gentle tug stayed her. Her eyes met his, and there it was, that same look, the one he had given her while rowing earlier that day, that look of desire and angst, and her breath caught in her throat.

This time though, she wasn't afraid of it. This time, she let it soak into her as she brought her hand up to his face. Her fingers traced tenderly along his jawline, the dark bristle of his unshaved skin rough against her palm, and before she knew it, she found herself leaning forward under the heat of his gaze. It lingered low over her mouth, and against all her good instincts, Sólveig brushed his lips cautiously with hers, her *amma's* words echoing in her mind that men only wanted one thing. But s*he* wanted this and the truth of it shocked her. She wanted to kiss him and had wanted it for a while now. He pulled her into him, his hands coming about her waist, and he pressed his lips firmly against hers, parting her mouth with his. Her hands found the back of his neck, and slid into the dark unruly mess of hair, his hat falling carelessly to the floor, and she found herself thinking—if this is what it felt like to be kissed, then she could do this again and again.

Helgi pulled back, a lopsided smile sitting softly on his lips. "So that's all you wanted, Midwife, a kiss?"

Her cheeks flushed with heat, and she pulled away from him, covering her mouth, a little stunned by her own forwardness. "I'm sorry, I don't know where that came from."

"Don't be sorry." He grasped at her wrist, gently tugging at the hand covering her mouth, slowly pulling it away from her lips and leaned into her, his mouth grazing hers once more, sending flutters deep into her belly. She closed her eyes, his kiss growing firm and persistent, quickly deepening once more. The spark between them, so tender a flame, grew in strength, but Sólveig knew that fire was a dangerous thing to play with and without caution could quickly blaze out of control. She felt the heat of him, the heat of his desire for her through his kisses, but when his hands trailed down to her bottom, pressing her body to his, a sense of panic rushed through her.

She stepped away from him so quickly, the room spun.

"What is it, Sólveig?" He reached for her again, but she put a hand up to stay him, the gap between them like a cold void after being in his fiery embrace.

"We—I shouldn't be doing this." She stumbled over her words, not sure what else to say. Flustered and light-headed, there was something gnawing at her, deep in her belly, something she hadn't felt before, and she knew that if she stayed any longer, she would lose all sense of sound judgment and let him put his hands all over her. Her body ached for it, and it was this feeling that scared her the most. Not him, but how much she wanted him to touch her.

"They'll be wondering why I've been out here so long," she said with apology, fleeing the croft before he could stop her.

12

The weather took a turn for the worst, and Sólveig was stuck at Keflavík for the following two weeks with seemingly endless days of blizzards, raging winds and poor visibility. Morning and night, the men returned from the sheep croft looking like creatures of winter, covered in flakes and frost, their clothes half frozen to them. They were forced to use a line of rope between the house and sheep croft to find their way during these storms, lest they lose themselves and walk over the cliff. They complained of the cold being the devil in disguise, the way it burned their flesh on the wind. But the cold could not be kept out, it crept inside the farmhouse, moisture from the turf walls freezing solid in the hallway, along with the urine in the bedpans. Water and much of the food in the pantry had to be defrosted over the cooking hearth to use, and the household clothed themselves in extra layers, even in the *baðstofa*. Most of the time, they simply wrapped their blankets about themselves, staying abed most of the day, sleeping two to a bed to keep the warmth locked in, unless they needed to prepare food or use the bedpan.

Stína shared her bed with Sólveig, and between the two of them they kept her little boy warm and snug, and he slept and fed as he pleased, unaware of the battle the rest of the household was fighting with the weather.

Stína rose from her confinement a week after the birth of her baby, her post-birth bleeding finished with no signs of puerperal fever. The child thrived and he had a healthy set of lungs on him. He wouldn't be given a name until his christening, as was custom, but they took to calling him *litli minn*—my little one.

The young mother struggled initially with the breastfeeding, the girl complained of aching breasts when her milk came fully in on the third day and then sore nipples almost to the point where she was crying because they were so tender when the babe suckled them. Sólveig encouraged her to carry on through the pain, explaining to her that it would settle with time as her body got used to feeding the baby. It was no new thing for a mother to feed her own baby. Women had done it through the ages, she told the girl, and though it was not overly common hereabouts, Sólveig had seen plenty of the women down south do it. Sólveig didn't have any *blývatn*, lead water, with her to bathe the nipples in, but she was able to ease Stína's discomfort by making her a warm compress to soothe the tender skin, when the baby wasn't feeding.

The end of December was fast approaching and Sólveig had hoped to be home in time for Christmas at Suðureyri, but she knew now that she would spend it at Keflavík with Helgi and his family. Helgi and Sólveig had barely spoken since their kiss in the sheep croft apart from the usual polite greetings. She made sure she always kept herself in a room with someone else, which wasn't hard in a smaller household such as Keflavík. Helgi went on as if nothing had happened between them anyway, and she wasn't sure this didn't irritate her because his kiss certainly tormented her.

Preparations were well under way for the Christmas meal and Mass that evening. It was a quiet affair, the darkness of winter kept at bay with candles and the glow of oil lamps. They dressed in their best clothes and ate a meal of *hangikjöt*, lamb newly slaughtered and smoked for the occasion. Afterwards, they all sat by the light of the room, with full bellies, listening to psalms and storytelling.

That night the wind rattled the windows and snow fell in fat flakes outside, but despite the weather, the mood in the *baðstofa* was high and there was laughter and singing abound. Sólveig sat with a weak coffee in her hands, the heat of the liquid warming her, as she listened to the sounds around her, letting the mood of the evening lift her along with it. Helgi sat on a chair in the centre of the room, all eyes and ears trained on him as he began his tale of the Yule lads thirteen.

"Beware the lads, the sons of the trolls Grýla and Leppaluði. They who have been travelling down the mountains these last thirteen days, one at a time. Perhaps you have heard them, with the slamming of doors or scratching at the windows? You see they've come for food. As it is so often in winter, food is scarce, especially high up in the mountains, and these poor lads are driven down the slopes one by one every year to fill their hungry bellies, for Grýla is a poor mother indeed. Now, the lads are not cruel like their mother, who steals children that misbehave, but they are devious lads, taking great pleasure in trickery, and every night beginning on the twelfth of December, one of the brothers journeys down from the mountains, a sack on his back to sneak about amongst men. However, it's not enough to simply know that they are coming, you must pay mind to which of the brothers it shall be, for they each have their own peculiarities. If it be Skyr Gobbler, make sure to keep the lid tight on the barrel of skyr. Don't leave the Christmas hangikjöt hanging for Meat Hook to grab through the chimney, and tonight of all nights, we must keep all of our candles near, for Candle Snatcher likes nothing better than a juicy, fatty candlestick to gobble down."

Sólveig finished her coffee and took up her knitting, listening in amusement as Helgi played out each of the Yule lads. He had the room in fits of laughter—the way he stole his mother's spoon from her hand

and pretended to lick it as Spoon Licker the Yule lad did or was suddenly on all fours sniffing around their feet like Door Sniffer.

When he finished his silly tale, he took a seat on the cot opposite hers, the one he shared with Elías, his breath coming hard, contentment in his eyes as he took up his own coffee. She was hard-pressed not to look at him. When she did, images of that night in the sheep croft came flooding to the surface, and she hated the ache it left in her. But as Tómas took Helgi's place with his verses of Christmas and winter longings, she found herself there again, her eyes on his, and when he finally met her gaze, the jest was gone. The smile faded from his lips as he considered her across the room. This time, she didn't turn away as she had the habit of doing. She found it strange how looking into a person's eyes, really locking onto them, was like baring a part of her soul. It made her feel vulnerable and exposed. Her belly fluttered and her breath came faster. She wanted to cast her eyes away from his, but she couldn't. She saw his desire for her, but it scared her to think that he could see the same in her. *So, this is how it feels?* she mused. This was how it felt to want to meet a lover in the night. Guilt drove itself hard into her then, guilt at playing her hand in stopping Inga's flirtations with him. *Hypocrite.* And here she was wanting to do the same. Frustrated and ashamed of herself, she finally tore herself away and turned her attention to Tómas and his words. She refused to become one of *those* women.

⊹

The weather finally abated two days later, and Helgi and Sólveig took the boat back to Suðureyri, leaving Keflavík early that morning while there was still light and the weather was fair. She farewelled the others inside, out of the cold, but Stína stood in the doorway as they left, waving to them, tears in her eyes, her babe bundled in her arms. Sólveig waved back. She would see them again in the spring for the child's christening. She swallowed down the lump sitting tight in her throat, knowing she would miss this place and the people she had come to know over the past two weeks. She had felt part of the family here and they had welcomed her with open arms.

Magnús and Elías followed Sólveig and Helgi down the narrow track from the headland to the beach and helped Helgi turn the small timber rowing boat they had stored against the cliff. Snow sat like a thick blanket across the base of the granite wall, trailing down towards the shoreline. They had a fair job of digging the boat out from the snow, but they got it in the water. Magnús held the vessel steady while Helgi loaded it with his and Sólveig's sacks along with her medical bag.

"Do come see us again, won't you, Sólveig?" said Magnús as she embraced him in farewell.

"Of course, if Helgi would be kind enough to bring me back sometime." She glanced over at Helgi. He winked and gave her a curt nod. "It doesn't take long for this desolate corner of the Westfjörds to get into your heart," she said, turning to embrace Elías in farewell.

Helgi stood by the side of the boat at the ready to lift her in. She tried to hide how his merest touch affected her. When he picked her up, the strength in his arms coursed through her, one arm about her waist, the other behind her knees. He held her close, and her breath caught. Her arms drew around his neck, but it was over all too quickly as he placed her carefully down inside the boat. She moved to the end and took up the spare oars where Elías had been seated on their way to Keflavík. Helgi jumped in while Magnús and Elías pushed the boat out into the water, saving Helgi the nuisance of getting wet, regardless of the oilskin sea pants he wore.

"You think to help me row?" he asked, eyeing the oars in her hands with amusement.

"And why not? I thought you could use the help. It'll be more work for you otherwise, and besides, it might keep me from heaving the whole journey home."

He took the oars from her, dropping them back inside the boat. "Let me do this one task for you, Sólveig."

"You think I don't have the strength?" she asked in mock offense.

"Not at all." He chuckled. "It's just a man's pride, woman. Let me row for you."

"Men's pride be damned," she muttered, but she sat. Helgi positioned himself on the bench opposite her, taking up the other set of oars. She crossed herself, praying silently that they would make safe journey back to Suðureyri. She had only eaten a small bite for her morning meal, but she was anxious nonetheless.

"Sólveig, stop with the fretting. We'll make safe passage. I promise you." Helgi regarded her as he pulled the oars through the water, and she took a deep, steadying breath.

"I'll have to take your word for it," she said, gripping the seat firmly.

The boat ride home was a quiet affair, both the ocean and Sólveig's stomach were calm, and she almost enjoyed the way the boat glided across the water and the land slid past her quickly. The air was cold, and cloudy white puffs formed about them with the heat of their breaths. Helgi rowed in silence, every effort going into pulling the oars through the water. His mood was sombre, and he watched her as he rowed. The wind was with them, which gave them good speed on their journey. It blew against her back, urging them onwards, and she looked past him, into the distance, refusing to meet his eyes again, lest hers betray the emotion she held simmering at the surface. The fjord came into view as they rounded Göltur's headland. It was shrouded in the morning mist, the turf crofts barely visible specks in the distance.

"What was that the other day in the sheep croft?" Helgi ventured between puffed breaths, finally breaking the silence between them. She stiffened and the flutter returned to her stomach. But why did he sound so irritated with her? His brows were knotted, and he rowed all the harder, throwing his frustration into the oars.

"The kiss?" she asked weakly.

"Já, the kiss! You're a right puzzle to me, Sólveig. I don't know whether to pursue you or stay away from you."

He paused, waiting for her to respond, but what could she say?

"I think you enjoy toying with me," he added with a wry smirk.

She shook her head. "*Nei*, it's not like that."

"Is that your way, then?"

Her eyes locked with his. "And what do you mean by that?"

He scoffed, almost bitterly. "Well, you constantly accuse me of being a philanderer and then you're kissing me. What am I supposed to think?"

"What shall you have me say?" A moment passed, the splash of the oars lapping the water, taking up the silence. "I—I guess I just wondered what it was like," she finally said.

"You've never been kissed by a man before?" There was a hint of surprise in his tone.

She decided that she didn't have to answer that question. That was none of his business, though she knew her silence was admission enough. Unable to bear the intensity of him, she stared down at her gloved hands, but she was irritated with all this, with him, with herself. "And what have kisses gotten any woman but a bruised heart and a babe growing in her belly?" she demanded. "I'm not that woman, Helgi."

"And there it is again," he said, rolling his eyes. "What is it about men that you despise so much? You say you've never been kissed, so how could you possibly have so much resentment within you for our kind? What's happened to you that's made you hate us so?"

"I don't hate men," she said in a huff. "You wouldn't understand. You haven't spent your whole life being the evidence of your mother's shame." She looked away from him, unable to meet his gaze—that surprised, pitiful expression she'd read on his face, and she wished she'd said nothing.

They sat in silence again, the heat simmering between them, such contrast to the frozen land around them. Helgi heaved the oars one last stroke, and the vessel washed into the landing. He jumped out of the boat, into the shallows, and dragged it onto the beach with her still in it. He was annoyed, but he bit his tongue, his lips pressed together in a tight line. He helped her down from the boat, and despite his apparent irritation with her, he was gentle with her, lifting her like he would pluck a delicate flower. When he lowered her to the pebbly sand, he didn't let her go.

"You're far from being anyone's shame, Sólveig, and I'm sorry you were made to feel that way, but *you're* the one who kissed me, remember. Sounds to me like your body's telling you one thing and your head another," he said tightly.

Albert was headed towards them from the fishing croft, and she knew this was her chance to escape. She tried to pull away from him. Helgi knew it too, and before he let her go, he said to her, plain as day, "I want you, Sólveig. I can't get it out of my head, the taste of you."

Her eyes met his. "Let me go" was all she could say, panic hitting her hard and he finally released her. Helgi turned away from her, pulling the

bags out of the boat as Albert approached them, passing them one by
one to Sólveig.

"*Blessuð og sæl*—may you be blessed and well," said Albert. "Welcome
back from your journey. Did all go well?" he asked, shaking hands with
Helgi. Sólveig leaned into Albert as he kissed her cheek in greeting, his
bristles rough on her face, and she plastered a smile to her lips, hoping
Albert couldn't see how flustered she was, how disturbed Helgi had
made her. She nodded politely.

"We made fair crossing," Helgi said, pulling the boat farther onto the
beach. Albert took one side to help him heave it up the beach to the sea
croft. "And this one even managed to keep all her breakfast down," he
said, nodding towards Sólveig as she walked alongside them, all signs of
his earlier angst and irritation wiped clear from his face.

"A strong, healthy boy was delivered two weeks ago," she informed
Albert proudly. "Mother and babe are both well."

"We would have come sooner, but the weather held us there," added
Helgi.

"I'm glad to hear that all are faring well at Keflavík and more so that
you've both returned. We've missed you here, Sólveig," said Albert. "The
girls will be mighty pleased to see you."

"What did you name her?" she suddenly asked, remembering the
christening, eager to hear what name Albert and Krissa had chosen for
their daughter.

"Sigurlína Sólveig is her name," he said.

"Oh, Albert," she gushed. Her heart swelled with pride. "Well, I do
feel honoured, if I say so myself. How beautiful!"

Albert smiled in thanks. "You two head on up to the house and get
something warm into you. You look chilled, woman." And he turned to
Helgi. "Thank you for bringing her back to us safely."

"*Já*, thank you," Sólveig added, glancing at Helgi. She caught his eyes and tried a smile, but it fell flat. She wanted nothing more than to escape. "Well—" she said, ready to excuse herself as a strained silence drew up around them.

"I'll be down here awhile longer," Albert stated, taking his cue, and Sólveig took her leave.

Heavy footsteps closed in on her as Sólveig made her way up the beach towards the house, and she increased her pace. She knew it was Helgi trailing her, but she didn't dare turn. She approached the back of the croft, hoping to enter through the kitchen, but when she reached the outermost wall of the building, she found herself pulled towards it, her back hard up against the cold wall of the structure. Her bags slipped to the ground.

Helgi had her pinned to the spot, his body blocking her escape, an arm on each side of her head as he beheld her, his green eyes burning into hers. His breath came hard, his chest rising with it, and then his hands came about her face as he drove his mouth onto hers. His kiss was rough and desperate. She whimpered, responding to him for a moment, but the reality of what they were doing was too stark in her mind, as were the repercussions.

What if someone sees us? She slapped him across the face and pushed away from him, her breath coming hard. He stumbled back a step, stunned.

"What good will this do us, Helgi? It's only going to end in heartache."

"Do you think I enjoy feeling this way about you?" he asked, the veins in his neck popping, his voice cracking. "Christ, you're tearing me up, woman! What is it you want?"

"It's not that simple!" she tried. "What would people think if they saw us now? I could lose my position here and you yours. You have somewhere to crawl back to! I can't risk that. This place, these people, are all I have now." She hated that she was hurting him, but she wanted him to understand what was at stake.

"I didn't ask you what *other* people think! God forbid, woman, that your high sense of propriety be compromised and your *precious* Albert finds out that his midwife is human after all. I asked you, what do *you* want?"

She couldn't bring herself to say it. Why couldn't she just say that it was him? But the words wouldn't come, and a heavy silence fell as he waited for her answer.

"You know what?" he puffed with finality. "So be it, Sólveig. When you've decided, you let me know." He shook his head, grabbing his sack, and disappeared into the farmhouse.

Sólveig leaned back against the croft wall with a stifled whimper, needing its cold, sturdy presence. Her hands trembled and she closed her eyes, taking in deep, steady breaths in an effort control herself, to control the powerful urge she had to chase him, to call him back and tell him exactly what he wanted to hear.

13

January 1882

The new year drew in with calm days and clear skies, and with the knowledge of a full moon fast approaching, the men of Suðureyri decided to take to the sea to hunt shark. They would use the light of the moon to their advantage. It would be their beacon, a guide for their vessels on the great ocean depths of the North Atlantic.

"They must take the days they're presented with," Krissa explained to Sólveig the morning of their departure. "It's a matter of survival."

Sólveig sensed the woman's anxiety over her husband leaving. Shark hunting, like any seagoing was a dangerous venture. The weather could change, cloud cover could mar their way. So many things could go wrong.

Sólveig had risen early with Krissa and Rannveig, leaving the others to their slumber. She couldn't help but yawn as she stood by the cooking hearth with both house mistresses, dishing out bowls of porridge with liver sausage and slices of rye bread for the small crew of men heading out.

The party of six was gathered in the kitchen—Albert, Björn, Einar, Helgi, Jói and Árni—ready to tackle their greatest predator, the sea, to bring in one of its toughest creatures, the Greenland shark. Their faces were still sleep weary, but they were in good spirits, knowing they would finally escape the indoors for what had been a monotony of weeks sitting by the lamplight with only odd jobs and sleep to occupy them, when men were used to keeping busy, unable to sit, as women were wont to do all day with their knitting, sewing and weaving.

They kept their voices low so as not to wake the others, a nervous, excited tension rippling through the room.

The Greenland shark was a deep ocean creature, valuable not only for its meat but also its oil, a commodity that fetched a good price. Krissa told her it would buy them much-needed supplies if they were to hit hard times again in the coming summer.

In the time since her return to Suðureyri from Keflavik, Sólveig hadn't managed to find the courage to face Helgi and tell him how she really felt about him. She always managed to talk herself out of it, for what could she say, really? That she wanted him as much as he wanted her. How could she when she'd been so against his flirtations with Inga? No. She had to resist those needs of the flesh. Helgi wasn't the marrying kind—he'd told her as much when he'd scoffed at the thought of marriage to Inga. He'd made himself scarce besides, and she was quickly caught up with duties of the household, but he stood in the kitchen now with the others, his presence like a splinter embedded into her skin. She tried not to let it bother her, tried to pretend that his being in the same room with her didn't affect her, that his last words to her weren't still lingering there between them, unaddressed. He filled the room so with his presence. She passed him his bowl without a word, too aware of how his fingers brushed hers, meeting his eyes only briefly and pulling them away, her face flushing with heat. She couldn't let him see the way he affected her. Couldn't give him the hope he sought.

She focused her attention instead on clearing and cleaning up.

"*Jæja*, very well, the tide waits for no man." Albert handed his bowl to his wife, thanking her, and the men bid their farewells to the three women, making their way down towards the sea croft, dressed heavily from head to foot in their thick woollens. Their oiled sheepskin sea clothes were kept at the sea croft, where they would suit up and take to the water. Albert and Helgi were the last to leave. The workman hovered in the doorway. His expression when she finally had the courage to look up at him was severe, a hurt lingering there in his eyes. But he said nothing to her. Perhaps he was waiting for Albert to leave, waiting for a moment to be alone with her. Would she tell him then? Could she let him leave without telling him how she felt about him? She should know better than to let a loved one leave without saying goodbye. It could be the last time she saw him. She waited for Albert, watched him pick up his sack of supplies, food that Krissa and Rannveig had gathered for their sustenance. Sólveig couldn't help but let her eyes linger over the couple as Albert took his wife into his embrace and kissed her. Krissa leaned her head against his hand as it cradled her head, and he grazed his thumb along her cheek.

"Come back to us, Albert," she said. "We'll be praying for you." And before Albert could say anything, Krissa quickly turned away, making her way back down the hallway, her eyes glistening with unshed tears.

Albert turned to Sólveig. "I know you'll take good care of them for me while we're gone."

"I'll do my best, Albert." She squeezed his arm in reassurance. "Good luck out there, and may God be with you."

Albert nodded his thanks and left, and it was only then that she realised Helgi had slipped out into the darkness. He had left without saying goodbye and she had let him.

The men would be gone for a few days, and those who were left behind felt their absence, but life carried on, and Sólveig pushed aside her regrets, soothing her inner turmoil with distraction. She helped Krissa's girls with their daily Bible reading and reciting of psalms, made salves and brewed teas to soothe the winter cough that had taken hold in some of elderly of the household, particularly old Leifur and Tobba. From Björn's household, Rannveig too, was poorly, and Sólveig went between the two *baðstofas* with her healing teas, but on the third day after the men left, a visitor came to Suðureyri in the late hours of the night.

The dogs had startled them all awake with their sudden barking from the entrance of the croft.

"It's Grímur come for Sólveig from Vatnadalur," Krissa informed the curious faces, roused from their slumber, but she directed her gaze to Sólveig. Behind her towered a man Sólveig had never seen before.

He was a big, hairy man, tall and not so much barrel-chested as his belly was paunchy, but Sólveig thought him much like a man stepped straight out from one of the old tales, bent over almost double as he did to enter the room.

"Björg at Hraunakot has taken to childbed," he said.

"Grímur, this is Sólveig, our midwife," said Krissa.

"I'm pleased to meet the new midwife of Suðureyri," he said politely, stepping forward and bending down to kiss her in greeting.

"Thank you, and I you," Sólveig returned.

"If you'll make yourself ready, I'll take you to Björg directly." He held his hat in his hands. His thick, curly mane, the colour of stormy skies, stood out at all ends, and he patted it down with a large hand. "Júlíus would have come himself, but my younger brother is bedridden with sickness of the lungs."

"But I thought Gróa was to assist her. Júlíus made it clear—" Sólveig started.

"Been over there already," he interrupted. "Gróa's too poorly to come tonight. The snow's too deep for her old legs and she's sickly besides. Jósefína is tending her, so she can't go over either. I'm afraid it's down to you, my girl. And never you mind old Júlíus. He's too sick to put up any sort of argument." His voice was deep and hearty, and she heard how it filled the room. "So, you will come with me this night?" he asked.

"Of course," she told him, and he left her to make herself ready, retreating to the kitchen with Krissa for a cup of coffee before his walk back into Vatndalur with the midwife.

It took them two hours of hard walking. Sólveig was thankful it was a clear night, the stars bright and the moon full, lighting their path to Vatnadalur, but the snowfall had been heavy of late and the accumulation on the ground was copious. She clutched the hem of her skirt with one hand, the other carried her medical bag. Her skirt was heavy, made more so when the hem became wet from melted snow. The fine white particles clung to it as she trudged through the thickly laden path, sinking almost knee deep in places. Grímur was well ahead of her, his strides much longer than hers, but she followed in the wake of his footsteps. She found him waiting for her by the headland, and seeing how breathless she was already, he took her bag, carrying it for her as they traversed the path along the cliffs, near the ocean. Her nerves were on edge crossing this track. The wind carried flecks of sea spray to her face from the ocean on her right, and she was acutely aware of the danger that lay on her left with the build-up of snow on the mountain that rose with the cliffs above them. She thought back to Leifur and his warning to be wary of avalanches this time of year, but Grímur assured her that the track was clear and the passage safe to cross.

When they reached Björg and Júlíus's croft deep in the valley, Sólveig thanked Grímur, and he made headway for his home farther down, near the lake. She was greeted at the door by Björg and Júlíus's eldest child, Herdís.

"*Mamma* is in bed. The babe's head is coming," the child blurted, her eyes wide with worry.

Sólveig rushed into the *baðstofa* to find Björg on the cot at the end of the room, her nightshirt pulled up past her knees, the babe's head crowning in her pelvis. An older woman, small of stature, sat by her, holding her hand, speaking words of encouragement.

"That's the girl," said the older woman.

Björg panted, her breath coming short and fast, her eyes closed, her face contorted in pain as she pushed the head through, letting out a gasp with its release.

Both women looked up at her as Sólveig approached the bed, and the older one smiled at her in greeting.

"You must be the midwife, the new one from over Suðureyri way." It was more of a statement than a question, and before Sólveig could answer her, the woman added, "I'm Katla, Grímur's wife. I've made some hot water ready for you." She pointed at the tub on the table next to the bed. "She's a quiet one, for sure. But as you can see, the babe is well and truly on its way now."

"Where is Gróa?" Björg managed, looking stricken. Sólveig followed her gaze towards her husband. Júlíus lay asleep on the cot opposite Björg's, totally oblivious to the task his wife was undertaking.

"She couldn't make it," said Sólveig gently. But now was not the time. "Will you accept my help, Björg?"

The woman nodded her head curtly in assent as a contraction took hold of her, and Sólveig put her bag down and cleaned her hands quickly

with warm water and soap. She took her place at the base of Björg's bent
knees, watching and waiting for Björg's body to do its work, to expel the
child's shoulders.

Björg was unnaturally quiet throughout her labouring, and like a
woman who had birthed many times before, she knew how to draw the
pain into herself, for the pain was most certainly there. It was expressed
through the strain in her face and the way her knuckles turned white as
she bore down, leaning into her knees. There was no screaming like there
had been at Sólveig's last delivery. There was no fear, just a few muted
groans, a calm acceptance and absolute trust in her own body to do the
work.

The child made a quick entrance and Sólveig inspected the baby. She
was small and dainty, the thick creamy substance smeared in patches over
her body gave Sólveig the indication that she was a couple of weeks early,
and then she wrapped the child up and placed her on her mother's chest
while Björg birthed the placenta.

Later, Katla helped Herdís bathe and dress the baby while Sólveig
settled Björg in a clean cot, clearing away the soiled sheets and making
sure there was plenty of cloth to soak up the blood that would come for
a few days after the birth.

"What is it?" They all turned to the rough croak of a man's voice. It
was Júlíus. Sólveig couldn't help but view him with distaste, knowing
the sort of man he was and wondering how poor Björg could bear it.

"I said what is it, woman, a boy or girl child?"

Sólveig had just passed the clean and swaddled baby to Björg, who was
settled back in her cot, and waited for the woman to say something. But
she didn't.

"Well," he demanded.

"You have a daughter, Júlíus," Sólveig answered for her.

"Another girl." He scoffed and turned his back on his wife and new child as he succumbed to a fit of coughing. It took much for Sólveig to bite her tongue, but she knew it wasn't her place to interfere.

"Here, take her. I can't." Björg held the baby towards her, her lips set into a firm line. "How am I going to care for another child?" she whispered. Unshed tears glistened in her eyes. "I can barely feed the six I have. Milk is scarce in this household."

Sólveig took the baby into her arms. "You can always breastfeed her. Your breasts are made to supply the child with milk. *You* can feed her."

"*Nei*, I want them strapped," she snapped. "I don't have the time nor the patience for it. With Júlíus so sickly, I need to be back on my feet as soon as I can. I struggle enough keeping the other children clothed and fed." She was quiet, and then: "I don't know if I can do this again, Sólveig."

The words took her by surprise. The heartbreak in Björg's eyes and the hollowness in her voice was unsettling.

"Everything will be alright," she said, patting the woman's arm, but Björg drew away from her touch.

Emotions were often high after the birth of a child. Sólveig knew how tired Björg was. The woman had been tired for a very long time. It was etched into the fine lines around her eyes, in the strands of grey scattered through her hair, and Sólveig worried about how Björg was going to cope with her new daughter, along with her six other children and no support or kind word from her husband. To Sólveig, this child was a miracle of creation, a wonder to her as it was every time new life entered the world, but to Björg she was another mouth to feed.

Sólveig asked Katla to prepare some milk for the babe. The child was restless in her arms, making hollow suckling sounds until she became frustrated by her hunger not being met and started to cry. She gave the child to Herdís to hold, and Björg's eldest pat the baby's bottom and placed her little finger in her mouth for the child to suckle, soothing the mewling cries, not wanting to wake the other sleeping children. Sólveig, in the meantime, strapped Björg's breasts to stop the milk coming in, and when this was done, the exhausted mother lay back down on her cot, turning away from Sólveig, her back to everyone in the room.

Sólveig sighed. Björg's disinterest towards her new baby worried her. "I'll feed the babe tonight and settle her. Things will look better in the morning, Björg," she tried with a heavy heart.

Katla returned with some milk for the baby. "Get this into the sweet wee thing," she said to Herdís, passing her the small wooden cup with a spout to hand-feed the baby with.

"Nice and slow," Sólveig encouraged Herdís. The baby suckled greedily at the milk offering, her tiny pink lips making a circular shape, her small tongue wrapped awkwardly around the wooden spout.

Katla left them then, heading back home for some sleep, informing Sólveig she would be back in the morning to help with meals and the younger children. When the newborn was sleeping in her older sister's arms, soothed with a full belly, exhausted after her entrance into the world, Sólveig took the child, herding Herdís to bed, and she watched the girl sneak into the cot beside her younger siblings. The poor girl was exhausted. She'd been up most of the night helping Katla with her mother and then Sólveig after she arrived. Björg was lucky to have her. She may not be able to afford a work maid, but she at least had Herdís. Sólveig lay the sleeping baby next to Björg and took her own rest on the chair beside the cot, waking to feed the babe when she stirred.

A baby was crying. It took a few seconds for Sólveig to realise that she wasn't in her bed back at Suðureyri. It was dark in the room, the hard surface beneath her bottom reminding her that she'd fallen asleep on the chair beside the cot Björg slept in. She stood and stretched her aching limbs, rubbing at a knot in her neck. The cry grew louder, coming from the cot next to her.

"Will someone pick up that squalling baby!" called Júlíus from his cot.

Björg's bed was empty. She sighed and leaned over to pick up the baby. Her skinny little arms had come loose from the wrap she was swaddled in, her small fists flailing freely in frustration.

Björg was already up and dressed, a woollen shawl crossed over her chest, her apron on, the key to the storeroom jangling off the belt around her waist. Sólveig found her in the kitchen preparing the morning meal, stirring contents in a black cast-iron pot. Sólveig had the child with her, patting her bottom, looking to prepare her some more milk, but Björg beat her to it, and she pushed a cup for the baby towards her.

"Björg, what are you doing on your feet so soon?" Sólveig scolded. "I must insist that you return to bed and rest. Let me do this."

"I've done this six times already. Júlíus is sick. I must care for him. The household doesn't stop just because I've had a baby. I have six other children to care for."

"Then let me do that. Let me take care of you and your family. Take your little girl and feed her." She held the crying baby towards her. "She seems to be taking to the milk."

Björg glanced at the child and away again, her mouth set hard.

"*Nei*, I can't take care of her, Sólveig." She moved past her, grabbing bowls from a shelf and dishing gruel into them.

"But you must," pleaded Sólveig, taking up the small jug for the baby and bringing the spout to her mouth. The baby suckled greedily, and Sólveig had to tilt the jug carefully so it didn't come out too fast. She finally glanced up to press her again. "She needs you, Björg." But it was no use, Björg was already gone from the room, her footsteps echoing down the hallway.

⊰⊱

Sólveig stayed at Hraunakot with Björg and Júlíus for another five days. Katla came later that morning on the first day and took over from Björg, Sólveig getting her way in her insistence that the woman return to her bed for rest. In that time, she helped Herdís with the children and Björg with Júlíus but mostly she took care of the baby, trying to get Björg to bond with her. It saddened her greatly to see how little interest the mother showed her new daughter regardless of Sólveig's efforts to get her to hold her and feed her.

It didn't take long for Björg to regain her strength, and by the fifth day, she was up and out of her confinement. Júlíus still lay sick in bed. His fever had finally broken but his cough still aggravated him and kept him up at night, making his mood even more unpleasant. Sólveig prepared teas for him to drink, to help soothe him. He would mutter and moan when drinking the warm liquid but would soon after settle back to sleep. The other children showed little interest in the baby, apart from Herdís and little Anna María. When she could be spared, Anna María took her little sister and Sólveig let her feed her and cuddle her, but she, too, was taken up most of the time with helping her older sister to feed and dress their younger siblings, along with feeding the sheep, with their father being ill.

On Sólveig's last night with Björg's household, the two women were in the *baðstofa* after the evening meal, taking a cup of hot tea before bed. With Björg out of her confinement, it was time for Sólveig to return home, but Björg was alarmed by the news of her departure.

"Sólveig, you must take her for me," she pleaded, her voice soft so as not to wake the sleeping children.

"Do you not love this child, Björg?" Sólveig asked, unable to understand how any mother could give her own child away. But, then she thought of her own mother, who'd had no say in the matter. "What will Júlíus think?"

Björg shook her head. "You probably think me heartless, but it's *because* I love her that I can do this." She reached for Sólveig's hand. "You must take her, Sólveig."

Silence fell around them. It sat heavily in the room. Sólveig never thought it would come to this. It was no strange notion for a child to be fostered out at birth, but what was she to do with a baby? Could she take her, look after her as well as manage her midwifery duties? She certainly agreed that Björg was in no state of mind to care for the baby, and she could see that the household did struggle with milk supply. Björg certainly had enough to worry about with Júlíus being sick and the other six children she was responsible for, but she was also concerned with Júlíus and his moods.

"I worry about you, Björg. Are you safe here with Júlíus? He's never laid a hand on you, has he?"

"*Nei*, of course not!" she said, drawing her hand away. "He's not such a bad man."

Sólveig wanted to scoff at the woman's admission, but she held her tongue. Björg smoothed down the loose thread at the cuff of her sleeve, avoiding her eyes.

"I know you must think that of him, or perhaps you wonder why I married a man so much older than me?"

"Björg, age has nothing to do with my concerns about Júlíus. It's how he treats you, how he speaks to you, his blatant disregard for his new daughter."

"*Já*, he's certainly gotten crankier with age, short-tempered and more stubborn, the old fool." She scoffed lightly. "But he's all I have, Sólveig. It's him that keeps this place going, heads out to sea to provide for us, keeps us fed and a roof over our heads. It may not look like we have much, but we survive because of him. If he were to die, God forbid—" And she crossed herself at that. "What would happen to us then? My children would be taken from me, scattered about the district, who knows where?" She puffed out a harsh breath. "Don't you see? That's why it's so important that he gets well again. That Júlíus is back on his feet soon. I need to care for my husband, and I don't have the strength to make sure he survives this winter and this little one too."

The woman broke down then, her tears flowing, her face crumpled in misery, her body shaking. "I wish I did! I truly do, but when I look at her, I think of having to get up in the night to another crying baby and I shudder. I—I just can't do it," she sobbed, shaking her head.

"Shh, Björg, it's going to be alright," Sólveig soothed, taking the woman's hands in hers again, waiting for her sobs to settle. "I'll take her for a few months. Suðureyri is a bigger household. There will be milk to spare there, with the three cows they have, but just to get her stronger and to give you more time to get Júlíus back on his feet, do you hear?"

Björg rubbed her nose, sniffling softly and nodded. "May God bless you, Sólveig. I know she will be well cared for in your hands."

14

February 1882

The men had not returned from shark hunting when Sólveig arrived back at Suðureyri carrying the sleeping bundle across her chest—Björg and Júlíus's five-day-old daughter. She spotted Albert's girls playing by the frozen lake as she approached the house. Rannveig's daughter, Margrét, and their foster son, Steinn, were also there. The four of them, the youth of the household, enjoying the fine weather. They were clothed head to foot in their winter woollens, throwing snowballs and grappling with each other as they shuffled across the frozen lake, their joyful giggles and squeals echoing throughout the otherwise silent fjord. She waved to them when they noticed her, and they came running to greet her, their faces flushed red with the cold, their eyes glistening. Her escort, Grímur had already gone ahead of her.

"Sólveig!" exclaimed little Dóra in a mighty breath, hugging her in greeting. Sólveig smiled down at the girl with affection, patting her head as the other children caught up. "*Mamma* has been so worried," the little one blurted, wide-eyed, her lips pursed in a sullen pout. "*Pabbi* and Uncle Einar have been captured by Ægir."

"Hush now, Dóra, *Mamma* said no such thing," Dísa admonished her younger sister.

"That's what Leifur *afi* told me! The sea king has captured them, and they must battle him so he'll set them free," she retorted.

"Is your father not returned?" Sólveig asked, dread settling into her at this news. It had been eight days already since Albert and Helgi had left with the others. Surely, they should be returned by now.

Dóra nodded. "I don't like hearing *Mamma* cry. She thinks we can't hear her, but we can."

"Dóra!" Dísa gave her sister another disdainful look. "*Mamma* says we must pray and be hopeful. They'll return any day now."

Sólveig smiled at them with sympathy, patting Dóra on the head. A red woollen scarf covered her blonde plaits. "Your *mamma* is right. We must stay true to our hope and pray for him—for them all to return to us."

The baby wailed, startling the children. They looked around and at each other, baffled by the noise, but when it came again, they gasped in awe as Sólveig opened her woollen shawl to reveal her secret.

The baby was awake and stirred against her chest. The child would be hungry. She patted her bottom gently, rocking her, hushing her back to sleep.

"Where did you find a baby, Sólveig?" asked Dóra. "Did the Hidden people give it to you?"

Sólveig laughed. "*Nei*, my darling. She's Björg's little girl. I'm taking care of her for a little while, that's all." And she bent down so they could get a good peek at her. "Now off you all go. I have to get her out of this cold."

Rúna met Sólveig at the entrance of the croft, and she kissed her friend on the cheek in greeting.

"Grímur, says you've got yourself a baby to care for?" She took Sólveig's shawl from her shoulders, hanging it on a hook to dry out, and Sólveig produced the child in question.

"*Já*, she's a sweet little thing."

Rúna pulled the baby out from the wrap tied across Sólveig's chest. The baby stretched in her arms, whimpering at the disruption, and Rúna cooed over the child.

"I'll help you where I can with her. It's a kind thing you've done for the woman, Sólveig."

"It means much to me to hear you say that, as I'm afraid I'll not be able to do this on my own. But what's this I hear about Albert and the men still not returned?"

Sólveig noticed the tremble in Rúna's lips.

"Eiríkur from Bær came by three days after they'd taken to sea and bore us the news that our men may have landed in some trouble. Eiríkur had his boat out that day too, you see. A storm hit on their second day out on the water. Both boats had to sit it out. He said Albert and his men had been sitting on the edge of their vision for most of that time, but when they saw them pull out their sails and head north into the wind—well, Albert would only have done it if they'd run into some trouble." Rúna lowered her voice to almost a whisper, leaning in close to Sólveig. "But when Krissa broke down before him, Eiríkur tried to assure her that they would have made for land somewhere."

"Oh, Rúna, I'm so sorry," she said, the knot in her own stomach growing.

"I'm afraid for them, Sólveig. Helgi is out there. I've already lost a father to the sea. I can't lose a brother too."

Sólveig pushed away at the thought they may never return, that the ocean had swallowed them up, as it had done with so many good men.

What could have happened that held them so? And then she thought about how she had left things with Helgi. The matter between them was a constant torment to her, a heavy weight over her, a feeling like something was lodged into her chest and someone held it there, twisting it. Was it too late? Had she lost her chance to tell Helgi how she felt about him? She shook those thoughts away. No, she couldn't think like that. What good would that do?

"We mustn't give up hope, Rúna. Like Eiríkur said, surely, they were able land somewhere, and we must cling to that, that they'll return to us when they can. They're skilled sailors—Albert, your brother, Einar and Björn." She squeezed Rúna's hand.

Rúna let out a reluctant sigh. "I suppose you're right." The baby grew unsettled and started to wail. "Come now, Krissa's in the kitchen, and we can find this little one some warm milk and a clean cloth for her bottom."

"Já," Sólveig agreed. "I could certainly do with a coffee, even a weak one, if there's some to spare." And she followed Rúna to the kitchen to introduce the newest member of the household to its mistress.

Sólveig was grateful to have the baby as a distraction. She nicknamed her Stella, a latin name, for the stars that had been so bright the night of her birth. Her true name would not be revealed until her christening day, and she hoped by then Björg would be in a better position to take her youngest daughter back. Krissa and the rest of the household were initially surprised to see her bring home the child, but they knew the sort of circumstances Björg and Júlíus lived in, and they understood. The household embraced this new child so that it was not simply Sólveig who took responsibility for her but the whole of Suðureyri. Albert's girls doted on her as they did their baby sister, Lína, and thankfully Krissa had spare clothes she could lend the child. Lína was nearly three months old and thriving. She had outgrown her earlier gowns and woollen leggings.

Sólveig was able to knit for the child, and combined with Tobba, Rúna and Rannveig's quick skills with the knitting needles, they were able to keep the child adequately clothed.

What else was there to do but knit and wait and fret? The days dragging on into what seemed an eternity of waiting for some news, constantly looking out the *baðstofa* window to see if their men were returned.

Stella slept next to Sólveig in her cot. She was a dream baby, often waking only once in the night to be fed and drifting quickly back to sleep with a gentle pat on the bottom to soothe her. Lína was still waking a couple times, and Sólveig often met Krissa in the kitchen preparing milk for her own daughter, her eyes heavy, but it was more than a waking baby that wore at her. Sólveig knew it, because she felt it too. They all felt it. That knot of worry lodged within them for the men of Suðureyri.

Sometimes Stella simply cried, and it was hard to settle her again. Krissa gave her advice, being experienced as she was with two older daughters, for Sólveig was new to the role of motherhood and welcomed any help with the child. Sure, she was a midwife, and she knew how to deliver babies, but she had never had to step in the place of *mother* before and have someone depend on her so entirely.

⁂

The weeks rolled into a month of their men being gone, and February drew in, the end of winter and the turning of the season, a time to ponder the coming spring and hope for better days, but the women of Suðureyri found no comfort in that. The more days that passed with no sign of their men, the more a possible future without them settled in their minds. It wasn't uncommon for the ocean to steal a whole crew of men in one gulp. In those frozen waters of the Westfjörds, what hope did they have of survival?

But their ghosts had not returned. Krissa surprised them when she spoke of it one night as they all sat gathered in the *baðstofa*, the children tucked into bed. The women folk sat up in the glow of the lamplight, pouring their worries into the click of knitting needles or the clack of the wheel of the spindle, chatting in hushed tones about a reality they needed to finally face, after nearly a month of silence, voicing a hurtful truth gnawing at them.

Krissa told of a time long ago, when the sea had taken her first husband, Þórður. He had drowned along with his entire crew and his ghost had come to her to let her know. It was as if by telling this story, she was reaffirming to herself and the others that there was still hope, even after so long.

"I heard him, clear as day," she said softly. "And though it is eight long years now, I remember it as if it were only yesterday."

Sólveig glanced up from where Stella was sleeping in her arms. Krissa's eyes were far away, as if the woman were there, at this moment, hearing it again. "He was calling my name from the doorway, my sweet Þórður. But when I came rushing to the entrance, the door simply flapped in the wind, not a man or woman in sight."

A shiver ran through Sólveig. Krissa continued, "I searched down the road stretching along the length of the farmhouses. We were expecting them home any day, but a storm had hit the night before and there had been no sign of them. It was as I turned back into the house that I saw them—two large footprints, like he'd stepped straight from the sea into the front room, and I knew then that he had come home to me. I searched the house, like a woman gone mad, thinking he had already made his way into the house, without me seeing him." Krissa sighed, a haunted look taking hold of her. "And he had been there, just not in the way I had expected him to be. Two days later, they found the missing sixareen washed up on the coastline between Flateyri and Staður, and the sea finally returned their bodies, my Þórður's among them."

They all bowed their heads in silence, and the piece that had lodged itself within Sólveig twisted a little more as she considered what this woman had already lost. She recalled Albert telling her of the child she'd lost shortly after Þórður's death. Dísa had been only three at the time.

Krissa broke the silence again. "What I'm trying to say is that their ghosts have not returned to us. I know they're still out there! I say we pay a visit to Eiríkur at Bær. Perhaps he can send a boat out to look for our men, to ask along the coastal farms. Their boat may have washed up somewhere along the coast. Someone must know something."

"They're not gone. I would know it too. I would feel it in my bones if my boys were no longer here," said Rannveig. "But I don't. They're biding their time, is all."

"How could they be alive?" asked Tobba. "It's been a month already, with no sign of them."

"Hush, *Mamma*, I won't give up on them—not yet."

"We'll go tomorrow to speak with Eiríkur again. Rúna and the girls will manage the children and the household," said Rannveig.

Krissa nodded and the matter was settled.

Krissa and Rannveig left at daybreak the next morning, walking to Bær, leaving Lína, the girls and the household under Tobba's care.

Later, as the remaining household members all gathered for their midday meal of skyr and rye bread, Leifur sat at the window smoking his pipe, peering out into the distance.

"They'll return tomorrow on the eve," he announced with his usual croaky drawl.

"Who? Rannveig and Krissa?" Sólveig asked, not looking up. She had little Stella propped up on a pillow on her cot, looking about the room, her tiny fist in her mouth. Sólveig caught her eyes and smiled at her, and for the first time, the child gave her the tiniest hint of a smile in return. Her heart warmed at the sight. Not much melted the constant worry she felt day in and day out, but this little child brought such innocent joy into the dark days they faced.

"Our men," Leifur said, still staring into the distance.

She drew her eyes away from the baby. "How do you know this?"

"I've seen it. My eyes are failing me, but I still see. There, on the horizon," he said, puffing smoke from his mouth, pointing towards the boat landing on the moor. "I see men walking."

Sólveig stood from the cot and peered out the window, following his gaze. There was only a small glimpse of the beach through this back window. She could see nothing. Perhaps he sensed their ghosts returning and she shuddered at the thought. They would know soon enough.

That very same evening, Jakob arrived at Suðureyri to collect Sólveig to Botn for the birth of his and María's child. Again, she was surprised to receive the beckon, when the woman had been so adamant that Gróa assist her, but by Krissa's accounts, she knew the old midwife was still unfit for travel. Rannveig and Krissa were still at Bær, and Sólveig had to rush out, leaving Stella in the care of Rúna and Inga.

Night had settled and the sky was overcast with no light of the moon to guide them, but Jakob knew the way. She followed him into the fjord, tracing the coastline hugging the sea, taking the trail she had walked with Albert the day she had arrived in Súgandafjörður. She glanced back at Suðureyri farm—this place and the people that were slowly making their way into her heart. What would she come back to after this birth? She couldn't help but hope that the men would be returned, or would there be sore tidings to bear?

15

Sólveig was held up at Botn for four days after the birth of María and Jakob's baby. The labour went on into the night, and María was delivered of a baby boy in the early hours of the morning. He was a small, weakly thing, born limp and lifeless into Sólveig's hands, and she worked quickly with him, resorting to the use of the *salmiak spiritus* drops she carried in her bag, and bathed the babe in warm water, massaging his body to bring more life to him. They christened him straight away, repeating the holy words over the child, in the place of the priest, lest the babe didn't survive the coming days. But as the days wore on the child grew stronger, taking the milk he was offered with more vigour. His parents gave him the name Albert Einar, for his uncles, who were yet to reappear with the other crew members of the missing sixareen. Sólveig noticed how the weight of uncertainty surrounding his brother's fate sat heavily upon Jakob, as it did the hearts of the whole community. She sensed that hope of the men's safe return was dwindling in those around her, and this unknown truth left her almost breathless with grief, to the point where she flinched whenever she heard the names of the missing men spoken. It would be a heavy blow for a community as small as theirs to lose so many men in one go, men in the prime of their lives, but Sólveig was determined not to dwell on it. Nothing was certain in her mind until they had word of them, or their boat, or God forbid the sea returned their bodies somewhere along the coastline. She could distract herself with the tasks before her, with fighting for the new life she had just helped deliver into the world. There was always a way to carry on, in the wake of even the smallest glimmer of hope.

It was past midday on her third day with the household at Botn when Jakob came striding into the kitchen, a wide grin on his face. "Sólveig, I've just had word from Suðureyri." He sounded so much like his older brother, so much so that it was almost as if it were Albert himself speaking to her, but for the wider set of his cheekbones and colouring of his hair.

Sólveig lowered the small jug of milk she was preparing for little Albert Einar, her heart pounding in her chest. "Well, what is it, Jakob?"

"My brothers are returned," he announced, his eyes glistening with joy. "Yesterday on the eve, they came in from Rekavík on the Hornstrandir coastline. They made land only three days after going out and have been biding their time up there for the past few weeks, fixing the boat and holding out for better sailing conditions."

Utter relief washed through her, and she clutched the edge of the bench, blinking back the emotion that welled up inside her. It was as if the piece that had been lodged in her chest for so long had just been released and she could finally breathe again. "After all this time," she said softly, her gaze fixed on Jakob standing in the doorway. "But, how do you know this? Are they all returned, the whole crew?"

He nodded. "*Já*, so I have been told. Helgi gave me the news himself just now."

"*Helgi?*" She couldn't help the way her heart leaped at the mention of him. "But where is he now? Did he not stop?"

Jakob shook his head, rubbing his chin. "*Nei*, I couldn't persuade him to linger. He was eager to be on his way again. He said Albert would have come himself, but Krissa won't let him out of her sight." He chuckled.

Her heart sank. But why hadn't Helgi the decency to stop and let himself be seen? Surely, he knew she was at Botn. "Jakob?" she said, her mind racing. She had to see him. If Jakob had come straight in with the news, he couldn't be too far towards home. "Can you take little Albert's milk to María for me?" she asked, pushing the jug of warmed milk towards him. She still had duties at Botn, but if she went now, quickly, she could see him—if only for a short while, and her anxious heart could receive the peace it had been seeking for the past month.

Jakob had barely uttered the word *já* before she took her leave and fled down the hallway and out the front door.

Helgi's lone figure trailed along the coastline. He was a sight for her weary eyes, and she ran towards him, clutching at her heavy skirts, treading across the snow-covered ground. The wind accosted her, tracing its icy fingers across her face and littering her clothing with flakes of white that fell from the sky, and she realised in her haste that she'd forgotten her shawl and mittens. Her long hair was carelessly released from the dishevelled plaits she wore, so that it flew wildly about her face as she ran, hoping to catch him. He had just passed the sea croft that belonged to the Botn men when he finally turned to her calling.

The land dipped and the croft sat on the bank, out of view of the farmhouse, boats lined up on either side of the stone and turf structure that housed their sea gear. Helgi made his way back towards her, and she slowed down as she approached him, breathing hard, trying her best to contain her excitement.

"I thought I would never catch you." She smiled unabashedly at him, greedily soaking in the sight of him. He wore grey slacks and a brown jacket, a hat over his mess of dark hair. He was truly here. Whole and unhurt, but he didn't return her smile. His face was composed and his eyes—they appeared almost pained. Had she seen the smallest hint of invitation in them, she'd have run into his arms and embraced him as she ached to do. She halted a few paces from him, less sure of herself under his reproachful stance, but the angst of the past weeks, of not knowing whether he lived or died, bubbled to the surface, and she found that she was suddenly angry with him for not stopping at Botn.

"You knew I was at Botn, and you couldn't come in to see me even for a moment? We thought you were surely perished," she scolded him, unable to control the wobble in her bottom lip.

He simply stared at her and then took his gaze past her in the direction of Botn, drawing out his breath in a long, tired sigh. The tips of his ears were red, as if burnt by the frost on the wind. She thought his face looked thinner, but he had grown out his moustache to a short, neatly trimmed beard. The green of his eyes seemed the starker for it, against the black of his beard, and it almost hurt to look at him.

"Go back to the house, Sólveig, you're turning blue with the cold. It's frost out, for Christ's sake."

She sighed impatiently, blowing out her frustration with him in a mighty breath.

"What happened to you all out there?"

His eyes turned soft and unsure. "Were you worried for me?"

She took carefully calculated steps towards him, like a man approaching a skittish horse. The void between them was but an arm's length, and she held his eyes, falling into their mossy depths.

"How can you even ask me that, Helgi? I've been sick to death with worry. Why did it take you so long to return to us? Jakob told me you made land up in Rekavík only three days after you went out?"

He rubbed his eyes. "*Já*, we did," he finally said. "Though nothing seemed to go right for us. The boat was in a bad way when we landed her. A young couple at Rekavík took us in, but they hadn't room enough for the six of us, so some of us went down to Straumnes and took up accommodation with the family down there. We met every day to make repairs on the boat, and when the time came to take her home, the conditions were never right, bad weather would set in, and then I took sick, a cough sitting heavy in my chest with a fever and chills." He was silent for a moment and wouldn't meet her eyes, looking instead into the distance. A muscle twitched in his jaw. "I told them to leave me there, but Albert wouldn't have it. He's a good man, Albert."

"Oh, Helgi," she managed. What an ordeal it must have been for them, and she was grateful Albert had waited, though it pained them all back here, not knowing their fate.

Helgi was so close to her, his breath a puff of white between them, mingling with hers and dissipating quickly. She wanted nothing more than to melt into the heat radiating off him, to hold him, to touch her hand to his face. "This is new," she said, referring to his beard, and she grew bold, tracing her fingers over his jawline, through the dark bristle of his beard, feeling the rough contour of him against her palm. He flinched, a strained look flashing in his eyes. "What is it? Are you still in pain?"

"Pain? *Nei*, not a scratch on me or the others, but by God, it hurts to be near you." His tone was low and raspy. He sighed deeply again and pulled away from her, taking her hands in his to still their insistent exploring. "I'm fine, Sólveig. Besides, I thought you indifferent."

"Indifferent? *Nei*," she said, almost breathless. She drew her hands out from his and let them fall uselessly to her side. "I—I've been so afraid these past few weeks. I hated how we last parted ways. I swore to myself that if you came back to me alive that I'd have the courage to tell you—" It came out in a rush of words, but she stumbled now, and she dragged her eyes from his, looking instead at the ground, afraid of what lay in them. Could she say it?

"To tell me what?" he insisted, and when the silence drew out between them, he slid a finger gently up under her chin. His touch was warm, and it sent a shiver through her as he tilted her face up to his, so that she had to look at him.

An almost pitied hint of a smile tugged at the corner of his mouth, but it was the want she saw reflected in his eyes that made her lean forward until her lips met with his.

He didn't respond at first. He held his frigid stance, but with a muffled groan, he finally softened his resolve, and his arms came about her, his resistance to her slipping so that his mouth opened to hers, and he returned her kiss with tender fervour. He tasted of the sea, of the wind and a hint of coffee, the bristles of his beard soft against her mouth. When they finally parted for air, they held each other at long last in an almost desperate embrace, as if they, at this moment, relived the tale of Ólafía and her Hidden man from the cliffs, clinging to one another, letting the tension and the worry of the past few weeks slip away.

Long moments passed where it was just the wind that blew around them. Sólveig shivered against Helgi, and his arms tightened around her.

"Come on then, Midwife, let's get you out of this cold before you freeze to death." He shrugged off his jacket and draped it over her shoulders, stopping to consider her, to push the dark hair that fell like a damp ruffled curtain about her face behind her ears. "My God, you're beautiful, Sólveig." And he took her hand in his, making to walk her back towards the croft at Botn.

"*Nei*, not just yet." Sólveig shook her head, staying him. She wasn't ready to relinquish him. A little longer in his company wouldn't hurt, but the clouds were low and a heavy fog lay over the fjord. The wind howled about them, picking up force, the snow turning to sleet, coming down harder so that it pricked their skin and left melted droplets clinging to his hat and beard, to her hair, and she steered him down the bank to the front of the sea croft for shelter.

The front door opened with a squeaky groan. Before them was a small, dark room, the smell of the sea embedded into every corner of the croft. The space was filled with ropes and nets, sea clothes, barrels and fishhooks assembled about the room on racks, shelves and hooks. Two small cots that also functioned as seats were built into the back wall, dressed in woollen blankets.

She'd thrown caution to the wind bringing him here, as if all they had was this moment, and in this moment, she was here, with him, alone in a croft by the sea. That was all her mind could contain. There was no past haunting her, no future to worry about. Just this moment.

He closed the door behind them, shutting out the frosty breath of the wind that had followed them in, and she let go of his hand, walking into the room, coming to stand at a wooden table up against the wall on their right. It sat under a small glass window facing out into the fjord, where she caught a glimpse of its dark waters and the mountain Göltur through the thick haze. Only a sliver of light streamed in through it, so that the two of them stood in shadows, and it took a few moments for her eyes to adjust to the dimness.

"You know this isn't a good idea, Sólveig," Helgi said, breaking the silence. She glanced back at him. He stood by the doorway, somewhat awkward and restrained. His brows were raised in question, but his eyes betrayed him as they travelled over her, soaking in the sight of her all too intensely.

"Isn't it?" she answered him softly, heat rising to her face, knowing perfectly well that he was right. "And since when have you been so worried about my propriety?"

He chuckled lightly at that. "Since you've been in a habit of running from me any chance I get near you."

"I'm not running now, am I?" She held his gaze, but her nerve faltered, and she turned away from him, distracting herself with the lamp at the table by the window. She lifted the glass cannister sitting over it and then replaced it again, knowing she had nothing with her to light it.

Heavy, cautious footsteps sounded from behind her, and she gasped at the sudden touch of his lips to her skin, tender and light, his breath warm on her as he nuzzled into her neck.

"You should be, because God help me, woman, I shouldn't be alone in a room with you right now," he murmured into her as his arms snaked about her waist. She pressed into him, and he ran his hands down the front of her skirt, over her apron, and pressed firmly between her thighs. Her breath caught in her throat, and she closed her eyes, leaning back into him and into the burgeoning desire he stirred within her.

"God, I want you, Sólveig," he growled, nibbling lightly at her neck just below her ear. "I've wanted you since that day in the valley."

The words he spoke cracked something within her, breaking some of the resistance she had been holding on to. She was tired of following the rules, and she ignored the voice in the back of her mind warning her not to let this go too far. He felt so good and the want inside her wouldn't subside. Surely, it wasn't meant to feel this way. Her *amma* had never mentioned to her how good it was to be held by a man, to be kissed by him. She had told her that it was a man's wants she had to watch out for, but what if *she* wanted this too, regardless of the consequences?

She turned in his arms to face him, pulled his hat off his head and dropped it carelessly to the floor. Her arms came up around his neck, and she combed her fingers through the short, dark mess of hair at the base of his head, meeting his lips with sudden desperation. Pushing aside the lamp, Helgi picked her up, hoisting her onto the edge of the wooden table, his body wedged between her legs, one hand sliding up to cradle her head and neck, pulling at her mouth so that it opened deeply, his tongue meeting with hers. The other hand slid up under her skirts, traveling up her stockinged leg to her bare thigh, where he gripped it firmly against him.

She had always thought good sense would prevail, but now it failed her completely. This time, she let the feelings within her rule instead of her overcautious mind. She couldn't stop her hands from exploring him, the way his explored her. His jacket slipped off her shoulders as she unbuttoned his vest, sliding her hands over the shape of him, over the coarse cream-coloured linen that was his shirt, running her hands along the contours of his broad shoulders and muscled arms. She relished the feel of strength in them, and he didn't stop her hands as they slid down, over his chest and around his waist, gripping the back of his shirt, bunching it into her fists as he pressed her into him, his mouth heavy on hers.

The door rattled, startling her out of her delirium, and they both came to an abrupt halt. In sudden panic, Sólveig tried to pull away from him, but he held her pinned to him and the table, his cheek against hers, his whisper of *shh* in her ear, soothing her worries. They listened for a moment longer, and the door rattled again.

"It's just the wind," he reassured her.

Her heart was racing, and she closed her eyes, tilting her head so that the white flesh of her neck lay exposed to his lips, and he leaned into her to kiss along its length, into the hollow of her throat, to the edge of her chin and up until he found her mouth again. His hands travelled over her hips, and down again, drawing her skirts up to her waist, and they gripped the bare flesh of her bottom as he moved his hips against hers, the gnawing ache in her groin growing as he pulled down his suspenders.

She was aware of his hardness against her, rubbing at her through the cloth of his pants. He groaned, a guttural, strangled sound, and plucked her up off the table, her legs wrapped around him, his mouth on hers and his hands under her as he carried her to the cot at the end of the room.

Helgi's eyes were fixed on hers as he lay her gently on the narrow bed, and in the dim light, she could see the restrained desire in them. She gasped at his touch when he lay over her, his hand locating her most private place, his fingers sliding into her, pressing, and stroking her, and she found herself opening to him, aching for more of him, arching against this unexpected pleasure.

When he pulled his fingers away, the absence of him left an ache in her.

"Helgi, please, don't stop," she breathed harshly, and he kissed her hard, deftly undoing his pants so that he was there again, leaning over her, the tip of his hardness against her, ready to push into her.

His eyes widened in surprise at her unexpected cry of pain, and he clenched his jaw, wincing, pulling back slightly. "I'll try to be gentle," he said, and she nodded, closing her eyes, gripping him to her. He kissed her eyelids, then across her cheek and down her neck, his hands gripping her bareness to him, slowly rocking his hips into her with a lustful rhythm.

The initial pain of his entry subsided, and she opened her eyes to find his gaze on her completely, filled with yearning. His breath came in short puffs, the sound of her own matching his—this, the only noise floating in the room about them as she melted into the feeling of him moving

inside her. His mouth took hers once more, and his kiss was hard and
rough, almost desperate, as he gripped her to him, his chest firm against
her breasts, his hands cupping her to him fiercely. Her body moved with
his in this strange rhythm, entwined as they were, meeting his thrusts,
deeper and faster, an intense ache building within her until he drove into
her in one final push, groaning as he did so, releasing into her.

Helgi lay over her, taking most of his own weight, puffing in
pleasure. The gnawing ache inside her had subsided—but why did it feel
unfinished somehow?

He rolled off her, tucking himself back into his pants. She caught a
look at it then, this intimate part of him, feeling her face grow warm
at the sight of it. She had let him inside her, and the reality of what
they had done hit her then. She tugged her skirts back down, almost
self-consciously, covering her bare legs, feeling his sticky residue there
between them, knowing that this coupling of theirs could well leave
a child growing inside her. And then thoughts of her own mother
came unbidden, and shame with it. Was this how it had been with her
father—two unmarried workers unable to keep apart? She blanched at
the thought and pushed it away.

"Are you okay, Sólveig? Did I hurt you?" he asked her then, squatting
before her where she sat on the edge of the cot.

"*Nei.*" She shook her head and gave him a reassuring smile, letting
him take her hands in his. The past few weeks of not knowing whether
Helgi lived or died had made it clear to her that he was the man for her,
that he was the one she wanted for a husband, but he wasn't sitting here
now asking her to be his, was he? Perhaps it wasn't just Inga he wasn't
intent on marrying. Yes, he said he wanted her, and she had given him
her body, but did she also have his heart? "I have to go, Helgi," she said

then. "Jakob's likely to send someone out looking for me if I don't return soon."

He nodded and stood up, pulling her with him, and she straightened up the tousled blankets on the cot.

They left the croft as they had found it, picking stray items of clothing that had found their way strewn across the floor, his hat, his vest, her scarf, stockings and shoes.

The fog still sat heavy over the fjord, and Helgi insisted on walking her back to Botn. She told him he needn't walk her, but he gave her an odd look.

"I wasn't asking, Sólveig," he said, matter-of-fact. "You shouldn't be walking alone in this, and besides, darkness is almost upon us. This fog is so damn thick, you'd just as likely walk into the fjord, for lack of direction, and no light to see you through it."

She took his offered jacket and they walked together, though they kept themselves apart, not daring to touch, after all the touching they had already done, crossing boundaries that shouldn't have been crossed. The silence drew up around them. She still felt him on her, the places where his lips had touched her skin, and she relished the memory of it, but it was as if what they had done together couldn't be spoken out loud. It had been done in the heat of the moment with no thought of what would happen next.

He stopped before they could go any further, turning to her as the outline of Botn come into view. "Sólveig?" he started.

"*Já?*" she replied meekly and stopped too.

"What we did this afternoon, giving ourselves to each other, it wasn't shameful, you know."

"What makes you think—" she tried, but he stopped her, before she could say any more.

"You don't hide your worries well, at least not from me, and you can pretend all you like that you're okay, but I wouldn't have stepped one foot into that sea croft with you without the intention of marrying you."

She was at a loss for words, and he reached for her hands, taking them into his, his eyes searching hers with earnest. "You will marry me now, won't you, Midwife?"

16

Albert was in the sheep croft when Sólveig interrupted his solitude, sweeping into the dimly lit croft on a rush of February wind.

It was still the early hours of the morning and Suðureyri lay in darkness. Soon, the winter sun would show itself for the first time, even if it was across the fjord on the mountain Göltur, leaving Suðureyri in the shadow of Spillir. However, it represented the hope of the coming summer and fairer days all the same.

Sólveig ducked her head under the low door frame, a scarf covering her hair and a thick shawl wrapped around her shoulders.

"Morning, Albert." She closed the door behind her, balancing a steaming cup of coffee in the other hand. "You're out early today."

"*Já*, I'm just checking on the rams," he said, returning her greeting. "It would be a sore sight to find them locked in a battle of horns for the females."

She peered over at the ewes milling about with the rams. "I've heard stories from down south of rams fighting to the death."

"It's not common, but it's been known to happen."

She thought the rams proud-looking creatures, muscular and beautiful with thick horns that curled about the side of the face. One was sniffing around the behind of a young tan-coloured ewe.

"But what brings you out here, Sólveig?" he asked.

She approached him where he stood leaning against a barrel along the wall of the croft, and passed him the cup of steaming black coffee, then reached into the pocket of her green-and-white-chequered apron, drawing out a small square bundle wrapped in cloth. "Krissa asked me to bring you some food. She saw you leave without breaking your fast this morning. I was heading this way, so I said I'd take it for her to save her coming out into this cold."

"Ahh," he replied.

"She worries for you, you know," she added sternly. "Said you don't eat enough."

Krissa did seem run-down of late, and Sólveig thought she'd grown thinner while the men were missing, all evidence of her pregnancy well and truly gone months before, but this was from more than just running a busy household. She'd taken her husband's absence hard.

Albert took a sip of the coffee. "She's a good woman, but I'm happy to go without a meal on occasion if it means the food stores last us through the winter." He sat the cup down onto the barrel and leaned back against the wall, his elbow resting on the edge of its surface.

"Hah, I'm not sure that plan will work, Albert," she chortled, unwrapping his meal of *slátur*, and rye bread for him on the makeshift table. "Krissa's watching you too closely. Probably more so now that she has you back. In fact, you'll be lucky to leave the farm again without her consent."

"Hmph," he managed, shaking his head, the lines around his eyes crinkling in pleasure, and he took a bite of the bread and liver sausage placed before him.

Noisy grunts sounded around them, the bleats of the ewes muted briefly, and Sólveig approached the sheep pen with curiosity, witnessing a big, horned black-and-white ram lift his front hooves to mount a tan

ewe in a bustle of thrusting and grunting, and then it was over as quickly
as it began.

"Oh." Sólveig stepped back from the pen as she realised what she had
just so intently witnessed, and she wasn't quite able to meet Abert's eyes
when she turned to face him.

He chuckled lightly, evidently seeing her discomfort. "It's instinct for
animals, raw and impersonal—nothing to blush over, Sólveig. He's got
a temper on him, as it is with rams, but he gets the task done."

"That was certainly quick. When will you be expecting the lambs,
then?" she asked, having composed herself once more.

"There'll be lambs come June. It's normally May, but there was no
help for it with our delayed return home from Rekavík. If the weather is
anything like last summer, it won't hurt being a little behind; in fact, the
lambs may have a better chance of survival with a late summer."

"I see," she said, and then her tone turned sombre. "We were so
relieved that you all came back to us."

His brows creased into a frown. "Well, we almost came back without
one."

"I'd heard—Helgi."

"*Já.*" He nodded.

"He thinks much of you, you know?" she said, then: "Rúna does too.
You did a good thing, not leaving him there."

"We almost did leave him, Sólveig. We knew the longer we stayed away,
the harder it would be on the people back here. Helgi came down with
an infliction of the chest so suddenly and his fevers raged on for days. He
seemed on the verge of death some nights, but he held on. He begged me
to leave him behind. The weather had been good, and I knew we'd make
good sailing home if we left him, but how could I return to my wife and
children and then face Rúna with news that I'd left her brother behind?"

He shook his head. "It was a woman from Rekavík who saved him. It was thanks to her skills that he survived—for all that I have to watch the women of the house around him." He winked at her, and her stomach dropped. Did Albert know? Were her feelings for Helgi that transparent? "He's a good man, Sólveig. He works hard and I'm not in the habit of leaving my men behind if I can help it, but he did say some strange things during his nights of fever-ridden delirium."

"He did?" She leaned against the sheep pen, curious to know what it was he could have said.

"Já, Guðríður asked me if I knew a woman by the name of Sólveig. I told her of our new midwife, of course, and it was likely she that he referred to."

"Oh," she breathed. "He was asking for me?"

"Já," he said, considering her carefully.

Perhaps Albert wondered about their relationship, or perhaps he knew already. Was the guilt of what they had done together written all over her face? She sighed inwardly, thinking now was probably a good a time as any to speak with him about Helgi.

"Albert, can I ask you something?"

"Of course," he said, a little surprised by her request. "Please, don't ever feel like you can't talk to me."

"It's just—" She hesitated. "Has Helgi spoken to you recently?"

"Not recently, at least not in any measure," he replied. "Why is that?"

"Well, you see, we are to be married, Albert," she said, on a puff of breath. "Helgi has asked me to marry him."

Albert whistled through his teeth. "Well, now, I knew it wouldn't take long for someone to snatch you up," he said lightly, his blue eyes crinkling in pleasure. He stood then, reaching out to take her hand in his, searching her face so that her eyes met his. "I must say I am surprised, but I am pleased for you, as I know Krissa will be. Have you told her yet?"

"*Nei*, I wanted to speak to you first. The thing is, Helgi hasn't enough saved for us to start out on our own, and there aren't any crofts around here for lease. We'll have to wait for something to become available. We heard that Vesteinn at Norðureyri is moving to Ísafjörður in July, so the household there may be an option for us."

"*Já*, I'd heard the same," he said, rubbing his hand through his beard again. "It may mean crossing the fjord for deliveries, but at least we get to keep you here in Sugandafjörður."

"Of course, Albert. You needn't have worried about that." She squeezed his hand. "It was never my intention to leave. This fjord is Helgi's home and it's my home now too."

"It's reassuring to hear you say that." He let go of her hand and came to stand beside her at the pen. "I meant to ask you this long ago, when you first told me your father left for North America—why didn't you go with him? You said there was nothing left back in Reykjavík for you, so why not go to America to be with your people, instead of to the ends of Iceland here with us?"

"You sound as if you're trying to convince me to turn back, Albert." She chuckled half-heartedly.

"Not at all. I'm just trying to figure you out is all." He smirked, folding his arms across his chest, leaning back against the pen.

"Well, Albert, I barely know my father," she explained, walking over to the barrel where he had been, and leaned against the wall of the croft opposite him. "My sister and I were illegitimate born, you see. My parents didn't have the means to marry. My mother managed to hold on to my older sister, Soffía, and upon my birth, I was sent to live with my father's mother until I was old enough to work in other households."

Sólveig wrapped her hands in the pockets of her apron as she spoke, unable to help the deep sigh that escaped her as she gazed out over the huddled sheep. Would he judge her now with the truth of her birth revealed? But she met his gaze once more and continued regardless. "To avoid more illegitimate children, my father and mother were separated, and my father was sent to another district. It was there he found another who had the means to marry and abandoned hopes of marrying my mother. Of course, times have changed somewhat, but I think my father never had the intention of marrying my mother." She shook her head. "I will never go to him, Albert." It was hard speaking this truth. She hadn't told anyone this before, having only indicated some of the story to Helgi. She wasn't sure why she told Albert now. Perhaps, simply because he had asked.

"I'm sorry to hear that," he said, holding her eyes with his, and she noticed the pity in them. "It's not easy growing up without a father. I know myself—my own father being taken by the sea when I was but a boy. And I do know what it is to be disappointed with the person who was supposed to be the one to love and support his family. You see, my mother remarried shortly after the death of my father, taking on a hired man to help her run the farm, enabling her to keep her sons with her, but it happened so quickly." He paused as if debating with himself, with painful memories that were hard to speak of. "She'd not had the chance for his true nature to reveal itself—that came after they married."

"What do you mean?" she asked.

"My stepfather was not a kind man. He had little affection for my mother. She was simply a means for him to gain property."

"I'm sorry, Albert. Your poor mother." It seemed his childhood had been just as troubled as her own, and she found she appreciated his confiding in her. Perhaps they all had shadows of the past hanging over them. "And Einar, he is your half-brother, is he not?"

"*Já*, that he is. He was the only offspring of that marriage and thankfully takes after my mother and not my stepfather." He chuckled lightly, glancing over at her again. "So, tell me, then, Sólveig, when will this wedding take place?"

"Helgi needs to speak to Séra Stefán, but we're hoping to marry in early July, before the haying begins," she said.

"*Já*, very good," he said, considering her. "There's a sense of comfort in knowing you're not facing life's difficulties alone. Marriage will give you that, Sólveig. I'm glad you've found that someone."

"Thank you, Albert," she said and meant it.

"Go on, then, go and tell Krissa the happy news. It's just what we all need after the last few weeks. A wedding to look forward to." Sólveig left Albert to the sheep, thinking as she walked how pleased she was to have Albert's blessing and pondering his words to her. Yes, she had finally found that someone she could belong to, someone to walk beside her through life's difficulties and celebrate its blessings with. She wouldn't become what her mother had been unfairly subjected to. She would marry and hold her head high. It wasn't everyone who was afforded that luxury.

17

March 1882

The days grew longer with the arrival of spring, but it seemed it had appeared in name only. The weather remained cold and snow still fell well into March. So, too, the birds of spring were late to arrive, late as the season was—the golden plover had still not shown itself to signal the arrival of spring, and the wind filled the silence where there should have been birdsong.

Early in the month, Grímur arrived at Suðureyri with news that his brother, Júlíus, at Hraunakot was much recovered from his illness, and Sólveig knew it was time she broached the subject of returning little Stella to her own family. The baby was two months old, and though she was small, she was a thriving and content baby. Sólveig had grown attached to the little one, but it was never meant to be a permanent arrangement, just a chance for Björg to nurse her husband back to health. Dishearteningly, neither Björg, Júlíus or their girls had been out to see the child.

Sólveig was alone in the *baðstofa* on the morning of her departure to Hraunakot. She had Stella on the bed, newly fed and wrapped in woollen layers, sleeping soundly, unaware of the changes ahead of her. Sólveig stood over the bed, lost in thought, ready to take the baby up, but she hesitated, her heart tender at the sight of the small child on the bed. She was a pretty baby, her features fine, her small pink lips pursed together in sleep. Would Björg be ready to take her daughter back? She was divided in her feelings about this visit. It was only right that the child be returned to her family, yet she couldn't help feeling sad at the prospect of seeing the baby go. She had, in truth, enjoyed the precious few months she'd had with her.

"Has the time come?" She stifled a squeal at Helgi's sudden appearance in the quiet, almost empty room. His arms snaked about her waist, his hard, lean body up against her back, as bristle scraped her cheek tenderly and soft lips nuzzled into her neck. "You can't go around keeping every baby you help deliver, Sólveig," he whispered in her ear playfully.

"I know." She wiped at the tear trickling down her cheek in the hopes that he wouldn't see the state she was in.

"Ah, Midwife." He chuckled softly. It was laced with pity, and he turned her in his arms, his hands coming up to cradle her face, his thumb catching another stray tear, and he embraced her, kissing the top of her head.

She looked down at the sleeping child. "What if Björg isn't ready? The way things are with them at home, with all the children and their hardships. Perhaps she's better off being raised here at Suðureyri with Albert and Krissa or—by us?" she ventured, posing this subtle question to him, wanting to know how he would feel about raising someone else's child.

Helgi pulled away from her, his eyes searching hers. "That's for Björg and Júlíus to say, Sólveig, but you know I would never turn an innocent away, if that's what you're asking." She caught the glint of humour in his eyes as he added, "Though if it's a baby you want, I promise to let you make as many as you like, once you've made a decent man of me—my body is at your disposal."

Now it was her turn to laugh, and she looked up at him, enjoying the mischief dancing in his eyes. "Oh, will you now? How kind of you to sacrifice yourself that way."

"Though—" He quickly peered around, dropping his voice so that it didn't carry across the room. "I'm happy to oblige any time, if you want some practise." He raised his brows in question, and pulled her to him, his kisses light, trailing down her neck and over to her mouth, creating tingles over her flesh. "I've missed you," he murmured against her.

Their coupling a month earlier hadn't left a child growing in her belly. She was relieved when her courses had finally come, and it was then that she'd decided not to let herself get so carried away with him again, at least not until they were married.

"Helgi." She pushed at him gently, pulling out of his embrace, putting clear distance between them, regardless of how much, in fact, she wanted the opposite. "Somebody may see us, and besides, I must be going while Stella is settled and newly fed."

Sólveig had made it clear to Helgi that she wanted to wait, to do things the proper way, but it was a struggle for them to keep their hands to themselves, as if that boundary that had been crossed was a magnet that pulled at them. There were stolen glances across the *baðstofa*, snatched kisses and restrained, ache-filled touches. She couldn't help the need to feel his touch—she couldn't help it any more than the ocean could stop itself lapping the shoreline, an invisible force pulling at their joining. She found the nights the hardest when she lay in her cot, feigning sleep, her own body ablaze and left wanting in the wake of the rustle and groans of the coming together of Krissa and Albert in the same room. She used to be able to tolerate that noise. It was a common enough noise growing up, but now that she knew the feelings personally—knew what it felt like for a man to put his hands on her body, to touch her most intimate parts, to move inside her, it awoke a desire within her so fierce it was hard to deny.

Sólveig brought her attention back to the source of her torment, Helgi's desire for her all too clear in his eyes and roving hands, but she relished the truth of knowing that soon he would be hers, and she his, and together they would make their life, with the promise of children of their own—a family of her own.

"Soon, Helgi," she whispered the promise to him.

He blew out his breath in frustration, but he surprised her by leaning over the bed, his broad hands coming about the baby and picking her up gently. One hand cradled her head, the other her bottom, and he rocked her lightly against his chest, to keep her sleeping.

"Soon just isn't soon enough," he said, glancing up from the sleeping baby, and he closed the gap between them again.

"I know." She reached up to kiss him lightly on the mouth.

He was impatient for sure. Despite Albert's blessing, Sólveig had decided it best to keep the news of her engagement to Helgi quiet. Helgi was against the idea. He wanted the news out in the open, tired of having to hide the truth of his feelings for her, to sneak around behaving as if he were indifferent to her, but he had relented, and only Albert, Krissa and Rúna knew of their plans to marry.

The wedding was to take place in July when the men returned from the yearly *kauptíð*. It was during this time that the farmers travelled to the merchant towns to trade their goods for supplies, just before the haying began. And besides, Séra Stefán wasn't coming out from his parish at Holt until April for the Easter service and the christenings, and they were yet to read the banns. This declaration of marriage had to be read three times in church before they could marry. Sólveig had also explained to

Helgi of needing time to sew herself wedding clothes. She wanted to look respectable before the community.

Helgi placed the babe into her arms. "Are you sure you don't want me to walk the two of you over there today?"

"Your sister will make the trek with me, but thank you, Helgi. Besides, I can't go stealing you away from Björn and your duties here." She tucked the sleeping child under her shawl, her slight weight a steady comfort in her arms, and sighed, looking back up at Helgi, soaking in the sight of him. "Just be careful out there today. No more lost anchors and drifting away. I don't think my nerves could take it."

He smiled at her, holding her gaze. "I'm not going anywhere, Midwife. I promise you."

The visit to Hraunakot did not go as Sólveig hoped it would.

"The child is better off at Suðureyri," Björg said. There were no tears this time. The woman held herself in check, her voice stern and emotionless.

Sólveig and Rúna sat in the *baðstofa* with both Björg and Júlíus, Stella in the arms of her older sister Anna María while they discussed the baby's future. Björg held little Soffía on her lap. The toddler was fevered and she lay asleep in her mother's arms, a deep, chesty cough disrupting her slumber all too frequently.

"Albert and Krissa will take her on as a *tökubarn*, a foster child," croaked Júlíus with confidence. He stood by the window at one end of the room, staring off into the distance, unable to meet Sólveig's eyes as he said it. Yes, he was much recovered since she had seen him last, but there was still a slight wheeze to his breathing. "Björg has her hands full as it is with the children sick. Our sheep are only milked in the summer, and we've not our own dairy cow to supply us with fresh milk."

"I shall speak with Albert," said Sólveig. "He's a generous man. But, please, take the extra milk and *slátur* Krissa packed for you. I've also some dried herbs to make a tea for the children, to help with their coughs, and there's some socks and shoes for the little ones too."

Júlíus didn't respond. He just kept on staring into the distance, and Sólveig thought perhaps he hadn't heard her, but she repeated herself and it was met once more with silence. She bit her tongue, silently cursing him. He was a proud man for sure, but then she turned to Björg, and the woman nodded curtly, accepting the gift.

"*Já*, best if Stella stays with us at Suðureyri," Rúna commented, and she passed Björg the packed bundle of goods she held in her lap. "I'm sure Albert and Krissa will take the child. You have enough on your hands."

It was settled. Stella would become a permanent member of the household at Suðureyri, with Albert and Krissa's approval.

Sólveig and Rúna left Hraunakot with a heavy heart, taking Stella with them. The hardship that some in their community suffered was hard to bear, and Sólveig offered to stay on a few days with them to aid Björg with the little ones, but Júlíus refused, stating that Katla, Grímur's wife, and their widowed daughter, Hallveig had been coming when they could. This gave her some comfort, but Sólveig worried about Júlíus.

"Björg." Sólveig pulled the woman aside just before they left. "I must ask you something."

"You want to know if he's resumed his marital rites with me, don't you?" she answered tersely, unable to meet Sólveig's eyes.

"*Já,*" she said gently. "Your body needs to recover. It wouldn't be wise getting with child again so soon, if at all."

The woman finally looked up. "He's keeping his distance for now. Grímur had words with him over it. I think Katla's been saying things. I don't know what I'd do without her." She sighed deeply. "But I know Júlíus, Sólveig. He'll demand what's rightfully his sooner or later, and I'm terrified I'll be with child again before the year is out."

"My dear Björg, is there anything I can do?"

"If there were a way to stop a babe from starting, then I could put up with his lying with me," she said meekly, and she covered her face with her palms as she broke before her. "But so help me God, Sólveig, I can't have another one. I just don't think I'd survive it!"

"I'm afraid the most effective way is simply abstinence, Björg."

"Oh, but there is a way," interrupted Rúna. She stood waiting near them at the entrance of the croft, peering about her. "I've heard *Mamma* speak of it. Said she used it to stop getting more children after Elías. She nearly died birthing him, you see, but this is something just shared among us women."

"*Já*, tell me." Björg took Rúna's hands in hers, hope lighting in her puffy blue eyes.

"Júlíus mustn't find out, Björg. If it makes its way to the ears of men, who knows what they could do."

Björg nodded in understanding. "Please."

"Very well." And Rúna's voice lowered to a whisper. "Crotchet yourself a small square of the softest wool and soak it in whey. Then before he beds you, slide it inside you, and it is sure to catch his seed and soak it right up."

"Rúna, that you know such things astounds me!" scolded Sólveig.

"I've not had use of it myself yet, but there's no harm in knowing it," she said, crossing her arms defensively.

Sólveig shook her head. "Björg, I'm not sure of this. Just know that you'll have to undergo the utmost care with cleanliness if you go ahead with this and remove it once the task it done, cleaning it thoroughly. There's always the risk of infection with this sort of thing."

Rúna shrugged. "It worked for my mother."

"I thank you for it, Rúna," said Björg. "I promise I'll be discreet."

Little Stella stirred in Sólveig's arms.

"We'll take our leave now," she said to Björg. "You will see the child christened, will you not?"

"*Já*, we'll be there in April to see her blessed and give her a name." Björg leaned over the baby, swaddled and content in Sólveig's arms, and kissed her gently on the head. "Thank you," she whispered, her eyes glistening. Sólveig noticed the tremble in her bottom lip before she set it once more into a firm line, and the woman turned from them, ushering her horde of remaining children into the hallway, closing the door behind them.

18

April 1882

In early April, Helgi's family made the journey from Keflavík by boat over to Staður for the christening of Stína's baby. Séra Stefán hadn't completed his once-a-month pilgrimage out to Súgandafjörður since December, so it was a much talked about affair, a gathering of the community after the long winter, and almost everyone was there, packed into the church to receive the word of the Lord for Easter and to witness the christenings of two babies—Stína's boy and little Stella.

Sólveig shivered where she sat in church between Krissa and Rúna, holding a sleeping Stella closer to her, patting her bottom to keep her content. Her eyes strained in the dimness of the cold room after being outside under the bright sun. It was an old church, clad with timber walls and flooring, but built like the rest of the crofts in the district—of earth and stone. The alter sat above the congregation on a timber platform where the priest gave his service. Everyone had their seats according to sex and what farm they belonged to.

The most important men, the heads of the households, sat towards the front of the church, workman towards the back, and women on the eastern side.

The crowd of people stood as the hymns began with the priest entering the church. Albert's voice sounded in the room as he led the singing. He was *forsöngvari*—the lead singer. Sólveig hadn't known he had such a strong voice. It was deep and smooth, and it bellowed throughout the small space.

A tall, neatly groomed man of middling years, dressed in the long black garb of a priest, with a thick ruffled white collar, made his way down the aisle, and behind him, as if his shadow, Stína proceeded. She held her son in her arms, her head downcast, a strained look on her face with the attention of the room on her as Séra Stefán cleansed her of her *lustful* sins with sprinkles of holy water. Björg would receive no such shameful ceremony because she was a married woman. The older mother had arrived late with Júlíus and her other children in tow, sitting towards the back of the church.

The Easter service was conducted, and then Sólveig stood before the community as Séra Stefán called the parents, babies and witnesses to come forward for the christenings. Her heart swelled with pride observing the two women standing next to her with the beautiful, thriving babies they had made. Such contrasts they were—both in age and their birth experience—and Sólveig couldn't help but marvel at the courage it took to bring a child into the world.

Björg and Júlíus chose the name Stella Björg, for their daughter and Sólveig was delighted by the name. Magnús stood in as witness for Stína's boy, and the child was given the name Örnólfur in honour of Stína's father.

Sólveig was seated back at her place with Stella in her arms once more. The service was coming to an end, the crowd becoming restless, younger children wriggling in their seats, mothers reprimanding them gently or patting bottoms, rocking whimpering babies who were starting to feel their hunger once more. Her own mind had started to wander somewhat, so she was momentarily caught off guard by the sound of her name being called before the congregation along with Helgi's name.

"I hereby announce the banns of marriage between *Helgi Sigurðsson* of Suðureyri, son of Sigurður Magnússon and Elísabet Helgadóttir, and *Sólveig Pétursdóttir*, of Suðureyri, daughter of Pétur Guðmundsson and Kristjana Margrét Sigurðardóttir," Séra Stefán announced.

Sólveig smiled in response to the hearty congratulations of the people seated around her.

Helgi had managed to speak to the priest after all, she mused, turning in her seat in search of her betrothed, and caught his eye. He winked at her, smiling broadly, but then she caught the scowl on Inga's face. The work maid was not pleased.

Much to the surprise of many, Séra Stefán also announced the banns for another union, and all eyes turned upon the young woman next to Sólveig, as the priest declared the banns for Rúna's upcoming nuptials to Einar. Sólveig gasped in surprise, turning to her friend. She was pleased for the work maid, and she raised her brows at her, with a knowing smugness.

"Oh, don't you start," Rúna scolded, but she was grinning, pleased with herself despite it.

Later, Sólveig was exiting the church with the rest of the congregation when Inga sidled up beside her.

"So, you wanted him for yourself?"

"Inga, please—" Sólveig started, but she was interrupted.

"I see you for what you are, Sólveig Pétursdóttir. You have the people here fooled with your decency, but you're nothing more than a thief!" And before Sólveig could reply, Inga pushed past her, taking Björn's eldest son, Jói, by the arm, and marched out the front door with him.

Sólveig glanced around, wondering who had heard the work maid accuse her, her face flushing hot with embarrassment. She kissed little Stella on the top of her head, holding her closer, trying to hide her shame. Of course, she'd known Inga would be upset. Perhaps that's why it had been important for her to keep the news of her engagement quiet until the banns were read, but Sólveig hadn't quite expected the reaction she received.

"Pay no mind to her, Sólveig." Rúna put an arm around her as they made their way out into the daylight, squinting at the brightness after sitting in the dim interior for so long.

Sólveig sighed deeply, rubbing at her eyes with one hand, but for more than the reason of it being so bright.

"I, for one, am glad it's you to be my sister-in-law."

"Oh, Rúna, me too, but I know how it must look. It was I who caught them together and warned Inga against the wiles of men." Sólveig couldn't help but roll her eyes as she said it. "And it was my fault that Helgi ended their flirtations—and yet, I'm the one he's marrying."

"You can't help who you love," Rúna said, her eyes filled with pity. "Don't be so hard on yourself. Inga can take her spite up with Helgi. You don't deserve it. My brother is a grown man, and if the girl's spite is the fault of anyone, it's his."

⊰║⊱

Sólveig stood outside in the cool air with Helgi, accepting the continued congratulations of the people around her for their upcoming nuptials. But when Stella began to fuss, her soft, distraught mewls speaking of her hunger, Sólveig had to find somewhere to feed the babe.

"Would you like some help with her, Sólveig?" asked Helgi, his hand at her elbow.

"*Nei*, you stay here with your family, before they row home. I'll take her into the church and feed her out of this wind."

His hand slid around her back, and he placed a delicate kiss on her mouth, happy to lay claim to her before all, but Sólveig squirmed under this public display of affection. The child wailed again, and she hoisted her medical bag up over an arm, sitting it in the crook of her elbow, Stella in the other arm, and made her way over to the church entrance to feed the child. She had just reached the doorway when her path was waylaid by two women.

Sólveig smiled at them in greeting. She hadn't been introduced to them before, though she had seen them in church during the service. The old woman smiled up at her, her pale eyes almost swallowed in folds of soft wrinkles, her skin brown and weathered, her face wrapped in a black woollen headscarf, and thin white plaits trailed down over her shoulders. A middle-aged woman stood beside her, her hands linked about the old woman's elbow in support. She wasn't much taller than the older one, fair of hair with deep-set eyes.

"My mother-in-law has been wondering about the young new midwife of Súgandafjörður. I'm Jósefína, Eiríkur's wife, and this is Gróa."

"Of course," replied Sólveig. "I've so been wishing to meet you," she added, shifting Stella to her other arm so she could take Gróa's gnarled bony hand into her own, and she leaned in to kiss the woman on the cheek in greeting.

"And I you, young lady." The old woman squeezed her hand in return, surprising her with her strength, regardless of her frail appearance, but as they pulled apart, instead of releasing her hand, the old woman held on to it, turning it in her own, inspecting it. *"Já,"* Gróa finally said with satisfaction. "These are good hands for catching babies. Small and fine boned. You have Frigg's blessing about you, and I see you are quickly earning your place within our community."

"Frigg's blessing?" she asked, somewhat confused, as Gróa released her hand.

"*Mamma* loves the old Norse tales and still pays her respect to the old pagan gods," Jósefína explained. "Frigg is the Norse goddess of hearth and home, the protector of woman, family and childbirth."

"No hurt in honouring the old ways," said Sólveig with interest, feeling honoured by the woman's words. "But I must say, you've left large shoes to fill, Gróa."

"You'll do, child." Gróa pat her hand, adding, "Remember this, and remember it well: *The strands of fate have already been woven, but its pattern we do not see. Do not blame yourself—for what has been and what is to come.*"

Her face was tender, but the words rang clear and strong, sending a chill down Sólveig's spine, and she tried her best to smile, not sure what the old woman meant by her strange words. Stella started to wail in her arms again, her hunger getting the better of her, reminding Sólveig that she was on her way to feed the child. She gave the women a look of regret, ready to excuse herself.

"Ah, but the child's hungry." Gróa leaned in for a good look at Stella. "I see you've taken Björg's little one under your care. I raised four myself—babes taken from homes that couldn't keep 'em, along with six of my own. Jósefína was one of them. Raised her like my own, and then she married my eldest, Eiríkur. Well, you best see to her needs, then, my dear, and welcome to our community."

The two women left her, and Sólveig made her way into the cold, dim church, struggling now with the crying baby, Gróa's strange words echoing in her mind. Was the woman addled in her old age or was she some kind of seer? She'd heard rumours of Gróa around the community. There was always much reverence for one believed to have been called on by the Hidden people to assist with the delivery of a baby. She had heard such stories before, stories of women falling asleep and dreaming they had helped a Hidden woman in childbirth and forever after being gifted with the *sight* or success as a midwife.

Gróa's words echoed in her mind: *Do not blame yourself—for what has been and what is to come.* Sólveig couldn't help but shiver again. Did the cryptic words refer to her sister, Fía, who was lost to her in childbirth? Did Gróa know of the pain she carried in her heart for that loss? It wasn't something she spoke about, and she couldn't recall having told anyone about it. This was her own private burden. How could the old woman know such a thing? Sólveig pushed those troubling thoughts aside, deciding it was surely just something the old woman herself had lived by, and she shouldn't take it so personally. Then Stella's cries brought her attention back to the matter at hand.

"*Já*, my little one, your milk is coming," she told the distraught child.

Sólveig was still fumbling about with the bag in a fluster when she noticed Albert walking towards her from the raised alter at the front of the church, where he must have been with Séra Stefán. She flushed with shame at disrupting them with the wailing babe. Stella's cries had increased in volume and fervour, her carer having failed to satisfy her hunger, trying to find the skin flask in amongst her things with no help for the poor lighting in the room.

"Is everything okay with the babe, Sólveig?" he asked.

"Oh, Albert, she's just hungry, is all. I'm struggling to find her milk in this bag full of things utterly useless to me at this moment."

Albert knelt before her and the baby where they sat on the bench in the last row at the back of the room, and he took the bag from her as she rocked the child, searching quickly through its contents to bring out the feeding cup and a leather flask with Stella's milk.

"Aha!" He grinned, holding up the item in question, deftly uncorking the flask and pouring the milk for her into the cup.

"Thank you, Albert." She took it gratefully, bringing it to Stella's mouth, her angry cries brought down to one final whimper as she gulped the milk greedily.

"Stella! Darling, slow down, child." She chuckled as the baby finished the milk. Albert poured her a little more, watching the child with satisfaction, the corners of his mouth lifted in a tender smile.

"Ah, she's a sweet thing for all that wailing," he said, gently stroking her fine head of fair hair. "There's nothing more pleasing than satisfying a crying baby."

"I'm sorry if I interrupted you and Séra Stefán just now. I didn't realise people were still in here."

"No need to fret." He stood up and took a seat on the edge of the bench on the opposite side of the aisle to them. "I could see you struggling, and Séra Stefán and I were finishing up besides. He needed the census lists I collected for him last December. We take it every year around that time, but I haven't been to see him until now."

"I see," she said with interest, thinking this must have been undertaken when she was away at Keflavík to deliver Stína's baby.

"And how did Helgi take the news of your fostering the babe?" he asked, meeting her eyes with interest, the subject changing quickly to the child before them. They had spoken on the matter when she returned from Hraunakot. Sólveig wanted to take on the raising of Stella.

"I'm not sure he had much say in the matter," she replied smartly.

He chuckled at that. "*Nei*, I don't suppose he did."

"But, in truth, he will be father to her as he will be husband to me, once we are moved into Norðureyri in July," she added, glancing down at the baby in her arms.

Stella's eyelids fluttered, lowering sleepily, having finished her milk and content with her meal. "Albert, you know Gróa well, do you not?"

"*Já*, I suppose I do. I've known her since I was a boy. Did you finally meet the old midwife?"

She nodded, not sure how to approach this, this sense of unease in her at meeting the woman. "She said some strange things."

"I've always been a little scared of her myself." He chuckled lightly. "There's something very ancient about her and it's not just her age."

"I've been told that she's had dealings with the Hidden folk."

He considered her, his brows knotting together. "*Já*, she's had dealings with them, but then Bæjarhvilft, the cliffs near the farmhouse at Staður, not far from here, is said to be one of their places. That's why they don't hay the fields there in summer. Bad luck has fallen to those who have done so."

"And do you believe in such superstition?"

"I'd say I'm wise enough not to disbelieve it," Albert said, matter-of-fact. "There is much we don't know of the world, Sólveig, of life and death and the hereafter. You see, Gróa's one whose had good reason to heed the Hidden folk."

Sólveig narrowed her eyes, intrigued to know more, and Albert continued.

"When she was a young woman, she lost her first husband to the sea. They were newly married and had just taken over the farm at Staður that spring. The summer before his death, a man came to him in his dreams, warning him not to hay the field at Bæjarhvilft, but the warning was ignored, and it was hayed anyway. It wasn't until Gróa too, was paid a visit in her dreams by the same man that she made him stop. You see, this *dream* man was the one and the same who'd collected her to deliver his child in the Hidden world. She knew to heed him. But the damage was done, and she lost her husband to the sea the following winter. Gróa remarried, of course, and never again has that field been hayed."

"Nei," she said softly, considering this story. "You wouldn't want to tempt fate that way." Gooseflesh rose on her skin once more, and she knew then there was more to the words Gróa had spoken, more to them than she could know, and it unsettled her deeply, down to her very core.

19

June 1882

On a rare sunny day in late June, Sólveig took to the mountain slopes around Suðureyri. There were still large patches of snow on the upper ridges, more than usual for that time of year, but then again, it had been so cold still of late. They'd had news of pack ice sitting off the coast of Iceland, sending cold chills across the land. It had stopped the men from taking to the sea as they'd liked, and the frosts that lashed the land in its wake had taken many of the new lambs released into the mountains in the weeks previous.

She walked a distance up the steep, rocky slopes and was surprised at how high she had come as she gazed out at the view of Suðureyri farm with the smooth waters of the fjord laid out before her. She was collecting *blóðberg*, mountain thyme. Its tiny purple petals and glossy green foliage only grew in the summers, and she'd found a decent patch amongst some rocks on the mid slopes of the mountain, before it rose too dramatically. She was pleased to find it, as the herb could be used to brew a tea to help reduce fevers.

She had only managed to collect a handful of the herbs when she spotted a man heading up the slope towards her. By his grey hat and casual lope, she knew it was Helgi.

She waved to him, and he waved back, grinning at her. Before long, he stood over her, blocking the sun. "So, this is where you're hiding? I've been looking for you everywhere," he said, catching his breath after the steep incline.

"Have you? Is something the matter?" she asked, thinking there was some incident or birth she must attend to now.

"*Nei*, nothing to fret about, Midwife. I'm just away to Ísafjörður for the *kauptíð* and then on to Keflavík to help with some supplies. We'll be gone for five days, maybe a week at the most."

"This day? You weren't to leave until tomorrow," she said somewhat sulkily.

"*Já*, but with the weather so fine, Björn wants to leave today."

"Oh, but it is beautiful, don't you think, Helgi?" She lay back on a patch of soft moss behind her, stretching out before him under the pale-blue skies, closing her eyes in the bliss of letting this rare glimpse of sun soak into her pores, warming her skin.

"My God, woman, you take my breath away." His voice sounded strained, but the words warmed her immensely, and she sat up onto her elbows, squinting up at him, one eyed, patting the soft grass next to her.

"Come, sit by me, and if you must be off, a kiss will do nicely," she said boldly.

Helgi squatted onto his haunches next to her. There was a moment of indecision when he glanced back down the slope, and then he turned back to her. His shirtsleeves were rolled up past his elbows, and she found that she enjoyed the sight of him, the sight of the smooth muscle on his forearms and the veins that rose in his hands, hands that swallowed her small, dainty fingers when he held them. She caught the desire clear in his eyes and couldn't help the way her body tingled at his nearness.

He leaned over her, pressing his mouth to hers. "The men are waiting for me," he said, smiling into her lips, but he didn't pull away. Sólveig leaned forward, her hands snaking about his neck, pulling him down to the ground next to her. She felt the rumble of his chuckle at her insistence and his kiss deepened.

They were partially hidden from the view of the farm where they lay on their sides facing each other, and once again the ache of restraint pulled at them, flesh begging to meet with flesh. Her head scarf slipped down off her hair to sit loosely about her shoulders. His hat fell to the grass behind them as she pulled her hands through his dark, unruly curls and her leg slid playfully over to rest on his.

His hands trailed along her clothed body from her cheek, slowly down over her neck and breasts, and she closed her eyes, enjoying the feeling of him touching her. His mouth met hers once more, and those tender touches turned suddenly ravenous and desperate. Helgi's hands pulled at her skirts, sliding up the length of her thigh to slip under the coarse woven material, and she gasped, his fingers suddenly there, probing gently within her. She spread her legs as he moved over her, and she found herself pulling at the opening to his pants. The past few months of wanting him and restraining herself was wearing thin, and knowing she wouldn't see him now for so many days was suddenly too much to bear.

"Are you sure you want to do this, Sólveig?" He stopped, his eyes searching hers for consent.

She nodded. She couldn't keep waiting. He pulled her to him, gripping her bottom, and entered her with a groan. There was no pain this time. Just a desperate need that demanded satiation.

This coupling was not gentle, nor tender. It was rough and desperate, a meeting of two bodies that had been too long apart, and it was a quick affair, her legs wrapped around him, taking him deep into her, their hips meeting in that strange rhythm. An ache was building within her again, but this time, it kept on growing. His eyes held hers, the green in his swallowing her completely. He watched her with unrestrained pleasure, a crease at his brow, and she sensed with his increasing rhythm that he, too, felt this strange ache within him. He gripped her tightly to him, and it was then that he groaned, puffing hard, rocking his release into her in deep strokes, and she stifled her own cry of relief as a glorious explosion within radiated from her core. Never had she experienced such a sensation, an indescribable pleasure that made her smile and feel suddenly lighter of both body and soul.

They lay in the grass puffing, side by side, their need for each other satiated for now, their hands clasped, dazed and content at what had just occurred again, but the moments passed too quickly. Helgi got himself up, buttoning his pants and straightening the disarray of his clothing after their tussle.

She sat up with him, pulling her skirts back down over the milky-white skin of her knees, tucking her legs up together so that she could wrap her arms about her legs and rest her chin against them, watching him. She already missed the loss of his touch, the feel of him inside her.

"Do you really have to go?" His hat lay haphazardly on the ground near her, and she passed it to him. "Cannot Björn just go himself or take Jói instead?"

He took the hat from her, then reached again for her hand and pulled her up to him, snatching a kiss from her in the process. "Björn is to go, but you know I have to stop by in Keflavík. Magnús is expecting me."

"You were right, you know." She wrapped her arms about his neck. "We should have married sooner. I'm so tired of this. Of having to sneak about as we do."

"Ah, Midwife," he said, his voice laced with sympathy. He gently tucked the loose strands of hair flowing about her face behind her ears. "We'll be an old married couple with eight children before you know it."

"Eight!" she snorted.

He chuckled. His eyes full of mischief. "Okay, ten it is, then," he declared and continued brushing his thumb along her cheek.

"You will have me for a dairy cow, heavy with child all my married life?" She laughed in return, if somewhat weakly.

"*Nei*, never." He shook his head.

Sólveig enjoyed the way his eyes crinkled at the sides, the way he looked at her like she was already his.

He cradled her head between his hands, but his expression turned suddenly intense. "In my heart, I'm already married to you, Sólveig Pétursdóttir, my troublesome midwife, but to share a bed with you as man and wife is what I crave." He kissed her deeply before she could say more. "To wake up next to you every morning and take our pleasure in each other as we see fit." And he nuzzled into her neck, cupping her buttocks, pulling her close again, the rough stubble of his beard tickling her, making her squirm.

"Oh, Helgi, off with you now, before you have Jói and Björn on a manhunt for you, and don't forget the scarf for my *peysuföt*."

"Never! A beautiful white silk scarf for my beautiful bride," he replied, and she let him kiss her one last time, slow and hungry, before he pulled himself away. She watched after him, her heart full as he loped back down the hill towards Suðureyri and the men who awaited him.

⚜

Two days after Helgi left with Björn and Jói for Ísafjörður, Jakob came from Botn to collect Sólveig. It was late afternoon, but daylight was still rampant as it was this time of year in midsummer. She was busy changing Stella's wet rags in the *baðstofa* when she saw Albert's brother through the window. Krissa was up to answer the door, and she listened to their conversation from the cot.

"What is it, Jakob? Please, do come in out of the wind, won't you?"

"*Nei*, I mustn't, but thank you, Krissa."

"Has something happened? You're supposed to be in Ísafjörður by now, are you not?"

Sólveig caught the worried edge to her voice.

"*Já*, I was, but it's Fríða. She's burning up with fever. I need Sólveig to come quickly."

Sólveig picked Stella up off the bed and made her way in a hurry to the entrance of the farmhouse, where the two of them stood.

"Of course, I will come," Sólveig said as she approached the door, moving Stella to her other hip. "How long has she been like this?"

"She came down with the fever last night, but for the past two days, she's been complaining of a sore throat." Jakob glanced at Krissa and then back at Sólveig. "She complains of a pain inside her mouth and the brightness burning her eyes." His tone was calm as he spoke, his voice deep and steady, but his eyes were tired with dark shadows beneath them, his worry etched deeply into his features.

"It was the croup and mumps that were running rampant last year, but María says she hasn't seen the likes of this before. She's beside herself with worry for the child."

"Are there spots?" Tobba asked suddenly from behind them, coming to the door so that all three women stood there.

He nodded his head. "Tiny white spots inside her mouth and a rash were just starting to appear on her brow as I left for Suðureyri. Do you know this illness, Tobba?

Tobba blanched. "It could be the dreaded measles. They came around in '46. I was just a girl of sixteen at the time. I survived it, but it took many children with it, including my two younger brothers—God bless their souls." She crossed herself.

Krissa stiffened beside her. "The children," she gasped. "They were playing together only two days ago at Botn while we collected peat."

Sólveig had gone too, to help collect the heavy, wet soil from the bogs near the farmhouse which was cut into logs and dried for fuel.

"*Já*, they were." Jakob looked mighty sorry.

"I will come with you, Jakob. There's not much I can do apart from help her fight the fever. If it's what Tobba says, then we're all at the mercy of the Almighty." She turned to Krissa. "Have the girls been around Lína much since yesterday?"

She shook her head. "*Nei*, they've been so good with playing outside. They haven't had much time for her."

"Thank goodness. You must get Rúna or Inga to take them away. Take Stella and Lína to the sea croft. Keep them away from the girls and the rest of the household. There's a couple of beds there. No one must go to them. It's very important to keep them away."

Krissa nodded, her eyes filling with fear at her words, but it was for the best. There was still a chance that the babies could be spared this, if they hadn't been in contact with the other children.

"But if Sólveig goes with Jakob now, she may bring the illness back to us and spread it amongst our household," said Tobba. "That's how these illnesses work. Spread from household to household with the movement of people."

"She's right, Krissa. If I go now, I won't return to you until the danger is over. Will you be okay? Albert and Einar only left yesterday. Perhaps we need to send someone for him. Get a message to him that we need Doctor Þorvaldur. Get him to bring the doctor home with him."

"I'll send Tóti," added Rannveig who had entered the front room, where the crowd of people stood, Jakob keeping his distance outside. "He's young, and fast. He'll make good time over the mountain to Ísafjörður."

Sólveig and Krissa nodded in mutual assent. Krissa placed her hand onto Sólveig's arm. "Go, then, Sólveig. Go and may God be with you and the household at Botn."

"You too, Krissa. Let us pray that Suðureyri will be spared this."

PART TWO

The days will come and so, too, the solution.

Það koma dagar og þá koma ráð.

—Old Icelandic proverb

20

June 1882

Albert

When Albert returned from Ísafjörður the following day with Tóti, he found his household much changed. Both Dísa and Dóra lay abed with a raging fever. Their noses ran and they complained of a sore throat.

Krissa was relieved to see him, but his wife had been quiet since he arrived home, bottling up the worry within her. A calm exterior, but the nagging fear was there in her eyes. She cared diligently for her sick children, going between the girls with cool rags, coaxing them to sip at the pungent tea Sólveig had told her to administer to them for the fever.

He had blocked the light from the window in the *baðstofa*, cloaking the room in darkness, because his girls cried, complaining of their red, inflamed eyes hurting with the brightness of the room.

It wasn't long before Krissa told him of the tiny white spots that appeared inside their mouths. Shortly after that, flat red spots rose at the hairline, first on Dísa and then on Dóra, spreading down the neck, trunk, arms and legs as the day wore on.

Albert hadn't been able to bring the doctor with him from Ísafjörður. The inability to ease his children's suffering made him angry and on edge. Their small, pain-filled cries tore at him, and he found himself in the smithy, where he knew he could do something. Just get his hands on something. He felt utterly useless in the face of this illness.

Albert thought back to the previous night, when young Tóti had arrived in Ísafjörður, requesting in a rush of words between puffed breaths that he was to come home directly and bring the doctor with him. But Doctor Þorvaldur, upon hearing Albert's request, had scoffed at him and told him in no uncertain terms that he couldn't possibly come. The illness had its grip on the merchant town, and many had already fallen in Ísafjörður to the measles.

"You have the midwife," the doctor told him. "She has a level head and she's a smart woman."

"She's no doctor. Are we to face this on our own?" He took a deep breath to calm his rising frustration. "Is there no medicine we can administer, no way to immunize against this, as we've done with the smallpox?"

Doctor Þorvaldur shook his head. He looked weary. His mouth was grimly set, dark shadows under his eyes as they narrowed in apparent annoyance. "There's not much more I can do to fight this *blasted* illness than you or any other," he snapped, rubbing at his brow. "Go back to Suðureyri, Albert," he said then, a little more gently. "You and your men. It's not wise to be here as things stand. The illness is spreading quickly."

"What am I to tell them, the people of my community? What am I to tell my brother and his wife, whose daughter lies in the grips of this?" Albert pressed.

"Reykjavik is swarming with the disease. Many hundred dead already. We're being advised to stay put, lest the illness spread faster. Keep the fever down and give plenty of fluids. Keep the rooms dark," he stressed to him. "And pray, Albert. Pray that your loved ones be spared this."

In his rush to get the news back to Botn, Albert left Einar and Árni behind in Isafjörður to collect the rest of the supplies they'd come for. There was no point in wasting a journey. Albert had taken up accommodation within his uncle's household and over the two days had managed to collect most of what they needed. He'd met with Björn on his way out. His neighbour was boarding at his brother's farm, just outside of the town, and was heading back to Suðureyri in the morning with Jói and their own boats loaded with supplies. They were shocked to hear the news he carried. That the illness had already made its way to their community. There'd been talk in town of people getting sick, but Björn hadn't paid it much mind. There was always some illness abound. But this one seemed to be getting serious, and all were eager to be back home with their loved ones.

When Sólveig answered the door at Botn, it was the early hours of the morning. The sun was just rising again, and Albert was thankful for the long summer nights, where the sun barely set before it rose again. He walked at a fast pace, Tóti managing to keep up, not stopping to rest, and he was puffing as he waited, relieved to have arrived, but he'd sent the boy straight home to Suðureyri with the news.

The young midwife looked taken aback at the sight of him, a dark shadow hovering at the entrance of the croft. She peered through the small glass window, her eyes narrowing in concentration and then widening in surprise as it dawned on her who had arrived.

"But where's the doctor, Albert?" she asked, opening the door to him before any greetings could take place. He could see that she'd had no sleep, the fabric of her yellow striped apron was crumpled and stained with dark patches, her face flushed with colour and her eyes—they were red-rimmed and glassy.

It pained him seeing the hope in her fall to despair at the news he brought with him, but she took it calmly, nodding her head, taking in a deep, steadying breath. He watched the emotions run through her as she tried to tame them, the sadness reflected in her brown eyes, the hopelessness and fear they echoed. But then her lips pressed together in a tight, thin line and her eyes took on a hard, steely resolve.

"Well, then, we must do what we can. Have you been to Suðureyri?"

"*Nei*, I've come straight here, but I'm heading there now. How does the child Fríða fare? Is she still with us?" he asked with apprehension.

"She survived the night. We managed to get her fever down, but it's Ásta and little Albert Einar. They, too, have a fever. The babe is so young, only five months old, and his cries grow weaker by the hour." She sighed heavily, looking past him as she spoke. "Albert, I fear he is not long for this world," she said then, her voice trembling with tightly held emotion. Her large, sad eyes met his, glistening again with unshed tears. "María and Jakob are with him now."

"Ah, Sólveig." He wanted to embrace her, if only to lend her some strength. "Is there anything I can do?" he asked with a heavy heart, and he couldn't help but think to his own baby Lína—to his own children and how they fared.

She shook her head. "*Nei*, you've done so much already." She reached for his hand, but hesitated, clutching the fabric of her skirt instead. "Albert? Perhaps you can tell me—what news of Helgi?"

"He left for Keflavík early yesterday with Magnús, who met him in town. Past that, I'm afraid I don't know."

She nodded quickly and he was sorry he couldn't tell her more.

"Thank you for coming so quickly, Albert. Go home to Krissa and the girls. She'll be in sore need of you."

Two days had passed since his return to Suðureyri and more in the household came down with the measles. It was the children who fell ill first—those in his household, his daughters, but as children were wont to do, they played together, and the sickness took hold of little Margrét and Steinn in Björn's household. Tóti, who had returned with Albert only days earlier, was next, complaining of a runny nose and a sore throat. He was abed and slept away the time, the only sound from him a dry, hacking cough.

The others returned from Ísafjörður by boat with their supplies and they, too, fell ill, but the sickness didn't hold on to them as it did the little ones. They were able to fight the fever even though it left them with an overwhelming exhaustion that kept them abed for days.

Albert was grateful for Sólveig's quick thinking to get the babies away. Rúna was holed up in the sea croft with eight-month-old Lína and six-month-old Stella. Inga and Tobba brought her food and milk for the babies, leaving it at the doorstep, until Inga, too, became ill. Tobba seemed immune, having already had the illness back in '46 along with her father, Leifur. Krissa found the separation from Lína hard, as he, too, did, but most of their worries were poured into young Dóra who had just turned seven.

Dísa was strong and was taking liquids and even a small amount of gruel. It seemed to want to stay within her, her body absorbing the much-needed nourishment for her recovery. Her fever had broken, and she slept and slept. It was little Dóra who was faltering. Her cough had settled deep into her chest, and the child still burned to the touch, no matter what they tried.

"It's the fever that will take her," said Tobba.

"Hush, *Mamma*." Albert heard Krissa reprimand her mother in the kitchen. "There won't be any *taking* in this household."

But the child couldn't keep any fluids down. She rejected the fever tea and so her temperature raged, and their child, who had been so full of life, her cheeks rosy with the bloom of youth, now lay limp in her bed, dark shadows under her eyes, her pale face covered in spots.

Krissa hadn't left her side since that evening, and she lay by their daughter on the small cot, stroking her soft cheek, brushing back the hair from her pallid skin, singing to her softly.

Dóra's breath became more ragged as the hours passed, and Albert knew his little girl was slipping away from them. His world was crumbling. It just wasn't right, and Albert struggled to look upon his own child. Seeing the battle her small body fought, willing it to keep fighting. Wanting desperately to take the struggle for her, to take it so that he as her father could do his rightful due and fight it in her stead.

Albert was dozing on a chair when he was awoken by a heart-wrenching wail. It came from beside him, and he startled awake in the dim room in the early hours of the morning. He turned to see his wife clutching the limp form of their child in her arms. Rocking over her.

"She's gone," Krissa sobbed, pressing her head against Dóra's, holding her to her bosom, clutching her with desperation. "Albert, our beautiful little girl. She's left us."

Albert staggered off the chair to his wife's side on the cot, taking them up in his embrace, cradling them to him, unable to quite believe that this was happening—that the life had truly gone from Dóra, his little girl who always had a smile for everyone.

The child lay peacefully in Krissa's arms, her eyes forever closed, her spotted face the pale, waxy shade of death. He brushed his hand along Dóra's cheek, smoothing her limp golden hair in tender strokes, a strangled *shh* escaping his lips as they pressed hard against Krissa's temple. He couldn't fix this, and the bitter truth of it tore through him. It was as if someone had their hand wrapped tightly about his heart, squeezing it, crippling him with the pain. There was nothing he could do but hold them, clutching them to him, his own heaving sobs mingling silently with his wife's.

Sólveig

It was early evening, the sun still many hours from setting outside, but the *baðstofa* at Botn sat in eternal darkness to keep out the light that hurt the eyes of the sick. It had been ten days since the measles took a hold over the people of Súgandafjörður. Sólveig was making the rounds in the *baðstofa*, with supper for the household. She had prepared fish soup. Those that were sick couldn't stomach much. She barely had interest in food herself, she was so exhausted, but she made herself eat, if only for the strength to keep going. She'd barely slept since she arrived. Sigrún, the mistress for the other household residing at Botn, nursed her sick husband and their teenage son. Her four-year-old daughter, Finna, was already lost to them, and their foster son, Gunnar, was faltering. The mother poured her grief into the business of caring for her loved ones. What else could she do?

Sólveig went between the households, administering cool cloths to soak the fevered brow and coaxing water into the sick for hydration. Some needed help with the bedpans, they were so weak. She worried constantly, but bit back the fear, not allowing it too close to the surface, not thinking too far ahead, just taking things one moment at a time. It fell to Sólveig to care for the sick of Jakob's household, with María abed, swallowed in her grief over the loss of little Albert Einar, and then two days later, four-year-old Ásta. María's eldest, Fríða lay recovering in bed, only just starting to regain her strength. Jakob barely left the smithy, coping in his own way—by throwing himself into the sorry task of making coffins to bury their dead.

It was during the night, while the household slept, that Sólveig was at last able to rest her feet for snatches at a time, but in the silence of the kitchen or in the dark *baðstofa*, the worry she had pushed down all day made its way unhindered to the forefront.

No one dared venture to other farms, lest they spread the sickness, not unless they absolutely had to. But the question remained—had the measles made its way to Suðureyri? Had they been quick enough to get the babies away? And then there was Helgi and not knowing what had become of him. Albert had said he'd travelled to Keflavík with Magnús. But how did they fare over on that piece of isolated headland? Had the illness been carried there too? She was desperate to know, and her only reply—the silence of the night and grumbled mutterings of the ill.

Sólveig finished spoon-feeding the liquid of the fish soup into young Hans, a boy of fifteen, one of Jakob's workmen. He was very weak, but he managed a few dribbles of it, his hands shaking, his lips trembling over the wooden spoon, before a fit of coughing took hold of him and exhaustion finally claimed him once more.

Leaving Hans to his rest, she took up the half-eaten bowl, passing a young woman who sat by María, the house mistress. She looked up at Sólveig and shook her head in defeat.

"She won't take it, Sólveig," the work maid said. "She's just set on staring at the wall."

The girl's name was Hulda. She was only seventeen, but Sólveig found she could rely on her, especially now with the mistress taken to bed in her grief.

"I'll talk to Jakob," Sólveig said with a sigh, and made her way to the kitchen, a sense of helplessness coursing through her. What could she say? The poor woman had lost two babies. Sólveig too, would want to curl up in her bed and perish with sorrow, but María still had Fríða. She had to live for the only child God saw fit to spare her. Could Jakob help pull his wife out of her desolation? But Sólveig's mind was a jumble in the exhausted state she was in. Leaving the bowl on the bench, she made her way towards the front entrance of the croft. She needed fresh air, needed to see the mountains, let their strength and steadfast presence seep into her. She didn't care that it was overcast outside and that the rain came in a steady, ceaseless patter. She thought only to escape, if just momentarily from the suffocating gloom that hovered over her and the household, but when she opened the door, she found Albert standing before her.

He startled her, appearing suddenly there before her, his tall, broad frame blocking the entrance, but it wasn't just that. It was his appearance, the grim set of his mouth, the haunted look behind his burning red-rimmed eyes that unsettled her the most.

"Albert, what are you doing here? Please, come in out of the rain."

He shook his head, the rain dripping off his hat and onto the shoulders of his brown jacket, where it rolled down the dark fabric in thick droplets.

"*Nei*, I've come for you, Sólveig." His voice was low and raspy. "You must come quickly."

She caught the emotion running through him, his pained features, a strangled sort of anguish making its way into him. "Ahh, I didn't know what else to do." He pulled the hat off his head and held it in his hand, running his fingers through his damp hair. "She's cramping something terrible—and the bleeding. There's just so much blood."

"What are you talking about, Albert? Who's bleeding?" The dread and hopelessness rose within her once more.

"Krissa. Had she not mentioned to you she was with child again?"

"*Nei*, she hadn't," she said, taken aback by this revelation. "Then she is probably losing the child," she added gently. "But what of the sickness? Has Suðureyri been spared?"

He shook his head. "I fear it's this damned illness that has brought this on." His voice had lost its edge and now it was low and desolate. "Our Dóra has been taken from us. Little Margrét too."

"Oh, Albert." She reached out to him, taking his hand, feeling the dark void within her tremble, a hollow ache that reached deep into her chest. The children. So many of the children were being taken from them.

"Only Steinn and Dísa seem to be over the worst of it," he continued, "but it's Krissa, she's been abed with a fever since last night."

"I'll come directly, Albert," she said, and returned to the *baðstofa* to gather her things. She glanced over at María, who lay asleep in her cot, facing the wall, and pulled aside Hulda informing her of her need to leave with Albert.

They made haste, Albert retreating into the downpour, waiting for her by the horse he had ridden to Botn, his face pale and grim. He'd had no time to saddle two horses, he told her somewhat apologetically, just took his faithful mare and rode with the wind. It was quicker by far on horseback, and Albert had Sólveig tucked up behind him, her arms about his waist, her head resting against his back to shelter her face from the onslaught of water as they rode along the windy, rainswept coastline back home towards Suðureyri.

21

July 1882

Sólveig

The dark days of summer drew ever on, nature itself echoing the devastating illness that drew its claws of death over the young lives of the people of Suðureyri—this illness that took from them the heart of their community—their babies, their youth, their future. All the while, storms and frost lashed a land that should be basking in summer's growth instead of hovering in an eternal winter. Sólveig so often felt like a fox caught in a snare, the sense of being trapped ever present. She was blind in the fog of darkness spread over them, desperate to see a glimmer of light, for an escape or an end to the stifling grief. What choice did they have but to hold blindly on to their faith, on to the hope that this would soon end? All they could do was to pray and give themselves solely into the hands of the Almighty and his grace.

Krissa lost the baby she was carrying. There was nothing Sólveig could do to stop it. Watching the woman writhe in pain on the cot she shared with Albert brought old wounds to the surface; that sense of helplessness she had felt with the death of her own sister, Fía, to childbirth. But

Sólveig was a trained midwife now and she had no time to wallow in that festering wound. With the unborn child lost to them, she had a fight on her hands, a fight to keep the mother from leaving them too. Krissa was half delirious, burning with fever, the rash of the illness spread over her skin like hundreds of glowing embers in the pit of a kitchen fire. In the dark of the room, Krissa's body contorted with pain and misery, a low keening, ceaseless moan from deep within her being. Her body had not long gone through childbirth. It was too soon to put her body through that trial again, only just healed as it was. Tobba fretted over her daughter, helping Sólveig clean up and clear away the bloodied sheets as the unformed child came loose. The hardest for Sólveig to control was the flow of blood, but it finally did ease, leaving Krissa deathly pale, and weak like a newborn babe. She took some of the sleeping draught she'd brewed for her, to help her sleep, if somewhat fitfully.

Sólveig needed to find Albert. He needed to be with his wife. To be by her side. She thought perhaps he had retreated to the smithy, busying himself as he so often did when she knew he was worried about something, but he was not to be found there. She would look for him in the outer houses, but as she passed one of the smaller rooms off the hallway that usually served as a storeroom, she caught a glimpse of the cradled bodies of Dóra and Margrét in the centre of the room and she stopped in her tracks.

An oil lamp sat on a shelf at the back of the room, bathing the room in a dull orange glow even though it was still the light of day outside. As it was with vigils, two women would sit with the bodies at night, keeping watch over them, making sure that they were never alone, that the light in the room would never blow out. Sólveig stepped quietly into the room, humbled to silence by the vision of two small timber coffins in the centre of the room, painted black, their lids resting beside them, with a beautiful white cross carved on each. The lids had not been placed over them, and she caught her breath at the sight of the two perfectly still pale faces of Dóra and Margrét, the delicate form of their small eyes closed, dark lashes sitting against waxy skin, their lips a bluish hue, the colour of death. No life stirred in their veins. It was truly gone from them. She performed the sign of the cross in the air just above them and ever so gently brushed her finger along the dull gold of Dora's hair. The lump in her throat grew harder to swallow, her bottom lip trembled, and her eyes blurred with tears. That familiar feeling of powerlessness washed over her. Who was to say who God decided to spare or take? But she had so often wondered why it had to be the little ones, so bright and innocent and full of life? She thought to the injustices they faced in life. She couldn't understand why they had been allowed such a short stay, why children had to fight so hard upon arrival into the world only for their little souls to be snatched up later with illness.

"We were to bury them tomorrow," said a deflated voice quietly from behind her. Sólveig spun around, clutching the base of her throat in fright. It was Albert. She hadn't seen him there, sitting on the bench in the dark corner of the room. He looked up at her through the short wheat-coloured strands of hair that had fallen across his furrowed brow, and she saw the tormented sorrow radiating from him.

"No service. No priest. Just Björn, Árni and I." He stopped and released a hard breath. "Ah, they deserve more than that, but what are we to do, Sólveig, when most in the household still lay abed?"

"Oh, Albert," she said, feeling the weight of his grief. She was about to say more, but she followed the direction of his gaze as it travelled to her hands, still raised in front of her where she clutched the fabric of her shawl, and saw as he did, the dried, smeared blood on the inside of her pale forearm. Her sleeves were still rolled up from when she had washed just now, but she must have missed this. She turned her arm to take it from his view, and that pained look crossed his features once more.

"And what of Krissa?" His voice was raspy with emotion. "Am I to lose her too?"

She sighed deeply. "We couldn't save the child, Albert. I'm so sorry." She knelt before him, her skirts bunching about her, grasping her hands in his, to hold them, to lend him comfort. He needed her strength as much as she needed his. "She's resting now. She's very weak from the loss of blood and the fever still has her in its grip. I don't know how much longer she will hold on."

He took a deep, exulting breath. "I never wanted this child, Sólveig. Not if it meant I would lose her in the process. My wife lies on the brink of death and—it's all my fault." His lips trembled and he crushed his head in the palm of his large hands, rubbing the long fingers through his hair in agony. "What have I done?"

"*Nei*, Albert, you mustn't think that!" His words stunned her. "This isn't your doing; do you hear me? You can't blame yourself. This is out of our hands. Please—" she begged him. "You can't—"

"But it must be." He stood suddenly, stepping away from her in one swift stride.

She straightened herself as Albert continued, his back to her, his voice restrained with the effort of not breaking. "I made a promise to God, that if he would just spare my wife in childbirth, then I would stay away from her—that I wouldn't bed her again." He turned to her then, his eyes a blue pool of suffering, his words stumbling. "But, Krissa—I should have tried harder—and now he's punishing me. Oh God, what I have I done?" His resolve finally broke, and his handsome face crumpled, his pain exploding in great, gasping sobs, and he fell to the ground, kneeling before her, clutching her to him.

"Sólveig, what am I going to do? Tell me what to do? I can't lose her too. There must be something you can do?" His arms were wrapped firmly about her waist, his head resting hard against her stomach. She struggled to hold herself together in the face of his grief and was so taken aback by him, by the strength of him against her, by this request of his—as if *she* held the power of life and death in her fingertips.

"Albert, *shh*," she whispered harshly, doing her best to control the wobble in her voice. "You've been so strong. Through all of this. You must be stronger a little longer yet—for Krissa, for Dísa and Lína. They need you now. Do you hear me?" She held him to her, his head resting against her, this big golden-haired man who she'd only ever seen rational and held together, a gentle, patient light in his eyes. But fear gripped him now. Fear and grief, and it radiated from him in waves. It trembled within him, and all she could do was let him cling to her until his heaving sobs subsided.

Sólveig took a deep steadying breath. "Come now, Albert." She pushed herself away from him, forcing him to look at her. "Krissa needs you now. You must go to your wife." She held his gaze until he nodded curtly, his lips set in a firm line, and she bent down to him, helping him to his feet. Albert hovered over her for a spell as if wanting to say something, but he held it back. Instead, he turned abruptly, and she was just as suddenly left standing alone in the room of the dead, her own silent tears slipping down her cheeks, knowing there was once again nothing she could do to keep away the reaper that hovered at Krissa's bedside. But Sólveig prayed anyway. She prayed silently and fervently that the woman would hold on for her girls and for Albert.

Albert

He kept his health. So, too, did Sólveig, Tobba, Björn and Rannveig, even old Leifur.

Krissa was buried the following Sunday, along with his darling Dóra and little Margrét.

Albert knew that in the world they lived in death lurked at every corner. The only thing certain in life was that one day death would come, but that didn't stop the pain that ripped through him at facing the loss—of being the one left behind. The grief that choked him was raw and heavy. It was unbearable at times, but he would pull himself together as they all had to. He must push the grief down into himself so that he could carry on. People were relying on him. He had a farm to run and two motherless daughters to raise.

It was a sorry sight to bear and an even sorrier task to perform, carrying his dear loved ones, cradled in their eternal beds, down the dimly lit hallway of his home. Árni and Jói carried Dóra. Björn and Tóti took Margrét, and he along with Einar carried Krissa. The mournful hymns were sung by the household as they exited the house. Steinn was waiting with the horses at the front. There should have been more people to farewell his loved ones. It should have been done with the holy blessing of the priest, but many of his household and Björn's still lay abed, over the worst of the illness, but still weak of body—not ideal for venturing out in the weather that greeted them, a constant wind and the sting of sleet. Those that were able farewelled them at the croft.

Albert held himself together. He wouldn't let the grief overtake him again, as it had that day in the vigil room with Sólveig while Krissa lay dying. Thinking back on it made him recoil with shame—how he had fallen in a sobbing heap at Sólveig's feet, expecting her to perform some sort of miracle to save his dying wife. He'd been so caught up in his own grief and the fear of losing Krissa, he hadn't been thinking straight at the time, but he knew it had been unfair of him to place that burden on the young midwife. She had stood heroically throughout all of this. Not once had he heard her complain, though he could see the exhaustion clear on her face, first caring for the sick at Botn and then at Suðureyri. He knew she had her own worries to contend with, how the lack of news of her betrothed would be eating at her. They were yet to have word of Helgi, and he wondered what had become of the people over at Keflavik.

It was a quiet affair at the churchyard at Staður, digging graves in the icy ground. The sting of sleet assaulted him with the onslaught of the howling wind, and Albert welcomed it. It took his mind briefly off the numbing pain within.

At the cemetery he'd met with others from the valley, also burying their dead. With the priest stationed at Holt, in the next fjord, and unable to travel, they'd had to do it themselves.

Júlíus was with his brother, Grímur, and Eiríkur from Bær helping to bury Júlíus's wife, Björg, and their two youngest children. Júlíus looked a shadow of himself, a broken man, like a snap of wind would simply split his thin bony frame into two.

"What will become of the children?" Albert asked Grímur.

"Júlíus wants Tómas and his eldest, Herdís, with him, but Anna María and little Kalli will come and live with us," he replied, shaking his head. "The downright sorry mess of this all."

Eiríkur looked as weary and downtrodden as the rest of them. He informed them of their loss—two children from Staður, and three little ones from Bær. They were yet to have word from the crofts across the fjord. Albert took it all in, feeling almost overwhelmed once again with grief at the news of more children being taken and that poor woman, Björg. Sólveig would be distraught with this news. Thank goodness Stella was with them at Suðureyri. So many lost to them, so many families left grieving and broken, and Albert knew he had no cause to feel sorrier for himself than anyone else.

Albert stayed back a while longer after the others had left, standing at the foot of the grave of his wife and daughter. He made sure his Krissa was buried next to her Dóra and the little boys that she'd lost shortly after birth. If there was any comfort to be taken, it was in knowing that she was there with her babies, watching over them. He stood in silence, his hat in his hands, his head bowed in respect, letting the wind carry his promises to them in the shadow of the mountains. He took his strength from those mountains, from their silent, solid presence. He spoke the words out loud, his tone sombre, speaking to them as if they could hear him—that the priest would be out soon to bless them, that he would be out to see them again with Dísa once she was well enough for the travel. He didn't even have proper headstones for them, just large stones he'd managed to drag up from the beach and engraved with the symbol of the cross, but he promised them, that would come too. To Krissa, he promised to stay strong and take care of their girls. He made a promise to Dóra that there would be flowers here soon, some of her favourite—the white ones with their large, silky petals that reminded her so of summer, *rjúpnalauf*—rock ptarmigan's leaf.

He smiled at the memory of her bringing him a bundle of them just last summer, and he wiped at the tears that came with it, knowing that these scars of grief for his wife and daughter were deep. He would carry their loss with him forever.

22

Sólveig

The summer had been a poor one as yet, but finally a reprieve from their suffering came and their hope reignited briefly with the appearance of the sun and fair, calm days in late July. Many had fallen ill, but those strong of body recovered just enough to keep on with the struggle of survival. Tasks were carried out as they were year after year. Milking was a daily affair, the fields would be taken to with the scythe and rake, the kitchen garden needed planting and tending, the men would take to the sea, food would be put away for winter, repairs to the farmhouse, the sheep crofts—it was never ending.

Sólveig wondered at the strength of Albert. He had just buried a daughter and a wife, and apart from his breakdown before Krissa passed away, he didn't dwell in his own self-pity. She watched him throw himself into his work. He was quiet and withdrawn after the burials, all traces of that anguish, that wretched sorrow and raw emotion, gone, and where before there had been humour and content in his blue eyes, there was now a courteous remoteness. Meals were quiet—too quiet—and Albert was often gone long into the night. Sólveig knew it was the silence that he couldn't tolerate, the little voices of the children no longer echoing within the walls of the *baðstofa*. She couldn't stand it either. It was a constant reminder of their loss.

The folk across the fjords finally arrived to bury their dead, some carrying their loved ones in coffins and some simply a body wrapped in a sack, for timber wasn't so easy to come by for all. They came across the water and then by horseback to the church at Staður. Sólveig counted them silently where she sat by the *baðstofa* window—six small bodies. But still there was no news of the people over the mountain at Keflavík.

Sólveig's worry for Helgi nagged at her, a deep ache in the centre of her chest. She longed to hear his voice, to feel his touch and to have his steady presence—for his comfort through this ongoing ordeal. But she knew that wanting him wasn't going to magically make him reappear. More and more as the days passed, she found a driving need to seek him out as, night after night, he came to her in her dreams. She feared his silence and, in her dreams, the haunted look in his green eyes.

With no new cases and the people of Suðureyri slowly recovering, the women of both households threw their efforts into cleaning the croft from top to bottom, scrubbing the sickness away, so that Rúna and the babies were finally able to return to them. The young woman was thinner about the face, her long midnight braids making her skin look paler than it already was. It had been hard on her, this separation, as it had been on them all. Though spared from the suffering of the household, she wasn't spared the knowledge of those who had suffered at its hands and the worry it had caused. But this reunion and having the babies amongst them again brought with it a renewed sense of wonder and hope to the household.

Sólveig was deeply saddened by the news Albert brought to her of Björg's passing, and her reunion with Stella was bittersweet. Stella had grown plump and clung to Rúna, shy in the face of these people she hadn't seen now for a month, and Lína a bright, happy baby, had started pulling herself up on furniture. She was mobile on all fours and was quick to fall into her father's outstretched arms. It was a tender sight, Albert taking his little fair-haired Lína into his arms. A rare sad smile lit his eyes as the child played and pulled at his short beard where the household sat in the *baðstofa*. Dísa sat silent next to her father, leaning into him, her head resting against his arm.

"Do you think she knows, *Pabbi*?" she asked timidly. Sólveig could see how the confident older sister had changed since her illness. She had drawn into herself more, taken to crying for her mother and sister every night. The child would often lay with her *amma* for comfort and followed her father about during the day, falling to anxiety and panic when he didn't come to bed at night, or she didn't know his whereabouts.

He turned to her patiently. "Does she know what, Dísa?"

"That *Mamma* and Dóra are gone to heaven."

He turned Lína in his arms, pulling her chubby hands away from his face. "I can't say. Perhaps she feels it, but how is she to tell us? *Nei*, my darling, it will be up to you and me to tell her about them."

Sólveig watched from her place in the *baðstófa*, finally holding Stella. The child squirmed, reaching out to Rúna, who sat beside her, whining for her.

"I fear she has forgotten me," Sólveig said dishearteningly as she passed the child back to Rúna.

"It won't take long for her to get used to you again, Sólveig. It's thanks to you that both she and Lína came through this dreadful time unscathed. But what of my brother? Is there still no word of him or my family at Keflavík?"

Sólveig shook her head. There had been no word of him or Magnús. "If he doesn't show himself soon, I'll be going there myself to find him." The idea had been sitting there within her since Krissa's death. How long was she to wait?

⁍

That night, Sólveig dreamed of Helgi once more.

He was walking down the slope of the mountain Spillir as he had done that last day of their parting back in June. These dreams always played out the same, as if she were reliving the moment again and again, vivid and stark, the memory of it imprinted in her mind:

The sun was warm on her face, the breeze cool through her hair. A shadow passed over her where she lay in the grass. It was Helgi. He stood before her, blocking the sun.

"So, this is where you're hiding? I've been looking for you everywhere."

"Oh, have you? Is something the matter?" she asked.

"Nei, nothing to fret about, Midwife. I'm just away to Ísafjörður and then on to Keflavík to help with some supplies. We'll be gone for five days, maybe a week at the most."

His words confused her. She shook her head as she sat up "Nei, it's been a month already, Helgi. It's nearly August and you are not returned to me."

He was unbearably woeful as he considered her. "I'm sorry, Sólveig, I must go," he said, turning from her reluctantly, making his way back down the slope.

Sólveig ran after him, and there before her very eyes he transformed into a raven, dark as the night. He flew down over the farmhouse at Suðureyri and back up the mountain, back towards the rock she had been lying beside. He circled it in the sky, his eery caw echoing on the wind, until finally he landed on the rugged grey surface. She strode back up the hill as quickly as she could, holding her skirts, even in her dream state, puffing with the effort, the raven's green eyes ever watchful as she approached him. She knew those eyes. They were Helgi's.

The raven sat before her, eerily still, as if he were part of the rock he perched on, and she found herself compelled to touch the big black bird. "Helgi?" She instinctively reached for him, to pet the silky black feathers of his wings, but it was then that he let out another caw and pecked her on the hand. Startled by the motion and the sharp pain that came with it, she pulled her hand quickly away. Blood, stark red against the paleness of her flesh, pooled into a drop where his sharp beak had broken the skin under the fourth finger of her right hand.

⬥

Three days later, Sólveig was in the kitchen garden with Tobba and Dísa, taking up some root vegetables, the thick, musty scent of manure stirred up with the rich, moist earth they were disturbing.

They'd been working silently side by side when she accidentally nicked herself with the small knife she was using to cut the green foliage off the swedes as she dug them out of the ground. It was silly, really. She'd been distracted by the voices coming from the front of the farmhouse. Was that Magnús's voice she had heard? She clutched her hand where the knife had sliced her palm, a drop of blood welling instantly from the cut, but she ignored it, feeling instead the rapid thump of her heart at his voice.

"Well, who might be coming now?" asked Tobba, stretching back up onto her knees, pulling out a bunch of swedes as she did so, her well-worn, knobbly hands stained with the brown of the earth.

Squinting, her pale eyes were swallowed up in a fold of wrinkles as she gazed towards the side of the croft where the voices had drifted from.

"Helgi," Sólveig gasped, and her eyes met Tobba's and Dísa's. They had come. He was home. Helgi was home. Dísa threw the swedes she carried into the wooden tub next to Tobba, and the child ran to the side of the croft, her blonde plaits swinging wildly with the movement.

"There's a boat pegged on the beach. Someone has come," she called to them with excitement.

Tobba stood up along with Sólveig, picking up the bucket of vegetables they had gathered from the garden.

"I'd best get some coffee on. Better get that cleaned up right away." She peered at the hand Sólveig clutched, where blood trailed and dripped onto the ground at her feet.

"Oh, it's only a nick," she said and almost ran to the stream a short way down the slope to wash her hands clean of the earth and blood that stained them.

Sólveig entered the room, a small smile lingering on her lips. They were finally here. Helgi was finally home.

When she entered the *baðstofa*, they all turned their eyes to her. Einar, Tobba, Dísa and Inga, even the babies on the floor, and there stood Magnús and Elías. She searched the room. But where was Helgi? Perhaps he had stepped out in search of her, she mused. But it was Rúna that made the gooseflesh rise on her skin, the sight of her in the embrace of her older brother, her face puffy and red.

"What has happened?" she demanded.

Why did they cast their eyes away? And then finally, Magnús took her gaze into his, his face solemn, his eye, the one without the patch, glassy and red.

"Sólveig." His voice was full of regret.

"Where's Helgi?" Her breath caught in her throat as she waited for the answer to come, the beat of her heart, so loud it thrummed in her ears.

"My dear Sólveig!" Rúna cried, breaking free from her older brother. She took Sólveig's hands in her own, her face crumpling in misery before her. "I'm so sorry."

"*Nei.*" Sólveig shook her head. Hadn't there been enough sadness already?

"The sickness has taken him," said her friend, her voice quivering.

It hit her like a slap in the face, and Rúna embraced her, the woman's tears flowing again, but she pulled away from her friend.

"When?" she managed. It couldn't be Helgi. They must have it wrong. He was young and healthy. In the prime of his life. He couldn't be dead. The measles couldn't have taken him too.

Einar took Rúna into his arms. She couldn't speak under the flow of tears, but she hiccupped and managed to get out, "Two weeks since."

Magnús spoke up. "He fell ill with it the morning he was to come home to you. We'd been back from Ísafjörður for five days. Must have picked it up when we were there. They say some sailors carried it in with them from Reykjavík." She heard the words he spoke, but it was as if from far away. "We all took sick, and God only knows how the child survived it, but little Örnólfur did and Steindór too. But Helgi—" Magnús faltered, struggling with the telling of this news, and she could see by his expression that he couldn't quite believe it himself. "He still hadn't fully recovered from the last sickness—said his lungs were still weak. He often felt it with a lot of walking, he'd told me. I'm so sorry, but he just wasn't strong enough, Sólveig."

She swallowed hard, forcing her voice to work. "Where is he now? May I see him? Did you bring him with you?"

Magnús shook his head. "He was buried back home, at Keflavík. Told me he wanted to be buried on the headland so he could see the sea from the rise behind the house. It was one of his favourite places as a child." A sad smile touched the corner of his lips as he recalled it. She hadn't known this about him. There was so much about Helgi that she would never know now. "Sólveig, I made sure he had a cross put up marked with his name for you to find him when you got the chance to return to us."

They all watched her, waiting for her to break in front of them, but she wouldn't.

Magnús turned to the table up against the *baðstofa* window and took something from it—a small square bundle wrapped in tissue paper with a green ribbon tied around it. "Helgi told me to give this to you and he said to tell you—"

"What did he say?" she whispered impatiently, desperate to hear his last words to her.

Magnús took a deep, trembling breath, his calloused thumb brushing at a stray tear sliding down her cheek. His tone was low and tender. "He said that he hopes you'll forgive him one day for breaking his promise to you, and he's damn sore about not marrying you sooner."

His words sent a cord of love and sorrow and regret through her, and her hand shook as it took the parcel from him, but she didn't open it. She simply stared at it, struggling to hold herself together before them. She had been right. Those dreams—the raven. It had been Helgi. He'd been trying to tell her that he was leaving her. She traced the broken skin of her palm with her thumb, where the knife had nicked it, and there under the fourth finger at the same place was the mark of the raven.

The room spun. The air was thick and heavy with grief. It was suffocating. She needed fresh air, or she was going to be sick.

"I'm sorry," she whimpered, dashing out of the room in a bid to escape, to get away from them, away from their pity and their sad, misery-filled eyes.

She made it to the side of the house where the contents of her morning meal came to the surface. Tears stung her eyes and the world spun again with light-headedness. The parcel was still in her hands. Though it was, in fact, light as a feather, the significance of it was heavy. It was the last thing he would ever give her. Closing her eyes, she clutched it to her, the ache in her swelling to a crescendo. Magnús was suddenly there beside her, helping her up, but she pushed his hands away, unable to bare his touch.

"I just need some air," she mumbled, walking as if in a daze down to the beach, where the waters of the fjord lapped gently onto the shore.

The wind harassed her, the cool sting of its breath on her face. There, moored on the sand at the small beach, was the boat Magnús and Elías had arrived in—without her Helgi—and then the memories came flooding to the surface. It was here they had rowed out from, that day to Keflavík to deliver Stína's child. She remembered how Helgi had teased her, lifting her into the boat over his shoulders, and the restrained desire she had seen in his eyes as they rowed. She would never see that look in his eyes again. She would never fall into their green depths again.

Why hadn't she just gone to him? So many times, she had wanted to leave, but duty bound she stayed.

The crackle of tissue in her hand brought her awareness back to the parcel once more. She held it before her and ripped it open, suddenly desperate to hold the last thing he had touched.

Her breath caught in her throat at the sight of it. A beautiful white scarf slid through her fingers, soft and light—ever so light. It was silk. The scarf he had promised her, the one for their wedding day, for the *peysuföt* she was making for herself. She clutched at the fabric, silent tears streaming down her cheeks as if the fountain of water within her was a bottomless ocean, but with the tears came a sudden burning flare of her anger. She gazed out at the fjord, clutching the scarf to her, gulping the air in deep breaths to still the tide of grief within, to stop it from spewing forth. She resented the calmness of those grey waters. How dare the ocean be so calm when a storm of anguish raged inside her.

Sólveig leaned against the boat, only just becoming aware of its hard timber surface against her legs. It sat there before her pegged into the sand, and rational thought all but flew by. Perhaps it was the weeks of exhaustion, of the endless nagging worry, of seeing the face of death over and over again, that was the cause of it and this news was the final straw. Perhaps people just snapped sometimes in the face of loss.

Why was it that, yet again, someone she loved had been taken from her? And all she knew at that moment was that she needed to get to Keflavík to see Helgi, even if all she would find there was his grave. She would do, now, what she hadn't done before. Leave.

Ripping away the thick wooden peg that anchored the boat, she strode to the stern, pushing all her weight against the small boat. It was heavier than she imagined, but she heaved into it, throwing her anger, her sorrow, into this one task—to get the boat out, to get it across the fjord so that she could go to him.

Helgi had always made it look so easy. What would he say now, seeing her attempt this? She pushed, her arms tiring, her strength waning, her breath coming in hard puffs. He would likely laugh at her foolishness.

The boat barely inched forward, and she hit and kicked it, letting tears spew forth, throwing her rage into it.

"Move, damn it, why won't you move?"

But it wouldn't budge. The pain in her chest was crippling and she finally sank to the ground in great, gasping sobs, exhausted from her efforts, clutching the silk scarf to her. She ignored the cold seeping into the cloth of her skirt at her knees, now wet from the damp, gravelly sand, as the thought of never seeing Helgi ever again sent an ache deep into her, tearing into her very being.

"Sólveig." A deep voice spoke gently behind her. It was Albert. He knelt carefully beside her, his knees in the wet sand, and she let him draw her to him, his arms coming around her, holding her firmly against him.

"He's gone, Albert," she muttered miserably against his course woollen jacket where she gripped it, and his arms tightened their hold on her.

"I know," he said softly.

"I should have gone to him, Albert," she cried pathetically. "I should have just taken the boat and gone. If I had known he was sick, I could have been there for him. I could have nursed him." Her throat was tight. It ached with the words as she spoke them.

"*Shh*, Sólveig, but you didn't know. How could you have known?" he soothed, his lips against her hair.

The wind blew against them for a spell, her sobs subsiding, and she let the sounds of the fjord birds come to her focus—the eiders, and the wild geese, the seagulls and the singsong of the pipits. She let the sounds sweep over her.

When she shivered against him, she heard his deep intake of breath, felt the rise and fall of his chest against her head.

"I will take you to him, Sólveig. I promise you. I will take you to Keflavík to see Helgi once the haying is done." He paused and his tone was firmer this time, almost stern. "But you must promise me to never take the boat out on your own, do you hear me? Promise me."

She nodded against him, feeling suddenly tired, so very tired, and he picked her up then, off the beach, holding her in his arms, cradled as if she were but a babe. He carried her home, back up the bank, back to Suðureyri and to those that remained.

23

August 1882

Sólveig

With August arrived the rain, a ceaseless patter, as if the tears that had been shed for the loss of lives now poured from the heavens and onto the land, cleansing it of the sickness that had ravaged them.

At Suðureyri, all their efforts were pushed into preparing for the winter ahead to ensure their survival. After all, they didn't get through the measles just to starve to death come winter. For Sólveig the busyness helped keep the thoughts of Helgi at bay, and on those days she could pretend. She could pretend that he was still just in Keflavík or Ísafjörður and would return to her soon, but there were times when she would wander the land, scouring the slopes and rocky crevices for herbs for her medicine stores, and all of a sudden, she'd find herself standing at the water's edge staring into the distance. She would scan the horizon where the sea kissed the sky, where the mountain Göltur stretched its earthly fingers towards it, as if trying to touch it. She longed to see the outline of Helgi's boat coming around that headland, the current carrying him steadily home to her, but his boat never arrived.

Sólveig realised towards the end of August that she had been at Suðureyri for almost a year. How she would have been shocked to know then that in only a year of being here she would become the shame she always thought to prevent. Pregnant and unwed at that. Her courses had not come since she had lain with Helgi at the end of June—that sweet moment on the slopes of Spillir. She had blamed its lateness on her exhaustion, of battling through July with worry and little sleep, but when the nauseousness arrived with it in early August, and she found herself hiding swedes in her apron pocket to battle the nausea, she knew his child had taken to seed and grew within her womb. The child had not yet quickened, but she felt the heaviness of new life inside her. It was there in the tenderness of her breasts, the pulling and stretching in her groin, as her body made room for the child. She was awed by this revelation, and she held on to the wonder of it, keeping this knowledge to herself, something that was hers alone for a little longer. It was a bittersweet feeling, and she had initially scoffed at the irony of the situation she found herself in, of the worries she'd had for Inga when she first arrived, when, in fact, it was her own propriety she should have been concerned with. Her emotions of late were like the ocean—unpredictable and difficult to navigate, calm and smooth one day and a roiling grey torrent the next. There were times when she was angry at him—at Helgi. Could you be angry at a dead person? He had promised her after all. He had told her time and again that he wasn't the sort of man to give a woman his child, and leave her. Well, he had broken that promise. But she often thought to those last words he had given Magnús for her. Helgi had wanted her. He had wanted their child and she found that the shame she thought would overwhelm her was not there. Rising alongside her grief was hope and purpose. She cherished

the life he'd left behind. Along with the scarf he'd given her, it was all she
had left of him.

Albert had been good to her. He'd been a comfort to her that day on
the beach. She had needed his strength and steady, calming presence.
She had felt somewhat alone throughout the sickness. With no doctor
on hand, the responsibility for the sick had fallen on her, and it was a
heavy burden. She was often reminded of Gróa's words to her back in
April—to not blame herself for what had come to pass. Albert had asked
her to save his wife, but she hadn't been able to. She hadn't been able
to save the children at Botn either. They'd lost lives and she questioned
herself. Was there more she could have done? That day on the beach
with the news Magnús had brought with him had been her undoing, but
Albert, even after his own loss, had been there for her. He had wrapped
his arms around her and poured his calming strength into her. He had
that effect on people. People looked up to him, came to him for advice,
seeking his opinion on matters of the land and house. He listened to
his people. It's what made him a good leader, the *hreppstjóri* for his
community. He had become a dear friend to her, someone she could
trust and rely on, someone whose opinion she valued. But what would
he say now, in light of her situation? She knew him to be a moral man.
Would his view of her change? Would he think less of her? She didn't
know why it was so important to her, but she wanted to keep his respect
and her place in the only home she had.

October 1882

With the approach of the *slátur* season, Sólveig was grateful the constant
feeling of nausea had subsided. She was hopeful that she would get
through the gruesome task of preparing the meat and offal from the
sheep without retching. But it did show itself again.

   Early one morning in mid-October, Sólveig was gathered with the
women of Albert's household—Tobba, Rúna and Inga—in the dim
light of the warm kitchen, having just taken her morning meal with
them. They were preparing themselves for the *slátur* work they would
undertake this day. Albert, Einar and Árni, with old Leifur for company,
had been busy. Many sheep had been culled and there was much to
prepare for smoking, boiling, and storing the meat. Sólveig didn't envy
the men the task of culling. She knew it was carried out for their own
survival, and nothing would be wasted, but she wondered if they found
it hard at times to have to take the life of a living thing, or was it one of
those things that became part of the everyday mundane, a necessity—just
another task to complete like plaiting one's hair or dressing for the day?

   The four women stood around the warm kitchen, chatting amongst
themselves, Inga informing them animatedly of how it had been
out there during those cold days on the mountain searching for the
sheep. Sólveig listened somberly. She'd had a strained relationship with
the young woman since her engagement to Helgi was announced in
summer. Inga had complained to Rúna of how she felt Sólveig had
betrayed her, and the pretty work maid said very little to her unless
she had to. Since the illness, she was thinner, the lustre and glow of
life she normally carried had dulled, as it had on them all, but her eyes
were bright as she recounted her story. She had joined the men on the
sheep roundup along with Björn's work maid, Hansína, but Inga was

interrupted as Albert and Einar walked into the kitchen carrying large buckets filled with offal and meat. The men were grim-faced and quiet as they entered the room, bringing a rush of cold wind indoors with them. Tobba coughed with the draft sneaking into the room in their wake.

"Are you planning on leaving us any warmth?" scowled the old woman, rushing to shut the wooden door behind the men. It hadn't escaped Sólveig's notice of late, the way the cough dragged on and settled into the old woman. She had been coughing with more frequency in the last few weeks, a deep, wet sound that rattled in her chest, her breathing heavy after exertion, and fits of hacking leaving her weak. Thankfully it didn't take hold of her this time, and with the door shut, she made her way back to the table following Einar and Albert.

"Here, you'd best start on this while it's still hot," said Albert, approaching Sólveig. She sat at the wooden table against the back wall of the croft, near a small glass window that let in minimal light. Albert's hands were bloodied, and he placed the bucket full of thick, steaming fluid before her. It sloshed against the pail, dark and red. The heat of it hit her, a warm, tangy, metallic smell that drifted into her nostrils, filling the room with its stench, and she found herself clutching the edge of the bench, trying to control the ill feeling rising within. Her morning meal of oats suddenly became a hard lump sitting at the top of her stomach.

"Why, Sólveig, you look as if you've been rocking too long on a boat at sea," remarked Inga. "Are you unwell?"

Rúna nudged the woman, and she scowled at her in response, rubbing her arm. "Would you just hush, Inga?" she whispered tersely.

Sólveig took up quickly, catching Albert's quizzical look as she rushed past him, her hand over mouth. She made it outside through the back door and to the side of the storehouse before it all came out. With her eyes closed and her breath still coming in deep puffs, she simply sat there,

letting the wind blow into her face, cooling the beads of sweat on her
brow that came with the effort of heaving. Breathing crisp, fresh air deep
into her lungs, she could already feel the nausea subsiding. She sighed.
She had been feeling so good of late. How was she to go back in there
and help finish the task before them without being sick again and again
as the smell overwhelmed her?

And it wasn't just the *slátur*. How was she to help, too, with the
washing of the wool in the coming weeks without retching at the
overpowering smell of urine they cleaned the wool in?

"Oh, Helgi. What have you done to me?" she muttered miserably
under her breath. What would she say to them when they questioned
her? She wasn't ready to tell them, though Rúna's comment before she
ran outside confirmed her suspicions that the work maid already knew
of her condition.

Sólveig wiped her mouth with the corner of her apron, kneeling on the
cold, hard ground just a spell longer, trying to summon the energy to face
the questions and comments she knew would come when she returned
to the croft.

Sensing she was no longer alone, she turned to see Albert standing a
few paces away, his hands now cleaned of the blood and folded across his
chest, a crease furrowing his brow.

"Are you with child, Sólveig?" The look on his face was one that she
hadn't expected, one of hurt, like she had somehow disappointed him.

Her hand lingered over her stomach protectively. "How could you
know?"

"There's been talk, as there always is. You think people haven't noticed
you running off to be sick in the mornings? The missing swedes, the way
you're constantly chewing on stale bread and dried fish throughout the

day." He cocked an eyebrow at her, adding, "I'm well aware of the signs of a woman with child, Sólveig."

"So, it was Inga, then?" She gritted her teeth together in annoyance. The maid had caught her a few too many times chewing on the foods that kept her stomach at ease.

"Is it Helgi's?" Albert asked, suddenly by her side, taking her by the elbow to help her to her feet.

She didn't like his tone, and she pulled her arm from his grasp, turning to face him, offended and annoyed that he should deem to ask who the father was—as if he didn't already know, as if she were one to give herself to just anyone, like a wanton woman.

"How can you ask me that? Of course, it's Helgi's child." She stared at him, searching his face for some sort of understanding. She hadn't expected this. Not his contempt. "What is it that bothers you so?" she asked tightly.

He shook his head, his eyes a dark, stormy sea, hard and cold, his words slow and careful. "I trusted you, and then you do this, under my roof—an unmarried woman giving herself before she's wed!"

She slapped him then, for words could not come to her quick enough.

He blinked hard, taking the blow she gave him. His face turned red, whether with anger or shame, she didn't know. The golden bristle on his jaw and cheek hid the welt where her hand had met his flesh. She had surprised herself, that her reaction had been to slap him, but his words hit a raw nerve. What right did he have to question her this way? She was her own person, not beholden to him or anyone. Her chin quivered as she spoke, and she found it hard to control the want to cry before him. Why was it that her tears flowed so freely these days? She used to be in much better control of herself.

"I know you're exhausted, Albert, and you're still grieving, so I'll see it as the grief speaking and not you. Helgi and I were to be married, our engagement was announced before the community. You know this!"

"You weren't yet wed, and you gave yourself to him. Do you not see how this looks, Sólveig? I am *hreppstjóri* here. I have to maintain some semblance of order within my household." He shook his head. "I expected better from you. A learned woman, an example to the young women in our community."

Though he had not hit her physically, it felt like a blow, and she stumbled back from him.

"That's not fair," she replied, her eyes burning with unshed tears. "Did I give myself to Helgi knowing he would die only weeks later? How were we to know what was to come? We were to be wed." She shook her head sadly. "I don't have any regrets. I loved Helgi. I still love him." She brushed irritably at the tear trailing down her cheek. "And this baby," she said, clutching the fabric over her stomach, "is all I have left of him." She paused, her breath coming fast, trying to keep herself together before him, wanting to hold her head high. She wouldn't let him shame her. She had nothing to feel ashamed of, but she was utterly disappointed by him.

Albert sighed, rubbing a hand over his face, the dark shadows under his eyes stark against the paleness of his skin, and she saw the way the anger and hurt in his eyes suddenly relented and dissolved into something else. Was it regret?

"Sólveig—" He reached out to take her hand, but she pulled it away from his touch.

"I'm grieving too, Albert." She pushed past him, too angry and hurt by him to stomach the sight of him any longer.

Despite the new life growing inside her, it was a hollow feeling walking back to the croft. Though she knew him to be a moral man, she had not expected that reaction from Albert. He was one of the people whose respect she'd earned and wanted the most to keep. Residing at Suðureyri with his family, she'd finally been gifted with some semblance of belonging. A place where she felt respected, and her opinion regarded. Was that lost now? He had made her feel so very little—like what she'd done with Helgi had been sinful and dirty, and it brought to the surface those old feelings of shame she'd had growing up. Was she not worthy of love and respect? Was that why all those she loved eventually left her? Her father, her mother, her sister and now Helgi.

She pushed at the self-doubt threatening to overwhelm her. She pushed against it as her anger flared suddenly, pulling her out of her own self-pity. But, of course, she was deserving of love! Wasn't everyone? Her shame had not been her own. Her parents being unmarried was no more her fault than it was this little one's growing inside her. But she knew it wasn't as simple as that. They lived in a world where people could be cruel. Those that didn't conform to the usual ideals were gleefully trodden on and put in their place.

She sighed deeply and made her way down the road, running along the row of crofts, thinking to enter the house from the front, avoiding the kitchen. The anger inside her simmered, the sting of Albert's words still lingered there, and she came to a decision. If Albert didn't want her at Suðureyri in the 'shameful' state she was in, then she would go to Elsa at Keflavík.

Opening the front door carefully, she quietly made her way down the narrow hallway to the *baðstofa*. Most of the household was still gathered in the kitchen dealing with the *slátur*. She could hear their voices from the kitchen, echoing down the hallway.

"The pity of it," she heard Tobba say.

"Not so high and mighty now, is she? Unwed and pregnant." Inga snickered. "I knew there was something strange going on with her. Albert will surely send her packing now."

"Inga! That's enough. Let the woman be. She's only ever been kind to you," Rúna scolded, but the words Inga spoke hit a nerve. She would pack her belongings and take her leave of them.

Was she being irrational? Perhaps, but she couldn't unsee the disappointment in Albert's eyes. She had let him down. He would send her packing anyway.

It was still early, but with autumn upon them, the days were shorter. There wasn't much for her to pack, and if she left now, she could make it to Elsa's place before nightfall. She wasn't quite sure of the way. She could skirt the fjord down to the farm Botn and follow the path up behind the croft at Göltur. That would take her over the mountain, as Helgi had told her once when she'd asked him about going by land. She could also ask Jói or Einar to ferry her across the fjord on the boat to make her journey shorter. She knew Elsa would take her in, at least for now, but the isolation and distance did present a problem if she was called out to births in the coming months. She pushed that thought aside. That was a worry for later.

Sólveig couldn't help the tears that fell now, unbidden, as she packed. She thought she'd had a friend in Albert, she thought he of all people would have some compassion. She didn't want to go, but she wouldn't stay where she would be judged and viewed with shame.

"Are you leaving us?" came a small voice. It was Dísa standing in the doorway with Stella on her hip and holding Lína's small, chubby hand as she stood, the eleven-month-old taking awkward, shaky steps. The child looked almost afraid to enter the room. "I heard *Pabbi* talking to you,"

she said, finally relenting to Lína's tugging to go forward into the long
room. She placed Stella on the rug on the floor, where she sat confidently
on her own, and Lína stood, using the bed to support her, making her
way gleefully across the wooden frame. Sólveig smiled half-heartedly at
the baby and sighed, drawing her eyes back to Dísa. She was a miniature
of her mother, with her long blonde plaits, but her eyes were a sky-blue.
Old eyes they were. Since Sólveig had come to know her, she had felt
the young girl was old beyond her eleven years, always a serious child,
ready to take on the responsibility that often fell to the elder sibling,
an example to the younger ones. She flinched, thinking back to Albert's
words only moments earlier about her being an example to the women
of their community.

"I'm not going far. Just over the fjord to Keflavík."

"Why does everyone have to leave?" Dísa's eyes were large, her
brow furrowed in concern. Regret swept through Sólveig at the
disappointment evident in the girl's tone. She had lost so much, and
now, here Sólveig was, yet another person leaving. Dísa almost ran to
her, clutching Sólveig about the waist, as if begging her to stay. Sólveig
embraced the girl, this suddenly motherless child who would be a young
woman in only a matter of years.

There was a quiet knock at the entrance to the *baðstofa* and both
Sólveig and Dísa looked up to see Albert's imposing frame in the
doorway.

"*Pabbi*, I don't want her to leave," she whined.

"Dísa, go to the kitchen while I speak to Sólveig, please. Take the babies
with you." Dísa did as she was asked, glancing back at Sólveig with a
pitiable frown.

With no desire to speak to Albert just yet, Sólveig turned her back
to him and kept folding her clothes, pulling her few items off the shelf

above her bed, her knitting, her book of Psalms and Bible, her midwifery textbook. Her life's belongings. She didn't own much. No household of her own, just these things, and keeping Stella was out of the question.

"Were you to just up and leave us this very day?" he asked from behind her, a note of astonishment in his voice.

"I won't stay where I'm not welcome, Albert, or in the household of a man who would look upon me and my child with disdain."

He exhaled harshly. "Ah Sólveig. You didn't deserve my anger, and I am sorry for it, but you were right. I *am* grieving sorely, and I'm just so tired of the fight—of how damn hard we must fight just to survive. I let my frustration get the better of me. You were simply the first person in the path of my wrath. It wasn't fair of me to put that on you. After all you've done for us."

She still had her back turned to him, but she stopped shovelling her things into her sack, not wanting him to see her in this state, the way she held her breath to stop the sound of her sobbing, the way the tears fell in big blobs down her face. She simply stood there frozen, a book in her hand, ready to put it into the sack.

He sighed with frustration, his feet shifting, making the floorboards creak. "Sólveig? Sólveig, can you look at me?" His heavy footsteps sounded behind her, and then his hands were on her shoulders, pulling her gently around to face him, forcing her to see him. She met his gaze with reluctance, not wanting him to witness her weakness, the uncontrolled state of her emotions.

His expression was a mirror of regret. "Ah, can you ever forgive me? It tears me up to see you cry and that I should be the cause of it. Of course, your child is a blessing. After all that we've lost, this new life is the hope we all need. Please don't leave us. You must stay. Your home is here with us. I told you that when you first arrived, and it still stands. We need you here. Dísa and Lína need you, and Stella too." He took her hands in his, bringing his eyes level with hers. "Sólveig, say you'll stay?"

24

Albert

Only a week had passed since Albert had asked Sólveig to stay on with them at Suðureyri, and he'd woken early one morning, as he did so often, before the rest of the household. Stepping out to relieve himself, he scanned the sky above him, the low haze of stars fading as the day dawned. It would be a good day for travel. It was time. Today he would take the midwife to Keflavík. To her Helgi.

They were a group of five that left the shoreline of Suðureyri beach as the sun rose, the skyline a blaze of orange, like glowing embers on the kitchen hearth. Sólveig, Rúna, Einar, Dísa and himself were seated in a boat, the smaller of their wooden sea vessels used for short-distance travel. Einar, like himself, was dressed from head to foot in his sea skins, helping him with the rowing. The two women and his daughter wrapped themselves in layers of wool, hair tucked under scarfs and across the chest for warmth, fingers gloved to take away the chill, knowing that the weather could always turn. It hadn't been his intention to bring Dísa along, but Tobba had insisted he take the girl. The old woman wasn't sure she could cope with only Inga to help her with both the babies, along with the child's anxiety about her father never returning to her. Besides, they would be there and back that same day.

Dísa sat on the bench next to the midwife on the boat, leaning against her, her smaller mittened hand clasping Sólveig's larger one. His daughter grinned from ear to ear in her joy to be included on this trip, to be considered along with the adults. Seeing it brought a sense of joy to him, but with it came an intense ache. How she looked so like her mother! This was an adventure for the eleven-year-old, and it pleased him to see the serious frown she often wore transformed into something light and youthful, as a child's should be. She had seen too much sadness of late, as had they all.

Sólveig had agreed to stay on with his household at Suðureyri and Albert was thankful for that. He couldn't do with losing her. Of course, there would be some talk. Inga had been only too eager to point out Sólveig's odd behaviour to him that day in the kitchen, of her morning sickness, and though he had his reputation as *hreppstjóri* to consider, he was also at a point where he was beyond caring about the callous opinions of others. She had been right to be angry with him. His reaction to her pregnancy hadn't been just, and he could see now how he had placed too much expectation onto her. She was young, and she, too, was struggling with the reality of the altered course of her life, as he was now, having had stolen from him the person he thought would walk beside him in life. Sólveig and Helgi had been on the brink of marriage after all. Of course, there was that temptation. Boundaries were easily blurred when you were with the one you loved. He knew that only too well. Hadn't he, after all, given in to his wife after he had vowed to stay away from her? He'd been in a bad state of mind that day after the culling of the lambs. One setback after another. Dragged down by the constant hollow grief that assaulted him day after day. Waking every day to an empty bed. At least, with Krissa, there had been someone to share the burden and the worries with. But she was gone now, and he felt at times so very alone, the weight of responsibility almost drowning him as he struggled to keep his household afloat, as well as his own head above water.

The boat pulled into the small landing at Keflavík, and Albert jumped out into the shallow water, his sea skins keeping the cold wet from seeping into him as he dragged the vessel onto the beach. Dísa was already standing, her eyes wide with wonder, eager to explore a new place, and he took her outstretched hands, chuckling to himself at the enthusiastic leap she took off the edge of the boat, onto the sand, with his help.

Albert heard a splash as Einar jumped out after him into the shallow grey water at the other end of the boat and reached up, taking Rúna into his arms, carrying her to the beach.

"Don't you drop me, Einar Sveinsson," she warned him, but Albert could see the work maid was smirking, her eyes creased in pleasure at being in the arms of his brother, and he couldn't help but smile at the pair.

"I wouldn't dare," Einar remarked dryly, placing her carefully on the beach, and then turned back for Sólveig.

Albert dragged the boat up the beach, away from the shoreline.

He was breathing hard when he finished, the boat pegged safely away from the sea's grasp. The others had already started up the trek to the headland, Rúna and Dísa leading the way, Einar not far behind, but Sólveig stood at the head of the path, her medical bag clutched tightly in one hand, looking up at the trail, but not moving.

"Before you," he said as he approached her, assuming she was simply waiting for him. He swept his arm up in a gesture to direct her forward, indicating the ascending rocky trail. It was a steep climb, and he wondered if she thought it would be too much for her. But the way she chewed the corner of her lip and the soft crease at her brows told him that it was more than that. Something was bothering her. "What is it, Sólveig? Are you unwell?" he asked, his hand coming almost instinctively to the small of her back.

"*Nei*, it's just—" She hesitated, taking a small, shaky breath, glancing up the steep embankment and then back at him, her eyes full of concern. "I feel now that I'm suddenly faced with it, that I don't know if I can do this. It all seems so final somehow."

He let out a sigh, understanding her hesitation. He had only been through it himself three months earlier. "I know it feels that way. It's a hard thing to face, standing at the grave of the one you love," he said gently. "And if you're not ready yet, then that's okay. You just say so and we'll turn back."

He studied her features as they took in his words, seeing the sadness there, mingled with apprehension, and she dragged her gaze away, out to the grey mass of the sea stretching endlessly towards the horizon.

"*Nei*, I think I need to do this, Albert." She gave him a curt nod, and he reached down to take the medical bag from her hands.

"Then let me carry this for you." She let him take it from her, this bag she insisted on carrying everywhere. Always ready in case she was called upon. He couldn't see that she would need it, but she was at least prepared. They never knew what life would throw at them. Sólveig turned from him and made headway up the track to Keflavík, Albert trailing her.

❦

"How have things fared here?" Einar asked Magnús, and Albert was grateful for his brother. Undressed of his sea clothes, he sat next to him on a cot in the *baðstofa*, a cup of steaming coffee in his hands. Dísa played with baby Örnólfur on the floor. The ten-month-old sat before her banging together sheep bones clutched tightly between chubby fingers. The child's mother sat beside Magnús on the cot, where she worked with a needle and thread stitching holes in a shirt.

"Much the same as you I suspect, a late harvest, poor yields. We lost ten lambs in the sudden freeze," Magnús replied. "It's been a tough year for everyone," he added, rubbing his good eye, a black leather band covering the damaged eye. Albert had only seen him once without it, the eyeball beneath still there, but the colour gone from it. He had heard the story about how he'd lost his sight—how when he was a boy of fourteen, a splinter of wood had embedded itself deeply into it while building a boat with his father. The infection that came with it had claimed his vision.

Elsa's sister, Salbjörg, sat quietly on her cot at the end of the room with her knitting, and the other workmen had just come in at the news of the arrival of visitors. Albert was sure it was always an occasion when visitors came to Keflavík, as it was at home. Their farm at Suðureyri had a more centralised location, and visitors passing through was a regular occurrence, unlike Keflavík, as isolated as they were in this part of the fjords. They were likely eager for news, but Albert found he had little taste for socializing, and he was grateful that Einar led most of the conversation.

"He was a good man, Elsa's lad. We're sorry to see the back of him." Salbjörg's words brought his attention back to the room. "And the midwife." She shook her head. "That poor girl. So soon to be her husband, but, of course, you'll know what that's like, Albert. We're all terribly sorry to hear of your own loss."

Albert flinched at her words but nodded his head curtly in her direction. He found it stuffy in the room, the eyes on him constantly filled with pity whenever they looked at him. He knew they only meant well, but he realised with sudden clarity that he hadn't the heart for social calls and was surprised at how hard he was finding this visit and the meaningless, endless chatter, simply for the sake of propriety.

"If you'll excuse me," he said, standing abruptly. He left the room in a hurry, escaping to the outdoors where he could breathe again, taking great gulps of air into his lungs to calm the thumping in his chest. He unclenched his hands, cooling the sweat between his fingers, and walked, needing to clear his head, wanting desperately to forget the hurt. To stop feeling it. He wanted nothing more than to just take the boat and row home, but that wasn't an option. This wasn't about him after all. This was her time, Sólveig's. He'd promised her, and he would stand by it. Making his way towards the back of the croft, past a small vegetable garden and a back door that led to a kitchen, he finally stopped at a rock wall, a windbreak for the vegetable garden. He leaned against the hard surface, seeking not only privacy but the view of the ocean, letting the sounds engulf his senses, feeling himself calm down, away from prying eyes and the chattering noise.

That's when he saw her, and he couldn't look away. Sólveig. He couldn't help but watch her. She looked so vulnerable out there, a lone figure set against the rawness of the land around her—as if a gust of wind could just blow her over and she would, like many others, disintegrate before his very eyes. She was a tender reminder of the fragility of life in this harsh landscape, a reminder of how insignificant they really were, her small frame set against the backdrop of the mountain Göltur rising stark and menacing before her. He noticed the slight hunch of her shoulders, her head bowed in respect before the small timber cross and the fresh earth settled on the mound, and he felt the depth of her loss. He had surely looked much the same, not long ago, at his wife's and daughter's graves, that same sad lone figure. She didn't deserve what life had thrown at her, but he knew she would bear it, just as he had to. He recalled her story of her father's abandonment, of growing up an illegitimate child herself, and he thought now to her unborn child. It would have the same fate. And he wondered then, had he been yet another man in her life to let her down? Her father with his abandonment, Helgi with his death, and now him, a friend, with his judgment of her. He cringed at the memory of the hurt he had seen in her at his reaction to her pregnancy, at his angry, hard words.

Albert closed his eyes, pushing the thoughts aside. The seabirds' persistent squawking came to his notice, carried on the wind from the cliffs, where they nested nearby. The sound of the ocean, the ceaseless lapping of waves against the shoreline, came to him too, but then his attention was diverted to the muffled voices of women coming from inside the croft.

"*Mamma*, she has a place with Albert at Suðureyri." It was Rúna and her tone was somewhat incredulous. This piqued his interest, and he directed all his concentration to the conversation taking place.

"And he's a good man, but I won't have my grandchild raised fatherless, treated as inferior to the those around him. Magnús is thinking to take Stína as his wife, but I'll speak to Elías. He's a man now. He'll step up to raise his brother's child. He'll take her as his wife."

"*Mamma!* You'll do no such thing. Elías is only *just* a man. He's a good seven years younger than Sólveig. He can barely look a woman in the eye, let alone step up to marry one—" She scoffed.

Albert dragged himself away from the conversation, somewhat taken aback by this proposal of Elsa's but amused at the same time. Granted, it was an honourable gesture, but he couldn't see Sólveig wanting to marry a boy, even if it were to save her reputation, but then she had surprised him many times, with her outspokenness and forthrightness. She carried a calm demeanour, not too imposing with her views, but he found, if she was pushed too hard, she reacted, and that backbone of steel showed itself. He knew she was not one to be coerced into anything she felt would go against her set values, and he admired her for that. But the thought of her marrying a mere boy, though it amused him, unsettled him too, as the thought of her leaving them did, after all she had seen them through. He let his gaze fall once more onto that lonesome figure out there in the open, vulnerable and exposed as she was, and he knew if nothing else, he just wanted to do right by her, to see her taken care of as she had cared for them.

⚜

Sólveig

Sólveig's visit to Keflavík was difficult. Just being at the farm around Helgi's family brought back many tender memories, but in coming, she also felt closer to Helgi somehow. She sensed him in the spirit of the place, this place he had been born to and raised in. Their time together had been too short—less than a year. It made her aware of how little time she'd had to truly know him.

Standing by his grave, the numb sorrow within burned into a fierce ball of anguish radiating from her chest. It didn't tear at her as it had done that day on the beach. It was a quiet, slow-burning sort of anguish, and she simply let it wash over her—the hurt and loneliness of his absence. She felt so defeated by his death somehow. She longed to hear his voice, to feel those mossy-green eyes of his heavy on her, to catch again the way his lips tilted in that lopsided smirk of his as he called her *Midwife*.

"Oh, Helgi, what am I to do now? I don't know if I can do this without you," she admitted out loud. With Helgi, she'd had a small taste of belonging to someone, of truly mattering to someone. They'd had plans. She would start her own little family with him. Her. A wife. The wife of someone, and he, the father of her children. Yes, her children would have a father—a somewhat foreign notion to her. Her hand lay gently over her stomach, where his child grew, where life and hope grew despite death, and though this new life filled her with a strength and will to carry on, it didn't stop the way it hurt, or the way she felt so cheated of sharing her life with him. She let the wind carry her woe, resigning to the bitter truth that there was no use in wanting so hard. She knew it wouldn't bring him back. She had tasted loneliness before. In fact, it was a feeling she was used to—this feeling of facing the world with only herself to rely on. Nothing was certain in life, she of all people knew that. With her mother gone and then her sister and her father's abandonment, it was a familiar, bitter feeling, and though she was scared, she *would* carry on, despite it. She would focus on her baby, on nurturing and bringing forth what remained of her Helgi—of the gift he had left her.

Elsa had teared up at the news of her expected grandchild. There was no judgment there, only a sort of pity for her, that things had turned out the way they had. The older woman even pulled her aside and reassured her that she would always have a place with them, and knowing that her son would live on in her grandchild had brought her a sense of peace. Sólveig, too, felt a sense of peace around her journey to Keflavik, and she was thankful to Albert for keeping his promise to take her.

25

Sólveig

It was Sunday morning, three days after their return from Keflavík, and the household was finishing up with their church readings.

With the priest only paying rare visits into their community, they were well used to practising their Lutheran faith in their own homes. Albert led the procession in the *baðstofa*, reading from the book of Psalms. Dísa, who was in training to take her confirmation in the coming years, took up some of the readings, the words read clearly and carefully, and many songs were sung.

Since delivering María's child in June, there had been no new births and no weddings. Einar and Rúna had delayed marrying, but there was news that Séra Stefán would visit the valley in November. He had only come in September with some of the rare fine weather to bless those that had been laid to rest, the people of the community too busy to stop, even on a Sunday, making use of the pause in rain while it lasted.

When the service ended, the household stirred back to life, the work maids off to prepare the midday meal. It was a day of rest, but a woman's duties were never done. For the work maids, there was still food to prepare and the men to see to. While the others took up books to read or small items of work, Sólveig lay Stella and Lína in her cot, sitting over them as they drifted off into a light day sleep, as babies needed. After much wriggling about and babbling, Stella fell asleep, and Lína was just drifting off when Albert asked her to take a walk with him.

Sólveig was apprehensive. It sounded serious. Had he changed his mind after all about her staying on at Suðureyri?

They strolled along the shoreline, in the direction of the sea croft, the wind pushing softly against them. The slopes of the mountain Spillir running alongside them were dappled with white where snow had fallen of late.

"Are you well, Sólveig? Are you happy with us here at Suðureyri?" Albert suddenly asked beside her.

There was a softness about his expression as he considered her, and she replied, feeling a sort of tenderness for the man, remembering how he had swallowed his own grief at Keflavík so that she'd had the chance to face hers. "The people here have become like family to me. *Já*, Albert. I am content."

He nodded, seemingly pleased by her answer. His hands were in his pockets as they casually strolled along the track, but he wore no hat, and the slight wind ruffled strands of his wheat-coloured hair. His beard had grown too. Krissa would be clucking her tongue at the sight of his unkempt state, but she was not here to see to him, and he'd brushed off all offers to tidy him up.

They continued along in silence, the sounds of the fjord cast into focus, the sharp cries of the seabirds, the gentle lull of the sea, their own footsteps, side by side. Sólveig waited patiently for him to begin again, knowing there was surely something important on his mind. She sensed he was trying to build up to it, that he had sought the outdoors for privacy. It was too easy to overhear conversations not meant for stray ears in the confines of the croft. Outside, only the wind, the mountain and the sea would bear silent witness to secrets told. They passed the sea croft and headed towards the end of the fjord, where the land met the wild open sea. It stretched out before them, a heavy mass of bluish grey, throwing itself against the rocks below them in a steady rhythm. To their right was the narrow path to Staður and Vatnadalur along the base of the cliff, but Albert stopped finally at the junction, gazing out into the distance, where they simply stood side by side for some time.

When he spoke his tone was soft, almost reflective. "There's a sense of peace in watching the sea, Sólveig, the steady, never-ceasing ebb and flow of it."

"Já," she conceded, sensing its power where she stood, then chuckled lightly as she added, "from land, I will agree with you, but out there, in her grasp, I'm afraid I have a much different view of her."

"True, she's a dangerous beauty." Albert smiled in turn, his eyes crinkling at the edges as he continued, "And she deserves our respect, but she keeps us going. When the land fails us, we must look to the sea. There she is beckoning us to her, to search her depths for our sustenance."

He turned to her then, all humour gone from his eyes, but they were soft as they held hers. "You know we must keep going, Sólveig. As hard as it feels at times. We are but the cliffs that are shaped and changed over time by the sea, and life has certainly twisted our path, has it not?"

"What is it you're trying to say, Albert?"

He took her hands in his. "I would see you looked after, you and your unborn child. Helgi was a good man, and I know he'd want to see you and his child cared for."

"Albert?" She was utterly surprised by him.

"I would be that man for you, Sólveig."

Not long ago, he had scolded her on her impropriety, and now here he was offering himself as a husband. She sighed, drawing out her breath, feeling both gratitude for him and pity. She squeezed his gloved hands in hers, meeting his eyes. Sadness lingered in their depths, but she could see that he was serious.

"You would marry me? But how can you ask me this when you're still grieving so sorely for Krissa?"

"I know this feels too soon. It is too soon, but the girls, they need a mother, and I'm not sure how much longer their *amma* will be with us to help me raise them. You must know it too. You must sense that she isn't long for this world."

She nodded. "I see how she grows weaker, but is that a reason for us to wed? What would people think?"

His eyes were steadfast as they held hers. "I don't make this decision lightly. I will step in as father to your child. You'll have my loyalty and my protection always. You've become a friend I can't do without." Hope sat bright in his eyes, but his Adam's apple bobbed in his throat, betraying his nerves.

Could she really marry another? Wasn't this all just too soon?

She shook her head, uncertain. "Albert, my heart is still sore for Helgi. I—I don't know if I will ever marry now, and to be a true wife to you—"

"It need only be a marriage in name and friendship," he cut in. "I don't expect you to carry out your marital duties, if that's what you're concerned about?"

"Oh, Albert." Her face grew warm at this suggestion, and she cast her gaze down at their interlinked hands, unable to meet his eyes.

He squeezed her hands in his. "Let us help each other. Let me do this for you and you can do this for me."

She struggled with the jumble of emotion that rose within her and wasn't sure what to say.

"Just think about it, Sólveig. Will you do that for me?" he asked. "At least just think on it?"

She nodded. That was all she could give him for now.

"Come, let me walk you back. We need to keep this cold at bay."

"You go on ahead, Albert. You've given me much to consider. I'll follow shortly." He nodded and left her, but with his absence came an overwhelming turmoil of emotion, and she was suddenly unsure of everything. It was as if she were the sea, as if those waves were her emotions being thrown against the rocks below her. They were in such a state at Albert's unexpected offer of marriage.

Sólveig walked the slope of the mountain, finding the spot hidden from view of the farmhouse that looked out into the fjord. The wind lashed at her this high up. It was cool on her cheek, and she was still puffing when she found a seat on a soft bed of moss. She closed her eyes, breathing in the cool air, allowing herself to remember, to remember that day on this mountain, in this very same spot, where she had farewelled Helgi, not knowing it was the last she would ever see of him alive.

Could she marry Albert? It felt like a betrayal to Helgi, so soon after his passing, and what would Krissa think, Albert marrying Sólveig?

She sighed deeply and wrapped her arms around her raised knees, resting her head on them—well, they weren't here to give her that answer, she thought wryly.

It had taken much of Albert to ask her this. She knew Albert didn't love her, not like that, and though he was an attractive man, she'd never seen Albert that way, in the way she thought of a husband, like she did of Helgi, who had made her heart beat fast and her belly flutter when he kissed her. But she knew that marriage wasn't always about love. Sometimes it was about survival. Albert was a friend, and she never thought she'd be faced with this sort of decision. She knew it to be true what Albert said. They had to keep going. She had to move forward. She needed to think on her future, on her child's future. With Helgi gone and Sólveig unwed, would she be looked down upon, her child considered a bastard in the eyes of others? Could she repeat her own fate with her child? Would she even be allowed to keep her child, or would the authorities take her baby from her, as they had taken her away from her own mother? She couldn't afford to care for a child and herself on her meagre midwife wages. And what would happen to her baby if she died delivering it?

With these questions suddenly came an overwhelming sense of understanding for her own mother, how she must have suffered being pregnant and unwed, not once but twice. The only difference was that her mother had never been presented with the opportunity she had now, of having a man of good standing offering to marry her regardless of her condition.

Albert had offered to be father to her child. That was no small thing.

Sólveig sniffed, wiping her eyes, and stood up. She was tired of the tears, of the sadness and helplessness, of the constant worry. Here was a solution that presented itself, a solution that saved her the shame she had always worried would follow her—the fate her mother had been subject to, that she had suffered growing up. At thirty-two, Albert was almost seven years older than she was, but she trusted him. He had been good to her. She knew he would be respectful and not cross any bounds with her. He kept his word. She knew this of him. She had seen the love and respect he gave Krissa in their marriage. He was a good father to his children and made sure they never went hungry, and she knew with grounding certainty that he would be good to her child too. He would step into this father role as he did with his role as a sort of father for their community, as *hreppstjóri*. Did her child not deserve that? A father. She had certainly felt the loss of her own in her life.

Sólveig made her way back down the mountain, feeling set in her decision. She would accept his offer. She would become the second wife of Albert Jónsson.

26

Albert

"You can't marry Sólveig, *Pabbi*," cried Dísa. "You already have a wife. *Mamma* is your wife."

Albert sat on his cot, feeling somewhat defeated. He rubbed a hand over his eyes, taking a deep breath to still his impatience with the child. She lay in her grandmother's arms, tears rolling in streams down her flushed cheeks.

With the chill of winter upon them, the old woman was too unwell to leave her bed for long. She was pale, her lips tinged blue with the sickness of the lungs, and though already thin, her bones protruded from her papery skin at sharp angles. The cough, when it took hold of her, shook her so utterly that it drained all her strength, and she simply slept most days.

Sólveig had accepted his offer of marriage, and Albert had wanted some time alone to tell Dísa, but Tobba insisted that she be there with him when he told the child of his plans. His mother-in-law was at first shocked by the news, and hurt had flashed in her eyes. "I knew it would come eventually, but I didn't expect it so soon," she remarked morosely. "It's been barely three months since we buried Krissa."

A sudden rush of guilt washed over Albert, but he pushed away at it with irritation. "You think that doesn't weigh on me every day?"

"You do this for the midwife?" Tobba asked, her tone full of accusation. "People will think the baby is yours, that you were unfaithful in your marriage."

"They all know she was to marry Helgi. I do this for our family, for the girls. Will you continue to run this household, step in, in place of Krissa? You haven't left your bed in days." He cast his gaze away, looking instead at his hands, away from the hurt in her eyes, willing himself patience and delicacy. "I need her to stay, Tobba. I trust her, and she's capable and kind to my daughters. I must think on our future, on how we are to carry on. Her needs match my own. That is all."

"You must do as you will, then." She nodded curtly in confirmation. "And you shall hear no more of my objection, but I warn you, now, that this news will not come easy to Dísa. I will be with you when you tell her."

That had been the day before, and Albert watched the old woman now, his daughter laying with her head on her lap, Tobba's long, knobbly fingers running down the length of her fair hair in tender strokes.

"I know, my darling. This is hard for you to understand. Your *mamma* is gone to the Lord and I'm an old woman now. I'll not be around forever and your *pabbi* needs help with Lína."

Dísa sniffed and sat up quickly, looking at Albert with desperate, hopeful eyes. "I will care for her. I can do it. I'm eleven now, *Pabbi*. I'm big enough now. Please, *Pabbi*, please."

Seeing her like this, hearing the way her voice cracked as she pleaded with him, almost broke his resolve.

Despite Tobba's warning, he hadn't been sure how his daughter would take the news. He knew she was fond of the midwife, and Sólveig had only ever been kind and patient with the girl, as she helped her with the babies, or hovered over the woman, questioning her about the herbs she dried and prepared in the storeroom.

Yes, Dísa was eleven years old, capable and mature in many ways, but he wouldn't rob her youth from her that way. It was true, he'd known children as young as her to take the role of mother for younger siblings when death met the family, but he'd felt with a firm knowing that it wasn't her place to step into that role. This wasn't her burden to take on. It would force her to grow up too quickly. By God, children were given little chance for childhood as it was with the hardships life brought along, he thought. He could see now that his decision to marry Sólveig would hurt the child, but what was he to do? He was head of the family, and acting on the wilful whims of the child wasn't an option. Sometimes hard choices had to be made, and they all had to live with them. In time, he hoped that Dísa would come to accept it and understand that it was for the best.

The child looked at him, her stark blue eyes shining with tears, so full of hope and dread combined.

"I know you could do it, Dísa, but this isn't what I want for you. Lína needs a big sister, just as much as she needs a mother. This is my decision. We must do what's best for our family. It doesn't mean that I love your *mamma* any less. Do you understand, child?"

Albert noticed the change in her expression. But what he saw did not comfort him. The dispelled hope on her dainty features transformed into a pinched, angry scowl, and she puffed herself up before him, her lips wobbling with emotion, her hands on her hips.

"Well, she shan't be my mother," she proclaimed, pushing past him before he could stop her.

"Dísa!" he called sternly after her, stunned at her outburst, shocked that she should react so strongly when before she had always been so obedient and courteous.

"Let her go, Albert." Tobba stayed him with a hand on his, adding gently, "She needs time."

27

November 1882

Sólveig

Four months after the measles devastated their community, not one but two sombre unions took place at the small turf church at Staður, a small spark of hope and light filtering through the dark cloud that hovered over the people. It was, after all, vital that they marry and repopulate or simply perish.

Sólveig and Albert would take their vows along with Rúna and Einar, who were to have married in July. Wedding licences were bought, and Séra Stefán was collected from Holt to perform the binding vows, ferried over by boat the day before the weddings were to take place.

The sky was heavy the morning of the weddings, the threat of snow lingered in its ashen, cloudy depths, the wind their constant companion on their journey to church. Sólveig sat on Albert's blue roan mare, her legs crossed demurely over to one side of the saddle, her black skirt cascaded down over her stockinged legs, the tips of her sheepskin shoes poking out. She wore her new wedding clothes, the ones she'd spent much time preparing for her marriage to Helgi. A black jacket with velvet cuffs and plackets, fit snugly over her arms and chest, the white chemise tucked beneath revealed at the opening of the jacket, and she wore the silk scarf Helgi had gifted her, tied into a neat bow at her throat. She had questioned whether she could wear the scarf. After all, it was meant for her union with Helgi, but it was too beautiful not to use, and Rúna had said as much to her, insisting Helgi would want her to wear it, no matter who she was marrying. Albert told her she looked beautiful as he lifted her gently onto the horse before they left, and she'd taken the compliment because for the first time in a long while, Sólveig did feel beautiful. Her breasts were fuller with pregnancy, and she wore the skirt high, tied at the waist with a white apron, so that it sat over the increasingly noticeable swell of her belly. She was early into her fifth month carrying the child, the evidence of it still hidden somewhat, however, it was certainly more evident when she sat.

She moved with the rhythm of the horse she rode, focusing on the steady clip clop of hooves on the ground instead of what was to come.

"Relax, Sólveig. You'll be fine," Rúna called to her from the horse walking beside hers, reaching to take her hand.

Was Sólveig's apprehension that evident? She sighed and smiled softly at her friend, who, regardless of her not marrying Helgi, would become her sister-in-law through her marriage to Albert, a fact that pleased her much. Rúna sat on Albert's dun mare, her own betrothed leading her. It was clear for all how smitten Einar was with her, and it was hard not to notice the tender touches and smiles they rewarded each other with, and though she was happy for her friend, it also just made the lack of it starker between herself and Albert.

Rúna was a vision of flushed beauty, dressed finely in her *peysuföt*, a yellow silk scarf with a matching apron. They had spent the morning plaiting each other's hair into an assortment of long braids that were looped back into the hair and tucked into a *skotthúfa*, a black shallow cap sewn of velvet attached to a long black silk tassel running down the side of the cap, sitting off-centre. The bridal party was at the head of the procession of people from their household.

Sólveig let go of her friend's hand, appreciating the gesture of encouragement, and her gaze settled instead on the tall man in front of her leading her horse. After today she would call him husband. Albert Jónsson. She'd never seen him so finely dressed. In a dark-grey suit with a fitted vest, and a white kerchief in the front right pocket. His *hreppstjóri* hat sat straight on his head, giving the impression once again of him being a sea captain. She remembered thinking that the first time she met him, waiting for her in Ísafjörður, just over a year earlier, and she mused now over the strangeness of life—how she would have been astonished to know then that she would become his wife. He was certainly an attractive man who drew attention with his presence, but it was more subdued somehow, not demanded. He'd always given her the impression that he was a man who knew himself. He was a capable man, as much of the land as he was of the sea, and though he'd been somewhat lost these past few months with the deaths of his wife and child, she was, in fact, impressed by him, by his thoughtfulness, that he was willing to step down this new path with her with such a sense of surety. It calmed her own anxiety over the leap they were taking for one another.

Dísa hadn't taken the news of their marriage well. The poor child was still grieving. She refused to attend, deciding instead to stay at home with Tobba and old Leifur to help with the babies, and perhaps it was the child's disapproval that played on Sólveig's mind as they made their way amongst the crowd of people outside the church just before the ceremony.

A group of work maids were gathered, and she noticed at the edge of her vision how they watched her, hungrily eyeing the rise of her belly where she sat on the horse as it stopped near them. Albert lifted her from her mount and Einar did the same for Rúna. Her friend was quick to make her way over to Stína, who was waiting with Magnús and Elsa near the entrance of the church, ready to coddle little Örnólfur. Sólveig took a little longer to readjust herself after the ride, straightening her clothes, tying her apron tighter, waiting for Albert as he and Einar tethered the horses nearby.

The feminine voices drifted over to her, the work maids not trying in the least to lower their voices, though they knew she stood near enough to hear them.

"Look at her, standing there all high and mighty," said one. "The rumours are true then, there's a babe growing in her belly."

"But wasn't she to marry that workman of Björn's—Helgi, wasn't it?" asked another.

"*Já*, and I warn you, don't let your sweetheart near her."

She was shocked to hear Inga's voice amongst them. Did the girl truly dislike her so much that she would say such a thing about her? They were no great friends, but the young woman had been civil enough with her at home.

"That's right! She'd told you to stay away from Helgi and then up and took him for herself, didn't she?"

"Probably did the same to Krissa, right under her nose, before she died—God bless her soul. It's his child she carries, why else would he marry her?" Inga added cruelly.

What lies! How could she? How could Inga say such vile things about her? Sólveig turned her back to the women, trying to control the way her hands trembled, but her resolve crumbled. Perhaps marrying Albert was a mistake. She moved away from the women, Inga's words going over in her mind, the hateful gossip of the maids taking her straight back to her childhood, when her cousins would tease her, naming her the daughter of a whore, but she was tired of playing the victim. No more would she cower under hurtful words, and before she had really thought it through, she found herself marching towards the group of gossipers, unable to control herself, her fury blinding her. Her hand met with skin, Inga's cheek flaming crimson and the woman held her face looking stunned, the other maids gasping in horror.

"How *dare* you? You know perfectly well that this child is Helgi's. He chose me, Inga!" she yelled, pointing roughly at her breast. "Helgi chose me, not you, and you can hate me all you like, but you'll not drag Albert's and Krissa's good names through the mud, do you hear me?" She puffed hard, sensing her friend suddenly beside her, along with Albert and Einar.

"You should be ashamed of yourselves, the lot of you, and you can think again about stepping inside that church," said Rúna, crossing her arms.

"Go on home, Inga," Albert said tightly, his hand at Solveig's elbow, and the red-faced women dispersed quickly, unable to meet Albert's eyes. He turned to her. "Are you okay, Sólveig?" But her bravado and anger were spent, and she found herself pulling away from him, away from the stares and disapproving faces of the onlookers, walking faster and faster, until she met with the stone wall at the back of the church. The sob she'd held in finally escaped in a rush of breath and tears, as hurt and uncertainty overwhelmed her.

"Sólveig?" Albert's voice came from behind. It was tender and cautious.

She turned suddenly, blurting in a puff of breath and misery, "You don't want to marry me, Albert."

"Don't I?"

"You think to save my reputation, but don't you see?" she pleaded, her gaze finally meeting his. "That I tarnish yours. I'm no good."

"So, people are talking," he stated, as if it mattered little to him.

"You don't understand. The things they're saying—the work maids, the housewives! They talk as if, as if—" She couldn't even say it. "As if you were unfaithful to Krissa with me."

"I see," he said, matter-of-fact.

"It was as you said, Albert, when you found out about my pregnancy. Your good name is being tarnished."

He puffed out an exasperated breath, shaking his head. "They're just words, Sólveig. The shock and gossip will die down with time. We know the truth of it, you and I, and I'll be ready to straighten it out with anyone should they dare face me with these accusations." He raised his brows at her, a smirk playing on his lips. "But by the looks of it just now, seems to me like you can handle your own."

"I was right mad, and I let my temper get the better of me," she admitted, feeling the shame of that public spectacle ride her now. "Oh, I don't think I can go in there. I can't face them all after that." She buried her face in her hands.

He sighed, his fingers peeling her hands away from her face, tilting her chin up, so that she was forced to look at him. "I didn't expect today to be easy for either of us. To be honest, I never thought to be here again, so soon, and I'm fairly shaking in my boots, knowing I'm about to walk down that aisle again."

"Really?" A sense of ease and pity washed through her with this revelation of his feelings. "You seem much better held together than me."

The church bell tolled, the sound startling her. It was time. Knowing the ceremony was imminent made her heart race and her palms clammy.

Albert held out his hand to her. "Take my hand, Sólveig, and hold it. I'll not break today, nor turn back, nor doubt, so long as you're holding it. Do you think you can bear it? I know I can, if you stand by me."

She nodded her head and took his offered hand.

They were the last ones to enter the church, holding hands as they were, and they took their seats, Sólveig on the eastern bench, with Rúna and the grooms on the western side.

Mass was conducted, and then the marriages took place as the couples were brought together one by one before the congregation. Sólveig and Albert were first; as *hreppstjóri* for the community, he took precedent. Sólveig took the strength Albert offered her in the clasping of her hands in his. Séra Stefán spoke the holy words over them, joining them as husband and wife. Sólveig found herself observing the smallness of her hands in his, how broad they were, work worn and calloused, the veins standing like fine rope under his skin, and she sensed the strength in them, as they were, wrapped in hers. Albert was a whole head taller than Sólveig, so that her eyes sat level with his chin, and she had to tilt her head to look up at him. His mouth was soft, but there were small signs about him that gave away his nerves, the beads of sweat at his temples, and the way the muscle in his jaw twitched. This step into another marriage was just as hard for him, he had said to her, and she held onto him for her sake as well as his. Together they could get through this. It was the best way forward, a way to heal the fracture death had caused in both his life and hers, a way for their children to stay with them and not be sent to other homes.

Time stood still as Albert produced a ring. It surprised her. She had expected no such trinket. Jewellery was a frivolous expense, especially in these times, and she was touched by the thought that he had likely fashioned it himself. He slipped the shiny metal band onto her fourth finger, his warm blue eyes holding hers as he spoke the binding vows, his tone mellowed and utterly sincere, and she returned them, her voice coming strong and steady, offering her promise to him.

The thin band was cool against her skin. His contract to her. Their union for the sake of survival.

The priest pronounced them married, and Albert leaned in, his lips soft on hers, and her heart fluttered just a little, a stirring of something, even as broken as it was.

❖

Sólveig was tired after the day's events, her body weary, her heart sore, but sleep evaded her. There were so many thoughts running through her mind. She was a married woman now. A wife, and yet here she lay in the same bed she always had, next to baby Stella, while her husband slept in the cot at the opposite end of the room. As one, Albert and Sólveig had decided it was for the best, with Dísa struggling over the changes and Sólveig heavy with child as she was.

It had been a subdued affair after the weddings. The folk of Suðureyri walked home together, with those from Keflavík that had come over for the wedding joining them at Suðurereyi for toasts to their health and happiness and a bowl of *grjónagrautur*—rice pudding with raisins and coffee—before they returned home across the water.

The sound of sheets rustling on the bed opposite hers pulled Sólveig out of her reverie. She stilled, her breath catching in her throat. The sounds were accompanied by heavy breathing and the soft moans of Einar and Rúna coming together, binding their own marriage with the joining of their bodies, and she tried not let it bother her. Instead, she closed her eyes, feeling childish as she covered her hands over her ears to block out the sounds. She told herself she was relieved Albert wouldn't seek her in the marriage bed. This is what they had agreed to—a marriage in name and friendship only. But it didn't stop her feeling the loss of her sweetheart Helgi, feeling somewhat cheated of her wedding day and the solace of coming together in married bliss.

The room grew quiet once more, but she was still wide awake. She held her hand up, flexing her fingers before her in the dark, and her thumb brushed over the ring on her fourth finger, feathery light, but solid and binding as the vows she had spoken this day. A man's offering of a ring symbolized his commitment and loyalty. Albert had promised today to give her that, as she had done to him, but he would not share his body with hers, and she couldn't help but feel a little empty, a little lonely, in the room full of people, as if everything had changed and yet nothing at all.

28

Sólveig

Over the following weeks after their wedding, Sólveig and Albert found themselves adjusting to each other in their new role as husband and wife. Their interactions were polite and almost timid at first, but with time, they were able to slip back into a respectful and easy friendship. Sometimes Sólveig found herself even questioning what had changed between herself and Albert, apart from the ring on her finger and the new set of keys jangling at her waistline. She was, after all, the new *húsfreyja* of Suðureyri, mistress of the household. It was a fact not lost upon Inga, who, after her hurtful remarks at church, was suddenly very obliging towards Sólveig in the days following the wedding. She even went so far as to apologise to Sólveig. When Sólveig remarked on it to Albert, he surprised her by telling her that he'd had words with Inga the day after the wedding.

"I merely reminded her who the woman was that held her fate in her hands, and that it would pay to make peace with her, if she wanted to stay on as a work maid here."

Sólveig appreciated Albert stepping in and supporting her, and the tension between her and Inga had finally eased a little. It did bring to light, however, her new responsibility at Suðureyri. She had never been a *húsfreyja*, the keeper of the keys for the pantry. The responsibility lay solely on her now to manage the work maids along with the children's learning, the upkeep of the croft, the food they prepared and stored and the hosting of guests. She also took over the maintenance of Albert's and the children's clothing, spinning and weaving cloth, mending and making sure their clothes were dry for the next day, and though she was pleased with the rise in her status, she had to admit, even if it was only to herself, that she was a smite daunted by it all.

⊹

Albert

In mid-December, Albert took to his *hreppstjóri* duties, collecting the yearly census. It would take two days to complete, but it required of him much walking and trips in the boat, so long as the weather allowed him to get over to the crofts on the other side of the fjord. There were thirteen farms in their parish, and it was a good opportunity for him to see how the people of his community were faring since the measles outbreak.

The morning of his departure, Albert found Sólveig in the storeroom going through her supply of herbs, an assortment of mess before her. Her coffee-coloured hair was plaited into two long braids; one ran down her back, and the other sat over a shoulder. She wore her usual black skirt with the green chequered apron, and a beige shawl criss-crossed her chest. It was cold in the croft, the only heat coming from the kitchen hearth and the body warmth in the *baðstofa*. She hummed to herself, and Albert stood in the doorway a moment, enjoying the soft, feminine sound. He couldn't deny that she was an attractive woman, the long, dark waves of her hair he had seen on occasion let loose, cradled a heart-shaped face with finely arched brows, a dainty nose and a lightly dimpled chin, but it was her smile that was her true beauty. When she smiled, it was as if her face lit up with all the love and warmth of the world in it, and he couldn't help but want to be near her. He sighed, guilt riding him at such thoughts. Besides, he knew he'd receive no such smile from her at this news he brought. He hadn't pre-warned her of his plans, and he wasn't sure how she would react. He had an inkling she'd get it into her head to accompany him. She had mentioned one too many times the desire to pay a visit to Björg's children at Vatnadalur.

Sólveig turned suddenly, catching him leaning in the doorway, watching her.

"How long have you been standing there?" she asked, a coy smile sitting lightly on her full lips.

"Not long. You have a sweet voice, Sólveig."

Her cheeks coloured, but then she raised a brow at him as she took in his appearance. "Are you heading out, Albert?"

He was ready to walk out the door, dressed in thick layers to keep out the cold, his *hreppstjóri* hat on his head and a thin leather satchel crossed over his body containing his paperwork, feathered pen and ink prepared for writing the census lists.

"*Já*, just the usual census rounds. I'm heading into Vatnadalur and Staðardalur and I'll be home before dark."

Her eyes flashed with excitement. "Well, why didn't you say so earlier?" And before he could answer, she wiped her hands on her apron, making to pack away her goods. "Oh, I've been so wanting to see Katla and the children at Hraunakot. To see how they're faring and take over a collection of clothing and food for them. If you'll just wait a moment, I'll get my shawl and—"

"This isn't an invitation, Sólveig," he blurted, stopping her before she could go on.

"I'll be no trouble to you, Albert. I so want to see the children, Herdís and Anna María." She shook her head. "Poor Herdís stuck with old Júlíus. We must ensure he's not working her too hard. I am worried for her there. She'd have been better off with Katla and Grímur."

He groaned inwardly, wishing now that he had just gone and left a message with Rúna to give to her of his absence. "I'll be sure to check on them, Sólveig, and pass on whatever you have ready to give them. If the walking were easier, I'd gladly take you, but as the weather stands with the heavy layover of snow, you'd only overexert yourself. And besides, I need to get this task done before the weather changes again for the worst." He chuckled, shaking his head lightly, trying to make light of his refusal to take her. "And you are trouble, woman. You'd most certainly slow me down with that little waddle you've started walking with."

"What waddle? I don't walk with a waddle." She seemed genuinely offended. "Is it because I'm with child?"

"Of course, it's because you're with child," he clarified.

"Albert, what do you think I'd have to do if I were called out now to a birth this very moment?"

"This isn't that time now, is it?" he replied evenly.

"I feel fine. I know I can walk it. The child's not grown so big that I am easily exerted with walking."

He'd heard enough, knowing there was no use in arguing with her. She would never concede to being a hindrance to him in the heavy snow out there. "If you'll ready the pack for them, I'll be sure to give them your best regards," he said instead, settling the matter and turning for the door.

"So, you'll not let me come with you?"

He stopped but didn't turn to face her. "*Nei*, Sólveig. I won't."

"Do you realise how stubborn you're being?"

He turned then, feeling exasperated by her. He'd had enough. Couldn't she see that he was trying to keep her safe? To keep her baby safe? He took another deep breath, trying to still his frustration with her, but he knew that perhaps he needed to be stern with her. He was her husband after all. "I would think as the new mistress of Suðureyri, you'd have enough to keep you here with two babies and a sick old woman to look after." His tone was hard. She looked at him as if he had taken his hand to her. "I need you here, Sólveig, not traipsing around in the snow with me, as good as your intentions may be," he added with a little more gentleness.

⁂

Albert stepped out into the frosty air, making tracks in the heavy snow. It came up to his knees at times and it was arduous walking. When he traversed the cliff road, the ocean was an angry swell, throwing itself heavily onto the path. It had frozen in places, where the sea had melted the snow and frozen it again, and he had to watch his step, lest he find himself in the swirling depths of that angry swell. He felt justified in his decision to make Sólveig stay, but he didn't enjoy how the guilt nagged him now. The look of hurt in her eyes tormented him. He'd not meant the condescending tone he had taken on as he spoke those words to her—*as the new mistress of Suðureyri*— and he cringed as he thought on it. It was the first time they had disagreed heatedly since their wedding.

She was impulsive at times. Ready to throw herself into any situation, but there was always good intention behind it. That wasn't something he could fault her for. She had a heart of gold, that woman, but it meant that sometimes she put others' needs before her own. He couldn't stand the thought of her having to deal with more loss, and perhaps he was being overprotective of her, but he wanted her to have this baby she carried. This child Helgi had left her. He wouldn't put her at risk because he'd agreed to her accompanying him, and wind up exerting herself on the hard trek it was to get to Vatnadalur during the winter months.

Thankfully Sólveig had relented, though he could see how she bit her tongue, her annoyance with him simmering just below the surface. She had even allowed him to kiss her in farewell, a quick peck on the cheek, and she had reluctantly wished him a safe journey, passing him the pack of goods she had gathered for the children—knitted sweaters, socks and shoes, some milk and bread. He recalled Sólveig's argument about being called out to a birth as he rounded the headland, heading into the valley, and it was then that he found himself thinking with a sinking feeling in the pit of his belly that it was only a matter of time before she would be called to her duty as midwife. He just prayed that the call wouldn't come until after she had delivered her own child sometime in March.

29

January 1883

Sólveig

During the first week of 1883, they were hit with the full force of winter, a raging wind and heavy snowfall. Sólveig felt its wrath in the constant rattle of the window frames and the slamming of doors. It howled against the croft, its rage directed upon them relentlessly, and she found herself contemplating the will of nature, its necessity to constantly challenge them. But they held tight. Food had been stored for winter. What little hay there was would feed the ever-decreasing size of their herd of sheep. The two households kept themselves indoors, only leaving the croft if they absolutely had to. Sólveig cared for Tobba, saw to her needs and made sure she was comfortable, dosing her with the supply of Hoffman's drops she had to help her sleep or brewing her *blóðberg* tea. That was all she could do for the old woman, who lay weak and sickly in her cot, and they all wondered how much longer she would hold on.

On his census rounds earlier in December, Albert had informed Sólveig of a woman at Gilsbrekka, by the name of Arína, who was heavy with child. Albert had managed to get out of her that the child was due to arrive early in the new year, likely in February, and they all waited anxiously for the call to come.

The call finally did come and, to their dismay, at the worst possible time. It was the third week into January when a boy arrived at the household at Suðureyri in the late hours of the night, his sharp taps on the window stirring up the dogs and startling the whole household from their slumber.

Sólveig rose with Albert while Rúna settled the babies and hushed old Leifur over his mutterings about it being one of the *Huldufólk* come. But it was Sveinn from Gilsbrekka, and as the tall, ruddy-cheeked lad undressed of his layers in the entrance of the croft, he told them how a blizzard sat on his tail the whole way. The wind started to rage around the house as they spoke as if taunting them, daring them to venture outdoors. He had come for the midwife.

"You came alone?" Albert asked.

"*Já,*" said Sveinn. He looked no more than fourteen, only just a man. "My step-father, Bjarni, is over the mountain at Ós in Bólungarvík, fishing all winter from there. It's just *Mamma*, little Hannes and me."

Gilsbrekka was Albert's childhood home. It was the next farm over from Botn, where Jakob and María lived, but on the northern side of the fjord. It was at least a three-hour journey by foot, perhaps longer in the weather that raged.

"When the pains came on this evening," Sveinn continued, "*Mamma* asked me to fetch María from Botn, and she delivered the babe right quick, but something isn't right. María sent for you. The pains are still something awful, and she said, the pla—Sorry, I can't right remember what she called it."

"The placenta?" she supplied for him.

"*Já*, that's the word. She said it was urgent. Oh, but you must come, I beg you," he said, worry etched into his handsome young face.

How could she not go? Sólveig nodded. "I'll make myself ready."

Albert left them abruptly, stepping outside into the dark night and returning to the room, minutes later, with a gust of wind and snow. Her husband shook his head, his expression stern as his gaze met hers, but he addressed the boy.

"You made it to us in good time, Sveinn, but I'm afraid Sólveig can't go anywhere with this storm upon us."

Sólveig blinked hard. She was indignant that he replied so on her behalf. This wasn't a choice he could make for her. This woman needed her. Arína's life was at risk, and they couldn't afford to wait too long.

"A trip across the fjord would mean you could be there in less than an hour, but it's too dangerous to risk the journey by boat. The landing would be hard in this wind," Albert clarified for them, and he continued, "but with this storm upon us now, you'd have to skirt the fjord. Even that has its risks. The heaviness of snow on the mountains means the chance of avalanche is high, and if you can't see two steps ahead, you could just as easily walk into the ocean."

"I must return to my mother, storm or no," said Sveinn, determination set into his young face. Sólveig admired his courage. She wasn't sure about heading out into the frosty night with no moon to guide their way and the storm raging, but a stronger urge called to her. The urge to heed the call to help. She trusted Albert's judgment. He knew the land here better than most. He was good at reading the weather, but they had to go now. Lives depended on it. Could she let the boy return without her, his journey to them in vain and his mother at risk? No. They must go now, regardless of the risks.

"Sveinn, do you think you can lead the way back to Gilsbrekka, through this weather?"

She noted the surprised look on Albert's face but focused her attention on the boy. He stood a little taller, puffed out his chest and pulled his shoulders back. "I'll do my best to find our way back."

"Let me prepare myself, then." Sólveig nodded towards Rúna, who lingered in the room where they all stood. "Go to the kitchen with Rúna to warm yourself, and we'll find you some dry socks before we head out. That's the lad," she said, sounding more confident than she felt.

"Don't look at me like that, Albert," Sólveig said, finally meeting his eyes when the others left the room. Disapproval radiated off him in waves.

"You'll not listen to your husband?" he said, his tone low and controlled, but he shook his head.

"This is my duty. This is what I came to the district to do. I must go regardless of the weather," she tried.

"I understand that, but would you just stop and think on this for a minute, Sólveig. He's just a boy. What good will you be to the woman at the bottom of the ocean or lying under a mountain of snow? Just wait. María sits with her for now. Wait for the storm to pass over us."

"Albert," she snapped impatiently. "I don't know if we have time to wait it out. The boy made it to us, did he not?" She puffed out a breath in frustration and closed the gap between them, taking his hands in hers. "Is there really no way we could manage this?" she asked, her tone low and calm. "This is my duty. I told you that if the call came, I would go, and that time has come."

Albert shook his head, pulling away from her, but not before she saw the fear in his eyes. He ran a hand through his hair in frustration. "My God, you're a stubborn woman, Sólveig." He scoffed, turning back to her, the fear replaced with anger. "And what of your duty to me, your husband? What of your duty to your unborn child, who you put at risk for this?"

She winced. She knew him only to be concerned for her, but she had already made her choice. How could she live with the knowledge of this request for her help and not heed its call? She had to cling to the hope that she would make it to Gilsbrekka, regardless of the weather.

"We could take the horse, Albert. If you're worried about the journey being too much for me in my condition."

He had been angry before, but his expression now was more of incredulity, as if he could not quite believe the words to come out of her mouth. "If *you're* worried," he mocked, repeating her words to her. "*You* should be concerned too, Sólveig. My God, woman! What is it you think could be happening over there that can't wait the hour?"

"It could be the placenta, Albert. It could be stuck or unwilling to come. That can lead to problems, to infection and childbed fever. I can't let that happen." She breathed heavily, feeling the rawness of an old wound being picked at.

He was waiting, waiting for more, and she relented. It came spilling out of her in a rush of words. "My sister, Sóffía," she finally said, the words feeling strange upon her tongue. It had been so long since she had spoken her name. "She died giving birth to her baby."

She saw the misgivings on his face as she said it, and that anger and incredulity transformed into something of pity. "I'm sorry, Sólveig. What happened?" he asked, his tone low, gentle, even.

She pulled her shawl tighter about her shoulders, suddenly feeling the cold in the room, or perhaps it was simply the memory of it all as it came rushing back to her. "She was unwed, Albert, a worker in the household at a farm in the south. The *húsfreyja*'s son got her with child, but he brushed his hands clean of her, claiming it wasn't his," she said bitterly. "When she went into labour, there were problems. The child was stuck. It presented arm first, and there was no midwife for the district, so they found a local man who'd had some success in delivering babies. He was no learned midwife but had read some outdated textbooks on midwifery. I didn't receive the news until two days had passed and the man had attempted to push the child's arm back into my sister, breaking the limb so that it hardened inside her body, killing the child." Albert winced at her words, but she kept on with her story, her voice flat. "In the end, they tore the baby from her body. When I was finally excused from the duties at my own household, I made my way to her. She was burning with fever and died just before I arrived from infection and the trauma of her child being ripped from her womb." Sólveig's chest ached with the telling of it, a rising, burning in her breast that threatened to burst from her if she didn't push it back down. She swallowed hard. "Albert, her death haunts me to this day, and I often wonder—if only there'd been a trained midwife with her, then perhaps she would still be here today," she managed as a tear escaped, rolling silently down her cheek. "Perhaps I would still have a sister."

"It's why you became a midwife," Albert stated calmly.

"Já." She wiped at the tear. "If only I'd had the training I do now, I could have been there for her. The man used an old method of delivery. If he'd had the new textbooks, he would have known that this method was no longer used." She lifted her chin and squared her shoulders back with bravado and determination. "Do you see now, Albert, why I must go? I must do my best to get to Arína, no matter the weather. I can't have a death on my conscience. Not one that could be prevented. With the weather the way it is, we may not get to Arína for hours yet as it is."

Albert rubbed a hand through his beard, his eyes searched hers as he considered her, and she could see the battle he fought with himself.

"I'll take you, then. My horse will carry you, at least as far as Botn. We've no mountains to cross tonight, but from Botn we'll have to traverse the marsh and walk to Gilsbrekka. It'll be hard going."

"Albert." She sighed, feeling relief at his relenting. "I'm not asking you to come. Sveinn can surely lead the horse. I don't know how long I'll be away. It may be a few days or even a week. You have the family here to think of. Tobba. They can't do without you."

"You'll risk yourself against my wishes, but won't allow me the same." He chuckled, though it was laced with irritation. "*Nei*, Sólveig, where you go, I go. I won't have a boy take you out in weather like this. I know the land here like the back of my hand. I could walk it blindfolded."

30

Sólveig

Albert traipsed before Sólveig, leading the horse through the blinding darkness. The wind was icy. It lashed at them and stole away their words, but they had no need for talking this night. How the man knew his way through it was a wonder to her, and she was immensely grateful that he insisted he come. They had managed to convince Sveinn to stay behind. Though reluctant, he was cajoled with a warm bowl of soup and dry clothes, finally accepting his own exhausted state, having made the journey to them in such haste.

The cold bit at Sólveig, sitting as she was on the horse, regardless of being wrapped head to toe in woollen layers and another blanket over her lap. They had smeared their feet in butter, an old remedy to keep out the cold if their shoes grew sodden with snow. She wanted to walk, knowing it would keep her warmer, it would keep the blood flowing in her limbs with constant use, but Albert was insistent upon her sitting on the horse so as not to exhaust herself too quickly.

The wool of her scarf was rough against her lips, it scratched the delicate skin of her cheeks, wrapped as it was around her head, covering both mouth and nose so that only her eyes were visible. The air was so cold it hurt to breathe, the gusts of wind so powerful, it tried to snatch away her breath. Albert was dressed the same, protecting himself against the wind and extreme cold, but she knew it wasn't for himself that he worried. She recalled how he'd fussed over her before he lifted her onto the horse and the betraying worry in his eyes before they set off.

She lowered her head into the wind, catching Albert and even the horse do the same. All around them, flakes fell thick and fast, sticking to their clothing, to the horse, to everything, blending them quickly into the landscape.

With the way the wind pushed at them, the going felt slow, the ground so thick with snow that Sólveig couldn't see the narrow track that usually skirted the fjord. How Albert could tell what was fjord and what was land, she didn't know, but she sensed they were rising higher with the coastline, the track leading them upwards, sloping with the land, leaving her nerves on edge. One misstep of the horse, and down she would go with it.

A dark shape rose before them, and Albert pulled the horse in close to a croft. Turning to her, his arms snaked about her waist, pulling her down to the ground, and they ducked under the low entrance and found themselves in a livery. The warmth of the croft enveloped her along with the overpowering stench of manure and the disgruntled noise of sheep.

"Have we arrived?" She pulled down the scarf at her mouth.

"Nowhere near. We've made it to Laugar," Albert clarified. "She's doing her damned best to slow us down out there." It was dark in the croft, and Sólveig stood by him, his face masked by the dimness of night.

"Laugar," she muttered, somewhat dispassionately. They were only halfway down the fjord. It had seemed an eternity out there already. In fair conditions, it would only have taken them an hour to walk to this farm. Sólveig stomped her legs, trying to will warmth back into them,

rubbing her hands together, her fingertips burning, even wrapped in
gloves as they were.

"Why are we stopping now?" she asked. "We must keep going."

"Settle down, woman. You may have the will of iron, but I need some
reprieve," he said sardonically. "I had to get out of that wind for just
a moment and get my bearings again. Here." He found her hands and
placed a flask into them. "Take a swig."

She opened it awkwardly with her thick mittens, thinking it just water,
but the fumes that met her burned her nostrils.

"Brennivín?"

"It'll warm you up some, and by God, you need it out there."

She hesitated. "Albert, I need a clear head."

"You also need to stay warm," he insisted, his hand under hers,
nudging the flask towards her mouth. He wasn't normally one to imbibe,
and it was certainly not a seemly thing for a woman to partake in, but
she knew that it had its benefits at times. It seemed this was one of those
times. She sighed with resignation and took a quick sip. She couldn't
help but shudder at the sharp taste, and the smooth liquid burned as it
slid down her throat, settling in her chest, but she found that he was right
once again, as in its place came a radiating warmth. Albert took the flask
from her and did the same.

"Best we keep going before the horse freezes to the post out there.
Ready, Sólveig?"

"Ready as I'll ever be."

⁂

When they arrived at the farm Botn at the bottom of the fjord, the cold
had well and truly caught up with them again. Albert tapped on the

window of the croft to wake his brother, hoping to get out of the wind, if just for a spell, to get some warm fluid into them so they had the stamina to keep on their way. Sólveig was numb to the bone. Her limbs were stiff and her back ached from tensing it against the cold, but the stop was brief, and they were on their way once more with Albert's brother Jakob for guidance across the marshland at the base of the fjord.

The path to Gilsbrekka was steep and so narrow that they had no choice but to leave the horse behind at Botn. The snow fall had stopped when they began their journey anew, but visibility was poor, and the wind still howled in mighty gusts. As they walked, Sólveig sensed the track leading them high above the sea, and then it descended suddenly in places where the frozen layers of the ocean groaned like a disgruntled troll over the pressure of the moving water beneath. It was hard going, and with the deep snow, her steps quickly tired her—one step felt as if it were two. At least the movement kept the cold at bay, but she did feel quite breathless. She was thankful Jakob had offered to carry her medical bag. It was one less burden to her.

"We've not much farther to go." Albert said to Sólveig, when they finally stopped again to catch their breaths. They sheltered in a small windbreak by a large rock on the side of the path that had at some stage tumbled down from the slopes above them.

"I'll just sit a moment, Albert." The babe in her belly hadn't stirred since she'd left Botn. She grabbed some snow, and sucked on it, sitting down before the two men on the snowy bank. Her child moved inside her, its soft nudges of stirring reassuring her that it was still with her.

Snow had melted into her outer layers, and her socks were wet, the bottom of her skirts damp. Her limbs felt heavy where she sat, and her eyelids drooped, opening and closing, her mind drifting into fogginess, the desire to simply lay herself down to sleep here, no strange notion.

"Sólveig." Someone shook her. "Get moving girl or you'll fall asleep and never wake up." It was Albert, kneeling before her, his hands about her face.

"Just for a little, I'm so tired," she muttered sleepily.

"I know." He shook her again. "Sólveig," he said, and she heard the urgency in his voice. "Keep your eyes open." His face swam back into focus, his eyes boring into hers, and she noticed then how his lashes were covered with little particles of snow, and she wondered if hers were too. "We must keep going, do you understand?" He pulled her up to her feet. The effort to stand was momentous. "Come on, now, Arína needs you. We're almost there."

"Arína? *Já.*" She perked up, the name registering and jolting her back to her purpose, to the reason she was out here in below-zero temperatures, in the raging weather. She let Albert take her hand, and he led her onwards, almost pulling her, along the narrow, snowy track.

The snow started again; the flakes this time were small, hard pellets that stung the skin with the speed at which they fell, the wind slapping them against her already white form. How long had they been walking? The thoughts ran lazily through her mind. One step at a time. One foot before the other. Surely, they would reach the croft soon. Would she be too late? No! This journey would not be in vain, she reaffirmed, but the cold had seeped into her. She felt it keenly, Winter trying to best her. Her movements slowed. She was so stiff. Thoughts of her baby fluttered through to her. *The baby is fine*, she told herself. The baby was cocooned in a bubble of warmth in her body—but why was it getting so hard to walk? Running her hands over the fabric of her skirts where movement was the hardest, she felt the stiffened outer layers. She tried to keep up with Albert. He was only a few steps ahead, but she was beginning to lag. It was an effort, when all her energy was just about spent, the snow so deep where she trod that she could barely lift her knees with the constricted movement of her clothing.

Sólveig stopped, her breath coming in hard puffs, her chest aching, feeling suffocated by the scarf at her throat. She wanted to simply drop to her knees and sleep, but she knew she mustn't. She had to keep going. Another heavy step and another. She ripped down the covering at her mouth.

"Albert," she called, to no avail. "Albert, I can't move," she tried again.

He finally turned and made his way back to her. He pulled down the scarf covering his own mouth. "What is it, Sólveig? Are you hurting? Is it the baby?" he shouted through the wind.

"*Nei*. It's just–I–I can't move Albert! My skirt is frozen," she said through chattering teeth. He gave her a cursory glance up and down, bringing his hands to the stiff material and she heard him curse.

"Is everything alright?" It was Jakob appearing through the torrent of sleet behind them.

"Her skirts are frozen stiff. She can barely walk, Jakob. You go on ahead and inform them of Sólveig's arrival. We won't be far behind." Jakob left them and Albert turned to her. "I'll have to carry you." His arms came up under her legs, and he lifted her off the ground with grunted effort.

Albert traced Jakob's steps in the snow. The man was surely exhausted. So close to his face, she caught the stern frown he wore, his scarf was no longer wrapped around his mouth, and she watched lazily how his beard caught the falling snow and turned quickly to ice with the heat of his breath. An overwhelming sense of gratitude for him filled her. This man. How was it that she had won such respect and protection from a man like him? He'd walked when she rode, became her eyes when she couldn't see through the storm, and now he carried her to their destination.

"Thank you," she whispered into his ear. He tried to wink at her with frost-covered lashes, but it came out as an awkward blink.

A dark shape loomed in the distance, but before she knew it, they had reached a low doorway.

Not bothering to knock, Albert simply barged through the door in a flurry of wind and snow, yelling down into the hallway, "The midwife is here."

⁘

Albert

Albert carried Sólveig down the hallway and into the small kitchen, setting her gently down onto a table near the radiating heat of the hearth fire. The burn and tingle of his own frozen flesh reminded him how low his own body temperature had dropped, but it was Sólveig he was concerned about. He wasn't happy with the way her body shook and her teeth chattered.

His sister-in-law María greeted them in the kitchen, her face drawn and pale, her eyes large with concern at the sight of them. "I wasn't sure anyone would make it to us through this storm. You don't know how pleased I am to see you all," she said on a gush of breath.

"You're half frozen, woman," Albert muttered as he undressed Sólveig of her gloves, barely acknowledging María. He took her icy hands in his, trying his best to rub warmth and feeling back into them.

"What's happened to her, Albert?" asked María.

"Her clothes are half frozen to her," he said tightly. "And the cold is making her sleepy. We have to get her out of these damp clothes."

"I'll fetch her something dry. Jakob, you get Albert and Sólveig some of that broth I've just warmed," María said as she passed her husband, who had already found a bowl himself.

It was a small croft and housed only Arína, her husband and their two children, little Hannes and Sveinn. Albert wondered briefly about Arína, how she fared and if they had made it to her in time. But at this moment, it was Sólveig who he needed to attend to.

He left her in the kitchen, storming into the *baðstofa* to snatch up a woven blanket off an empty cot. Entering the room, he was assaulted by the familiar scent of birth—of sweat, the tangy metallic smell of blood, and fluid. He caught a glimpse of the woman whimpering in her cot at the end of the dim room and a swaddled babe sleeping next to her in the cot, but he hurried back to the kitchen draping, the blanket over Sólveig's shoulders, and proceeded to undress her out of her frozen skirts and stiff, cold clothing. He made her stand before him, and she clutched the blanket to her, and perhaps he crossed some boundaries, undressing her as he did without a thought to her propriety, but if she thought his actions a breach of conduct, she showed no sign of it. He sat her down on a chair, kneeling before her, pulling her feet out of her damp stockings, and noticed the large blotches of red skin around her thighs and calves where the cold had seeped in for too long. He cursed under his breath.

"Why did I let you come, woman?" He knelt before her, shaking his head at her in dismay.

"Albert, I'm fine," she replied weakly, her doe eyes soft. "We made it, didn't we? I just need to catch my breath, is all."

"Stubborn down to the bone, is what you are, but *já*," he relented. "We made it."

Jakob came over with two steaming bowls of broth. Albert took one and brought it to her trembling lips for her to drink.

"Thank you, Albert, but I can manage." She took the bowl from him. "Go and undress yourself. You're about as frozen as I and stubborn enough to say you're not."

"Okay, okay." He held his hands up in mock defeat and proceeded to undress of his own wet items.

"Here, get you into these." María was back with a bundle in her hands. "Arína is needing you in there with her, Sólveig."

María placed some dry clothes before them—pants and a long-sleeved shirt and sweater for Albert, and for Sólveig, a new skirt and shirt, clean dry socks and a woollen shawl.

"The pains are something terrible," María continued, "coming and going as they did the first time and the placenta still not delivered. She's mighty worn out in there."

"And the child?" Sólveig stood up, reaching for the new clothes to dress herself. She faltered, swaying on her feet.

Albert threw his arms out to steady her. She was in no state to be on her feet now. "Sit down, Sólveig. You need to rest a little longer."

She squeezed his hand lightly. "I just stood too quickly, Albert. I'm fine, really. I *must* see to Arína, now." Her eyes met his, her expression somewhat pleading, asking him to trust her.

He nodded and let her go. He didn't have to like it, but he needed to trust that she knew her own limits. She did have a little more colour to her lips and the chattering had stopped. She had a job to do. It was why they'd come in the conditions they had. It would do no good to delay. The weather had delayed them long enough.

Albert pulled on the clean, dry clothes, feeling warmer by the minute, listening on as María relayed the events of the evening.

"A little boy was delivered near four hours ago, breathing fine, but he's on the small side. Arína says she's a few weeks earlier than what she had calculated with the due time."

Sólveig finished tying a new apron around her waist, and Albert watched as she cleaned her hands with soap and boiled water and gazed about the room as if trying to locate something. He found it first, her medical bag half hidden under the pile of discarded wet clothes they'd been wearing, and passed it to her, a hand at her elbow. "Just call out if you need anything. I'll be waiting down here with Jakob."

"What would I do without you?" Sólveig said, her eyes glistening with gratitude, and he watched after her as she navigated the narrow set of stairs, following María into the *baðstofa* to assess the situation better.

<hr />

Sólveig

The child lay limp in her arms, almost lifeless, but not quite. There was still colour to her, no sign of blackened skin, indicating rot. But the child had yet to take her first breath. A second child. That was what an internal inspection and Arina's continued pains indicated. She had been carrying twins.

There was still the glimmer of a heartbeat within the tiny body, but she was turning blue. The lifeless image of her sister's baby flashed before her. *No! This one will live.*

Arína, who was still recovering from pushing the child out only moments earlier, was waiting for her new baby to be passed to her. They all waited, holding their breath for the child to take its first natural intake of air, but it wasn't coming.

Working quickly, Sólveig lowered the child into the tub of warm water beside the cot, massaging her tiny limbs, rubbing her chest with her bare hands, stroking hard the soles of her little feet.

Nothing.

She slid an index finger into the baby's mouth, slowly, deeply, turning it in her throat, removing the mucous from the airways. *Just breathe, little one*, she willed. *Just breathe.* Arína whimpered, María held her hand, but Sólveig wasn't about to give up. She drew the baby out of the water, exposing her to the cold air, and turned her, head down, shaking her carefully, slapping her bottom.

The baby squealed, taking in a gulp of air, her cries angry and sudden, and Sólveig was sure there had never been a better sound until now. Relief flooded her as she turned the baby once more and lowered her back into the warm water, the colour of life spreading into her little body, a flushed pink hue.

⚜

Albert

Albert sat by the table in the kitchen with Jakob as the hour drew on, dozing fitfully, exhausted, but the chill finally gone from him. He heard the cries of the woman in the other room, a long, drawn-out silence and then a baby squalling.

"It's another babe," María called, rushing into the room, and he startled fully awake. María's face was one of awe. "It's twins. A little girl. Can you believe it? All this time, she had two in there."

"Does the babe live?" asked Jakob, rubbing at his own sleep-weary features opposite him.

"There's life to her, though Sólveig had to encourage her a bit. She came out a little blue, but she was able to revive her spirit, like she did with our little Albert Einar." María's voice wobbled as she recalled the memory of her own baby boy, lost to them now with the measles. "She was amazing, Albert. Sólveig knew exactly what to do, knew straight away that there was another one in there. You can come in for a look now, if you like?"

Albert hadn't realised he'd been so anxious with the waiting, but relief washed through him at this news—relief and a sense of awe. Twins. Imagine that. A double blessing.

He entered the dim, quiet room, trailing Jakob and María, but he found himself seeking Sólveig first. There she was, sitting at the end of María's cot. She turned to them, and her tender gaze found his. Her face was flushed with colour, her eyes betraying her exhaustion, but he could see the pleasure she radiated too. He smiled at her, feeling something akin to pride for her, shaking his head in awe. She had done it. Her determination had won out against the adversity they'd faced. No storm would stand in this woman's way. She held one of the sleeping babies in her arms. Arína looked exhausted, her wide-set cheekbones flushed with colour, fair wisps of hair standing at all angles, having escaped their plaits hours ago, but she lay content with the other baby suckling at her breast.

"My Bjarni will certainly be in for a surprise when he sees them," Arína said, her eyes shining, and a hint of disbelief still in them. "He's been wanting a little girl of his own." A child stirred in the cot opposite hers, and Albert peered over to see the small form of her two-year-old boy, Hannes.

"I'll check the passes tomorrow. But I've a feeling they'll be no good. Bjarni's not likely to hear the good tidings until he returns home in the spring," said Albert.

Jakob and María sat with Arína for a while. Sólveig placed the sleeping child into María's arms and turned her attention to the soiled bedsheets and bedclothes on the floor at the end of the room, but as she stood, he saw the way she swayed again and had to grab the timber frame at the end of the bed for support.

"These can be dealt with later." He was quickly there beside her, steadying her, taking the sheets from her arms. "Let me take them for you." And he dropped them back on the ground. "You get yourself some rest," he said, leading her to the one of the spare beds near the doorway.

"It seems it's all catching up with me now," she conceded.

"You can't go all night, as much as you insist otherwise," he said dryly. "You're with child. You need your rest, woman."

She let him sit her on the edge of the bed, then squat in front of her, his hand sliding down her calf to her feet, gently pulling her sheepskin shoes off her swollen feet, rubbing them for her briefly.

She closed her eyes. "You can keep doing that." She smiled, titling her head back as he did so, and he rubbed them a little longer before stopping to help her out of her shawl. "But Arína. I must keep an eye on her. She may need me—"

"María, Jakob and I can watch over her for now."

She nodded in reluctant assent, and stood, slipping out of the skirt, so she was once again only in her thin underdress before him. This time he couldn't help but soak in the shape of her, the way her nipples stood hard against the woollen layer covering her naked flesh. He swallowed hard and looked away, instead pulling back the blanket on the cot for her to slide her feet in.

She lay down, resting her head on the pillow, and let him tuck her in. "You get some sleep," he said.

"Please wake me should there be anything amiss."

"I promise I'll wake you if you're needed."

The hint of a smile fluttered over her lips. "Thank you, Albert."

"You did well, Sólveig." He smoothed his hands over her hair, but her eyes were closed, and she was already drifting into sleep.

***

Sólveig

She woke to soft breathing against her hair and was aware of a warm, solid form next to hers, an arm slung over her, cradling her against a firm chest. She opened her eyes with a start, forgetting where she was for a moment, then remembered. It was surely the early hours of the morning, the room sat in darkness, the soft stirrings of sleeping bodies in the room taking up the silence. A chill hung in the air, and she wanted nothing more than to stay in the arms of this man, letting his warmth envelop her some more. If she closed her eyes, she could pretend it was Helgi. She could imagine that the last six months hadn't happened. That the man next to her was the husband of her heart, this house their own as well as the child stirring in her belly. She closed her eyes again, and a tear escaped, rolling lazily down her cheek. She could pretend, if just for a moment. She hadn't realised how much she'd missed this—being in the arms of a man—and it sent an ache deep into her being, reminding her that she never really had this with Helgi. Life had never given them that chance. She remembered back to the time Helgi had declared wanting to wake next to her every morning. But this was not Helgi. It was her husband who had come to her bed—her husband, Albert, and it was he who stirred against her now, holding her to him, muttering in his dream state, his hand trailing dreamily down over her breasts and swollen waistline. His lips found their way to the tender place behind her earlobe, and she shivered, leaning into his light kisses, enlightened by how her body betrayed her heart, her skin awakening under his touch. It had been so long since a man had touched her this way. The heat of his large, calloused hand burned through her thin underdress, her skin tingling in its wake. Albert mumbled again, something incoherent, and slipped his hand over her hip, trailing it down towards her inner thigh, resting there briefly between her legs, before pulling her hips towards him, pressing her so close to him that she could feel his pulsing hardness against her bottom. She closed her eyes again, torn, knowing she should stop him, but not wanting to relinquish this illusion just yet, and he nuzzled into her neck, into her hair. "Ah, Krissa," he groaned breathlessly.

She opened her eyes with a start, the illusion shattering.

He was just dreaming. This was not Helgi, and she was not Krissa. He had no idea what he was doing.

"Albert, it's me, Sólveig." She turned, running her hand over the course bristles of his beard, hoping to wake him from this lustful slumber, and he startled awake, his blue eyes seeing her for the first time, his forehead wrinkled with lines of confusion. She could see it the moment it dawned on him, his hand still heavy on her thigh, his hardness pressed firmly up against her, and he pulled away from her so quickly that he toppled out of bed, landing with a thump on the floor.

She stifled a giggle. "Well, that's one way of getting out of bed."

He stood before her, slightly baffled, his face still sleep heavy, his erection showing through his underclothes. He shoved one hand over himself, grappling for his pants at the edge of the bed. "Ah, please forgive me, Sólveig. It probably wasn't a good idea sleeping next to you. It's been so long since—" he struggled to get out, and she sensed his embarrassment.

"Albert, it's fine. I must be up, is all, to check on Arína and the babies." She got up too, finding her own clothes, and pulled on her long skirt. Albert nodded and left the room, Sólveig watching after him, feeling conflicted, guilt and pleasure mingling together—at odds with one another, but the soft mewling coming from the end of the room pulled her out of that reverie. Her duties here as midwife had only just begun.

31

February/March 1883

Albert

Tobba passed away during the time of *Þorri*, the midwinter's feast—during the darkest, longest days of winter.

Sólveig had only arrived home from Gilsbrekka two days earlier, going straight from keeping twin babies alive to giving some small comfort to a dying woman.

His mother-in-law had teetered on the brink of death for months, and Albert was relieved that her suffering was at last at an end, but this farewell he faced was harder than he thought it would be. She'd had much to bear in her sixty-three winters of living. The woman had been so long part of his life, the mother of his first wife, and grandmother to his children, so it was strange seeing her empty cot, and he couldn't help but feel it was another piece, another part of his wife Krissa, gone from this world. Dísa was once again faced with the loss of someone dear to her. But the child, who had seen her grandmother wither away before her eyes, had somehow stepped into her maturity and consoled herself. She was the first to her bedside the morning they all woke to discover

Tobba's spirit gone. The old woman's face was pale, her eyes resting in eternal slumber, and his daughter sat solemnly by her, her eyes red and swollen, holding her *amma*'s pale, weathered hand in her own, stroking it softly.

"I opened the window for her. She can go to them now, to be with *Mamma* and Dóra and God," she said, and Albert wasn't sure who this child was that sat before them, so calm with her big, sad eyes, wiping her other hand across her nose. He'd expected the same reaction she had given him when he married Sólveig—tears and tantrums, but there was none of that. And when old Leifur woke to the news, Dísa took herself to her great-grandfather, lending comfort to the man who'd outlived all his children.

A week later, they honoured the old woman by singing her from Suðureyri and she was buried in the frozen ground at Staður next to her daughter, as she had requested. Séra Stefán would be out in the spring to bless those who had passed from the world over the winter.

Winter finally released its hold on them, and the days slowly grew longer along with their stilled hope for the coming summer. Sólveig had stayed with Arína at Gilsbrekka for two weeks, helping the woman with keeping her twin babies alive. There had been no way to reach Bjarni at Ós, with the thick snow over the mountain paths and the weather too precarious to venture by sea. The man would simply find out, as many men did when they became fathers, when he returned from his winter duties. If the twins managed to survive, he would likely not see them until late spring, when he was called home to the haying and the tasks of summer. Sveinn accompanied Sólveig home in early February along with Jakob. They'd waited for a fair day and taken her across the fjord by boat. Albert found himself relieved to have her back under his roof. He was somewhat surprised at how much he had felt her absence—the lack of seeing her around the croft, her empty cot when he went to bed at night. He'd missed her voice, the tender smiles she gave him, their easy conversation, and he found himself constantly reliving that moment at Gilsbrekka, the feel of her body against his that morning in his half-dream state. He'd thought of it many times as he lay waiting for sleep at night, struggling with his physical need for Sólveig, but also with the guilt that arose with it, telling himself it was simply just a physical reaction being so close to a woman's body. It had only been seven months since he lost Krissa. Was it wrong of him to crave the touch of a woman again, of wanting her soft, supple body beneath his, taking him into her in shared pleasure? It was certainly hard not to want such release when he was all too aware of it happening in the same room, night after night. Surely, his brother had gotten his child onto Rúna by now.

⚜

Sólveig wasn't home for long before she was called out again. In late March, Eiríkur came from Bær to fetch her for the birth of a child by one of his work maids. Sólveig was getting close to her own time, so he couldn't help but worry for her walking the long distances with that heavy waddle of hers. She refused his offer of a horse, informing him that it was too uncomfortable to sit on the horse as big as she was.

"It's not my time yet," she tried to console him when Eiríkur came to collect her. "This one will stay for a little longer yet. I feel good, Albert. I've had some time to rest, since Gilsbrekka. Please don't worry for me."

But Elsa arrived from Keflavík while Sólveig was gone, ready to assist her grandchild into the world, and she scolded Albert for letting her go.

"My Rúna could have gone and called for her if there was any trouble. She's too far along to be traipsing about the countryside with that babe in her belly."

"Have *you* tried talking to the woman when her mind is set, Elsa? There's no swaying her. You know how she was the day she received news of Helgi's death. She thought to take to the sea on her own, just to get to him," he said wryly.

She sighed and nodded in agreement. "*Já*, Magnús told me. I do suppose you're right. There's a fire burning in her, under all that calm she's normally in possession of."

"She's been gone almost three days. There's been no report of any trouble. Any day now, she'll be home," reaffirmed Albert.

Sólveig

Sólveig was returning home from the birth at the farm Bær in Staðardal Valley when her labour started. The pain was similar to the cramps she sometimes had with her monthly bleeding, a dull, nagging ache across her upper groin. She had been getting them sporadically all morning, but she had pushed the worry to the back of her mind, convincing herself that it wasn't time yet. Besides, she had been getting similar pains these past few weeks on and off.

Eiríkur walked before her, a few strides ahead. He kept glancing back at her, and she tried her best to walk a little faster. He was short and stocky, but he kept a quick pace.

"I'm afraid it will be slow going," she had told him that morning before they left. She hated having to take the time out of someone's busy day just to walk her a way she was perfectly capable of walking on her own.

"I won't have you walking on you own, in your condition, Sólveig. Albert wouldn't be pleased to hear of it," he admonished.

The wind picked up, and they were only ten minutes off when the drizzle started.

Eiríkur was talking and talking, finally slowing his pace to match hers.

"Hafsteinn—a father! I'm still gettin' over the shock of it. Mind you, I'm still gettin' over the shock of Halldóra being with child. She managed to hide it well under those skirts of hers."

"What will happen now?" she ventured.

"He'll marry the girl. No son of mine will make babies and not take the responsibility that comes with them. If he's man enough to make 'em, he's man enough to step up and be a husband to the child's mother."

It was true. Eiríkur's youngest son, a man in his late twenties, still resided with him and his wife at Bær, ever the eternal bachelor. He'd shown no interest in taking a wife, but it appeared that hadn't stopped him from taking his liberties with the house maids. Halldóra kept tight-lipped about who the father of her child was. She refused to let it be known. Though once the babe was born, it hadn't been difficult to see who his father was. The little boy looked like him, nature's strange way of declaring a child's paternity. No other man in their community had hair as red as Hafsteinn's. The child's flame-coloured hair had betrayed the secret.

Hafsteinn had owned up to it then, but he'd not known of the pregnancy. There was a heated argument in the croft, Hafsteinn claiming that if he'd known, he'd have taken responsibility for the child. Jósefina, his mother, was livid, unmarried as they were, the copulation occurring under her roof, but Sólveig kept them away from Halldóra and her new baby until their anger had settled some.

Sólveig and Eiríkur walked the cliff path, the long stretch of road along the base at the very edge of the mountain Spillir, the salty notes of the sea drifting heavily towards her, as it always did when she walked this path. The seaweed beds were visible today with the tide being out, a shiny tangle of copper in the gentle lull of satin blue. Soon this place would be teeming with life as the eiders returned to make their nests amongst the dulse and granite rocks. Relief coursed through her, knowing she was heading home. She was somewhat exhausted after the past three days attending to this birth, being so close to her own confinement time. Her back ached with the heaviness of child. The babe stirred less these days, and she sensed the space within was getting cramped, his jabs and kicks sharp and pronounced.

They had only just started down the narrow ocean path along the cliffs when the pains began again, but this time they dragged on—longer and deeper, so that she was forced to stop and catch her breath, and it was then that she felt the oddest sensation deep within her groin, like a cork had just been unplugged from a flask. Warm fluid trickled down her legs. It soaked into her woollen leggings under her long skirts.

"Is something the matter?" Eiríkur halted on the path as she did.

"Oh, Eiríkur," she gasped, gripping his arm as pain surged through her with the release of the waters. "The waters—the waters have come loose," she puffed.

"The waters? You're not making any sense." His thick grey brows knotted together with concern.

"The baby. It's coming."

His face drained of colour. "Right now?"

She nodded, closing her eyes as a contraction washed through her, her whole body clenching into itself. *Not now*, she willed. *Not just yet.*

"Do you think you can make it back to Suðureyri?"

"I'm not sure." Her lips trembled, and she pulled the shawl tighter about her shoulders, knowing it wasn't really the cold that made her body shiver. The contraction left her as quickly as it came. She sighed with relief. "We'll keep walking."

Eiríkur strolled beside her, keeping to her slower pace, and they had made good progress before it happened again. The child lay heavy and low in her groin, and her stomach hardened as the pain burned through her.

Eiríkur gripped her elbow to steady her as she stopped to breathe through the pressure and stretching within. "I don't like this, Sólveig," he grumbled.

"Keep going," she told him once the pain receded, and they continued along the seemingly endless cliff path, only making it another ten steps before it tore through her loins once more.

She shook her head, the pain bearing down on her. Closing her eyes again, she drew her focus inwards, waiting for the wave to subside. "I can't," she moaned finally. "You have to go for help. It's coming so close together now. I don't think I'm going to make it back."

"It don't feel right leaving you here like this, Sólveig."

"I'm afraid you don't have much say in the matter," she snapped. "I need you to go now. It's better this way. Please. I'll keep walking, for as long as I can, but I need you to get Rúna. Leave the bag with me and bring her to me."

He reluctantly passed her the bag. "I don't like this one bit," he muttered, but he ran ahead regardless.

⊹

Albert

Albert was outside with Árni, fixing a leak in the roof over the kitchen that had come through during the winter. Einar had gone with Björn to Flateyri on the boat for more salt. He wanted to be nearby in case Sólveig needed him.

The salt they would need in the weeks to come as they went out for more fish. Their food supplies were quite dwindled, and they now relied heavily on the soured foods they stored in barrels of whey—*slátur* and preserved shark, and cod heads. They all looked forward to the summer to replenish their food stocks, for juicy mountain berries and tangy sorrel, fresh vegetables, and meat in the autumn. Albert knew the children looked forward to it the most. They'd just gotten through the midday meal, Rúna frustrated with Lína's refusal to eat the soured liver sausage, Stella imitating her and refusing it also. It was a struggle to get them to eat the soured foods at times.

It was just after their midday meal when Árni noticed a man approaching the farm.

"Someone's coming in a hurry down the beach from Staður," his workman said, pausing beside him and staring off into the distance. Albert turned and stood for a better view. There was indeed a man heading for Suðureyri in a hurry.

"It's Eiríkur from Bær. I'd best intercept him." He passed Árni the hammer and climbed down the ladder against the wall and made his way towards the sea croft.

"What it is, man?" He clasped Eiríkur on the shoulders as the man bent over, coughing, trying to catch his breath.

"Albert, it's Sólveig," he said. "On the ocean road. The child is on its way."

"What do you *mean*, man? She's out there on the cliff road?" he asked, incredulous.

"*Já*, the waters have come away."

"And you left her?" Eiríkur flinched at his words.

"Said she'd been having strange pains since the morning but thought little of 'em. Thought she could get home before they got any worse." He shook his head in dismay. "I'm sorry to let you down, Albert. I told her I wouldn't leave her, but she was adamant. She bid me to go for help."

"Ah, Eiríkur. She's not always the easiest to reason with. You carry on up to the croft. Take the news to Rúna and Elsa. Tell them to bring some blankets, rags and hot water with them. I'll hurry to her now."

Albert cursed under his breath. If she'd been having pains since the morning, why had she not just stayed put? Who did she think she was? She always had it in her head that she could just manage. Didn't she realise that she was a mere mortal like the rest of them? Did she not understand the risk she constantly put herself in? The woman sure made it hard for him to do his duty by her, to keep her safe. Isn't that what he had sworn to do on his wedding day? Albert willed himself patience as he ran. The cold air he inhaled deep into his lungs helped distil the burning fear within, but it washed through him afresh as a light drizzle started. A dark gathering of cloud crept down over the mountain Göltur towards the head of Spillir where his wife was walking. More rain and fog would be upon them within the hour.

Sólveig

The wind blew at her, and she noticed the menacing haze of cloud sitting over the mountain Göltur, slowly descending upon the fjord. She was alone and that scared her. Left to the mercy of the wind and the sea and coming rain, the mountains watching on in their regal silence. Would they bear witness to her child's birth? Eiríkur had left her upon her insistence, but now, she wanted him back by her side. Her vulnerability out here exposed to the elements was suddenly starker.

"Why now?" she asked her baby, rubbing a hand over her belly. She continued her shuffle onwards, stopping when the cramping ravaged her, then kept on, her progress towards home painstakingly slow. What other choice did she have but to keep going?

Sólveig was halfway down the ocean path when the rain started heavy and thick, and she pushed on faster. The damp wool of her stockings scratched against her thighs where the fluid still trickled from her body. She scanned the cliff wall she walked alongside, looking for somewhere, some sort of windbreak, some form of shelter from the elements, should she have no choice but to birth her child here.

The next pain hit her with such force that she had to halt and rest her hand against the rock wall, her bag dropping to the ground beside her as she tried to breathe through the pain, like she insisted her patients do. Her legs shook and the fear of facing this ordeal alone hit her hard. This baby would not wait for her arrival home to Suðureyri.

"Not here. Please not here. Just wait a little longer," she moaned, letting the wind carry away her plea.

Her legs trembled as she walked, straining with the effort to carry the weight of the child when she was already tiring so, and she conceded finally to the need to stop. Fog was rapidly descending upon the fjord, the mountain engulfed in its hazy embrace, and she was unsure of what she should do. The birds in the cliffs high above circled their own nests, but she looked beyond those birds, sending her prayer to the Almighty, her plea for herself and her child. *Let him live. Let me keep this one thing he left me*, she prayed, and then she heard it. The sound of water rushing down the cliff face nearby. The waterfall. It wasn't too far away. She could make it there. There was a small cleft in the rock wall, where a long, thin stream of water had carved a hollow into the solid surface over countless years. She had seen it many times on her way to and from the valley.

It was her only option—some form of shelter from the wind and the rain.

Sólveig staggered along the wall, willing herself ahead. Walking even through the agony, the child bearing down into her, making it known to her of its will to enter the world.

She stumbled through the narrow opening, finding before her a green sanctuary, the hollow much wider than she'd thought at first. The cliff wall here was padded thickly with patches of moss, soft and spongelike beneath her sheepskin shoes. Dropping her bag down beside her, she leaned hard against the damp wall, succumbing to another rippling contraction. It surged through her, and she blinked back the tears it brought to her eyes, closing them in a bid to bear down on the pain, and with it came the first urge from deep within her to push.

"*Nei*. I can't do this." She shook her head, fighting it, the panic rising again, knowing that with this sensation, the child was getting close to crowning. "Oh, God, please," she moaned. Where were they? Why wasn't anyone here yet?

The pain subsided and she rested her forehead on her hands for a moment, against the moss embedded into the rock wall, far enough from the falling stream that its spray didn't reach her, the sound of water rushing in her ears. With chattering teeth, she turned slowly, sinking down awkwardly into the soft bed of moss at her feet. It was cool and damp, but there was no help for that now. She removed the woollen shawl wrapped over her chest, ready to bundle the baby in it. And then she waited for the next wave to overcome her, scanning the faint outline of the sea through the white mist of rain from her place of shelter, using this moment to catch her breath. A pang of grief ran through her. How uncanny it was that she should have her baby out here, amongst the cliffs—these cliffs! Thoughts of Helgi came to her unbidden as she remembered the story he'd told her shortly after she arrived in the Westfjörds.

It was along this path that he told her the story of the man in the cliffs, and she found her mind clinging to that memory as the pressure within her built up again, growing and growing, reaching a crescendo until it crashed through her, this internal tide working to bring forth her child. She found herself in the delirium of this ongoing pain, thinking perhaps the Hidden man from the cliffs would come to her now to deliver her of the child and take him from her. Leaning back against the wall, she pulled up the wet hem of her skirt so that her legs were free of it. Fluid continued to leak from her, and she placed her hand over her opening as the need to push came again, and she finally let go of her resistance, allowing herself to be carried along with the growing urges of her body.

The head was there. She puffed as the pain subsided, reaching for her medical bag, and opening it so that it was ready with the tools she would need—scissors and string to tie the cord, and she drew the woollen shawl closer to her, ready to swaddle her child in it, and she sat back, waiting.

This was her first baby. She had never imagined it would be like this—that this was truly how he should enter the world—and she cursed herself for not listening to the cues of her body. She should have known better. She should have just stayed on at Bær and delivered her baby there.

Hopelessness threatened to overwhelm her, her strength waning with each wave. Fear closed in on her, and she found it harder and harder to keep it at bay as the thoughts running through her mind convinced her that this was no less than she deserved. This was her punishment. This was her punishment for her sister. For not having the skills to save her, or perhaps it was her punishment for Helgi, for not being there to nurse him back to health? Now she would die too, out here alone, giving birth to her baby, exposed to the elements. "I can't do this alone!" she cried.

"Of course, you can, Midwife!" a voice replied on the wind.

Sólveig opened her eyes with a start. Peering through the grey mist of rain, she saw a shadowy figure walking towards her. She caught her breath, a shiver running down her spine. She knew that casual lope.

My God, what is becoming of me? Am I dying now? Has Helgi come to take me to the Almighty? She shook her head, her heart thrumming wildly, tears streaming down her face so that she was sure it was raining inside her hollow. She took a deep breath, trying to shake his image away, and pulled herself up into a squat. "Pull yourself together, woman," Sólveig told herself sternly, but when she looked up again, the figure had drawn nearer. She knew those green eyes full of humour and mischief and that dark, unruly hair. She closed her eyes, shutting out her illusions as the wave within built up to a crescendo once more. Her heart broke all over again at the sight of him, her need for him at this moment so strong that it threatened to overwhelm her. "You were supposed to be here for this," she cried as if in reply to him, as if it were really him before her in the mist. Her Helgi. And with the burning in her body came the burning anger she felt at his abandonment of her. "You weren't supposed to die," she yelled, her voice drowned out by the gush of water falling from the cliff beside her, but she had opened the floodgates to the pain of her heart, and it came pouring out with the waves in her body, working to expel her baby. "You promised me, Helgi, you promised me. You said that you wouldn't leave me!" The void of grief within trembled and ached, along with her body, but there was no answer. "You should be here to see your child into the world," she whimpered finally, her strength leaving her along with her will to fight. Her legs trembled beneath her weight, and just when she thought she would collapse, she sensed someone supporting her, holding her steady.

"But I am here, Sólveig, I will always be with you and our son."

When she opened her eyes again, there was no one there apart from the wind and the sea, and the mountain behind her but he was *here* with her. She sensed his presence, and drawing strength from this knowing, she finally surrendered to the waves of pain bearing down on her once more, understanding that there was no use in fighting this. She bore down again, panting, feeling the head of her baby crowning in her opening, the burning, searing pain ripping through her as her body opened for the child's head. When it was released, her hands searched along the child's neck, feeling for the cord, making sure it wasn't wrapped around it, but the urge to push came again, and she pushed in one final effort, releasing the child's shoulder and arms. It slid out of her in another gush of warm fluid, and she reached for her baby, pulling him out, bringing her child to her chest in one final heave.

Her son.

His hair was as black as the night. An angry squall filled the small hollow, along with the falling water, and her heart burst with joy at his sound. His tiny shrieks continued—the child being exposed to the cold air after the warmth of his watery cradle was almost too much. Sólveig reached quickly for the woollen shawl next to her, wrapping it snuggly

about him, and closed her eyes, leaning against the moss-covered rock
to catch her breath, a burst of elation coursing through her. Tears of joy
and love and grief mingled into one as she held her baby to her. Son of
Helgi. His parting gift.

"Sólveig!"

Her name was being called through the swirling mist. The rain had
stopped, and the sun was trying its best to disperse the fog. It danced in
light dapples along the path, but then came the sound of footfalls, the
crunching of stones beneath feet.

"Albert," she returned. Her voice was raspy, and the babe was crying as
she rushed to undo the jacket she wore and pull up her shirt, her breasts
tingling and heavy, helping the child find her nipple.

Albert appeared before her, puffing hard, rain dripping from his beard
and hair, his face pale. "My God, Sólveig." He fell to his knees before her,
his eyes growing wide at the sight of the bundle she cradled against her
breast. "You did this alone?" Albert seemed almost afraid to touch her,
but he pulled back the corner of the wrap revealing a head of matted
black hair.

"Not quite alone." He gave her an odd look. "He was here, Albert,"
she explained. "Helgi was here with me."

Perhaps she sounded like a crazy woman, but Albert smiled at her with
knowing and with love, his eyes watering. "Is it—?"

"Helgi has given me a son, who is now, by marriage, your son too,
Albert," she answered for him.

He shook off his jacket and wrapped it around them. "Well, little
Helgi, you made quite the entrance." He chuckled lightly, gently
stroking the child's head, but he glanced up at Sólveig, his brow furrowed
in concern. "You're at least out of the wind here, but we need to get you
both home."

"*Já*, though I'm yet to deliver the placenta." The pains had dulled down, but they were still coming at regular sharp intervals, and she knew it was close.

"What can I do for you?" he asked.

"The scissors. You can cut the cord and tie it."

"Rúna and Elsa won't be too far behind me. Should they not do that?"

"*Nei*, Albert. You're as capable as they. You can do the honours with your new son. There's a bar of soap there, too. for your hands," she instructed.

He knelt by the rushing water, scrubbing his hands before turning back to her, finding the scissors and making a quick job of it, cutting the cord and, in turn, accepting this role he would play in this child's life as his father.

Rúna and Elsa arrived not long afterwards and Albert took his sleeping son while they assisted Sólveig in delivering the afterbirth. It came clean away from what Sólveig could see. They let her rest some more before wrapping her in the blanket they brought with them, and then Albert took Sólveig into his arms, carrying her home, back to Suðureyri, Rúna and Elsa trailing them with their new child.

32

Spring 1883

Sólveig

The months following the birth of her son were a haze of days and weeks mulled together in the bliss of family life, of nurturing and loving her little boy along with the rest of the family. He was a robust, healthy baby with a hearty cry, quick to fuss and demand his food.

News of his birth spread and the women of her community came one by one in the days after, women who she had helped through their own deliveries—Arína, María, Halldóra and even Stína—bringing with them small gifts of food or clothing, even when they had so little to give after the hard winter they'd suffered—a pair of sheepskin shoes for Sólveig, stockings for the baby, freshly baked rye bread—whatever they had to offer, and Sólveig was deeply touched by their generosity. She had never demanded payment for any of her deliveries, but now they paid her in kindness. It touched her deeply, how her community embraced her, and she was overwhelmed by a sense of belonging to this place and these people.

Elsa stayed with Sólveig and Albert at Suðureyri for two weeks after Helgi's birth, enjoying her grandson and helping Rúna with the running of the household while Sólveig was still abed and taking on lighter duties after the birth.

In late April, Sólveig's little boy was christened along with Arína's twins and Halldóra's son. Many in the community turned out for the service, and there was a general air of joy flowing through the people, with summer on its way and the land around them blooming with new growth. Her son was given the name Helgi in honour of the man who sired him. When Albert asked her to marry him, he had promised to give her child his name, but Sólveig insisted her son be known as Helgason, son of Helgi. She wanted it known who fathered him. It would put rumours to rest, and Helgi deserved to know who his father had been, though Albert would be the only father he would truly know.

Sólveig found her strength returning and a new sense of rhythm for life, but the women of Suðureyri saw little of their men over the following months. They took to the sea for the fishing season and were gone for long days, returning later and later each night to be fed, then falling straight into their cots, exhausted after the day. Those who came from farther down the fjord, Laugar and Kvíanes stayed on at the sea crofts, going home on weekends. They took positions on Albert's and Björn's boats, as they did year after year, taking their cut as the catches came in, salting, drying and barrelling as they went.

With the men out rowing, it fell to the women and young ones to take on the duties of the farm, and as May approached and with it the lambing season, nights were spent in the sheep house, keeping watch over the ewes, the younger ones and the work maids taking turns sitting over the flock, coaxing new life into the world.

May brought many changes and during *fardagar*, moving days, much to Sólveig's dismay, Rúna and Einar left Suðureyri to manage their own household across the fjord at Norðureyri. Rúna was with child, the babe due to arrive in autumn. Sólveig found the separation hard, though her friend was, in fact, not far away, just a trip in the boat across the water, but Albert was yet to find new workers to replace them and Sólveig was swamped with running the household and taking care of the children.

The change that came as most unexpected to Sólveig though, was when her husband asked her to share his bed, six months after their wedding day.

He'd caught her at a bad moment, labouring over the hearth fire in the smokey haze of the kitchen, Helgi squalling in her arms while she stirred the contents of the evening's meal, one-handed. Dísa had done her the favour of taking Lína and Stella out with her to inspect the lambs. She had tried taking the baby too, but it had been no good, and Inga was busy with the evening milking.

Feeling fragile and drained, Sólveig hadn't meant to snap at Albert. Tied to the baby with his need of the milk her breasts supplied, she was beginning to understand more and more why many house mistresses simply bottle-fed their children.

"Mm, that smells delicious. I'm famished!" Albert's voice came from behind her. And before he could say another word, she shoved the crying baby into Albert's arms.

"Well, it's not ready!" she snapped, turning back to the fishy broth, throwing in some dried herbs for flavour.

"That bad, is it?" he asked wryly.

Flustered and perturbed, feeling that sorry for herself, she had to take a few moments to school her face before turning to Albert again.

The man crooned softly, his voice low and soothing, and the crying had stopped. The baby lay stomach down along his arm, Helgi's head resting at the crook of his elbow, a broad hand curling up over his bottom, the other patting it. It seemed to soothe the child, and he simply hiccoughed and peered around the room calmly as Albert held him.

The sight softened her irritable mood, and she sighed with resignation, shame filling her at her outburst.

"I'm sorry for snapping, Albert. Sigga only just left, Helgi's been fussing and I'm afraid your meal is late." She rubbed a hand over her brow and shrugged in defeat. "I'm not sure I'm doing too well at this house mistress role you've entrusted me with."

"Ah, don't be so hard on yourself. I'd say you're coping just fine. You've three little ones and a household to manage, short staffed at that. But tell me. What's this about Sigga?"

"She was all in a state. They've run out of kindling at Laugar, down to burning grass and balls of dirt, unable to keep a fire burning for long." She wrung her hands, anxious about telling him, not knowing if she'd done the right thing. "I know we're running low ourselves, but I gave her some of our peat, just to see her through until they get out to collect and dry more at the end of May."

"Don't fret over it. You did right by her, Sólveig."

"It's so hard seeing others struggle as they do. I just wish I could have done better for her, but I'm afraid we still have to survive ourselves."

"*Já*, it's a fine line to walk. Were you worried I wouldn't approve?"

"It's just, Leifur's been muttering at me about giving away all our supply, but I can only imagine that Krissa would have done the same."

"*Já*, she would." He nodded. "But, Sólveig, I trust you completely with the decisions you make for our household. You have a sensible head on your shoulders. Thinking not just about ourselves is the only way we can survive here. We all need each other. In fact, I need to see to the matter of getting the licence approved to open a store here. Since the measles, it's all but been a waylaid idea."

"*Já*, I remember you spoke of it when I first came to Suðureyri."

"Well, with the *kauptíð* upon us soon, I can inquire again. I'll pick up some more of the medicine vials you need from the doctor while I'm there, and then there's your midwifery wages paid by the district."

"*Já*, and I want you to use them to make the purchases we need for the household."

He winked and she smiled in return, then he sidled up to the table where a loaf of rye bread lay half sliced, and he snatched up a piece, popping it into his mouth. "I do have some news that's sure to please you," he said while chewing.

"I could do with some good news." She scooped some of the freshly boiled *lúða*, halibut, into his *askur* and cut two slices of rye bread for him, buttering them too, waiting for him to elaborate.

"You now have two new work maids."

"But who?" she gasped.

"Sif, my maternal aunt from Skálavík, and Jóhanna, María's niece from Bólungarvík. I've been asking around. They'll be arriving tomorrow, and Valli, my new workman, the day after. So, what do you say to that?" he asked, rather pleased with himself.

"*Já*, well, I am pleased and relieved. It will certainly help lighten the workload. Now come, take your supper, and I shall give this little fellow his." She reached for the baby.

"*Nei*, you sit. Take your feed while you can, before the others come in and this one demands his milk again." He indicated the bowl she'd just dished up for him.

"*What?* I couldn't, this is yours."

"Sit and eat, woman. I won't have another bite until yours is done."

"Albert!" she scoffed in mock outrage, but it pleased her, this gesture of his, and she sat at the table by the window with her bowl of fish, relieved to rest her legs and aching back.

Albert stood by, still rocking and patting Helgi. The baby's eyelids drooped sleepily, and her heart warmed at the sight. Her husband and her son—their son. Albert was good with the baby. The way he looked at the child, like he was truly a son of his own loins, filled her with such love for the man, it almost surprised her.

"Sólveig." Her name on his lips was spoken with quiet reverence.

"Já?" She cast away her eyes, focusing instead on her meal, her cheeks growing warm at being caught watching her husband with such tender thoughts. Had he noticed?

"Perhaps with the new workers coming, it'll be time for us to show a united front."

"A united front?" His statement baffled her.

He chuckled deeply. "You look confused. I just thought, with the new workers coming in, that perhaps it's time we share a bed as man and wife."

"Oh." He took her by complete surprise.

"That is, if you feel you're ready?"

She shovelled a forkful of fish into her mouth, unable to answer him, so she simply met his eyes and nodded her head.

"It's settled, then," he said, sending a flutter deep into the pit of her stomach.

Their first night sharing a bed was surprisingly uneventful. She had been nervous all evening leading up to the night, so much so that Inga had questioned her more than once if something was bothering her. She was on edge and distracted, playing over in her mind how it would be to have Albert share his body with hers. Was she ready? Would she enjoy it? Would she fall asleep? That was a possibility, she mused—she was that tired! But that night, Albert went back out to the sea croft with Árni for more barrelling and salting and returned late. She *did* fall asleep, her babe at her breast as he was used to, but she stirred awake when Albert lay himself into the cot next to them.

The cot could sleep two adults, but it was narrow, as all the beds in the room were, and Albert lay close to her, so close that it was impossible not to touch, his warm, solid form next to hers, his familiar earthy scent mingled with salty notes of the sea, a strange and reassuring comfort. She lay on her side facing her sleeping baby; he was tucked between herself and the wall, and her breath caught in her throat, too nervous to move. She tried breathing normally, feigning sleep, and waited. She waited for him to touch her, for his hands to slide to her waist, to pull her towards him as he had done in his lustful dream state back in January. Instead, she heard the steady rhythm of breath behind her, of a body sinking into sleep, and she turned to see that he had indeed fallen into slumber.

Sólveig had imagined that when he asked her to share his bed, it meant that he was ready to share his body with hers, that it was time to bridge that physical gap between them, but he did not seek his release with her, and she wasn't sure if she should feel relieved or disappointed by this.

When he made no move the following night or the nights thereafter, it became clear to her that Albert was keeping to his promise of a marriage in name only.

Sólveig knew she should be grateful. After all, she wasn't ready to fall pregnant again. Helgi was only three months old. So why did she feel so foolish and ashamed lying next to him night after night, waiting, as she did, for him to make his claim on her? She had misunderstood him that day in the kitchen. Regardless, she found herself recalling that morning back in January—how it had felt to wake in his arms. He'd always been there for her, and she realised that, with him, she had a partner, an equal, and with everything they had been through, she felt very close to him. He was her friend, and she often found herself wondering if it could be more. Could they truly open themselves to one another in the way a man and wife should, in matters of the flesh and heart combined? Would there come a time when one of them would dare cross that void?

33

July 1883

Sólveig

The summer wore on, the days growing longer, the sun setting at midnight and rising again at three in the morning. The fields around the farm burst with new growth, the stalks of grass growing long, ripening under the glare of the sun and swaying in great ripples with the wind, the pulsing lifeblood of the land. With the peat collected from the swamplands left to dry out, and the sheep herded to the mountain pastures to fatten up, the men of Suðureyri took to slashing.

It was on the third day of haying, with the sun shining, that Sólveig decided to take half a day for herself from the household duties, leaving the little ones with the new work maid Sif so she could help with the haying. There was much chatter and laughter as the women worked alongside the men, turning the grass as the men slashed it, letting the sun dry the stalks before they could be raked into bundles and transported back by horse and stored for the winter. It was hard work, and Sólveig quickly tired, her back sore from bending, her breasts filling as the day wore on, ready for her son to release the pressure and take his fill of milk, but for the first time in a long while, Sólveig felt lighter of heart. She found herself more than once drawn to the tall, broad frame of her husband. She couldn't help but admire him as he worked, stealing glances at him all morning. Albert had scrapped his shirt like the rest of the workmen, heated as they were from their labour, and Sólveig noted how just a few days in the sun had left his milky-white skin golden like the strands of hay they cut. His well-muscled body glistened with sweat, the effort of his labour, and she enjoyed perhaps too much the way his muscles bunched in his arms and shoulders with the rhythm of the swinging scythe. Albert was in a good mood, and she enjoyed this lighter version of him, his easy deep-throated chuckle echoing about them at something his workmen had said, or the glint of humour in his eyes when he caught her watching him.

"We're catching you," Sólveig would taunt him playfully as they crossed paths.

"That'll never happen." Albert laughed, knowing that his manhood was at stake if the womenfolk caught up to them with the raking.

Sólveig returned to the croft just before midday to help Sif prepare food for the workers, flat bread and soured liver sausage, coffee aplenty, after Albert's trip to Ísafjörður for more supplies at the end of June.

She took up her baby, who had just woken from his sleep in the baðstofa, his little pink lips turned up at her in a smile, and the love radiating in his hazel eyes melted her heart as she changed his wet rags. When she was done, they made their way back outdoors with Lína and Stella in tow to join the rest of the household, everyone sitting out in the fields at the back of the farmhouse, enjoying the sunshine.

They had just eaten, and Albert lay on his side next to Sólveig, dozing in the grass while she fed Helgi at the breast.

Dísa came running over to them, her hands full, her face lit up with excitement.

"I just found a nest full of brown spotted eggs. I almost stepped on it, it was hidden so well on the ground."

"Ah, a meadow pipit's nest. And how many were in there?" Sólveig asked, thinking back to an old tale her *amma* had once told her.

"I counted five before the mother came back."

"You know, it is said that the number of eggs in the first nest you should come across will foretell the number of children you will have one day."

"I shall have five children some day?" The girl's eyes were wide with wonder.

"Perhaps." Sólveig shrugged, enjoying the child's enthusiasm.

Lína stood up from her place next to her, her meal of buttered bread complete, and she inspected the still form of her father, lying near them.

"*Pabbi* sleep." Lína pointed at her father. The child was enjoying finally being outdoors. Sif said she had been whining all morning, standing at the window in kitchen banging on the glass to go outside, where all the fun was.

"*Já, Pabbi* sleep," she said to the child, bringing a finger to her lips to keep quiet. She whispered, "Shall we wake him?" The child giggled along with Dísa who held Stella in her lap, watching Sólveig as she leaned over, Helgi still at her breast, plucking up a long golden stalk with a bushy head. Lifting it high, she brought in down delicately towards Albert's ear.

His large, workworn hand swiped irritably at his ear where the bushy stalk had touched, but Albert continued to doze. Sólveig waited and then did it again, Lína drawing ever closer to her father, leaning over him as his hand came up to swat again at the place the stalk met skin. This time he slapped at his neck.

They all giggled and Lína called loudly, "*Pabbi*, wake up."

Stella stood, too, then, wanting to join the game, her beaming smile lighting up her dainty features, golden curls bobbing up and down where she stood next to Lína.

When Sólveig brought the stalk down a third time, Albert sprang up with a roar and snatched it from her grasp. Sólveig squealed with fright, her nipple popping out of her baby's mouth momentarily, the child so startled that his mouth was downturned to cry his anguish at this sudden disruption, but he found the nipple and latched on again, suckling more vigorously. Sólveig glanced up to see a devilish grin across Albert's face, his stormy-blue eyes glistening with challenge, and her stomach swirled with anxiety, his expression telling her all too clearly that he would get his payback.

For the time being, though, Albert grabbed hold of the two little girls closest to him, taking Lína and Stella into his arms and tickling them, their hysterical giggles infecting them all.

Moments later Albert lay on his back, squinting up at the sun, laughing as Lína and Stella took turns throwing themselves upon him again and again, and he continued to tickle them in this new game they found so amusing. Stella, who imitated the older toddler, called Albert *pabbi* too, and he was happy to play that role, as she had become *mamma* to both little girls.

"May I hold him?" Dísa asked Sólveig. "I want to show him the flowers,". She sat next to her on the grass. The babe was finally full—fed and content, gazing about at the commotion and his surroundings, a bright smile lighting his features in response to Dísa's.

"You may, but don't wander too far with him, I'll be taking him back for his sleep soon." Dísa took her brother in her arms.

"Me too," piped Lína in her baby voice, tugging on her older sister's skirt to get her attention. Stella followed suit.

"Come on, then, you can pick some flowers for *Mamma*," Dísa said, and the little girls trailed her excitedly.

Sólveig wasn't sure she'd heard right. Did the child just refer to her as *mamma*? The child had taken to calling her *Veiga* most of the time. She was okay with that, but it touched her heart, hearing Albert's older girl refer to her with that title. She brushed away at the moisture brimming in the corner of her eyes, catching Albert observing her again.

"Dísa's so good with the children." Her stepdaughter was making her way back towards the croft, where the wildflowers grew along the stone wall near the vegetable garden. "She seems to be at more peace with me these days, Albert."

"*Já*, I see the change in her." Albert considered Sólveig for a long moment. "And how many eggs did you come across?"

She narrowed her eyes, the corner of her lips lifting into a smirk. "And here I thought you were sleeping."

Albert caught hold of her gaze from where he lay in the grass, now on his elbows. His long legs were stretched out before him, one knee raised, the straw she had used to tickle him with earlier there in his mouth where he chewed the end.

"Why do you look at me so?" she asked warily.

He sat up then, his knees bent, his hand shifting so that his fingers rested over his mouth, but he continued to stare.

She shuffled away from him ever so slightly, his unwavering gaze sending a flush of heat through her, and she squirmed under it, sensing some mischief abound.

"Just stewing on that spiteful little trick you played on me."

"Spiteful? Me?" she tried with as much innocence as she could muster. "We can't have you sleeping on the job now, can we, Albert? What sort of example would that set for the workers?"

"Is that so?" he asked all too casually.

"Mm-hmm," she muttered, with less conviction, ready to flee at the look he gave her.

She tried to stand, but he caught hold of her. "Oh no, you don't." He pulled her back down and pinned her to the ground with his body, tickling her in turn.

"Albert," she squealed, unable to contain herself. "*Nei!* Stop, please." She struggled against him, her stomach aching because she laughed so hard. He laughed too, his easy chuckle deep and echoing about them, but he stopped his roving hands, their bodies pressed together, his legs tangled with hers. He was puffing hard as he leaned over her, taking his weight on one elbow, his breath warm on her lips.

She caught the look in his eyes, one that told her of the sudden change in him, and she found herself waiting for him, waiting for his lips to meet hers, but he hesitated and instead brought his hand up to her hair, where he proceeded to pull something from it, brushing her cheek tenderly as he did so, bringing it into her line of vision. A strand of hay sat between his index finger and thumb.

"If I didn't have a full day of haying ahead of me, a tussle in the hay would probably do you some good, woman." His tone was husky but matter-of-fact.

"Would it, now?" she challenged, her breath catching at the thought of lying with him.

"*Já*, it would." Blue eyes bore into hers and stayed there for moments longer than she dared count, until finally she looked away.

Albert stood then, helping her up and brushing the grass off her with a sneaky pat on her bottom. He reached for the scythe leaning up against the stone wall near them. "Back to work," he called to the workers scattered around the field.

"Albert, it was six," she yelled after him finally.

He turned and winked at her, and Sólveig swallowed hard, a nervous excitement fluttering through her, unsure she had meant to start the game they now played.

⁂

Later that evening after the workers had retired for the day, Sólveig found Albert in the pantry, cursing under his breath as he rubbed his hands, a tub of tallow beside him.

"Albert," she said carefully, not wanting to startle him. "What have you done to yourself?" She wanted to smooth away the line of concentration between his brows. Instead, she came up beside him, inspecting his work. The pads of his hands were blistered and rubbed raw.

"That looks sore." She took his hands in hers.

The ghost of a smile flashed across his lips. "Ah, it's nothing that doesn't happen every summer from many days at the scythe."

"I have something better than just tallow," she offered, though it was more of a demand than a request.

"Well, now, that would be appreciated."

Reaching into her apron pocket, she pulled out the small salve she kept stored in a used tobacco tin. It was tallow mixed with yarrow to soothe and heal the skin.

She moved closer to him, taking in his earthy scent, of ripened hay mingled with stale sweat and mountain air. She recalled his comment earlier that day about a tussle in the hay doing her good, and her face flooded with warmth. She pushed it from her mind, focusing on her task, gently feeling with every nerve of her fingertips the rough flesh of his palm, but along with it, the strength in them, how these same hands worked so hard for the survival of this farm, this family. He winced.

"Sorry," she whispered and continued to massage down each finger, knowing how these strong hands welded, mended, built boats and crofts, and ploughed fields. How they had gently cradled her newborn son, how they could caress a woman's body, how they had felt on her body earlier that day and then back in January, in that rare moment of disillusion.

Sólveig became aware of his slow, deliberate breathing, but her own heart sped up. How could such a simple act feel so intimate? How could it awaken within her such a longing? This simple touch heightened in her a craving, a craving that had ignited today out in the haying fields and made her realise what she was missing—what she had been missing for the past year. She swallowed hard, hoping he didn't see how heated she was for the second time this day.

"Sólveig." Albert's voice came to her as if from far away. A calloused finger rested lightly under her chin, tilting her head towards him. *Look at me*, this gesture said. *Look at me*, it pleaded. Unspoken tenderness and desire burned through him, that same burning look she had seen earlier that day. She stopped the circular rhythm of her thumbs on his palm, and her breath caught in her throat as his hand trailed along her jawline and up to her cheek. She closed her eyes, leaning into the feeling of his touch on her face, the way his hand moved up towards her ear and into her hair to cradle the base of her head, pulling her towards him. His lips brushed lightly onto hers, the tenderest of touches, his beard tickling her upper lip and chin, his breath mingling with hers for the briefest of moments. A little stunned, she pulled away, but she didn't want it to stop. She leaned into him, this time his lips meeting hers with more insistence, her mouth opening as she wished to open her body to his as his hand moved down to her waist, gripping her to him.

"Veiga!" a child's voice called into the kitchen, shattering the moment. Sólveig and Albert separated abruptly, Sólveig knocking the salve to the floor in her fright, and they both stooped to pick it up, his head colliding with hers, just as Dísa entered the room.

"Here you are." The child's eyes darted between the two of them, somewhat puzzled, and Sólveig and Albert both straightened themselves, rubbing at the place where their heads had met.

"*Já*, here she is." Albert cleared his throat, passing the salve back to Sólveig. "She was mending my hand, but now I have a sore hand and a sore head." He winked at his daughter. "I thought you were in bed, Dísa."

"Oh, *Pabbi*." She shook her head as if she pitied him, and then turned to Sólveig. "Helgi has woken again. I can't settle him back to sleep."

"I'll be there in just a moment," Sólveig said to the little girl, and Dísa disappeared as quickly as she came, leaving her alone with Albert once more.

"I didn't get to do your other hand." She frowned, not knowing what to say in response to his kiss.

"We'll finish this later." He shrugged, somewhat sheepishly, and she left the room, unsure of what he really meant by that.

She pondered it while she sat on the bed, her child at her breast, soothing him back to sleep. Did he mean the salve for his hands, or the kiss? Her heart fluttered. The kiss had certainly surprised her. She had not expected to feel so moved by his caress, by the tender feel of his lips on hers. She hadn't realised that touching his hand in that way could be so intimate. Did she want him to finish what he had started? Could a man and woman really be married and live in the same house and be content with just friendship? She found more and more lately that she was fighting with herself, pushing away at the rising feelings of attraction she felt towards her own husband, feeling a nagging sense of guilt, as if by loving Albert fully, she somehow betrayed the memory of Helgi. But she couldn't deny the feelings that arose when he touched her, when he looked at her as he had done today. Did Albert suffer the same sense of guilt? They were married, were they not? He was her husband by law. Would it be so strange for the household to see the two of them act with each other like a proper man and his wife, or would they disapprove?

Was there truly anything more in his mind for her apart from doing what had been an act of kindness? It was, after all, only a marriage of convenience. She had only done it to save her son from bastardy, and he to provide his children with a mother. But the way he looked at her and his actions today told her otherwise. And why did he not seek her out now? The rest of the household had gone to bed, but like she had done so many nights before, she lay the sleeping babe next to her and waited for her husband to join her.

Albert never came. Dread settled into the pit of her stomach. Perhaps he was still not ready; no matter what the body wanted, perhaps the memory of his first wife was still a barrier between them. Sólveig drifted off to sleep, trying to swallow her own sense of guilt and disappointment.

34

Sólveig

The next day Albert and his workers hayed his portion of land over the mountain in Vatnadal valley. Sólveig decided to remain at the croft with Sif and the babies, but she packed them all food to take, and didn't expect to see them until late that night.

Albert was stiff with her when he departed that morning, and it left her a little befuddled. She realised that he hadn't made it to their bed last night, and she must have fallen asleep once more waiting for him.

"And where did you sleep last night, Albert?" she asked, passing him his *askur* filled with porridge. It came out like an accusation, though she hadn't meant it to. Dísa and Inga glanced down at their meals, an awkward silence drawing about them all as Sólveig waited for an answer.

"There were blades needing tending to last night. We can't cut hay with blunt blades," he said gruffly, spooning a mouthful of creamy cooked oats into his mouth.

He hadn't answered her question. She waited for him to say more, give her something more, a tender word, a small hint of the affection he'd had for her the day prior, but it was as if a different man sat before her, cold and dismissive. It was clearly his way of pushing her away. She turned from him and removed herself to the kitchen to collect Stella's and Lína's bowls. Helgi was still asleep, thankfully.

Perhaps what Albert said was true, but it hurt her, and she found herself annoyed by him, by his moods of late, trying to constantly gauge where she stood with him. How could he be so playful and warm with her, kiss her as he had done, and then just as suddenly pretend it never happened?

Albert gave so much of himself to her and at the same time could close himself off so completely. Rejection and bitter loneliness rose within her, so sharp it threatened to overwhelm her.

She held back her tears until Albert left, asking Sif to watch the babies while she collected water from the creek for washing. Her tears fell hard then, and she let her frustration with Albert flow through her, and out, feeling better for it, and as she was returning to the croft, she caught a glimpse of Rúna across the fjord at Norðureryi. Almost throwing down the buckets she'd just filled, she ran down to the small beach near her own farmhouse and called across the water, jumping up and down, her arms raised high, waving to her dear friend. Rúna waved back, and it was then that Sólveig decided that she would pay her a visit. Oh, how she missed her! She hadn't seen Rúna or Einar since they moved to Norðureyri in May, and she was eager to know how they had settled into their new household and how the pregnancy was faring. It was almost torture seeing the woman standing there and not being able to talk to her or embrace her like she wanted to. She needed the comfort and the good advice of a friend. She needed it today, more than ever.

But Sólveig battled with herself over the decision. Why couldn't she go? Surely, it would be no problem to whisk herself across the fjord to see her friend. The water was calm and there was no wind. She could take the smaller rowboat they often used to ferry people across. She could manage that, even if the thought of getting into a boat made her belly quiver with fear. Of course, deep down, she knew it went against Albert's wishes. He had warned her about not taking the boat out on her own, but she felt a streak of rebellion run through her, a small reclamation of her lost independence. She didn't need his permission to see her friend. She could do this, and besides, she'd seen the young lads do it, lads of only twelve and thirteen. She wouldn't be long, she reasoned—Albert needn't even know. She would be well and truly back before the men returned from haying at Vatnadalur.

⊹

Albert

By God, he wanted her. He wanted her so much it hurt. It had weighed on him all day, those playful and tender moments they shared the day before. The teasing glint in Sólveig's brown eyes, the deep satisfaction he felt hearing her light tone of laughter, the way her hands had massaged his so intimately, pouring herself so deeply into him with only her touch. That kiss. The feel of her soft, full lips against his. The taste of her. It was torment.

He threw his frustration with himself, his physical need for her, into the effort of haying, stopping only for brief moments to quench his thirst and answer the void hunger demanded be filled. There was some relief in that, but remorse ate at him now. He'd not failed to notice the stung look in her eyes that morning at his absence from their bed the night before, but he knew it had been better to stay away. She had only just given birth, for Christ's sake; the child was still so attached to her for his

sustenance. It had only been four months. It wasn't fair of him to ask
her to give herself to him so soon. He had done so with Krissa, and look
what had happened. It was simply easier this way. But as the day wore
on, the way he had treated Sólveig ate at him. Albert had been married
before, so he knew perfectly well that if their marriage was to work, there
had to be honesty between them, no matter how hard it was to speak. He
had been holding back from her this morning and he was determined to
make amends.

Their day of haying ended early. Albert and his workers were resigned
to the fact that bad weather was on its way, and he found himself
somewhat glad of it. The day had started out fair, but it had turned so
suddenly. It was raining by the time they returned, a dreary grey gloom
set over them as the fjord and the mountain Göltur disappeared under
the veil of fog.

Though it set back the drying of the hay, Albert was glad to be
home, and after washing the day's labour off himself, he strolled into
the *baðstofa*, hoping to see his wife, not wanting to wait any longer to
console her and apologise to her for his behaviour that morning.

Lína ran to him as he entered the *baðstofa*, squealing with delight
when he took the child into his embrace. Sif looked up from the cot
where she had Helgi, changing his wrappings, Stella sat on the bed next
to them playing with animal bones of various shapes and sizes.

"Where's Sólveig?" he asked. He hadn't seen her in the kitchen. The
other work maids, Johanna and Inga, had gone straight from haying to
preparing the evening meal.

"I told her she shouldn't go, Albert," his old aunt said, shaking her
head, not meeting his eyes. "Not on her own in the boat like that, never
know how the weather could turn."

"What do you mean on her own?" Albert said, his tone sharp, dread rushing through him.

"She took the rowboat over to Norðureryi to see Rúna. Said she would only be an hour or so. I did see the boat heading back across the waters. I thought perhaps she was biding her time down by the sea croft to wait out the weather."

⁘

Sólveig wasn't at the sea croft, neither was the smaller of the boats.

Albert wasted no time in taking a boat across the fjord with the help of Björn and his boys. The conditions to take to the sea weren't favourable, but they made safe landing on the beach at Norðureyri.

Rúna answered the door when they arrived, her eyes wide at the sight of them.

"What are you lot doing out in this weather?" she asked, wiping her hands against her apron.

"Is Sólveig here?" Albert managed through ragged breaths. "Sif said she took the boat over at midday but she is not yet returned."

Rúna blanched. "She left here hours ago. The waters were calm and the sky clear, when she took the boat back. I thought she made it across. Einar and the boys were haying all day. I told her to wait, but she insisted she not be a burden. She insisted, Albert, and I let her go." She shook her head, clearly distraught, her lips trembling. "I would *never* have let her go, knowing the weather would turn so."

"You're not to blame, Rúna." He squeezed her hand with reassurance but felt none himself.

Einar strode into the entrance, along with another burly man in his early fifties, Guðmundur, but he was known to them all as Gummi, the owner of the other household at Norðureyri. He was a robust, energetic man with dark hair, greying at the sides and deep lines etched into the corners of his eyes, and luckily for Albert, in the predicament he was in, he was a man known in their community for his skill at sea.

"What's happened, brother?" asked Einar, his eyes darting between Albert and Rúna.

"We think Sólveig may be stuck out in the fjord or God forbid, drifted out to open sea," Rúna piped in weakly, coming up to Einar. He put his arms around her, his eyes, as they sought Albert's, went wide.

"You can't go back out in this, Albert. You shouldn't have come across as it is." He shook his head, knowing where his brother's thoughts lay.

"My wife is out there, Einar." His voice sounded strained even to his own ears. "I'll not sit by and wait this out only to find her body washed up on the beach tomorrow. I can't, Einar, I just can't do it again," he said, trying his utmost to hold himself together, not giving the dangerous thoughts lingering in the edge of his mind room to debilitate him. He would find her alive. He had to.

"We'll find her, Albert," said Gummi, his grey eyes suddenly fierce. "We'll get a crew together and take out the sixareen. We'll have a better chance out there in the bigger boat. I've sailed in worse than this."

35

Sólveig

She lay in the rowboat, curled into herself between the two seats, the
sea soaking into her clothes along with the pouring rain. Her eyes were
closed, but it wasn't helping with the dizzying, swaying motion as the
rolling waves, like grasping claws, taunted and teased her. Perhaps if she
could keep herself small, the boat would stay steady on the current and
the sea wouldn't simply decide to upend her into it.

Luckily as the rain subsided and the wind dropped, the boat managed
to stay afloat, and she within it, the vessel falling into a steady rhythm,
rocking and lulling her so that her eyelids grew heavy, along with her
limbs, weak from exerting all her strength in rowing earlier. That was
before she lost one of the oars. Before that, she'd had some hope of
rowing herself to shore.

But curse her weakness at sea.

Her mind ran lazily over the events of the day. She had been so full of
confidence and bravado on the way over to Norðureyri that morning,
feeling empowered by her decision to see her friend on her own terms.
Sure, the rowing had been hard, and she was quite breathless when she
reached the landing beach, but she was proud that she had been able
to do it, regardless of how it frightened her. Rúna was overjoyed to see

her, her belly so full with child that it was hard to embrace the woman
properly, and Sólveig spent the hour in her company. It was clear to her
how happy Rúna was running her own household, and she proudly led
her to the *baðstofa* and introduced her to the work maids and occupants
of her household. The men were out in the fields farther down the fjord,
busy with the haying, and Rúna and Sólveig were able talk of all matters
in relative privacy—of how Helgi thrived, how Dísa was warming up
to her, the new workers at Suðureyri, even of her conflicting feelings
towards Albert. Sólveig in turn, was able to quell some of Rúna's anxiety
over the upcoming birth of her child, due in late September. She had only
stayed the hour. Rúna tried to convince her to stay longer, to wait for
Einar to come home to ferry her back across the fjord, but the weather
had been fair, the sun shining and only a little wind about. She hadn't
wanted to burden him with that task after his day of haying, and besides,
they'd likely not return before midnight. She certainly couldn't wait that
long.

So, she had gone.

Drawing the oars through the thick water had been difficult. Her
arms, already sore from the first trip across, were quick to tire and she
was left breathless. The rowing became even harder as she crossed the
undercurrent, where the water flowed fast towards the middle, and in
trying to cross it, the current dragged the boat further up the fjord,
towards the open sea. Sólveig didn't have enough strength to pull herself
across it with any ease. Not only was she farther from Suðureyri than
before, but the wind had also picked up. The sea grew rough, and the
boat rocked vicariously, feeling suddenly very flimsy and small in the
palm of the sea. The coffee and flat bread she'd eaten at Rúna's quickly
came to the surface, and she'd found herself at the side of the boat, her

stomach heaving. In her moment of weakness, one of the boat's oars slipped and slid into the water.

"*Nei,*" she whimpered pathetically, lurching forward to grab at it, almost tipping the boat in the process. Using the remaining oar, she tried to reach the other floating in the water, but it was swept quickly out of reach.

With the long days of summer ahead, Sólveig knew it would be many hours before sunset, but the sky darkened regardless as a thick fog crept down over the fjord, and it wasn't long before she could neither see the shore she had left nor the beach she was headed for.

The boat heaved in the surging sea, and she retched again, and then she simply sunk to the floor of the boat, exhausted. What else could she do but curl up into herself and wait it out? Would someone find her, or would the undercurrent drag her out to the open sea?

How long had it been since she had left Norðureyri? She thought of her baby, and her breasts tingled, filling with milk, leaving them aching and hard. He would be hungry again. Did he cry for her? Would he know it if the sea took her? The wind bit down into her bones where she lay, hopelessness threatening to overwhelm her.

"*Don't tell me you're giving up now, Solla?*"

That name, that voice. Only one person had ever called her that.

Her sister, Fía.

She sat on the timber seat before her, a swaddled baby in her arms. It could have been her mother, she looked so like her with her long golden tresses. They blew around her, like a halo.

"Fía," she gasped at the sight. Her sister was so full of life, so achingly real. She looked as she had the last time she had seen her alive, and Sólveig soaked in the sight of her, her presence both calming and disconcerting. "I can't." She shook her head. "The sea will swallow me if I move again."

"If you do nothing, the sea will take you," she said, her soft voice taking on a sterner edge. *"Take up the paddle, Sólveig."* She followed her sister's gaze to the remaining oar lying near her on the floor of the boat.

"I can't." She trembled. "I can't, Fía. The sea is too strong. What's the use of it now? There's no surviving this."

Fía shook her head, clearly displeased with her answer, but her tone was gentle and calm, the comforting older sister she had always been to her. *"What about all those women you're yet to help? Would you give up on them so easily? You have a purpose here. You are not done."*

Sólveig wanted to touch her but was afraid to in case she disappeared. It was enough just to see her, enough just to hear her voice. Fía had always been good to her. She had always made the effort to see her on her days off, no matter that it was half a day's walk to get to her, sometimes farther.

Her sister glanced lovingly down at the baby in her arms, stroking its fair head tenderly. *"What about your son?"* she asked then, her sad brown eyes meeting hers. *"He needs his mother, and those little girls over there. They've already lost enough."* Fía seemed annoyed with her now. *"And Albert. Will you break his heart all over again?"*

Shame filled her. Fía was right. She mustn't give up. Not yet. Death had already taken so much from her. It wasn't her turn. She wouldn't go without a fight. And she had so much to fight for—her son, her stepdaughters, little Stella, the mothers of her community and *Albert.* Her heart ached at the thought of him, the thought of the worry that surely filled him, of him coming home from haying to find her gone, and she could see now how reckless she had been to take the boat on her own.

"Follow the raven," Fía said, nodding her head in encouragement, hope and love shining in her eyes. *"Call to him, Solla. He's coming for you."*

The boat lurched, and Sólveig woke with a start, the taste of bile in her mouth, and the bitter tang of salt on her parched lips. The seat before her was empty where the vision of her sister had been, and her skin rose in gooseflesh.

Had it been just a dream or had her sister truly come to her? She recalled the story Albert had told her long ago of old Gróa and the dream man who had warned her husband not to hay the field, and Sólveig knew no good would come of tempting fate. She must heed the warning.

Scrambling to her knees, she grappled for the remaining paddle, wondering how she was going to manage saving herself. The boat had taken in some water, but she couldn't let that worry her now. She lowered the oar into the sea, and as she did so, it made contact with something hard. A long timber paddle bobbed in the water alongside the boat.

The missing oar!

But how? Leaning over the lip of the boat, she took it up, relief gushing through her as she held it in her hands, so wonderfully solid.

And then she rowed.

Where she found the strength was a mystery to her, but she rowed through the thick fog, unsure in which direction she was headed, still blind in the mists, the sea swirling and angry beneath her vessel. After a while, she stopped to catch her breath, tiring once more, defeat edging its way back in.

But then it came, the caw on the wind. His call was hollow and haunting. Above her, circled a large black bird, his raucous caw calling to her.

"Follow the raven." Fía's words echoed within her, and with trembling arms, she pulled the oars through the water with renewed vigour, following the flight of the raven, chasing his haunting cries until he finally disappeared.

"*Nei*, don't go," she called.

"Call to him now. He's coming for you." Her sister's voice came to her loud and clear.

"Albert," she croaked. Her voice was hoarse from disuse. "Albert." This time her voice was louder and clearer. She closed her eyes, listening for him, hoping and praying that he was out there. The sound of the wind met her ears, the slap of the waves against the wood of the boat, and then—

"Sólveig!" It came on the wind as if from a dream. But then she heard it again, a little louder. "Sólveig!"

"Albert, I'm here," she yelled through the veil of cloud, her heart in her throat, and within moments came the sound of deep male voices and the heave of a large boat through the water.

It was Albert. He had come for her. He stood at the bow of their boat, his expression stern as he struggled to tie the end of her boat to theirs in the restless water.

"Thank God you're here, Sólveig. Here. Take my hand."

She took his outstretched arm, his gloved hand wrapping around hers, gripping her hard and steadying her as she leaped across onto their boat. "My God, woman, you're really here," he said, lifting her gently down, taking her into his embrace. His lips pressed firmly against her hair, and then he pulled away from her, his gaze searing, scouring her up and down, her head in his palms, his brows creased into lines of concern. "Are you hurt?"

She shook her head. "Just a little cold."

He sat her down, wrapping a blanket around her shoulders, and seated himself next to her, taking up an oar. Einar and Gummi were with them in the boat along with Björn and his boys, all dressed in their sea gear, watching their exchange. They regarded her with relief and pity but said nothing. Having tied her boat to theirs, they dragged it behind them and rowed, the strength of them forcing their vessel through the dispersing fog and strong current to land on the beach on the Suðureyri side of the fjord.

Albert helped her down off the boat, and the others dragged it farther up the sand.

"Get yourself up to the house for warmth," he said, his tone suddenly cold and dismissive. "That baby will be needing you something sore."

She turned, somewhat awkwardly, feeling small, knowing Albert was displeased with her, but she thanked each man in turn for coming out to find her, knowing they would wait out the weather a little longer and warm themselves with coffee before heading back across the fjord.

"I'm just relieved we found you," said Einar, squeezing her hand with affection. "Rúna will be happy to know you're safe."

"Please tell her I'm sorry, Einar, and that she was right."

"No trouble at all, Sólveig," said Gummi, giving her a friendly wink when she thanked him. "You sure put the fright into Albert. I haven't seen him in such a state before. That sort of worry would put grey hairs on any man," he added before making his way towards the sea croft.

Guilt wrenched through her at his words, but she picked up the hem of her wet skirts and made her way towards home, not waiting for Albert's scolding, which by his sudden change of demeanour, she knew was coming. She was tired, cold and wet, her breasts full to bursting, and she couldn't stop shivering. All she wanted was some food in her belly, the warmth of her bed, and her baby in her arms, with his baby smell and tender smiles to fill her heart. That, and to release the pressure of milk in her breasts. She sighed and almost ran the whole way home.

Sólveig sat on the cot she shared with Albert in the *baðstofa* in dry clothes, with a fed and a content baby asleep next to her. The rest of the household was preparing for bed and the little girls were already asleep. It was just before sunset, the sky outside through the small square window a purple haze. The fog had finally lifted and the sea outside in the distance seemed calmer. She shuddered at the sight of it.

Both households of Suðureyri were much relieved to see their mistress returned, the girls overjoyed, Lína and Stella not really understanding the fuss, but Dísa hugging her tight and Helgi crying at the very sight of her. Later, when the men had all returned, there was much chatter while they took their coffee in the *baðstofa*. Albert hadn't said a word to her since disembarking the boat at the beach, his manner towards her abrupt and cold, and it worried her.

The front door shutting below pulled her out of her reverie of the afternoon's events. Albert was home from seeing Einar and Gummi off. She listened, waiting patiently for him to join her, expecting to hear his steps heavy on the stairs leading to the *baðstofa*, but she didn't. She sighed heavily and got up off the bed, making her way down the hallway towards the kitchen. She needed to explain, knowing it was time to face him and whatever scolding he had in mind for her.

"Can I help you with that?" Sólveig hovered at the entrance of the kitchen.

Albert sat by the table at the window, his jacket draped over the chair, pulling off his socks. "I can manage."

His curt reply was just a reminder of how he'd treated her that morning and Solveig's frustration with him rose, along with her temper. "Have you naught to say to me? After everything that's happened today?"

"I just don't know what to say to you right now, Sólveig." He stood, socks in hand, walked over to the fireplace and draped them over the hearth stones to dry them. "I'm still just *that* perturbed with you right now."

"*Já*, clearly, you're upset with me." Was he not relieved to have her home? "I don't deserve your silence, Albert. Just talk to me. You've no right to be angry with me."

"I have no right to be angry with you?" He scoffed, finally meeting her eyes. "Well, I am angry with you. In fact, I'm furious." He took a step towards her. "Do you have any idea how long we were out there looking for you? What in God's name were you thinking taking the boat out on your own?"

"The day was fair, and I wanted to see Rúna. I thought—" she stumbled, "I thought I could handle the boat on my own." She let the words drift away pathetically.

Albert's lips thinned and his jaw ticked, his tone low and controlled as he spoke. "I thought I'd made it clear to you that you're never to take the boat out on your own. You're to ask for help."

"And what was I to do? Just wait for you to come back from your day haying in Vatnadalur?"

Albert threw his arms in the air. "*Já*, just wait! Or better yet, you could have walked to Norðureyri, or come to Vatnadalur and found me or one of the workmen to take you."

The veins pulsed in his neck as he spoke. Unbridled anger radiated off him and it scared her. He was not often angered. She had only seen it on the rare occasion, but to have it directed at her made her feel small, and her heart pound wildly.

"The sea takes men all the time, Sólveig. Strong men used to its temper. You think it wouldn't do the same to you?" His tone was scalding, and she flinched at his words. "Your damn independence! Why can't you just ask for help? You get it in your head that you can just manage—"

"Because I have to," she interrupted him, exasperated by this attack on her character.

"You know that you can rely on me. Have I not proven to you time and again that you can ask for help?"

"I know this, Albert, but I just can't." The truth of the words burned her. She wanted to tell him, she truly did.

"Why can't you?"

She wanted to say to him that she was afraid of letting herself need him too much when she'd always only had herself to rely on. In truth, she was afraid of loving him, even if her body was a constant betrayal to her. Would he not leave her in the end too? As they all did. Her mother, her sister, her father and Helgi. Was Albert not holding himself apart from her, because he, too, was scared to open his heart to love again? She couldn't form the words to tell him.

He turned away from her as if exasperated by her lack of reply, running his hands through his already dishevelled hair. When he finally spoke again, his words were strained. He sounded weary, almost defeated. "Damn it, Sólveig, I thought I'd lost another wife today."

Wife. Sólveig blinked hard, a little stunned by the word.

"*Another* wife. Am I a wife, Albert?" she asked.

He turned to her then. "Of course you're my wife."

She shook her head. "But I'm not! I'm not a *true* wife to you. *Já,* I tend your house and look after your children, but that's all it will ever be." She couldn't believe the words to come out of her mouth, but she couldn't stop them either.

"What's that supposed to mean?" he asked evenly. "I thought that's what you wanted. I thought we were both clear on what this was?"

"And what is this? Because I'm not sure what it is you want from me, Albert. When you kissed me like that the other day in the storeroom, it was certainly more than a *married in name only* thing to do." There was more sarcasm in her tone than she'd intended. "And there I was waiting for you, like the fool that I am, thinking that my husband finally wanted to claim me as his." She shook her head, breaking her gaze from the fierce blue of his, and she made to walk past him, feeling petty and fragile, finally done with this conversation.

Albert stepped before her, his hand at her waist to stay her.

"Look, just forget it." She wished fervently she hadn't lost her temper, that she hadn't said anything at all.

His hand at her waist barred her escape. "You think because I haven't bedded you, you're not mine?" His words were slow and deliberate. "You want me to bed you, woman? Is that it?" It came out half strangled, his brow raised in question as it dawned on him what she was really telling him, what she was really asking of him.

Sólveig swallowed hard, heat burning her cheeks as she met his eyes, her answer clear, and then just as suddenly, Albert grasped her face with a stifled groan and pressed his lips to hers.

It stunned her. It was no innocent kiss, no delicate, gentle peck like their wedding kiss had been. It was full of unspoken want. They pulled apart, both breathing hard, his eyes searching hers, a frown creasing his brow.

"Christ, I want you, Sólveig. I want you in my bed. I want to love you as a man loves a woman, to claim your body as much as you have laid claim to my shattered heart." He pulled her to him again, his hands in her hair, cradling her head as his mouth sought hers hungrily, and Sólveig responded. Gooseflesh rose over her body that had nothing to do with the draft in the room but everything to do with the feel of his lips on

hers, and his hands in her hair bringing with it a stirring deep into her
core.

She pulled away from him, taking his hand in hers. "Then, come,
husband, and take me to your bed."

"*Nei.*" He shook his head, staying her once more. "Not in there."
He indicated the *baðstofa*, the room full of sleeping people down the
hallway. "I want to see you, Sólveig. I want to see all of you." He led her
from the kitchen and into the room she used for drying and preparing
her herbs.

The comforting array of flowery and woody tones created by the dried
herbs hanging around them heightened her senses where she stood in the
centre of the room, but her eyes were on her husband as he closed the
door and lit the lamp on the table by the window. She was acutely aware
of the flutter in her belly, of the racing thud of her heart, the heavy rise
and fall of her chest, and she closed her eyes to still her nerves. When she
opened them again, Albert was leaning against the table watching her,
his gaze soft. He reached for her, pulling her to him. "You're trembling,"
he said, planting a kiss on her open palm, one, and then, the other.

His mouth against her skin left it aflame regardless of the coolness
of the room, and she took a step back, her eyes locking with his as she
slipped out of her skirt and unbuttoned her blouse before him. He stood
too, following her lead, undressing of his own attire, until they both
stood naked before each other in the dim light of the room, shadows
dancing on bare skin—man and woman in the bloom of life.

Albert drank in the sight of her. She unabashedly took her fill of him,
in all his masculine form, and then she closed the gap between them,
moulding her body to his. She pressed her full bare breasts against the
hardened planes of his chest. The soft auburn hairs tickled her skin,
and his arms enfolded her, strong hands kneading the soft flesh of her

bottom, pressing her to him as he kissed her deeply. His mouth trailed down her neck and to her breasts, tugging at her nipples, and then back up to her lips once more, staking their claim over her, as his fingers made their way to her most private place, stroking the soft folds of her womanhood.

She tore herself away and moved towards the cot in the corner of the room, laying herself on the bed, ready for him. Albert followed, lowering himself over her, holding his weight, and she relished the sight of him, the soft shifting of muscle in his upper arms, the length of his lean, rugged body covering her completely. She opened herself to him then, her cooled skin warming with the friction of his body against hers as they found each other and created their own rhythm, filling for a time a void they had both long suffered.

Albert knew his way around a woman's body. They were eager and hungry for each other, for the touch of flesh with flesh, urgent to be joined, but he reigned it in and slowed the pace. And then he was unrushed and gentle with Sólveig as he gave her his body, and she gave him hers, their satisfaction voiced in soft whimpers and groans. A marriage bound in both body and soul.

Afterwards they lay tangled in each other, a blanket roughly draped over them. Sólveig was strangely content. She had been dreading this moment and wanting it, and now that it had happened, there was no remorse, no guilt, simply a simmering sense of peace as she lay her head against Albert's chest. She ran her fingertips through the soft fuzz of hair on his muscled chest, feeling the solid form of him, the comforting rhythm of his heart beating beneath her ear.

"Don't scare me like that again, Sólveig," he said quietly, his voice gruff. The sea incident was clearly still hard on his mind.

"I'm sorry. I know it was reckless of me to go across the fjord on my own. I truly thought that I could manage it..."

She looked up at him and caught the pity there in his expression and cast her eyes away again, laying her head back down onto his chest.

"I thought I lost you today and all I could think was—" He stopped as if he struggled to say the words. "That I hadn't let myself be a true husband to you, the way you deserved—for the guilt I felt at wanting you, for the guilt of those gone before us. I've been holding back from you." He kissed the top of her head and rubbed a hand along her back. "But what kind of life it that? We aren't honouring the memories of the dead by fearing to carry on in their absence, Sólveig. We honour them by living our lives to the fullest. Life's too *damn* short to do anything but."

"*Já*, I've been afraid too," she conceded. "I'll admit I've been stubborn and insistent on doing things myself. It's just been me for so long, I get it in my head that I must manage, as we all do. Life *is* short, Albert—and will you not just leave me in the end too?"

She felt the deep exhale of his breath against her head. "Ah, Sólveig, I don't know when my time will come. No one knows these things, but know that as long as I live and breathe, I will walk beside you. You *can* rely on me. You and those children in there are my life." She stretched up and kissed him tenderly, then pulled away, but his grip on her bottom tightened, halting her, his mouth hovering seductively over her lips, his breath mingling with hers. "You're mine and I am yours if you'll have me. Will you have me as a husband in more than just name?"

"*Já*, I will." She smiled against his lips, opening her mouth to his, and he began his exploration of the delicate contours of her body once more, sending a familiar ache through her. She moved against him, letting him love her, giving herself completely to her husband.

Epilogue

September 1883

Sólveig

"Something's abound tonight, is it?" asked Albert, strolling into the kitchen from the *baðstofa*. It was the late hours of the night and the rest of the household was abed.

"*Já*, I think it must be Rúna's time." Sólveig rubbed her eyes, and yawned from where she stood over the hearth fire, warming milk in a pan for herself in only her night dress and a shawl. She couldn't explain to him the strange hunch she often got over an impending callout for a delivery, but her husband smiled at her, sympathy written over his own tired features, rubbing a hand through his dishevelled bed hair.

"Milk?" she offered, ready to pull a cup down for him, too, from the shelf above the bench.

"Not for me," he replied, taking a seat next to the table by the window.

She could sense him watching her as she poured the heated milk for herself into a cup, then turned to him, sipping at the thick, warm liquid.

"I hope you're wrong. I'm not ready to face an empty bed for the next few nights," Albert said, reaching for her, drawing her onto his lap.

"I'm sure Lína would love to snuggle her *pabbi* for the next few nights," she suggested cheekily.

"I'm sure the little rascal would." He chuckled. "If only she didn't end up kicking me all night with her legs in my face. I don't know how Dísa puts up with sharing her bed."

"*Já*, Dísa is good to her, but I must admit, I'm not in any hurry to leave you either, though I am sure Rúna is eager for her child to enter the world. I know only too well the feeling. I will, however, be relieved to leave the *slátur* preparations to Inga and Jóhanna tomorrow."

"Is that so?" He sounded surprised.

She hesitated, feeling suddenly shy about bringing this up with him. "*Já*, I honestly didn't think it would happen again so quickly, especially with little Helgi just weaning off the breast, but it appears to be so." She took his broad hand into hers and placed it gently over her lower abdomen, where she believed his seed had taken hold and another child grew.

His eyes widened. "Are you sure?"

"My courses haven't returned since Helgi was born, so it's hard to know, but I think so. The smell of blood yesterday with the sheep offal had me rushing for a bucket, and I've been so tired of late."

"Ah, this was one of the reasons that I held back from you for so long, Sólveig." Now, it was his turn to hesitate. "And how do you feel about it?"

She could see he was apprehensive, but she took his head between her palms. Her thumb smoothed the frown lines etched into his forehead, and she leaned forward, bringing her mouth to his, kissing him tenderly, then pulled back, holding his blue gaze in her own.

"I'm happy, Albert," she said, running her hand over his beard, stroking the fair bristle covering his face.

He leaned into her, his mouth hovering over hers. "Then I, too, am pleased." He pressed his lips to hers and shifted her on his lap so that she straddled him, like a man would ride a horse, a leg on either side, bringing their bodies closer together. His mouth claimed her throat, travelling along the edges of her jawline as he gripped her bottom, pressing her to him. A quiet angst began to build within her at his touch, at the gentle tilt of his hips meeting hers in slow rotation through the thin material of their woollen underclothes. He was hard against her, his desire for her evident.

Three knocks sounded from the entrance, and the dogs started barking. Albert groaned, pushing her upright, and they both looked at one another with knowing, breathing hard. Sólveig smiled with satisfaction at being right about expecting visitors this night, and Albert laughed, shaking his head in both resignation and frustration.

It was Einar. His breath came in heavy white puffs, dispersing quickly into the cold night air.

"Ah, Albert. Sólveig's needed over at Norðureyri! She must come. It's Rúna," he said, his agitation and excitement clear.

"Well and about time too," said Sólveig, coming up behind Albert. "Have her waters come away?"

"Not yet, but the pains have been coming on strong for the last hour."

"Come in while I get myself ready."

All angst for her husband quickly dissipated, and Sólveig dressed herself in the dark of the *baðstofa*, leaning over to kiss her children as softly as she could on the tops of their heads as they slept—Dísa, Lína, Stella and her little Helgi. Looking at them each in turn, she felt the fullness of her heart and, in taking her leave from them, prayed that they would be watched over in her absence, knowing, if anything, Krissa and her Helgi watched over them all from another place. There was a sense of comfort in her belief in that.

Retrieving her medical bag, she wrapped herself in layers, a head scarf and gloves, a thick shawl, dressing warmly for the trip over the waters of the fjord, following Einar and Albert out into the cool night. She was filled with her usual mixture of emotions at a birth call out—wonder, excitement, and apprehension. Crossing the fjord didn't help the apprehension side of this matter, it only added to her anxiety. She hadn't been across the waters of the fjord since July when she had taken the boat out on her own. But this time, she had Einar with her. She knew she was in good hands, so she pushed the fear aside, praying silently to the Almighty for their safe deliverance to Norðureyri.

The night was clear, and star filled, with a three-quarter moon shining a path of light for their sea vessel across the deceitfully calm waters of the fjord.

Albert accompanied her to the boat with his brother. The old sailor, Gummi, waited for them and took Sólveig's bag as Einar jumped into the vessel, and then her husband turned to her. He stooped, lifting her into the boat, cradling her with his arms up under her knees, but he didn't set her down straight away. He held her to him a moment longer, leaning his forehead against hers, their breaths mingling as one. "I'll be waiting for you, wife," he said, and kissed her quickly before setting her down into the timber sea vessel. "No solo trips back across the fjord." His tone was light, but there was a hint of warning there.

"I think I've learned my lesson, Albert. Trust me. I do not want to tempt the sea again on my own."

"Good," he replied, seemingly satisfied.

"I'll bring her back myself, brother," Einar reassured him, eager to be on his way, and Sólveig watched the tall, broad figure of her husband grow smaller on the beach as the boat heaved across the waters with the stroke of the oars until he was swallowed up in the darkness.

⁕

Rúna was delivered of a baby girl, strong and healthy. The child's hair, black as a raven, sent a squeal of delight through Sólveig as she witnessed the child's head crowning. The baby entered the world as the sun rose into the sky. It streamed into the *baðstofa* at Norðureyri, cleansing the day and, most surprising of all, cleansing Sólveig's spirit. Sólveig had entered the croft with anxiety in her heart, fearing the unknown—what if something went wrong? What if there were complications and she lost her dearest friend? The world was so unpredictable at times, and this lingering fear took hold of her as she crossed the fjord with Einar and Gummi. She found doubt within herself for some reason, as if her confidence had been jolted since the sea incident, but upon seeing Rúna on the cot, breathing calmly through the waves of pain, all thought went instinctively to her friend and her unborn child, her mind set on the task of delivering the baby into the world. There had been no room for doubt then, just the sheer hope and faith that all would go well and that Sólveig had the knowledge and training to do what she could if problems arose.

Rúna laboured well, tackling the waves of pain as her body stretched and opened itself for the babe. At the climax of her pain, she cried and cursed Einar for putting the child inside her, but her anger just as suddenly turned to tears of relief when her baby slid out with a final grunt of effort and was placed into her arms. The startled cries of her new daughter pierced the morning silence, bringing Einar rushing into the room, unable to keep himself away any longer. His face transformed from anxiety to pure joy and love at the sight of his child in Rúna's arms.

Sólveig's heart filled with warmth, reminding her of the moment she first held her own son in her arms, a bittersweet joy.

After cleaning up, Sólveig sat on one of the cots nearby with a coffee in her hands and watched Einar and Rúna interact, quietly reflective, admiring the love they shared for one another and their new baby. She recalled Albert's sentiments about having someone to walk beside in life, to share both life's blessings and difficulties with. Albert was hers to walk with, and so, too, her son and stepdaughters and the realisation of what she had overwhelmed her with gratitude and love for them all. She didn't need to face life alone.

There would be death, as surely as new life would be born, and she knew with a burgeoning sense of certainty that she would no longer live her life fearing the uncertainty of it.

She thought to her sister, Fía, to the mothers and babies lost in childbirth. Life was often hard and cruel, and she wasn't so naive as to believe that birth was always beautiful. Not every birth ended with joy. Sometimes it was raw and unforgiving, but today it was a blessing. Today it reaffirmed to her the beauty in life, of the sheer little miracles that life saw fit to gift them with and the love and hope that came with them, and she couldn't help but smile too. This moment. It was all she really had, and she would take it for what it offered and each moment after that.

She looked back on what she had with Helgi, and though their time together had been short, she was grateful for it, for the son that resulted in loving him. But she was also grateful for Albert, for his love—the patient, loving, trusting kind that he constantly offered her, that he had given her for a long time now, even when she thought she walked alone.

Her hand rested instinctively over her abdomen, knowing how she already anticipated the birth of the child she grew there—new life. A child that represented the tender healing of two broken hearts, a child of hers and Albert's making. She wasn't alone anymore. She had a family again. She had found her place, her home, her people, and she was grateful.

Author's Note

Mother of Light is a work of fiction, including the characters, incidents and dialogue. However, many of the events and characters in this story were inspired by real people of the times. Every town and farm named in the book was an actual place in Iceland in 1881, with the exception of the farm Hraunakot, which did exist, but prior to 1881.

No offence is intended towards living relatives of any character whose name I have borrowed for the purposes of this story, or any representation of towns and places mentioned.

Sólveig is inspired by my own great-great-grandmother Guðrún Þorðardóttir, who was the first educated and registered midwife for the Suðureyrar district from 1880 to 1905.

Albert was inspired by the man who became Guðrún's husband. She was the second wife of Kristján Albertsson, my great-great-grandfather. He lost his first wife, Kristín Guðmundsdóttir and their two daughters to a measles epidemic in 1882, and his boat did happen upon trouble during a shark hunting expedition, though it occurred ten years earlier.

Helgi Sigurðsson was an actual person. He was engaged to my great-great-grandmother and died during the measles epidemic in 1882.

Doctor Þorvaldur Jónsson and Doctor Jónas Jónasson were real practising doctors in Ísafjörður and Reykjavík in 1881.

The measles epidemic is an event that did occur in Iceland in 1882. In Súgandafjörður, they lost twenty-five people, mostly children, a tragedy for such a small community. Biographies written by people who lived through this epidemic talk of this time as being one of the hardest years they'd ever lived through.

Many of the birth situations in Mother of Light have been drawn from biographies written by Icelandic midwives of this era:

Íslenszkar Ljósmæður Æviþættir og Endurminningar, a triple volume set of biographies written about and by Icelandic midwives compiled by Séra Sveinn Vikingur was a great source of information and inspiration.

Levy's Kennslubok Handa Yfirsetukonum written by Doctor A Stadfeldt, translated by Doctor Jónas Jónasson and published in 1871 was the actual midwife manual used for practising midwives of this period. This book was referenced extensively for accuracy in birthing methods, tools and medicines used at the time for birthing mothers, as well as general attitudes towards breastfeeding and care of the expectant mother.

Other books and resources referenced considerably were: *Súgfirðingabók: Byggðasaga og mannlíf* by Gunnar M. Magnússon, *Firðir og Fólk: 900-1900: Vestur-Ísafjarðarsýsla* by Kjartan Ólafsson, *The Little Book of the Icelanders in the Old Days* by Alda Sigmundsdóttir, *Wasteland with Words: A Social History of Iceland* by Sigurður Gylfi Magnússon, *Plants of Iceland: Traditional Uses and Folklore* by Guðrún Bjarnadóttir & Jóhann Óli Hilmarsson, *Horfnir starfshættir og leiftur frá liðnum* öldum by Guðmundur Þorsteinsson, *Þeir vöktu yfir ljósinu: Saga Karla í ljósmóðurstörfum* by Erla Dóris Halldórsdóttir and the newspaper archives timarit.is

It is important to understand that many Icelanders of this era believed in ghosts, symbolic dreams, and the *Huldufólk*—the Hidden people. Icelanders lived very closely with nature and life was dictated by the seasons. If you've ever spent a winter in Iceland, you'll get an understanding of why Icelanders were open to such beliefs and stories, and storytelling such a vital part of their daily life.

The folk tale about Ólafía and the Hidden man told by Helgi to Sólveig, is an old Icelandic folk tale, and the inspiration for this retelling was drawn from the book, *The Little Book of The Hidden People* by Alda Sigmundsdóttir.

Lastly, please consider leaving me a review on Goodreads and Amazon (or wherever you purchased the book from). Aside from purchasing a book, leaving a rating and review is one of the best ways to support an author. Your feedback is valuable and will help other readers both find my book and decide whether to read it.

Thank you, from the bottom of my heart, for your support.

-Elin de Ruyter

Acknowledgements

Without the continuous support of the following people, this story of my heart, Mother of Light would not have been told. Thank you to my family for your constant love, support and patience. To my husband, Mark for always believing in me, and especially for being brave enough to move with me to the other side of world to reconnect with my roots and discover this writer within me.

The four little humans I brought earthside, Lucas, Cora, Ella and Svala. The beautiful pregnancy and birth experiences I had with you all, fuelled my passion for birth, pregnancy and midwives, and discovering the stories of the courageous women in this profession.

My parents Johanna and Omar for taking the adventurous leap to create a life for my sisters and I in Australia. Without that I don't think I would have had such an intense drive to discover myself through understanding where I was born and who my ancestors were.

To my four sisters Tinna, Maria, Carol and Margret, for your continuous encouragement and enthusiasm in both life, and writing, and for being my valued alpha readers as I navigated my way through the first draft of this story.

My valued writing friends through the Instagram writing community, particularly Amy DeWolfe, Sarah Wibrow, Bethany Garcia, Roger Marsh, Elles Lohuis and Jennie Ryan, along with my other betas for this book: Linda de Ruyter, Lisse Egilsdóttir, Kristrún Steinarsdóttir,

Þórdís Edda Guðjónsdóttir and María Weinberg Jóhannesdóttir. My dear friends Nadine Beckhouse, Krystal Lording and Kara Cuskelly, for your unwavering support and belief in me and this book, and for your constant friendship, advice and much needed coffee dates.

Icelandic Roots and its volunteers, particularly Sunna Furstenau for allowing me to be part of such a wonderful genealogy organisation, honouring our Icelandic ancestors and preserving their stories. Also, Helga Margrét Reinhardsdóttir, Natalie Guttormsson and again Þórdís Edda Guðjónsdóttir who have encouraged and helped me with historical and Icelandic related details, writing mechanics and research directions.

My cousins in Iceland, Kristin Salome Jónsdóttir, Sigrún Edda Edvarðsdóttir, Eyþór Eðvarðsson, Sigríður Hanna Jóhannesdóttir, Hanna Maria Siggeirsdóttir, Magnús Sigurður Jónsson and Birkir Friðbertsson (who sadly passed before I was able to meet him in person) for your enthusiasm in reconnecting our large Suðureyri leg of the family tree and sharing your memories and insights into our ancestors who lived for many generations in Súgandafjörður where Mother of Light is set.

About The Author

Elin de Ruyter was born in Iceland and grew up in Australia. She has worked as a professional genealogist and writer and has written articles for the genealogical organisation Icelandic Roots where she specialises in the history of Icelandic midwives.

In August 2020 she moved back to Iceland for two years with her husband and four children to reconnect with her Icelandic roots and to write *Mother of Light*. She currently resides in Brisbane, Australia.

Mother of Light: A Novel is Elin's first book. She has a passion for reading and writing women's historical fiction and particularly likes her novels to have a romance sublot.

Visit her website and sign up for her newsletter to stay informed with upcoming book releases and writing updates at www.elinderuyter.com

Ísafjörður

Printed in Great Britain
by Amazon